ALSO BY WILL WIGHT

*For the most up-to-date bibliography, please visit **WillWight**.com*

THE
CAPTAIN
THE LAST HORIZON
BOOK ONE

WILL
WIGHT

HIDDEN GNOME PUBLISHING

CHAPTER ONE

LET ME TELL you how I died five times in one day.

We were on the planet Nezarin, and I don't blame you if you haven't heard of it. If you're not a student of rare astronomical phenomena, there's no reason you should have. Standard blue-green planet with a mid-sized yellow sun.

Its native sentient population moved on centuries ago, but they left behind records of an unexplained Aetheric occurrence. Every thousand years or so, the planet experiences something you might call a kind of eclipse.

For reasons unknown, the Aether gathers around the planet, forming a concentration of magic that manifests itself in the sky. In this case, a natural spell blots out the sun regardless of the viewer's perspective.

But you don't see the sun as a black disc. Instead, it's like the sun is cut out, and you can see...beyond.

The sun of Nezarin becomes a clear lens, through which you can see the future.

Wizards throughout history have left behind a sizeable body of work about this phenomenon, which the locals had a dozen names for, from the Eye of God to the Future Fall.

All mages have a particular interest in unique magical events, as they can be used to magnify spells.

Which was why I came to Nezarin in the first place.

Employees in the silver-and-blue uniforms of the Vallenar Corporation bustled around me, setting up equipment in a wide circle. Industrial lights loomed overhead, ready to activate when the sun gave up. Aluminum crates were stacked at specific points around the circle, precisely where I had indicated.

The circle was one hundred yards in diameter, drawn in ancient stones placed by the locals. This was one of the thousands of sites around the planet where they had come to view the Eye of God, in the days before they'd abandoned their home planet entirely.

In the center of that circle, I had marked out a new pattern. An intricate seal of complex magical meaning, with lines workers now traced by carefully pouring glittering dust from open containers.

The dust was made of powdered diamonds. No, let me rephrase, because just about any planet has diamonds. These were made from Dornoth night-diamonds, one of that planet's most prized natural substances. We'd had to negotiate an exemption with the planetary government before they would allow us to purchase a single night-diamond.

Every half-second that a worker dispensed that glittering dust, they dumped out treasure worth more than the city of their birth.

And the night-diamonds weren't even close to the most valuable component the Vallenar Corporation had found for this ritual. The expense would bankrupt many civilized systems.

Which was why I had double-checked, triple-checked, and had a team of experts in orbit verify my placement of every inch of the magic circle. And still, my stomach churned with worry and anticipation.

I was about to reach beyond the limitations of the universe. To get a glimpse further into the Aether, further into magic, than anyone ever had. And to bring knowledge back with me.

But we only had one shot.

The sun started to fade from view, light dimming gradually. Our

Vallenar Corporation camp occupied a large outcropping close to the peak of a mountain, but the air was still; magical barriers kept the wind from getting anywhere close to us. To an outside observer, it would look like a subtle, invisible dome over our entire operation.

I pointed out directions to my team, guiding them through steps we'd practiced hundreds of times. As an experienced Archmage of sealing and binding magic, I had designed the program they were following. I'd written the spell we were all about to cast. They didn't need my guidance, but still I drummed fingers on my thigh.

In less than an hour, my life's work would be complete.

A shuttle slowly lowered from the sky, landing outside the wind-barrier so it didn't kick up dust. A ramp extended and more workers in silver and blue came out in pairs, each carrying another aluminum crate or massive work of art between them.

After six or seven pairs, my father strode down the ramp.

All the members of the Vallenar Corporation straightened at the sight of him. He wore a tailored gray suit and carried himself as though he owned everything here.

Some would say he did.

We weren't a military organization, but still some people saluted. Most of them had never seen the President of the Vallenar Corporation in person. Though, since everyone here was part of my team, they saw another Vallenar every day.

Benri Vallenar ignored everyone else and marched my way. He looked like the older version of me: his dark skin had more wrinkles, and the sheen of his silver hair and eyes had faded slightly with time.

Neither the eyes nor the hair were natural, of course. Our resemblance was no accident, either.

My parents had been eager to design the perfect heir to the Vallenar Corporation, which was a virtual copy of my father.

He ignored everyone else until he reached me, and even then, he didn't immediately speak. He stood next to me, looking over the bustling swarm of scurrying workers. He pulled out a cigarette, lit it with a snap of his fingers, and put it into his mouth.

Only after letting out a long puff of smoke did he say anything. "How's our condition, Varic?"

If I had eaten anything, I would have vomited an hour ago from sheer nerves. At the same time, I had never looked forward to anything quite so much...nor had I ever been so afraid that something would go wrong.

"We're ahead of schedule," I reported. "I've confirmed the structure of the spell and the Aether is strong. It all looks good." I raised my hand and blocked out the sun, trying to get a glimpse of the approaching Future Fall. "Won't be long now."

"I saw you went over budget on the Kyraxian Spirit-Orbs." He took another drag of the cigarette.

I had hoped he wouldn't discover that until after the ritual was over. "Now's not the time to hold back. With the Spirit-Orbs, I'm confident we can get five reflections."

"That's up to you, isn't it?"

Benri Vallenar's silver gaze wasn't focused on me, but I felt pierced as though it was. In the same way, he didn't need to remind me how much expense went into this ritual.

There was no practice run. No second chance, and no refunds. Magic didn't function that way. The spell would work as intended, but that didn't mean we would like the results.

Either we completed something that no one in galactic history ever had or we threw a thousand fortunes into a black hole.

And it all came down to me.

Everyone else there wore blue and silver, but I alone wore a white, padded jumpsuit. Aetheric sigils covered the cloth, magic symbols I'd drawn myself in black marker.

I may have been the second-best mage on this planet, and the one who had designed the ritual, but I wasn't the caster.

I was the target.

"Don't think about the money, Dad. Think about the magic!" Between my fingers, I gazed up at the sun. "Even if we don't make a profit, we're going to make *history*."

"It's all about the money. That's our family motto."

"No, it isn't."

"Then I'll pay to have it changed." He glared at me through a cloud of smoke. "You're on the hook for all this. Don't forget."

"I'm the one in the chair!" I took a deep breath. "Never mind. Dad, if I...if something goes wrong..."

Spells never went *wrong*, exactly. They always worked as intended if you cast them correctly. But they often had unintended consequences.

We had done everything to minimize risk, but it was still possible that the Varic Vallenar who walked out of that circle wouldn't be the same *me* that walked in.

As I tried to put my feelings into words, my father turned to me with raised eyebrows. "What do you mean, if something goes *wrong?*"

"No, everything looks good, I mean—"

He jabbed a finger into my chest. "I'm investing a hundred billion standards in *you*. Don't show me doubt, show me *skill*. Show me confidence. If you can't handle it, you'd better say so right now."

I started to snap back at him...but deflated. He was right, after all. As usual.

I was a Galactic Union-certified Archmage of sealing and binding. This was *my* ritual, my magic, and there was no room left for doubt.

After steadying myself, I pointed to the head of the circle. "Finish your preparations and get in position. Preliminary incantation begins in twenty-four minutes, so I want you with staff in hand ten minutes early."

He released another breath of smoke. "That's more like it."

I took my own advice, walking the edge of the magic circle as the sun overhead gave off less light. It wasn't being obscured, but rather fading. Now that it was dim enough to glance at, the star gave the impression of collapsing in on itself. Like it was a sinkhole, slowly crumbling into a tunnel beneath.

Every ritual component rested in its designated spot around the circle, most still inside the aluminum crates in which they'd been shipped. I passed a tank of water with one gleaming fish inside. Its mirror-bright scales reflected different versions of me, possibilities unrealized, and I couldn't resist a quick glance as I strode by.

One open crate held golden coins heaped inside, a massive chest of treasure from an ancient empire. Each coin contained a day of life, and I ran my hand over the gold without touching it.

A stone slab, taller than me, that had once rested on the tomb of an ancient wizard now stood propped up by a titanium frame. It bore an Aetheric formula that allowed for rebirth and faced the center of the circle.

Everything I passed was a priceless artifact that had turned out to be not-quite-so-priceless when the Vallenar Corporation threw open its bank account. Any one of these could become the cornerstone of a once-in-a-lifetime ritual, and they were all great mysteries of magic. It felt disrespectful not to give each the admiration it deserved.

We had forty-nine of them. Seven sevens.

They spiraled inward to the center of the circle, all facing one very mundane item at the center: a padded chair.

When I'd finished tracing the complex symbols within the circle, I finally reached the middle and lifted the console strapped to my left forearm. The device's screen flickered as it shifted to transmission mode.

"Ritual subject in position," I said. "Ten minutes to preliminary incantation."

Then I unstrapped my console and handed it to an attendant. There couldn't be anything on me that might interfere with the spell.

I sank into the chair and leaned back. Now, in one sense, my part was over. Years of research, planning, calculation, and preparations culminated in this moment.

Excitement and worry wove together until I couldn't tell where one ended and the other began, but there was nothing else my concern could accomplish. The mages performing this ritual were professionals, and I'd trained them myself. They wouldn't make a mistake.

Now, I just had to lean back and enjoy the magic.

"Oh, wait!" I said, before the attendant left. "Do you have a marker? I think I left one by the—oh, you do! Thanks, just let me..."

The man handed me the marker and I leaned over to a set of lights next to my chair. It was just a box of seven lights at the top of a waist-high pole; my team hadn't wanted to put it there, but I'd insisted.

The number of shining lights would show me how successful the spell was.

Currently, only the left-most light was lit. One was the default state, and seven would mean the spell had gone perfectly.

One light, because I had mastered one magic.

I started to circle the fifth light but stopped after putting the marker to glass. I could be a little more optimistic. After another second of hesitation, I circled the sixth light. Then I capped the marker and handed it back to the attendant before settling into the chair again.

I had never expected the full seven. Five would be excellent, and six would exceed all our hopes.

My father hadn't wanted me to have the light. It was an unnecessary distraction. But the initial incantation took long minutes, and I needed something to distract my mind. This, at least, would give me something to watch.

A voice from a nearby speaker echoed over the ritual site. *"All personnel in place. Thirty seconds to ritual initiation."*

Six mages spread around the outer edges of a circle, evenly spaced from each other, but leaving a gap for the seventh: my father.

The silver-eyed Archmage, the President of the Vallenar Corporation, carried a silver staff topped by a blue crystal. At precisely the correct moment, my father slammed the butt of his staff into the ground and began to chant.

All around him, above and beneath physical reality, the Aether shook.

Benri Vallenar's every syllable resonated with magic itself, silver-gray symbols flickering in the air around him as the Aether responded to his call.

Though it would make no difference, I ran over the entire ritual in my head. I couldn't help it.

The spell my father chanted was a variation on his signature spell: the Mirror of Silence. Ordinarily, he could manifest temporary copies of his targets, reflections of possibility brought into being.

I could see the influence of that spell even now, as flickering gray ghosts began to appear like shadows around all the artifacts in the circle. They buzzed like static, appearing and disappearing.

The spell functioned by manifesting alternate possibilities. Dreams made real.

This time, we were reaching further than that. Instead of bringing shadows of myself *out* of me, we were going to summon them *into* me. I was about to channel knowledge from my alternate selves.

Spells I *could* have known, but never did. Skills I *might* have trained. Talents I never developed. Sights unseen, lessons unlearned.

Wizards each specialized in a single magic. The more they advanced in skill and power, the more focused they became. One mage could only ever master one discipline.

Until this ritual.

We were about to break that rule.

If everything went well, I would unite the skill of seven wizards in one body. I would see further into magic than any mortal ever had and master more spells than anyone else in history.

Here, today, I would glimpse the heart of magic itself.

As the chanting reached a crescendo, the entire circle around me shone bright silver. All the artifacts were surrounded by black-and-white reflections, like holographic duplicates. I should have been relieved—the spell was on track—but I had left my analytical mind behind. Initial success only heightened my nerves.

Especially when restraints wrapped around my wrists and ankles and the chair began to lean backwards.

That was all part of the plan I'd devised myself, but it still wasn't comfortable being strapped into place and made to look into the sky.

Until I saw God's Eye slowly open. Then I was left with only wonder.

The sun crumbled into nothing more than a bright ring, leaving me looking into a tunnel beyond the world. A hole into eternity.

The spell reached its apex, the voices of the seven chanting mages blending into a transcendent song echoing through the Aether itself. The mundane world fell away, and finally I saw past the limits of mortal magic.

And there I saw...

...failure.

I was someone else. No, I was still myself, but another version. I'd lived an entire life, and I remembered it all. In fact, I forgot the version of myself strapped to a white chair, and this became my entire reality.

I knelt on the sticky floor of a disgusting chamber, one that was equal parts grown from bioengineered flesh and hammered from steel. I wore a suit of powered combat armor, but my visor blared crimson warnings. It was all damaged, just dead weight holding my body down, and one of my eyes was glued shut with blood.

My weapons were empty, I was exhausted from casting spell after spell, and my wand was shattered beyond repair. Disgusting abominations of cybernetics and undead flesh held me down. They forced my head up, looking at the edge of a metal table.

I shuddered back from the Aetheric symbols that shone over that table. Or rather, at the monster those symbols crowned.

A ten-foot-tall fusion of man and machine rose from the table. He opened blazing eyes and looked at the woman next to me.

Because of the angle of my head, I could only see glimpses of her, but I heard her struggle. She screamed at him, and I felt the total failure seeping into my soul.

We had fought a long crusade to stop the Iron King. First, to stop him from being born in the first place, then to stop him from gathering power, and finally to stop him from eating through the galaxy like a raging fire. We had suffered through too many defeats. And now, one more.

Still without looking at me, the Iron King put his metal hand through my chest.

I died in failure, leaving the galaxy to be killed and raised again as an army of the shambling cyborg dead.

Then I came to, gasping while strapped to a white chair.

I strained and struggled, trying to get out. The Iron King had strapped me down! Where was I? How did I get here? I tried to cast a pathfinding spell, but my navigational magic was restricted by binding circles on my restraints. I had to get out.

As I wrestled with the straps, I saw the seven lights.

Two were lit.

That triggered a memory, and I froze with realization. Somehow, I had gone back in time. It wasn't too late, the King hadn't been born yet, I could still stop—

Then more memories came back, and they struggled with one another.

I hadn't traveled backwards. I had seen another life, one that was years further into the future than this one.

But that wasn't how the spell worked.

I wasn't supposed to be summoning memories of entire lives, just the spells. This wasn't even on my list of possible outcomes.

Now, I remembered living two lives. Was this a memory? Was it still a vision? Which set of memories was the real one?

I had mastered two disciplines of magic, sure, but it did not feel at all like a victory. Had the Aether decided for some reason that I *needed* to live two lives? Why?

Before I figured it out, the collapsed sun drew me back in.

This time, I wore solid blue. I piloted a massive humanoid mech of the same color, and I fought side-by-side with others of my order.

We were the Knights of the Titan Force, and we defended the galaxy from monsters.

As the Blue Knight, I clashed with alien magic and wielded elemental water as a weapon. I provided balancing wisdom to our hot headed leader, the Red Knight. He and I were opposites in many ways, but our united purpose forged us into friends.

Until, one day, we failed.

A planet-sized insect bit down on the Yellow Knight, swallowing her and her mech whole. The Swarm-Queen raised one titanic claw, and fire from a nearby star began to stream into its mouth. As the creature fed on the corona of a local sun, swarms of insectoid monster-spawn rushed past us and began to strip the biomass from the closest planet.

We were defeated. I took off my armor and retired.

Insects from beyond the universe ruled the galaxy, and I lived the rest of my life knowing I had failed to stop them.

Once again, I woke in a panic, sweating and staring into the third light. I wanted to scream the abort code, but I couldn't remember what it was. I could barely remember who *I* was.

I remembered my name. That was one of the only things consistent through every life.

But what it meant to be Varic Vallenar changed. I had three different definitions. And three different magics.

The vision swallowed me again.

I saw the Galactic Union, the largest interplanetary government in civilized space, take over and start a civil war in pursuit of galactic dominance. Freedom became a distant memory, and I was executed in a secret prison.

Four lights.

I fought a crusade against an invincible warrior, hailed as a hero, as he turned his powers against those he once defended. He killed me to send a message, but at least I died before I could see the galaxy bow to him.

Five lights.

I guarded a towering Karoshan queen, whose power was so great I sometimes wondered why she needed bodyguards at all. Until genetically altered super-soldiers came for her. I told her I could defeat them with curse spells. No one was my equal in magic. She trusted me, and I died knowing that my pride would be her downfall.

Six lights.

Six childhoods, six apprenticeships, six sets of fears and hopes. I learned more lessons than anyone else, and I learned the same lessons more times. I saw myself die and I saw the galaxy fall.

Six lives swirled in my head, and I cried out to the Aether for mercy.

At that moment, all the lights went out. The motors in my chair screeched. The phenomenon in the sky dimmed.

And I blacked out.

CHAPTER TWO

BENRI VALLENAR CHANNELED a greater spell than any he'd ever cast. Any that had *ever* been cast, at least in centuries. Aether twisted the entire sky, centered on the God's Eye that had replaced the sun, and dozens of irreplaceable artifacts shone like silver stars all around the ritual circle.

He could see it. Anyone half-trained in magic throughout the whole sector could probably see the effects of this ritual on the Aether.

Their spell was a *masterpiece*.

His son, Varic, convulsed on the chair restraining him, but that was as expected. He was channeling enough magic through him to blight planets or douse a sun. Next to him was the display of seven lights that Benri had cautioned against. Varic shouldn't have a distraction next to him, and they would know how well the ritual succeeded after it ended.

Now, he was glad for it. Six lights showed there. *Six.* Almost perfect.

The spell collapsed, silver light dying in an instant, machines blowing out all over the ritual circle. His jaw clicked shut, biting off the incantation, as the Aether itself stopped his speech.

The site went dark, but Benri felt like celebrating. He would have been satisfied with four lights, but he'd gotten *six*.

Now he controlled a sixfold Archmage. The only one that ever existed—that ever would exist, surely. No ritual like this could be duplicated. Six sets of magic, when the Aether only allowed one.

Benri's son had become the most valuable asset in the galaxy.

Varic was slumped in the chair. Understandable. Benri looked to a nearby medic, who consulted a screen on her console.

She gave Benri a thumbs-up. "Vitals are good. Contingency spells didn't even activate."

"Well done," Benri said. "Security measures are in place?"

"It doesn't look like they'll be necessary."

"Better to be safe. How long until he wakes up?"

"Computer estimates just a few seconds."

"Good. Let the psych team know." Varic had just gained the results of five extra lives of magical training. There shouldn't be any significant risk—it wasn't as though the ritual had really changed him—but one never knew what effects stress could have. And the Aether often had unexpected consequences, at least for spells this complex.

It would be days, maybe weeks, before they understood the full import of this spell. Before they knew exactly how valuable Varic had become. Varic would need practice, surely, to become used to his new abilities.

Benri had to be patient...but even so, he couldn't help but glance at a wizard to his left.

The man, a visibly aged half-Aethril with lights that sparkled like stars in his hair, stared at Varic through a spinning circle of magical symbols.

"We got six, didn't we, Teranon?" Benri asked.

Teranon adjusted his vision-spell. "I don't...I'm not...Ben, I don't know what we got."

Benri froze. They *couldn't* have failed. That wouldn't make any sense. It would violate every principle of magic he knew. The Aether always responded to power, to skill, to effort, and to sacrifice.

"The meter registered six reflections," Benri pointed out, trying to keep the desperation from his voice.

Teranon swallowed hard. "Take a look." He grabbed the slowly spinning disc of Aetheric symbols and slid it over like a lens.

Benri looked through. Certain symbols flashed, while others shone brightly. This analysis spell wasn't his area of expertise, but he was educated enough to get a general reading.

And he didn't see a problem.

He slammed his staff into the ground, unable to contain his pride. "Six! *At least* six! We did it!"

One Archmage with the magic of six wasn't worth *just* six other wizards. He would climb the heights of magic farther than any before him. Varic would go down in history as the greatest magical genius of all mankind, and Benri was the one who created him.

He watched his masterpiece come together through the mystic lens. "How soon can we have him..."

Benri's voice died slowly when he saw what else the spell revealed to him.

The center of the circle showed six lights inside of Varic. Representations of different magical styles he'd learned, the powers he'd stolen from different lives.

They were stretching, weaving into one another, twisting around like ribbons. Into a knot that was growing in complexity every second.

Teranon ran a hand through his own star-speckled hair. "I think we got more than we bargained for, Ben."

Six separate sources of magic were all bleeding into one another, each strengthening the others. Evolving.

In his stunned thoughts, Benri couldn't come up with an appropriate analogy. It was like mixing random chemicals and seeing them spontaneously create life. He had been trying to paint a portrait only to see the image crawl off the canvas.

It looked like the spells were...*learning*.

"Brain activity," Benri snapped.

The medic responded immediately, "Looks good, sir. He's about to wake up."

"I can't imagine Varic controlling all this," Teranon said. "We'll need to be patient with him for a while."

Teranon was a wise man, a longtime Archmage, and one of Benri's mentors. And he was thinking too small.

The man thought they had just burdened Varic with great weights while trying to give him extra strength. In his mind, Varic would need help to carry them until he got used to things.

Benri had cast the spell himself. He understood the theory better than anyone.

Something more had happened.

The spell had acted according to its nature and the intention of the casters, as it was supposed to, but it had gone far deeper than they had ever imagined. They'd broken new ground.

New ground could be dangerous.

"Security one, go," Benri said.

An attendant relayed his order, and a moment later, further restraints wrapped around Varic's body.

Teranon held out a hand. "Wait, I don't think this is—"

"Security two, go."

Four walls fell from a ship above Varic, slamming down around him in an impromptu cage. The walls lit up with shining magic symbols, cutting him off from the Aether. Varic had asked for these measures, though they weren't supposed to be activated at the same time.

"You think you got him?" Teranon asked bitterly. "Come on. Now, when Varic wakes up, he's going to think you—"

"He's awake!" the medic reported.

Benri braced himself...but he saw only the cage. There was no explosion, no magical eruption. Not that there should be, of course. He had just expected something to go dramatically wrong.

Wizards learned to trust such instincts, but even so, Benri hesitated. Logically, this was overkill. Varic hadn't gotten any *stronger*, which Teranon's analysis spell confirmed. A wizard's strength was determined by knowledge, skill, and accomplishment, not by sheer magical weight, and that much remained true.

Despite the strange reactions of Varic's internal magic, he wouldn't be able to get out of his chair without assistance.

One of the cage walls tipped over. It hit the ground with a crash, and Varic walked out.

"Security three through seven," Benri shouted, but his attendants were already on it.

Another cage of magic and metal erupted from the ground beneath Varic, sealing a wide circle inside a steel dome. Seven pillars dropped from the sky, spreading a field between them. Hovering drones sprayed a magic-dispersing mist over the outside, and a half-ring of armed men rushed out, pointing rifles inward at the dome in case of a breakout.

"How long until he passes out?" Benri asked.

"The gas takes three seconds, the spell takes five," the medic responded. "Between the two of them, he should have been out before you...asked the..." She trailed off, looking at her console.

Benri dusted off his hands and braced his staff, ready for battle. "He's not out, is he?"

"I think he's *casting*."

The interior of that dome should have been completely cut off from the Aether, but Benri nodded as though it made perfect sense.

A second later, the side of the steel dome exploded outward, and Varic strode through the newly created doorway. His white jumpsuit was unscratched, and he brushed pieces of his restraints from his arms like cobwebs.

The anti-magic mist in the air around him drifted away as though repelled by his very nature. He strolled up to the barrier spell outside, glanced at it, and then waved a hand.

The spell parted as though he'd swept aside a curtain.

Teranon made a choking sound. *"What?"*

That hadn't been a display of raw power. It was skill, but on a different level than anything they had ever seen. It was like watching someone perform molecular surgery with a kitchen-knife.

Security forces opened fire. They released stun charges, not bullets or plasma bolts—Benri didn't want his investment damaged, not to mention that this was his son—but every one of the shots stopped at arm's reach from Varic. The blue shells whined in the air, where he was holding them.

With crude telekinesis.

It would only have been a little harder to catch the shots with his bare hands.

Varic tilted his head and looked at his father, and a chill ran up Benri's spine. This wasn't an alien creature or a being of pure magic inhabiting his son's body. This was Varic.

But he looked at his father with distant eyes.

Varic levitated up, drifting over to Benri, then settled down back to the ground to talk face-to-face.

Benri pretended he hadn't noticed anything out of the ordinary. "What happened to you?"

"Memories," Varic said, and his voice was dry. "The magic came with memories."

"That doesn't make any sense. We only summoned the spells and—"

"And everything necessary to use them," Varic finished. "Yeah. Apparently the Aether thought I needed to live six lives."

Benri toyed with that realization for a moment. It was a possibility they'd never considered, but it came with both obstacles and opportunities.

"How was—" he started to ask.

"It wasn't fun," Varic answered.

"Let's get you to the psych panel," Benri said. He signaled the medic.

Varic waved a hand. "Nah, I'm leaving. Where's my ship? Never mind, I see it."

He walked heavily away, trudging through the bare grit of the mountainside. Benri was having trouble keeping up with the reality of the situation, but he still gestured the security team back. They looked only too willing to try another volley of stun rounds.

"Varic. What did you see in there?" He had to get his son talking, to keep him here, and Varic was always willing to talk magic.

Varic sighed heavily. "No matter what I say, you'll try to keep me here. I'd rather skip the long conversation and get right to the part where I leave."

"You cost me a hundred *billion* standards! You owe me an explanation! What did you see? And where are you going?"

Varic waved a hand toward his ship, and the Aether flickered in a dozen deftly manipulated symbols. While Benri was still in awe at the display, the ship rumbled to life and extended a docking ramp.

Varic looked back at his father with dull silver eyes. "I'm going to save the galaxy, but I'll probably just die trying. I usually do."

Then he leaped off, a burst of telekinesis carrying him to his ship like a gentle wind.

CHAPTER THREE

ONE YEAR LATER

LIKE I SAID, I'd already lived through five deaths. I didn't want to make that six.

So I kept the output of my starship down as I crept around the edges of the battle. Streaks of light lit up space all around the local star system, plasma bolts slashing through the darkness in both directions.

The system had been divided into two neat halves. The Galactic Union fleet controlled one half, their gray ships hanging in formation between me and the local sun.

They traded blows with a swarm of abominations. Ships that were equal parts metal and flesh, machines forcibly fused with living beings. The Iron Legion stole its ships and infected them with meat, so their fleet was a haphazard collection of gruesome trophies that were nonetheless coordinated with mechanical precision.

The Legion orbited one structure in particular, a bulbous slab the size of a small moon that was the beating heart of the Iron Legion's fleet. This Iron Hive even somewhat resembled a heart, though one with a collection of battleships half-melted into it, sticking out here and there like they'd been shoved into place by a gigantic child.

A shimmering emerald jewel of a planet hung in the shadow of the Hive. Much of its surface had been scorched by the invasion of the Legion, but the timely arrival of the Galactic Union fleet had brought that invasion to a halt.

Timely was a little generous, but at least they had eventually acted on my repeated warnings. If they had taken my calls weeks ago, they could have had a fleet here to intercept before the Legion ever came out of Subspace.

Now, because they had waited until the last possible second to listen to me, they were about to be too late.

The Iron Legion wasn't fighting aggressively. Their ships held defensive formations around the Hive, dragging out this engagement as long as possible.

While there could be a number of reasons for that, which Union tacticians would no doubt be debating to death, I knew what was happening. There was a weapon aboard that Hive, one that would turn the battle for the Legion. They were buying time for it to be completed.

The Iron King was about to be born.

And that's why I was crawling around the edges of the battle and toward the planet, coming closer and closer to the Iron Hive.

I'd seen what a King could do. Not only had he led the expansion of the Iron Legion throughout the galaxy, billions captured and made into cyborg zombies, but he had killed me. I could still feel the cold of his steel arm in my chest.

But that was another life.

This time, I was here to stop that invasion before it began.

Darkness spilled over the viewport of my ship as I slipped into the shadow of the Hive. The Legion's attention was captured by the battle, so I had an opening.

Not that any approach to the Hive was undefended. Fighters, scout-ships, defensive drones, and weapons platforms on the surface of the Hive itself all scanned nearby space for intruders like me. This approach was lightly protected only by the standards of an active battlefield.

A wedge-shaped Hunter ship covered in an insectoid carapace passed over me, so close I could see the segments of its armor. Each Hunter had enough firepower to shred *Moonfall,* my personal starship, in a single volley.

But the Hunter flew right past me.

"Invisibility spell is holding," *Moonfall* informed me.

If it wasn't, I'd be floating in space amidst the wreckage of my ship, but nonetheless I nodded to acknowledge the computer.

Then I patted the glowing, twisting ball of nebulous energy hovering over the ship's console.

"You're doing great," I told the invisibility spell. "Hang in there."

The twisting knot of shining cyan magic gave what I imagined to be a tired chime. It had worked hard these past few hours, and it wouldn't last much longer. It wasn't my spell, just one I had borrowed, so I could only stretch its life for so long. Soon, the spell would die, but it burned the last of its life for my sake.

By the way, spells aren't conscious. I just like to imagine they are.

Maybe I've been working alone too long.

I tapped my forehead in a brief salute to acknowledge the invisibility spell's brave sacrifice, then I took the starship controls again to begin our approach into the Iron Hive.

While I did, I spoke to my ship. "I'm going to crack open a passage. On my mark, give me a fourteen-minute timer and then shoot your way through the Hive toward my position. You'll have to run the forward guns hot. Burn them out."

"Firing on the registered pilot is a violation of safety protocols."

"I'll be fine."

"Safety protocols—"

"Override." We were angling for a shot on the thinnest part of the Iron Hive's armor. I muttered a quick pathfinding spell, which made a tunnel through the Hive light up in my vision. That was the route I needed to take, and I lined *Moonfall*'s cannons up with that shining white line that only I could see.

Moonfall was dark gray, with a shape that somewhat reminded me of a scorpion with its tail raised. Its forward cannons were positioned where the 'claws' would be, but a little closer to the center.

I was about to tighten my finger on the trigger, but I hesitated at a sudden thought. *"Moonfall,* to be clear, don't shoot me. Shoot *toward* me."

"Safety protocols have been overridden."

"Shoot in my direction until you see me, then fire on whatever else is in the room. Not me."

"Parameters unclear. Clarification required. Identify 'whatever else' and 'room.'"

This is why machines are never as good as magic. You have to be so exact.

"Any living being you see is a hostile except for me. Is that clear?"

Moonfall started to respond, but something changed in that moment. The entire Iron Hive quivered as though it had been struck, and my pathfinding spell dimmed, fuzzed, and shifted slightly as it picked out a different path.

Inside that Hive, the King was being born.

If I waited any longer, I'd be too late.

I cut off my computer by shouting "Mark!" and squeezing the triggers for *Moonfall's* forward plasma cannons.

Bolts of bright, superheated orange plasma chewed into the side of the Iron Hive in a destructive river. There were no shields on the Hive, as it needed to allow the free entry and exit of its fighters, so my guns sent blood and debris gushing into space as they ate through steel and skin alike.

The invisibility spell hovering over the console glowed a little brighter. From the outside, we'd look like nothing. Maybe a little liquid and dust coming off the Hive, if the debris drifted too far.

Best of all, the spell hid me from more than just sight. Scanners, infrared, and detection spells would be just as blind as the naked eye. To the magic, invisible meant *invisible.*

That's why magic is better than technology.

If I'd picked a random spot in the Hive's hull, the process of drilling inside might have taken half an hour. The pathfinding spell showed me the weakest entry point, so instead, I tore open a wound in the Hive within thirty seconds.

As soon as air began gushing out, I rose from the pilot's chair and began striding to the airlock.

I equipped myself as I walked. Onto my left hand, a levitation ring. On my neck, a shield amulet, shining orange. My Lightcaster IV plasma pistol went into its holster on one hip, and my wand—which glowed like neon sapphire and buzzed eagerly—onto the other.

Finally, I slid into my blue mantle. Once I felt its protective magic settle over me, I flipped up the hood and pressed my hand to the panel to open the airlock.

The screen flashed.

Locks Engaged – Verbal Override Required

I faced the microphone and stated my own name. "Varic Vallenar. Let me out."

Metal bolts thunked as they slid open, and the airlock hatch hissed open. It closed after me when I stepped inside, and there was a pause before the computer released the external hatch.

It was a brief pause, only a second or two, but it was one of those moments that seemed to stretch. The fingers of my right hand twitched, tapping on nothing, eager to draw a weapon. I stared through the viewport and into the distant battle, or at least what I could see of it from around the curvature of the Hive. Impatience boiled in my chest.

I couldn't wait to be spilled out into space.

Just when I was about to ask the computer what was taking so long, the external hatch opened. There came a sudden rush of sound as air huffed out into the void, and then there was silence.

I drifted in vacuum, my hood fluttering with the remains of the air escaping around me. Spidery runes around the hem of my mantle glowed softly silver as its protection spell engaged.

The mantle was meant to protect me from everything. Even the vacuum of space.

I activated my levitation ring, which caused an invisible cushion to spread out from me. Somehow the effect sounded more silent than silence, like my ears had been stuffed with cloth. Using this telekinetic force, I spun myself around to orient toward the Iron Hive.

It loomed over me, closer than I'd realized. *Moonfall* hovered only a few dozen yards from the bleeding surface of the Hive, nose-down, as though it had halted itself just before crashing into the surface.

The ship's shields had protected it from flying debris as it tore into the Hive, but now they were down, allowing me to drift quickly toward the open gash in the alien surface.

I flew past molten metal and torn muscle, both of which had already started to squirm as the Hive healed itself. Past the mangled wound made by my ship's cannons, there was an iron walkway leading deeper inside.

Thanks to the effect of my pathfinder spell, the road glowed white. This was the way to go.

I lowered myself down to the intact portion of the metal road's surface and checked the timer on the computer strapped to my wrist. Obedient to my thoughts, it displayed the countdown transmitted by *Moonfall*.

12:11

12:10

Before it could tick down any further, I set out at a sprint down the hall.

The levitation ring could carry me, but in a straight shot like this, it wouldn't be much faster than running. And the ring had a limited power supply I didn't want to waste for no reason.

Not to mention that I knew I wouldn't run far. As I'd expected, I rounded the corner to face a makeshift door.

Tendrils of flesh holding metal plates had rushed out of the wall to seal the corridor after the hull breach, preventing the loss of any more atmosphere. Fortunately, I had expected this, so I was already chanting the right spell.

No one could hear my incantation in the vacuum, not even myself. But spells don't need air. They need the Aether, and that's everywhere.

I whipped out my wand, its metal plates buzzing eagerly in my hand and blue light shining from its core. I pointed it at the door and completed my incantation, and the Aether resonated, manifesting my spell.

It bloomed into a circle of white light, complex symbols and diagrams spinning inside it. The symbols had very intricate and subtle meanings, but it all translated to 'stop.'

This wasn't the spell to unlock the door. It was the spell to deal with what came next.

I tucked away my wand and pulled out my Lightcaster IV. Plasma pistols often didn't work in vacuum, but this one did.

In fact, that was the weapon's tag line from its famous marketing campaign. *Lightcasters. They work anywhere!*

An orange streak erupted from my pistol's barrel, hit the white circle of my spell, and froze.

So did all my follow-up shots, until I had an entire volley of plasma bolts locked in the air in front of me.

Then and only then did I chant the spell unlocking the door. Sealing magic was my original specialty in this life, and that, of course, includes spells to *un*-seal things.

The door rushed open at my word to reveal the small flesh-and-steel army that had been pushing at the other side. Just as I'd known they would be.

In an Iron Hive, you have to expect a horde of Pawns behind every door.

They were eager to spill out and devour me, heedless of the fact that they would suffocate and die in seconds. If they could tear me to pieces first, they would die satisfied.

It's hard to describe the instinctive revulsion you feel when you first encounter an Iron Legion Pawn. They're vaguely humanoid, twisted and molded so grotesquely that it's impossible to tell whether they used to be human or some other species.

They are usually made of parts leftover from the creation of other Iron Legion creatures, so it's probably a mix.

Anyway, the result is a squat minion of muscle and bone whose missing pieces are completed by machine parts. Some shamble on one elephantine leg and one wheel, others crawl on four elongated limbs.

They have little brain left. Not enough to feel pain or self-awareness, which is the one blessing for victims of the Legion. They can only fulfill the most basic functions and are commanded like tools by those higher up in the Hive hierarchy.

In this case, someone had ordered them to go hurl themselves into the vacuum. Which they did with slavering, single-minded ferocity.

But they didn't get a chance to suffocate. The instant the door opened, I dropped my sealing spell.

All the plasma bolts I'd trapped in the seal flashed out and tore through the Pawns at the same time.

They still rushed out after me, but now they were only twitching corpses pulled by vacuum. My levitation ring shoved them aside as I dashed up the river of half-metal bodies and into the hurricane winds gushing out from deeper in the hallway.

If it's your *first* time seeing a Pawn, the revulsion can be bone-deep and crippling. Training programs for troops going into combat with the Iron Legion are designed to acclimate people to this level of shock.

But it wasn't my first time. I brushed past the dead Pawns without noticing them any more than it took to shove them aside with telekinesis.

I was an old hand at this. I had faced the Legion more times in my lives than I could remember. In fact, I only knew one other person with more experience fighting the Iron Legion than I had.

We battled side-by-side for years. We even died together.

Of course, none of that had ever really happened. She was probably out there among the Galactic Union now, pursuing her never-ending war against the Iron Legion while having never heard my name.

The six sets of memories do get confusing sometimes, but in the Hive, they were certainly an asset.

As the timer on my wrist continued to tick down, I pushed deeper inside, following the white line of my pathfinding spell. I wasn't distracted from the eyes that would slide out on stalks from metal panels in the walls, nor the sickening screams—or perhaps mechanical squeals—that echoed from other hallways.

I had seen all of it before. And had been trained for worse.

As I jogged along the metal road, I held my wand in my left hand and my pistol in my right. Curious drones or eye-stalks got the pistol while doors or anything else suspicious got a blue flash from the wand that sealed them in place.

That wouldn't kill them alone, but it would lock them in place. At least until the timer on my wrist hit zero.

The metal path sloped up and led to a larger door, this one looking more like a standard starship hatch than a horror show monstrosity. It was guarded, however, by a pair of Sentries inside sheet metal booths that extended from the wall.

Sentries are the big brothers of Pawns. At least they're usually made from a single corpse apiece.

They tend to be bigger, smarter, and capable of things like guarding positions and firing from cover. Which they did as I approached, filling the hallway with overlapping streams of fire.

I recognized their weapons as VC-21 chaos rifles. Two shots were ordinary plasma bolts, but every third was a magically accelerated bullet. The result was an interesting sound as the high-pitched snap of a plasma rifle alternated with the louder, deeper crack of a projectile shot.

The theory behind the chaos rifle was simple. Some shields and protective spells were effective against plasma bolts but fell to shots of solid matter, while others were the reverse. Chaos rifles fired them both, which would overwhelm most commonly used personal protection systems in seconds.

I walked out and all their shots pinged off the sphere of protection surrounding my body. That was my shield amulet proving its value. The shield was only visible where struck by a bolt or bullet, at which point it flared to life in a burst of crackling light.

My personal protections are not commonly available.

Under fire like this, I could stand here trading shots forever, or at least until reinforcements showed up with bigger guns.

Instead, I waved a hand and disrupted the Aether around their weapons.

The acceleration spells that fired their bullets swelled with power and suddenly performed their jobs with four hundred percent power. Both chaos rifles exploded, and magically driven shrapnel shredded the Sentries holding them.

That wasn't a spell, just a little trick. It helped that I was familiar with the rifles.

After all, my family made them.

The door past the two dead guards was locked, but flashes of eye-searing light passed through it, immaterial symbols reflected in the Aether. There was a big spell underway on the other side. A huge ritual, only minutes away from completion.

Wards, curses, and huge physical locks barred the door. I tore them away with a word.

The door hissed open, and I was met with the sight I had been waiting for. Six robed figures strode around on mechanical tendrils, the magic around them sparking into visible light and strange Aetheric symbols that floated in their auras.

These were Shepherds, the mages of the Iron Legion, but they weren't worth my notice. It was the subject of their ritual that sent a shot of adrenaline through me.

The six formerly living mages surrounded a figure strapped to a table. He resembled a ten-foot-tall human man. He had no visible skin, being wrapped in chrome armor, and his back was connected to long strands of many kinds. Electrical wires to charge his cybernetic components, pulsing umbilical cords carrying chemicals, and mystical streams of light supplying complex workings of Aether.

While his eyes were closed, his head wasn't. His skull was a transparent tank containing a swollen brain, which flickered with lights. Lights that indicated thought.

He was starting to *think*.

In a few more minutes, this Hive would have given birth to a functioning King of the Iron Legion.

That would have meant, at very least, the loss of the entire Galactic Union fleet in this system. And if the King made it out of the system, and was given a few months or years to expand his power...

The Iron King that had killed me was fully mature. The first death I remembered.

But it wouldn't be the sixth.

The voices of the Shepherds rose together, chanting in an ancient language now used exclusively in ritual magic. They saw me enter, but they didn't stop their incantation. To them, stopping would be just as bad as letting me interfere, and they had multiple layers of shields protecting them.

Their voices overlapped in eerie unison, and I knew the meaning of their alien words. *"Rise now in steel, King of Death, King of all that—"*

I shot them.

I fired my Lightcaster IV as fast as I could pull the trigger. They had shields up, but I'm an Archmage in sealing and binding magic. Nobody's shields can keep me out.

I had already stripped away their protections, so my shots landed where they were intended: on the cords sustaining the life of the newborn King.

Electrical wires snapped, spraying sparks. Severed organic tubes squirted fluid, and non-physical Aetheric connections frayed away to nothing.

The metal-shrouded King convulsed on his table, and the Shepherds screamed. They turned to me, joining their magic with inhumanly perfect cooperation.

Of course, before they could cast a spell, I had shot three of them in the head.

I could strip away protective magic faster than they could cast. They had no defense against me unless someone else intervened.

The moment I thought so, someone intervened.

A metal panel came away from the wall and deflected the bolt that would have taken the fourth Shepherd through the head. That interference bought them enough time that the remaining three Shepherds finished their spell.

It was just a fireball. Shepherds aren't creative because creative mages don't get captured alive.

Still, it was a fireball formed by three people calling on the Aether in perfect unison. It swelled and filled the space between us, howling toward me. The heat rose until it got uncomfortable, but it didn't rise past that.

My mantle was enchanted with protection, which meant protection from all things. Including sunburn.

It could be overwhelmed by directed attacks, though, including the concussive force of this fireball spell. That was where my shield amulet came in. Between those two layers of protection, there was no gap.

In other words, the three-person fireball came to a crashing stop a few feet from me as it hit my shield and washed over it. While that alone didn't concern me, the fire in all directions blocked my sight.

I chanted rapidly, drawing the Aether into a spell. The boss of the Shepherds had shown himself.

Sure enough, when the fire finished spilling over the shield, I found myself face-to-face with a Bishop of the Iron Legion.

And when I say face-to-face, I mean it.

The Bishop was a giant face.

Technically, Bishops are a consciousness bound to manage certain Iron Legion Hives, but they tend to form faces out of the walls in order to converse. One of its eyes was a cluster of cameras high up on the wall, while the other was a bunch of living eyeballs shoved together.

It even had a nose, made from a bulge in the wall as though an actual giant pressed its face against the surface from the other side.

The skin-and-steel of the wall split horizontally into a mouth, and the Bishop spoke. Its voice was half-mechanical and shook the floor. "SURRENDER. YOU WILL BE ALLOWED TO SURVIVE."

Bishops aren't stupid. He just wanted me talking in case that might buy him some time.

I finished my incantation and leveled my wand.

"Absolute Burial," I said.

My strongest sealing spell responded to its name and surged into being, surrounding its target with swirling white discs of Aetheric sigils. After a brief second, the seals collapsed, carrying their target out of reality and into an isolated pocket of Subspace.

Obviously, my target was the King lying on the table. It was the only thing this Bishop cared about.

Sure enough, the room shook with the Bishop's fury. Guns emerged from the walls all around and more spells began to form from the Aether. Not my spells, this time.

Not only were Bishops not stupid, but they also weren't weak. It hadn't expected me to be able to do anything to the King so quickly, but I knew it wouldn't make that mistake again. Every second that passed gave the Shepherds time to cast, the Bishop time to overwhelm my defenses, and an army of Pawns time to get here and drown me in flesh.

Worse, the Absolute Burial spell had an anchor. The spell was a ball of twisted white seals combined together, which hovered like a moon over the table where the King had once lain.

A spell anchor like that was very difficult to destroy or unravel, but the Bishop could manage it, given enough time.

I had to defend myself, defend the spell, and get the anchor out of here before they could break it.

I shattered spells, deflected bullets, and fired into metal-fused flesh. Sweat stung my eyes, and every second felt like an hour. My lips never stopped chanting, my wand never stopped moving, and my trigger finger never rested.

My shield amulet burned against my chest, its spell stretched to the limit under the incessant barrage. The shield itself began to crack. The heat from encroaching magical fire pressed on me as my mantle's protective enchantment took up more of the burden from the failing amulet.

It was very stressful. For about two, maybe three minutes.

Then my timer ran down and I threw myself to the side.

The wall opposite the Bishop's face turned red. Then orange. Then it collapsed inward in a spray of molten metal.

Air rushed out of the chamber, grabbing several Pawns and dragging them into space. *Moonfall* emerged in the gap, plasma cannons incessantly roaring. Everything in the room was flash-cooked in seconds.

Everything except me.

When the plasma cannons spun down, I saw their barrels were white-hot and deformed. They'd need to be replaced.

Worth it.

I stretched out a hand, calling the Absolute Burial spell anchor. The white ball leaped obediently into my palm, having suffered some damage from the ship's bombardment but being no worse for wear.

Moonfall's voice sounded in my audio implant. *"Twenty seconds estimated before the Bishop patches the hull."*

Time to move, then. I strained my levitation ring to fly toward the airlock faster.

It wasn't the Bishop I was most concerned about outracing. It was my father.

He'd be here in minutes. An unborn, inactive Iron King was worth a fortune; almost as much as my ritual had cost. I'd sent him warnings, but he'd ignored them, as I'd known he would. He would never destroy the King. Not when there was a profit to be made.

So I'd do it myself.

Benri Vallenar stood on a steel outcropping looking over the mangled ruins of what had, until earlier that day, been an Iron Legion ritual room.

The Hive was dead now, subdued by Galactic Union troops. Soldiers were running throughout the structure, subduing Pawns, but this section had been secured by Vallenar Corporation personnel.

It was difficult to make out details in a room this devastated. Shredded by plasma cannons and then exposed to vacuum, there was little intact.

But one thing was missing that *should* have been there. Something durable enough to survive point-blank starship fire and valuable enough to be worth the fortunes he had sunk into funding this entire fight.

A young employee climbed up to him, wearing a sleek, helmeted spacesuit of blue-and-silver in spite of the fact that this room's atmosphere had been stabilized and pumped full of breathable air.

"Sir," the man reported, "we have confirmed signs of a major ritual involving at least five Shepherds and a Bishop."

"But you didn't find the King," Benri said. It wasn't really a question.

"We believe the ritual collapsed. There was a huge Aetheric disruption here, and if that failed ritual was focused on the King, that could account for the body's disappearance."

Benri pulled out a pack of cigarettes from his jacket pocket. He tapped one out, lit it with a quick twist of magic, and put it between his lips.

"Varic took it," he said at last.

The new employee looked confused. "Your...son? Is he working with the company again?"

"Yes," Benri said through a puff of smoke. "Yes, he is. Draft an announcement and put it on the Union Subline. My son, on behalf of the Vallenar Corporation, stopped the creation of a new Iron Legion King. The ritual failed and the body was lost. You can send them feeds from our cameras here to prove it."

The young man muttered into the console on his wrist, dictating the report. Benri left him to it.

This was only an attempt to salvage what he could. Varic had gotten away with an irreplaceable prize. Benri had sunk a fortune into an operation with nothing to show for it.

Again.

Now, at least the Union would think that Varic was working for them. It would save face for the Corporation, would make their rivals wary, and might even drive Varic back home. The Galactic Union would certainly put some pressure on him to see if the King's body really had been destroyed.

All in all, though, Benri had lost. That thought made the taste of the cigarette bitter, so he tore it out of his mouth and threw it against the wall.

The employee flinched but continued dictating.

Varic Vallenar was out there somewhere, mocking his father and preparing some grand magic with the Legion King's body. This was the second time he'd taken a priceless magical artifact from under his father's nose.

Benri would make sure it never happened again.

I unscrewed the torpedo, slid the spell anchor for the Absolute Burial inside, and then capped the torpedo again.

I patted the side. "Just hold on a little longer," I said to the spell within. "You're almost there."

Then I slid the torpedo into its tube, locked it, and ordered the computer to fire.

A flash of light erupted from *Moonfall's* launcher, carrying its magical payload forward...and into the sun that blazed nearby.

"Impact in sixteen minutes," the computer reported. The torpedo was Subspace-capable, vanishing here and there as it went in and out of a dive, skipping most of the journey between me and its destination.

I sank back into my chair and watched the torpedo as a red light on my monitor. I was still tense, staring at that blinking light. I wouldn't be satisfied until I saw it plunge into the star myself.

Then another monitor flashed a warning at me. It was a Subline alert; someone had mentioned me on the Union's public network.

I gave the okay, and a projector popped up with an image of my face. A handsome face, if I do say so myself, thanks to the best genetics money can buy.

A woman's voice came from the speakers. *"We're just learning that one of the unexpected heroes of the Galactic Union's victory in the Evven-Fahr system is Varic Vallenar, licensed Archmage and former heir to the Vallenar Corporation. Perhaps he isn't as far removed from his family as reports indicated, because it seems he participated in the battle on the Corporation's behalf.*

"Our sources say that he was the one who prevented a ritual intended to raise a new King of the Iron Legion. The disruption of the ritual led to significant damage to the Hive and the loss of the King's body, which is..."

The report went on after that, but I only listened with one ear. My father was publicly taking credit for me, trying to rope me back in.

He had made things hard for me in the last year, as I'd traveled around the galaxy. It hardly mattered now. The blinking red light that contained the Iron King was the only thing I cared about.

Once that torpedo burned up, I hoped I would sleep easier.

That was one of my deaths flying away from me, after all. It would make me that much safer. Then again, I could only prevent the fates I knew about. At least this would help a little.

I had spent the last year staving off impending doom. This was the last item on my list.

I'd pushed back every threat to the galaxy I knew about. In a way, I was safer. In another way, I was blind; who knew what else was out there?

Moonfall's smooth voice interrupted my thoughts. *"Awaiting navigational data. Where would you like to go, Captain?"*

I started to answer before I realized I had no idea. Other than warding off the imminent threats to the galaxy—not to mention my own death—I'd made no plans.

Honestly, I hadn't expected to have a future at all.

A few minutes later, *Moonfall* inquired again. *"Where would you like to go?"*

Even later, the torpedo containing the Absolute Burial spell crashed into the star.

"Impact confirmed. Target eliminated."

The spell anchor would be destroyed, releasing the lifeless body of the Iron Legion King. Which would disintegrate instantly in the heat of a star.

I watched the point on the monitor where the torpedo had disappeared. Everything had worked.

"Where would you like to go?"

I didn't know.

CHAPTER FOUR

A FEW MONTHS after the destruction of the Iron King, I crouched in the mud as it bubbled up. My eyes locked on the largest of the bubbles as it grew as big as my fist.

"This is it!" I whispered. "Everybody pay attention! Get ready!"

I didn't hear anything back, but I wasn't listening for their response anyway. My enthusiasm carried me off into a speech.

"The Theluusian aurora toad's unique Aether pattern is swelling now. If you look closely, you can see it gathering around the external shell of the mud. Do you see that glistening pattern? It's not reflecting the light, and the rain is avoiding it."

I indicated the column of uninterrupted air over the mud bubble. Not a drop of water fell on it, as though the clouds had decided to spare this patch of soil in particular.

"Notice how this is distinct from our weather protection magic," I continued, tapping my mantle. It kept me dry and warm, the air clear and temperature pleasant around me, but the mantle only stopped the rain. It didn't prevent the rain from falling in the first place.

"We noticed," one of my students said.

I glanced back to see her shivering in the rain. I had told them we were doing field observation today, and she had worn boots and a flight suit, but she hadn't prepared for the rain.

None of the students had. Some of them, the ones who had undergone military training, looked like they didn't mind standing in the wet. But even they didn't have waterproof gear.

My prepared lesson was broken by confusion. "What's wrong?"

"The Weather Authority said no rain," the young woman said.

"It's magic," I responded. I felt like they were missing the point. Obviously this rain wasn't natural or planned, or we wouldn't be here to observe it.

Another student stepped up, "You could have told us to prepare for rain, Professor."

"Just...cast a protection spell," I said. I really didn't see the problem. Why would I have warned them? If they weren't qualified mages, they wouldn't be studying at the Magic Tower in the first place, and certainly wouldn't be taking my class.

"None of us are weather mages," another student said. "Or protection mages."

I finally understood their problem, but it stunned me. "*None* of you know how to stay dry?"

One of the Union military trainees stepped up. "Our spells are optimized for combat, sir."

"Combat often takes place in the rain," I pointed out.

He looked dissatisfied with that answer, so I waved him down. "I understand. Well, good news, because closely observing this event will solve your problem. Get your cameras ready."

I pointed at the light on the muddy shell of the bubble, which was now almost the size of my head. "Observe the luminescence on the mud. Who sees the pattern?"

The girl in the front raised her hand. I remembered her, as she was one of the few mages in class who stood out.

Mariala Brechess was a human woman whom I suspected was half-Aethril. Her black hair was pulled back but looked dyed, her eyes drifted occasionally as though she was watching the Aether, and she was supposed to be in her thirties but looked ten years younger.

All of that added up to Aethril blood, in my mind, but I understood why she kept it to herself. Thanks to my genetically altered hair and eye color, people often assumed I was half-Aethril, and that caused all sorts of annoyance.

Some looked down on me as inhuman, some thought I could do miracles, and others wanted to use my blood as a magical catalyst.

So I wasn't going to blow the whistle on Mariala anytime soon.

"It looks like an Aetheric sigil," she said.

"Yes! As original spells were derived from natural patterns in the Aether, we're going back to our roots today. Can you see the meaning of the symbol?"

She hesitated, and no one else piped up, so I went on. "*Context.* Just like real language, magical symbols are all about context. We're standing in the mud, in pouring rain, watching an aurora toad hatch from a bubble. In that context, how is this symbol interpreted by the Aether?"

A different young woman, who at least had brought a wide-brimmed hat, raised a hand hesitantly. "Rain control?"

"Yes! Almost! I mean, very close!" I was going to explain further, but the symbol on the top of the mud bubble had begun to shine. Now, even an untrained observer could tell that this was some kind of magical sign.

It lasted only a second, and I hoped the students would record the moment for later observation.

Then the bubble burst, sending droplets of mud in all directions. The front rank of students were splattered with muck.

I stayed clean.

Rainbow lights rose from the bubble that had contained them. They drifted up the column of air that had remained dry, twisting around one another in a helix pattern.

While the lights started slowly, they moved faster and faster as they went higher, and they reached the clouds in only seconds. As soon as the lights passed beyond view, they exploded.

In one heartbeat, the clouds transformed. They were all turned from fluffy masses of water vapor to billowing stretches of rainbow light.

I let out a breath of appreciation. "Beautiful. I haven't seen that in years."

Technically, I had never seen it. I only remembered it as if I had. Same thing.

The rain was gone, vanishing a couple of seconds after the clouds did. Now a gorgeous aurora filled the sky over us, outshining the late afternoon sun.

I lowered my gaze to the creature that had caused all this. The toad was pure white and bigger than both my hands put together, with colors dancing over its slick skin like a coating of oil. It glanced toward all of us, determined that we were not insects, and then hopped away.

"The aurora toad absorbs mass and nourishment from the rainwater in order to grow so quickly," I explained. "That's why it induces the rain. But once it hatches from the mud, the rain would wash away the coating you may have noticed on its skin, so it clears up the weather to prevent this from happening."

I plucked the edge of my mantle. "By integrating the toad's magic into my own seals, I was able to expand my enchantment's definition of 'protection' to include 'protection from weather.' That's why I'm dry and you are not. Now, who can think of another way to apply this spell?"

I turned to the class, many of whom were still observing or recording the aurora, but the response I got wasn't the answer to my question.

"Sorry, sir, but is this a combat spell?"

The smooth course of my thoughts was jarred once again. "What?"

"You did say you were going to teach us a combat spell," Mariala pointed out.

"I've heard of weaponized weather spells," one man piped up.

I scanned their faces. They were missing the point so badly it physically pained me.

But I had made assumptions about their understanding of magic. And of combat. As their teacher, I should have made myself clear.

"Combat magic is not about using magic as a weapon," I said. "Don't use magic as a weapon. Use a gun."

One of the Union military cadets stepped forward, hands clasped behind his back. "Excuse me, sir, but we have been instructed otherwise. Most of us are here to learn as many combat spells as we can."

"You shouldn't be! If you want to be a full wizard, and maybe an Archmage someday, you don't need to learn a collection of random, disconnected spells. Master the spells you know." I gestured to the sky. "I'm trying to teach you how."

"Sorry, sir, but we don't have time to worry about *someday*. We're expected to see live combat within two years. We need to be ready."

Several students nodded approvingly, even some of the ones from mage families.

A small worm of despair ate away at my heart. I knew how important it was that they be prepared to fight. Far better than they did.

But this wasn't the way.

I had seen mages like them on battlefields yet to come. Faceless, generic spellcasters who provided mediocre support and then died. I didn't want that for my students. They *could* be better than that, and they *should* be.

In my previous lives, I had never made enough of a difference. Maybe they could.

I took a moment of silence to control myself so I didn't let too much darkness leak into my voice. Instead, I spoke in a very measured tone. "Not long ago, I raided an Iron Legion Hive. You may have heard the news."

Some murmured an affirmative, including the cadet in the front.

"What the Subline report failed to mention was that I did not accompany the Union or the Vallenar Corporation. I went in alone."

They were quiet. I didn't know if that was out of respect or skepticism, but I pushed forward. "When you're in a Hive, you have to be prepared for anything. Pawns can hit you from any angle, Shepherds can cast before you ever see them, and the ceiling can open and drop a Reaver on top of you. The walls themselves are alive."

I tapped into elemental water, gathering some of the water on the ground into a ball that hovered over my outstretched hand. "When you're in the heart of a Hive, you don't want a thousand spells. You want one spell with a thousand uses." I spun the water, creating a disc. Then a loop. A figure eight. A rain cloud.

All the while, I continued speaking. "A spell you know so well, you can use it without thinking. In any situation. In all situations. When your life is at stake, you want to be ready for anything."

I expanded the water until droplets hung over all the students. "And not one of you can handle rain."

I didn't drop it on their heads. I'm not cruel. Once I was sure my lesson had sunk in, I tossed the water back into the trees.

The cadet who had moved forward slowly slid back into the crowd, face red.

I sighed and stood up. "Let's get back to the ship. You can dry off and I'll show you how you can apply this spell to your individual disciplines."

Forty students crammed into *Moonfall* was a tight fit, but we weren't flying far. The artificial moon that was the home of the Galactic Union's Magic Tower wasn't especially big, so although we'd gone to a jungle on almost the opposite side of the moon than the Tower itself, we'd make it back in a few minutes.

There weren't enough seats aboard, so most of the students just hung on to something as I piloted us out of the atmosphere. The ship's gravity compensation spells were decent, so the force on the students wasn't so bad, but still a few lost their grip and took a tumble.

I heard their curses and groans from the cockpit, and once again I found myself shocked. Why didn't they catch themselves? Aether telekinesis was the most basic of basics. They wouldn't be as strong or precise as my levitation ring, but catching yourself as you fell was simple.

As *Moonfall* broke atmosphere, I added 'telekinesis' to my list of future lessons.

That list was getting depressing. If they didn't know how to

expand the function of their spells and they didn't know fundamental Aetheric manipulation, I wouldn't be able to teach anything
worthwhile. Not in the little time I had with them.

Moonfall's AI took over navigation, the ship skimming the
atmosphere into the full daylight side of the moon. I used the
break to answer student questions, which were mostly variations
of "Can't we learn something other than weather magic?"

I didn't expect to have to explain to a bunch of adult, practicing
mages why weather was important for planetary combat.

I took over the controls again, steering *Moonfall's* scorpi-
on-shaped bulk back toward the ground. Hangars stretched to
either side of the Magic Tower, with ships—mostly smaller shuttles
and other personal craft—docking and departing at every second.

There was little other development on the moon, the whole environment being reserved for magical research. The Tower was the
only site of interest in the whole system.

The moon didn't even have a name of its own. Officially, it was
called "the Magic Tower grounds."

And the Magic Tower itself lived up to that reputation. It towered over the moon, piercing the clouds, a polished spire of steel
burning in the sunlight. It hurled flares of Aetheric radiance in all
colors, crowned by light.

My students may not have been able to read the significance in
the aurora toad, but anyone could read this one. The Tower radiated
magic and majesty.

While the only docks were on the ground, the Magic Tower was
a vertical city equal to any colony. Though it was known across the
galaxy as a school, only a small percentage of its space was dedicated to educational facilities.

The rest was taken up by housing, centers of magical research,
manufacturing, food production, and everything else necessary for
self-sufficiency. If the rest of the moon exploded, the Tower could
float indefinitely until recovered. Its entrances would even seal in
the event of an emergency, making it airtight.

It was the beating heart of the Galactic Union's magical

community. Hundreds of millions of mages had come here to study from all over the galaxy, going on to do great things as Tower-certified wizards.

To most, this was a place of great mystery and untold power.

I found its reputation, uh, inflated.

As I steered *Moonfall* toward the nearest open hangar, I thumbed the Subline transmitter. "Varic Vallenar of *Moonfall* requesting permission to dock."

"Professor Vallenar, redirect yourself to Hangar 14-C. The Director is waiting for you."

I had a ship full of students with me, and I was almost out of fuel. If it weren't for those two things, I'd have turned around and flown away.

Actually, it was only the students that kept me there. I'd have still left on no fuel.

Compared to a conversation with Director Porellus, being stranded in a dead ship wasn't so bad.

I slid myself into the air traffic over Hangar 14-C and let the AI take over the landing. I equipped myself with my mantle, ring, amulet, and wand. My hand hovered over my plasma pistol before I, with great reluctance, left it aboard the ship.

When we finally docked, I let every one of the forty students walk down the ramp before I followed.

As expected, Director Porellus was fuming as he waited. One pair of his soft, flabby arms was crossed, while another pair rested on his hips. Or where hips would be on a human; I don't know much about the biology of his species.

Porellus resembled a giant, beige slug, with two pairs of what I would call arms and perhaps a dozen more pseudo-legs that helped support his fleshy bulk. He wore a mantle wrapped around his shoulders and glasses over his eyes, which made up his only clothing.

He glared at me as I finally came down, oozing across the tile of the hangar, limbs slapping as they pulled him forward. "Make our conversation private, Professor," he ordered me.

Too lazy to resist, I complied, creating a quick barrier against sound that floated around us in a cloud of drifting symbols. The runes all said the same thing, in my eyes: 'Quiet.'

Once my spell covered us in a dome, Porellus got closer, looming over me until I was eye-level with his pale underbelly. "You are to teach them *only* the spells they need to fight, Professor Vallenar! That is a condition of your employment!"

"I can't believe they never learned the basics," I said with a sigh. "They don't know how to master their own spells."

"That's not your concern! This is your second infraction, and I told you—"

"But what's more fundamental than observing magic in nature? They're all practicing mages, so they at least know a spell or two."

"They aren't wizards yet! You can't take them along for random—"

"They don't see *why*." I snapped my fingers, feeling illuminated. "I need to show them what they can do."

"Are you...are you listening to me?"

"What?" I half-heartedly covered myself. "Oh, yes, of course. But I'm getting them ready for the battlefield, I promise. This is all critical combat magic. I can prove it."

Porellus had begun to turn red, starting from his face and creeping down. It was a much brighter red than any human, but I suspected it still meant anger. "Stick to the curriculum we agreed upon! Teach them standard combat spells and move on!"

I scratched the back of my head. "But that's...I mean, it's trash. We both know it's trash, right? Nobody else can hear us, it's just you and me. If they take that curriculum onto the battlefield, they're going to get killed. They'll die."

"It is a foundation upon which they must build."

"Director, they can't handle bad weather and flight turbulence. How are they going to build on a foundation if we haven't taught them how?"

Porellus clapped his lower pair of hands in front of my face. "New magic is not your remit. The collection of combat spells we instructed you to teach will be *more* than sufficient for the battlefield."

"How would you know?"

That was why I hated talking with him. I tried to ignore him, just brush him off, but he still got under my skin until I snapped back. There were *real* threats out there, and here I was trading insults with a bureaucrat.

The man had earned the title of Archmage, but he'd never seen a conflict more intense than an academic debate.

Not that he seemed to realize that. His eyes flashed, and one of his hands drifted down to his wand. "Perhaps you need a lesson of your own, Professor."

I almost laughed, but his demonstration was more sad than funny. My wand buzzed with pity against its holster.

Without responding, I turned my back to him and waved away my barrier against eavesdropping. My class was bunched up nearby, whispering to one another and clearly wondering if they were dismissed. When I emerged, most of them turned my way.

"The Director wants me to stick to teaching you the standard suite of spells for combat mages, and I know many of you feel the same. Clearly, I have failed to illustrate to you what a combat spell is."

I pointed. "Mariala, come forward. What's your specialty?"

"Fortune magic," she responded.

"Fantastic. Cast a fortune spell, adapted to the spell you saw on the toad."

She hesitated. "I haven't had time to study—"

"Doesn't matter. Wing it."

The class muttered in surprise, and she gave me a longer look to see if I was serious. When I didn't say anything else, she started a hesitant incantation.

You're not supposed to cast a spell you aren't familiar with. It can fail, but more importantly, it can have effects you don't intend. "Winging" spells is a great way to end up turning someone inside-out. Maybe yourself.

But as she cast and I saw the rainbow aurora flickering around her, I nudged the Aether here and there, pushing it into the right patterns. She got it close on the first try; she must have been paying attention.

I didn't know whether she noticed my corrections or not, but she finished the incantation with much more confidence than she had begun. Though she still flinched as a cloud formed over her head, an aurora that was just as much gold as it was rainbow light.

She looked at the beautiful crown of shifting lights over her head for a moment. "So this will give me good luck...with the weather?"

I grabbed a water bottle from my still-open ship with my levitation ring. It floated toward me as I spoke. "This is how you should be learning new magic. Use new patterns to push the boundaries of what you can already do. Expand your capabilities."

The bottle of water hit my hand and I unscrewed it, then called the water out in a stream. With only casual elemental control, I condensed it into a cloud over Mariala's new aurora.

The rain fell directly toward her...then got caught by a 'random' gust of wind, avoiding her entirely.

Around her, her classmates shouted and stepped back in protest as they were splattered with rain. But she remained protected.

"You should all be able to keep yourself dry in the rain, once you've integrated the pattern of the aurora toad into your spell," I went on. "And beyond the obvious application of keeping you and your gear safe from the weather..."

I hesitated for a second then, because my next action was going to get me suspended.

Still, I went through with it. This would be a good demonstration, and not just for my students.

"...this has other battlefield uses as well."

I began to chant, blending the aurora frog's weather control spell with my sealing and binding magic.

The spells of the Weather Authority resisted slightly. They were supposed to be the ones in charge of the weather, and they didn't recognize me.

But I incorporated them into my own spell. I wasn't just taking over the weather, I was *sealing* the weather to myself, locking out all other influences.

A different interpretation than Mariala's, but the same result.

On a much larger scale.

All around the Magic Tower, the Aether bent itself to my will.

Director Porellus shouted at me, drawing his wand, but I ignored him. A rainbow aurora began to twist around the entire Tower, taking over the sky.

When my spell was complete, there was an aurora dancing in a halo around the crown of the Magic Tower, made of Aetheric symbols as big as star cruisers. The weather for miles was under my control.

I couldn't have handled a working so large on my own. I was borrowing the spells the Weather Authority already had in place.

Speaking of which, the wizards of the W.A. were probably panicking at that moment, but no one else was. Traffic wasn't even interrupted.

This was the Magic Tower. They were used to seeing strange things in the sky.

Well, *one* person was upset. Director Porellus quivered like a bowl full of jelly and he had his wand shoved against the back of my head.

Some of the students looked alarmed at his actions, while others were awed—or frightened—by my demonstration in the sky.

"Now," I said, "who can tell me how this might be useful in combat?"

I snapped my fingers. Behind me, lightning flashed. Deafening thunder rolled across the campus at the same time.

"Security!" Director Porellus roared.

I released the weather after that. Half an hour later, I was in the Director's office while he called the system's Galactic Union representative, comparing my spell to an act of terrorism.

"Have you lost track of the asset?" the woman on the other end of the call asked.

I, the asset, sat in my chair opposite the Director. I stared at the restored, perfectly clear weather out the window and wondered why I bothered with any of this.

"No, but he's out of control!"

"Were there any casualties?"

"No, but—"

"Any damage to Union property?"

Porellus transferred the call to his private earpiece at that moment and I lost the conversation. I could still hear him passionately arguing for my removal.

When he finished the call, he seethed, his tiny legs slapping in irritation against the floor.

"You knew they weren't going to let you fire me," I said.

The Galactic Union welcomed every ounce of leverage they had over me. I was known as an Archmage of seals and bindings and a skilled water elementalist, which already put me ahead of just about every other wizard in the galaxy in their estimation.

Throw in my connection to the Vallenar Corporation, and the Union was *very* motivated to keep their hands on me.

Of course, if they knew the real breadth of my capabilities, I'd probably be locked away already.

Director Porellus turned around again, and while he looked calmer than I expected, I knew his anger was burning not far beneath the surface. "Why do you stay here, Vallenar? You didn't train here, and you have no respect for Tower traditions. What are you doing here?"

I looked back out to the clouds. There were a lot of things I could say.

The Galactic Union had agreed to keep the Vallenar Corporation away from me as long as I stayed here, for one thing.

For another, the next generation of wizards was likely to determine whether the galaxy as we knew it survived or not. As I'd said, there was only so much I could do on my own.

But the fact was, I didn't have anywhere else to be.

"What am I supposed to do?" I asked him. In spite of myself, I did faintly hope that he might come up with some idea.

Naturally, he proved those hopes foolish.

"Jump out an airlock for all I care," he said. "One month's suspension."

CHAPTER FIVE

I LAY ON the floor of *Moonfall*'s bridge, staring into the ceiling. "What do I do?"

"You are restricted to the system," my ship told me.

Legally, that was true. Director Porellus could suspend me, but he still couldn't let me leave. I was bound to the Magic Tower on something like parole, and my ship was enchanted to prevent me from leaving.

I wiped away the spell binding me there with a gesture and a simple syllable. "Hey look, I'm free."

"I must recommend that you not defy Galactic Union law."

I sighed. "I wish you were a person."

"I am not."

"Yeah." I seized the arm of the pilot's chair and used it to awkwardly haul myself into the seat. "Get me a list of all the jobs on the Union Subline requesting experienced mages."

"Civilian, corporate, or military?"

"Blacklist Vallenar Corporation requests. Otherwise, doesn't matter. Prioritize listings with a danger warning and higher requirements."

"One moment." Then, only a breath later, a ping. *"Ready."*

"Put it on the monitor."

A file scrolled across the screen, including a picture of a menacing-looking black robot with one shining red eye.

"Summarize it for me," I ordered.

"This is a bounty request for a criminal who calls himself Dragonslayer. Wanted across the Galactic Union for corporate sabotage, mass murder, and ecological devastation over several planets. Analysis estimates he's an Archmage in illusion magic inside an Aethertech war-mech, and his bounty is up to fifty million standards."

I gave a low whistle at the amount. The Union wanted him *bad*.

That was a little intriguing, since the Union had plenty of mages competent enough to track him down. If it went beyond them, I might really be necessary. Maybe I could do some good after all.

"The request is posted by Starhammer and the Advocates, who have thus far failed to—"

"Pass!" I called. A shiver passed through me. "I'm not getting within five systems of Starhammer."

The Advocates were self-proclaimed guardians of galactic civilization, and they provided a valuable public service for those who were outside the protection of conventional police forces.

Their leader, the illustrious Starhammer, had also hunted me down and killed me in a previous life. There was plenty of bad blood there...or at least there had been, with another version of myself.

I couldn't get rid of him, but I could stay far, far away.

The file on the monitor blinked out, replaced by another. The picture this time was of a towering ancient obelisk, made of stone, but drifting in space amidst a cloud of its own debris.

"The Lost Temple of Merduua, in orbit outside Heliogoth IX. Its orbit has been decaying, and this time the planetary government has placed an open request for any mage able to undo the seals and inspect its contents."

"Done that. Pass."

There was nothing in the Lost Temple of Merduua. Just dust and some dried corpses. I had undone those seals in a previous life and the government of Heliogoth IX had skipped out on payment, convinced that I had magicked away their priceless cultural treasures.

Another file appeared, showing a widely grinning Lichborn man in a suit. Like every one of his species, he had gray skin and eyes that shone with green light, and he had the effortless good looks of a Subline celebrity. Lichborn tended to do well in politics.

"Senator Jom Harbridge of the Galactic Union was killed by a spell in his private apartments two days ago. Local investigators determined magic was the cause, and initially submitted a request to the Magic Tower. Now they have opened the request, looking for civilian experts on curses or biological magic who are willing to lend their expertise to the investigation."

"Nope. It was the Union that had him killed."

Technically, it was the organization *controlling* the Galactic Union who killed him, but I wasn't willing to say as much even to my own ship's AI.

Sometimes, paranoia was completely justified.

"An archaeological dig on the border of Dark Space reported a cluster of unknown eggs. Hours later, contact with the dig was lost. The Karoshan Alliance has put out a call for mages to seal a potential D'Niss incursion."

"It's not them," I said confidently. "Just a couple of bugs."

I happened to know that the last of the titanic insects known as the D'Niss were under control. The Titan Knights had taken care of them, and their queen wouldn't start an incursion into our universe for years. If she woke up early...well, she ate entire stars, not archaeologists.

"Universal Manufacturing has issued a request for an Archmage in sealing and binding. They didn't list the reward, but there is a danger warning."

"Pass. My father put them up to this."

U.M. was one of the Vallenar Corporation's biggest rivals. They worked together almost as often as they worked to tear the other to pieces.

"An Aether Technician by the name of Cinnal has requested a wizard to recover a shipment of abyssal iron."

"Pass. She'll have plenty of help on that one."

"There's a storm on Dornoth Two…"

The requests kept coming, and I spent less and less time on each one before turning them down. The ones that weren't dead ends were traps, and the ones that weren't traps were too easy. They could be handled by any competent wizard.

Not one of them was worth my time.

Not even the latest file on the screen, showing a weathered stone pyramid. It was chipped and pitted, writing chiseled into every facet, and its tip had been broken off.

"A coalition of explorers from across the galaxy has entered Karoshan Alliance space searching for a Zenith Device. Many independent crews have put out a request for a mage."

"Pass." I yawned as the screen changed. Then I waved at the monitor. "Wait, go back."

The file with the broken pyramid flipped up again. I can't say I was interested, really. I only asked for more out of boredom.

Zenith Devices were the original Aethertech. Mythical treasures from an era beyond reliable history. Actually, not *mythical*. They had existed once, they just didn't anymore. No one, in all my lives, had proven the current existence of a Zenith Device.

I had probably lived through this expedition in each of my five previous lives, and it had failed every time. How did I know? Because I'd never heard of it. If they'd really found one of the original Aethertech devices, it would have been galactic news.

But *because* I had never heard of it, I was mildly interested.

"Which Device?" I asked.

"The Zenith Starship," Moonfall answered through its speakers. *"They believe they have found* The Last Horizon."

I took in the words. I scanned the report on the screen.

"That's stupid," I said.

"Treasure hunters began gathering approximately two standard months ago. The Union has issued a travel advisory intended to prevent civilians from traveling into hazardous Alliance territory, but some of the more reputable explorer and scavenger companies have taken this as their primary contract.

"On the Corporate Subline, the Vallenar Corporation hasn't made a statement, but Antarion Transportation and U.M. are said to have dispatched agents."

That was a surprise. If there was one thing major galactic corporations hated, it was losing money.

So what were they doing financing a massive treasure hunt?

"What prompted all that?"

A green border appeared around the weathered pyramid, highlighting it. *"Three months ago, a billionaire living on one of the Free Worlds died without an heir, leaving his estate to auction. This artifact was among his belongings, and it purports to depict the location of* The Last Horizon. *It has been dated back to the Zenith Era and identified as originating in Alliance space."*

I snorted. "And that's enough to get them digging? Stupid." I zoomed in on the pyramid. "Wasting their time," I muttered as I scrutinized the letters.

The carvings were weathered and the resolution of the image was low, but that wasn't a language. At least, it wasn't *just* a language.

"Those are Aetheric symbols," I said. Any decent computer could read a written message, but magical signs had to be interpreted by a mage. The treasure hunters had no doubt replicated the pyramid itself, but that wouldn't be enough.

A normal person reciting the words of a spell would accomplish nothing. You had to *cast* the spell, which meant causing the meaning of the words to resonate with the Aether. It was the same thing here. If you wanted to make a functional copy of this pyramid, you'd have to understand the meaning behind it.

"...do we have more pictures of this?"

If we had images of the pyramid from multiple angles, I could make one. My insight into Aetheric symbols was without peer.

Any one wizard could only see magic from one perspective. Unless, of course, you had lived six separate lives, training along six entirely separate, parallel lines. It was like I had six eyes, each at a slightly different angle, while everyone else had one. In a manner of speaking, I could read magic in three dimensions.

But why would I? *The Last Horizon* wasn't real.

"Never mind, forget about it," I told *Moonfall*. I flipped to the next file.

...then I flipped back.

What if it *was* real?

"Hypothetically, if it did exist, what are *The Last Horizon*'s capabilities?"

"The Zenith Starship, known by its ID The Last Horizon, *is the original Aethertech—"*

"Not that I'm thinking of replacing you," I interrupted. "This is a purely academic exercise. You don't have to worry."

"...the original Aethertech starship," Moonfall went on, unbothered. *"It is said that colonization of the stars by early humanity was only possible thanks to the creation of* The Last Horizon.

"Legends attribute quite a number of abilities to The Last Horizon, *some of which are contradictory to one another and most of which are likely exaggerated. Notable capabilities include the ability to transport crew members across the galaxy without passing through Subspace, to conjure copies of the ship itself from the Aether, to pierce through planets in a single shot, to freeze the motion of planetary bodies, to construct entire colonies in seconds, and to terraform systems in a matter of weeks."*

While I was still mulling over that list, *Moonfall* concluded its speech. *"A further list of the Zenith Starship's reported functions is available on request."*

I drummed my fingers on the side of my chair. "I've heard some of those stories. How reliable are they?"

"Unlike most of the other Zenith Devices, the Starship does have a long history of reported sightings after the Zenith Era. Most of these are not considered reliable, but many scholars and Aether Technicians consider The Last Horizon *the one most likely to have survived into the modern day."*

A new image appeared on my monitor. It was the cover of a book, showing a printed title in block letters that read: *THE SHIP OF HEROES*.

Moonfall's summary of the book scrolled next to the cover, and I could tap on it to read the book itself. I did neither. Instead, I continued drumming my fingers against my chair as I stared at that title.

It seemed that there were no good places to use my talents. I could easily solve unimportant problems, but the ones that *did* matter—the ones that lurked in the galaxy like armed proton bombs—those were far beyond me.

"But with that ship, I could do anything," I muttered. *The Last Horizon* might even keep me alive. I straightened in my chair. "And besides, I have a month to kill. Right?"

"*That is correct,*" *Moonfall* responded dutifully.

I clapped my hands together. "Right, let's make that pyramid."

Then we could fly off chasing legends.

CHAPTER SIX

OVER THE NEXT month, I searched fourteen boring planets across eleven boring star systems. I had almost given up the search when I finally found danger.

It was less adrenaline-pumping thrill and more *"I hope they don't blow up my ship."*

Plasma bolts slammed into my ship's shields, which flickered a pale green. *Moonfall* was a scout frigate, made for speed on long Subspace runs. Not for tanking military-grade firepower.

Lights on the console flared, warning me that I had only a shot or two left before the shields went down.

I thumbed the local Subline channel. "Repeat: I am not a Dornoth scout! This is a civilian vessel with no cargo."

I knew they wouldn't believe me, but my spirits still brightened when my speakers hissed to life. If they were willing to open dialogue, maybe I could talk my way out of this.

The voice from the other ship was deep and growling, and surprisingly eloquent, as was typical for most Karoshans. "Open your shields for boarding and prepare for genetic scan. Resistance will be met with annihilation."

"I'd be happy to lower my shields if you'd stop shooting me," I said.

Another shot against the shields rattled me in my seat. "A genetic scan would be very inconvenient for me. How would you feel about a bribe?"

A pair of squarish black Karoshan fighters swirled around me. They added more yellow-white bolts to the attack, which were the last the shields could take. The shields crackled and folded, the monitor showing them at zero percent.

I braced myself for further impact, but none came. That was a relief. *Moonfall*'s armor was in a class that the salesman had compared to tin foil.

The ship's weapons were formidable for its size, though my plasma cannons were still warped after the battle at the Iron Hive. But I hadn't fired a shot.

That would only make things worse.

A Karoshan battlecruiser loomed over me, blocking the light of the nearest star. Like every other ship built on Karosha, it was blocky, black, and bristling with guns. Not only that, but a standard cruiser came with a squad of four-to-six starfighters.

Two such hovered in front of me, visible through the viewport, weapons hot and waiting for any signs of resistance. Two more circled their cruiser in a defensive formation. In case I had a fleet in my back pocket, I guess. For one scout frigate, this response was obscene overkill.

I activated the Subline channel again. "If you'll accept a video transmission, I'll prove to you I'm not a Lichborn. Please don't—"

Moonfall shook and echoed with a metallic screech as clamps latched onto the ship, locking in place for boarding.

"—damage the hull," I finished pointlessly. If they were going to board, I had *really* been hoping they would use magic.

For one thing, magic wouldn't break my cargo bay doors. Those were expensive.

The Karoshan voice came through the speakers again. "No video required. I will inspect you myself. I advise you not to bear weapons. You will be forced to test them against my own."

His confidence was understandable. Karoshans were superior to humans in virtually every respect.

"I'd much rather keep it friendly," I responded, but once again they ignored me.

Metal clanged, ringing my ship like a bell. I drummed my fingers on the console and wondered if it was worthwhile to continue trying to talk.

I *really* didn't want them to blow up my ship.

I had been flying fully armed, in case I had to make a hasty exit, which meant I now had to disarm for any chance at a friendly negotiation. I pulled out my wand and placed it on a metal shelf, though it buzzed and shone bright blue in irritation. My Lightcaster pistol went next to it.

Though I knew I had to leave the weapons behind, I felt like I was abandoning my own limbs. As one of my mentors had said, *"To survive in this galaxy, you need a wand in one hand and a gun in the other."*

Although, come to think of it, she'd been shot to death by Karoshan soldiers. During an inspection very much like this one.

I patted myself down to see if I was carrying anything else they might take for a weapon.

All I had on was a gray flight suit and blue mantle. I flipped the hood down but kept the mantle on. There was no way I was going into a potential gunfight without its protection.

For the same reason, I left my levitation ring behind but kept my shield amulet on. It would be too embarrassing to lose my last life to a random shot, fighting over nothing.

There wasn't much to *Moonfall* besides the bridge. Quarters for four crewmen, or eight if they wanted to double-bunk. Not much chance of that, since I traveled alone. I had filled one of the quarters with magical plants, and the others were mostly boxes of junk.

I also had one central multi-purpose room complete with a kitchen unit, one largely empty cargo hold, and the engine room.

Other than some subsystems and minor nooks and crannies, that was it. The boarding party would be able to search the whole ship in minutes.

Fortunately for me, they had properly latched onto the frame of my cargo bay doors. For a Karoshan boarding party, that should be counted as polite.

They hadn't started melting their way through the door yet, which meant they intended to pry the doors apart. I appreciated that too. Clearly, they meant to keep me intact, so at least we agreed on that.

But the clamps would leave a mark, and my doors would need repair after they were forced open.

With that in mind, I dashed to the console and swiped the cargo door access. The doors hissed apart, revealing a kneeling, helmeted Karoshan holding a mechanical device that resembled a battering ram with a pair of mechanical hands on the end.

"I got that for you," I said, with what I hoped was a charming smile.

The one in charge of breaching the doors fell back, and two of the others marched forward, carrying rifles trained on me.

"Hands up," one ordered. The voice was distorted through helmet speakers.

There were four troops here. All helmeted and anonymous, though they were clearly Karoshan. They were nine feet tall, for one thing, looming over me and every other human in the universe. Their hair ran from the backs of their helmets in cable-thick strands, each shining brightly like lit neon.

The one closest to me had hair-cables of shining pink, and his partner shining green. They could tell each other apart by the color, and the helmets were still airtight. The fashion of leaving their hair out had great traditional significance on Karosha.

Belatedly, I remembered to stick my hands in the air.

Once they had finished securing me, meaning four giant Karoshans had surrounded me with rifles raised, they called in their commander.

He strode in from the red-lit hallway of his own ship, hands clasped behind him. He wore a uniform rather than a helmeted combat suit. His skin was a dull, leathery red, and his hair-cables shone bright crimson. One sharp eye scanned me up and down.

The other eye, like the entire left half of the man's face, had been replaced by machinery. It looked like a mechanical spider had latched over one side of his head.

That eye shone blue and scanned me much more deeply.

On my wrist, my console blinked a warning. It transmitted into my ocular implant, showing the details so that only I could see: *ID Request Incoming.*

I allowed it.

A digital model of me floated in the air, complete with a fabricated name.

"Julian Derrimore," the Karoshan commander read. "Journalist specializing in interplanetary journalism. Should I be pleased to meet you, Julian?"

"It's a fake identity," I said.

The commander rolled his neck as though the cybernetic half pained him. "I think you may have misunderstood the purpose of a false ID."

"It's not meant for you. I'm always happy to cooperate with the throne of Karosha."

"Hm. Meant for whom, then?"

"Would you be offended if I didn't say?"

"That depends. If this isn't you..." the commander waved a hand and dismissed the digital image. "...then who are you, exactly?"

"Not a Lichborn!" I gestured to myself. "One hundred percent pure, home-grown, living human."

"The hair? The eyes? One might mistake you for an Aethril."

"My parents would be pleased to hear you say so. It's purely cosmetic."

In some places, silver hair and eyes had made me stand out as rich enough to afford genetic modification. As my family had intended. In others, they hadn't stood out at all.

At the corner of my vision, an alert warned that I was being scanned by another of the men, who turned as though speaking to the commander. I heard nothing, as the helmeted man's words had been transmitted on a private channel.

One of the commander's hairless eyebrows went up at whatever he heard. "We don't have you in our ship's database, stranger."

They were looking for something.

Not showing up in their database was normal. Why would they have up-to-date knowledge of millions of human ship IDs?

However, I was *technically* flying through their territory, so I played it cool. "Sorry, but I'm trying to stay off the scanner. Just passing through!"

"If I let anyone pass through just because they were human, the Lichborn would begin hiring human smugglers. I'd prefer you give us your honest identity, but fortunately for both of us, I brought an alternative."

Another helmeted Karoshan hurried from their ship, this time carrying a shining box. Its metallic corners were rounded, its facets transparent, and within there were a thousand flashing lights in many shades of blue. It resembled a storm of sapphire lasers.

I began to sweat.

This far from inhabited planets, it was almost impossible to get decent Subline access. If I wasn't in their ship's database, they would have no way of figuring out who I was.

This, however, was high-grade Aethertech. Probably a masterwork. A materialized miracle. It had no such limitations as "range."

I didn't know whether this one was a scanner or a Subline terminal. Either way, they were about to tear through my disguise.

And there was another, more immediate problem. Masterwork Aethertech was *insanely* valuable. They wouldn't let word of its existence reach the Lichborn.

They weren't letting me leave.

I pointed to the shining box. "Are you allowed to show me that?"

"Why not?" the commander asked innocently. "You wouldn't tell anyone, would you?" He gave me a wide smile.

So this was going to be the adrenaline-pumping kind of danger after all. My heart rate picked up and I began mentally rifling through spells.

Light passed from the box and swept over me while my console sent another warning into my vision. Still, I didn't cast anything.

I was trying to stay off someone's scanner, but not theirs.

I kept my voice low and calm. "I'm sorry, I didn't explain myself well. Please shut it off, I beg you. Under the Aether's light, I'll tell you whatever you want to know."

It was too late.

A digital image flashed in the air. It was clean and modern, a V and an A merging together into a design that resembled a stylized bird of prey. Our company's motto floated beneath.

Vallenar – Everything. For everyone.

The helmeted figures shifted uncomfortably and glanced up for orders. The commander initially looked stunned, and then a moment later lit up like he'd just been gifted a planet.

"A son of the Vallenar Corporation? I'm tempted to bow. Did you outpace your escort, Vallenar?"

I let my left hand fall, but wiped my face with my right hand.

I had taken a risk in leaving Galactic Union space. My father was one of the people I was trying to avoid. But now, the Karoshans had tapped into their Subline and found my identity. There would be a record of that.

A record that the Vallenar Corporation would discover in seconds, if they hadn't already. Soon, Benri Vallenar would know exactly where his son had been.

But the Corporation was only one of the organizations I was avoiding. The Galactic Union wouldn't be happy about me leaving their space, which was a headache I'd have to deal with eventually.

Unfortunately, the Union wasn't the most dangerous fleet after me.

"I'm still happy to bribe you to leave me be," I said. "You might be disappointed by the amount, though. I'm not with the Corporation anymore, and my family won't pay a ransom."

"I hope you don't mind if I try that for myself," the commander said. He chuckled, as well he might; in his mind, he'd just found a treasure chest floating unclaimed through space. "Why don't you join us on our ship, Mister Vallenar? You will be treated to our finest accommodation, I assure you."

I considered it. First, I was worried about leaving my gear. Most of it was irreplaceable. But after a moment, I decided to go with it. I nodded and started walking onto the Karoshan ship.

Having to recover my wand, staff, and ship from lockdown or the vacuum of space was far from the worst-case scenario.

My full identity was still secret, and I hadn't done anything to attract attention. Eventually, I might find a way out of this.

"Wait a moment," one of the Karoshans said aloud, and I shut my eyes.

We were approaching the worst-case scenario.

The commander leaned over the terminal of the Aethertech scanner. They didn't share the data with me, of course, but I could imagine what was happening.

My imagination was helped by the soldier, who continued to talk over the speaker instead of using a private channel. "We have several Subline news articles about an Archmage Varic Vallenar in our registry, but I found no personal records beyond that."

"I would be surprised if you had," the commander said. He would believe that the Vallenars could afford to hide any number of secrets from the public Sublines.

And that belief would be correct. However, if they searched a little deeper...

"Yes, sir," the soldier went on, "but then I checked the scanner itself. You should see what it's telling me."

I sent a mental command to my console. *All right. Hack it.*

There would be no hacking the scanner. It was Aethertech. But the soldier's helmet was standard Karoshan infantry issue, while the processor in my console was the best the Vallenar Corporation could produce.

I broke through his security in seconds, and then I could see everything he did. My three-dimensional image was now accompanied by much more information.

Varic Vallenar
Species: Human
Age: ERROR
Physical Traits: Silver eyes (modified), silver hair (modified).
Planet of Residence: ERROR
Personal History: ERROR

The commander looked into the air, where he was seeing the same thing I was. "Would you mind telling me why your age comes up as an error in my scanner, Varic? I've never seen Aethertech make an error before, you see."

"Multiple contradictory results," I told him. "The device doesn't know which is correct."

"Do you?"

"They're all correct." I looked down to the soldier punching keys on the scanner. "Just stop what you're doing. Stop, one second, and I'll explain."

The commander snorted. "That sounds like an ord—"

The soldier finally checked the scanner's assessment of my estimated threat level. I had been hoping he wouldn't do that.

The soldier's helmet was consumed by flashing red text. Since I was tapping into his feed, I saw the same thing.

WARNING — Fleet-class threat. Emergency response required on contact. DO NOT ENGAGE.

I laced my fingers together and stretched. "I *really* didn't expect you to have decent Aethertech. I would have handled this differently."

Four Karoshan rifles were already trained on me. The commander pulled a gun from a holster at his side. Sized for his species, the weapon was bigger than my face.

"Hands up!" the commander roared. "Up! Get them up!"

I gave him a skeptical look. "Listen, I'm trying not to hurt anybody, but I'm going to need you to scrub the navigational data on your ship. Personal devices too."

"Fire!"

Plasma rifles roared in the cargo bay.

My shield amulet flashed.

Four globes of plasma, fired from the rifles, stopped in midair a foot from my body. The shining, superheated balls were held in place by golden ripples in the air.

The energy in the amulet depleted from holding the plasma blasts in place, but not by much. The amulet had better performance than *Moonfall*'s shields did.

I pointed to the plasma bolts. "Normally, these would have bounced off my shield. I stopped that from happening. You're welcome."

The commander's pistol roared, and soon a sparking slug was floating in a golden field next to the plasma bolts.

"Did you not see the warning?" I asked, irritated. "'*Do not engage.*' This is engaging!"

Having seen that the projectiles were stopped, the commander lifted a wand instead. It looked more like a club, longer than my forearm, and made of bones that looked as though they had been braided together somehow.

The Karoshan spoke a slithering trigger word that echoed in the Aether, and a bloody serpent made from crimson light erupted from the tip of his wand.

I held up a hand.

It wasn't a bad spell. I'd give him a passing grade in one of my classes. The wand brought it forth faster than the commander could cast unaided.

This spell evoked a constricting serpent. It was a live binding spell, flexible and adaptable, intended to make a prisoner of virtually any target.

I knew the spell in an instant. It was as easy as reading a single digit.

And with a wave of my hand, I turned it around.

The world went black-and-white for a moment, and reality seemed to glitch. Then the red serpent was lunging back *toward* the wand instead.

The Karoshan commander was bound by a nest of writhing red serpents composed of Aether so dense that the reptiles looked real.

I nodded to him. "I appreciate that you used a non-lethal spell. Though you did try to shoot me."

Give me a countdown, I silently ordered my console. Mental commands were harder to send and less accurate than inputting commands physically, but of course the soldiers wouldn't let me tap away at a screen while they had me under guard.

A two-minute timer appeared on the device strapped to my wrist. Two minutes was only an estimate, but it should be accurate enough.

In two minutes, I had to be out of here.

The Karoshan soldiers were pulling their commander away as their plasma bolts were slowly eroded in midair by my magic.

"Stop," I ordered, and they did.

"I don't have much time, so answer quickly. What are you looking for?"

The commander grunted, struggling against the crimson snakes binding him, and forced his way up to a sitting position. "We're looking for a fugitive. We have reason to suspect this person may be hiding aboard a human ship."

"Who?" I asked.

His red organic eye and his blue cybernetic one were equally cold. "I will not tell you that. Even under threat of death."

"Fair enough." I didn't really care about Karoshan criminals anyway. But I did nod to his wand. "That's a nice wand. Where did you get it?"

I didn't recognize the wand itself, but any magical focus of its class was only assigned to commanders by the royal family. Or their magical advisors, at least.

"The King Regent authorized me to use this wand and granted me Aethertech for my hunt. More than that, I cannot disclose."

My mind was sent reeling. That disturbed me more than this random Karoshan commander could have possibly known.

"The King Regent?" I asked. "What happened to Queen Shyrax?"

The commander glared at me in a way I found difficult to interpret. "You don't keep up with the news?"

I can't make complex movements without my levitation ring, but I'm still capable of basic Aetheric manipulation. I seized the man with telekinesis and hauled him over.

The soldiers shouted, but the commander flew to me like a slab of meat launched from a catapult. I caught the ten-foot Karoshan with both hands.

And liberal support from telekinesis. The man was heavy.

"Tell me," I demanded.

My console ticked down to a minute and a half.

"She was deposed," the commander answered. "Convicted by the Dragon Court of high treachery and imprisoned about eight months ago. This was on the Union Subline, I'm certain."

He seemed more curious than afraid, if I read him correctly, peering into me with his one natural eye as though trying to see the truth of my soul.

My world was spinning, and I'm sure I did a bad job of hiding it. I shoved him away, and two soldiers caught him. It was hard to support so much weight without my levitation ring, but I wasn't thinking about the strain.

My fifth life had been spent as an advisor to Queen Shyrax's royal guard. She should have stayed in power years longer than this, even in the worst-case scenario.

Something had gone wrong.

I remembered being crushed by a Karoshan mage. Literally crushed alive, beneath a magical weight I couldn't overcome. That fate loomed over me again.

"Go," I said absently. "Get off my ship."

There were still thirty seconds left on my timer when they fled.

I could have demanded they leave the Aethertech behind, but I didn't. Having the Karoshan Empire on me for theft of military property wouldn't help anything.

My mind was still churning, but my body was on autopilot. I climbed back into the cockpit and took my seat, dimly aware of the Karoshans pulling off to a safe distance for a dive into Subspace.

Now the Karoshans had made open requests for my identity and information. The Vallenar Corporation would have intercepted those requests, but they weren't the only ones looking for me.

Ten seconds left on my timer.

"Plenty of time left," I said aloud, which was my mistake. I should have kept my mouth shut.

Just as the Karoshan ships left, there came a multi-colored twist in space. A Subspace distortion.

That distortion spat out two silvery wedges, covered in shell-like insect carapace. Hunter-ships.

The Iron Legion had found me.

CHAPTER SEVEN

MY PATHFINDING SPELL stretched in front of me like a golden river flowing into the endless night of space. This was the pinnacle spell of my navigational magic: the Cosmic Path. It didn't have much use in anything but space travel, but it was perfect for situations that required precise starship navigation at high speeds.

Like, for instance, when I was running from Iron Legion Hunters.

I slipped *Moonfall* into its path and slammed all the power I could spare into my engines.

This was the reason I'd invested into a fast ship instead of a strong one. Hunters were more maneuverable than I was and fighting them was pointless. If I destroyed them here, the Legion would only send more next time.

But on a long trip, I could outrun them.

Triangular Hunter-ships angled for a better shot, but I wasn't watching. I'd cast my pathfinding spell to search for a safe route, so when the danger shifted position, so did the path.

The golden river bent to the side, so I followed suit. Orange plasma bolts streaked past my hull.

The shield's auto-repair systems had done enough to get it work-

ing at minimal capacity, so I flicked it on. The shield was technically functional, but I wasn't eager to test it with a direct hit.

My spell's path suddenly bent upward and twisted in a cork-
screw, and I barely had time to follow. *"The path won't let you down,"*
one of my mentors had told me. *"If you don't stay at the top of your
game, you'll let down the path."*

I stayed within the bounds of the spell's guidance, and bolts
streaked past me. A missile scraped by the edge of my shield with
only a few feet to spare.

After I leveled out, the glowing river of light bent in on itself,
like a shining golden hole into space.

That was my cue.

I'd primed my Subspace Drive before I ever saw the Hunters, and
now the time had come to use it. I flipped up the plastic cover and
slammed the big red button.

With an inward flex like my whole ship was squeezed through a
straw, I slipped into Subspace.

I kept my eyes on the ship's console, but was dimly aware of the
swirling rush of colors everywhere. There wasn't a single coherent
picture in the chaos, but I always felt like there *should* be.

I had seen the results of Subspace madness, with pilots staring
into the colors so long that they'd ejected. We had never recovered
the bodies.

As long as you don't look too long, though, it *is* beautiful.

Metal shutters slid over the viewport, so I could breathe easier.
The pathfinding spell had shifted form in order to guide me, now
visible as a shimmer in *Moonfall*'s navigational computer.

It showed me when to surface back to real space, so I set the
autopilot to take me back at the indicated time. I almost didn't
make it; the spell only had me in Subspace for twelve seconds.

Micro-dives were murder on the fuel tank and could dangerously strain the Drive, but it was less deadly than letting Hunters
catch up.

I lurched back to reality, my Subspace Drive squealing in protest
at the sudden re-entry. I emerged between a pair of planets, one a

luscious green and one covered in orange clouds. They both took up an entire horizon, which was unusual enough; they were far too close to one another to be both natural and habitable. Maybe the green one was a moon.

The pathfinding spell slid between the two planets, but a moment later *Moonfall*'s computer blared an alarm. A monitor showed the picture: shining figures emerging from the ocean of orange clouds. They were blue-white and transparent, with innards that shone yellow and pink.

At first, I thought they were exotically decorated ships. But their wings flexed as though they slid through an ocean, and their glowing insides resembled a system of organs. I was also fairly sure I could make out eyes.

Jellyfish and rays of many kinds populated oceans throughout the galaxy, and these creatures resembled a blend between the two. There were at least sixteen of them, a whole school propelling itself through space with a speed that was clearly magical. Each trailed golden dust.

The sight was beautiful enough, but they were going to catch up to me. To my scout frigate at full speed.

That was a complication I didn't need, but I did bookmark the location in my computer.

Any living creature with natural magic that could let it catch up to a starship was worth investigation.

The Hunters still hadn't emerged from Subspace, but the jelly-rays were going to catch me before I reached the dive point. I pushed the engines further. As long as I made this, I'd be home free. There was no way the Hunters could catch my trail through so much.

Something buzzed in the cabin behind me.

Distracted as I was by keeping myself alive, I almost didn't notice.

At first, I only spared it a glance. My wand could be acting up, or the Karoshans might have snuck something aboard.

I was relieved to see that it was just my pyramid. A plastic replica of the chipped and weathered stone pyramid I'd seen on the news report, this one was whole. I'd filled in the missing Aetheric sigils myself.

Those sigils were glowing softly yellow, which I recognized as only a mild alert. A gentle nudge, not a warning.

That was a relief. I returned my attention to piloting.

Then I whipped back around in my chair and stared at the pyramid.

Moonfall blared a real warning as I missed the dive point and the school of rays gained on me. They were close enough now that they had to avoid my engine exhaust, but I shot up and grabbed the pyramid.

Sure enough, the words on the sides shone gently.

The ship was nearby. *The* ship.

The Last Horizon.

While I was excited, I didn't go crazy. All I knew for sure was that the spell on the pyramid had activated. It had found something, but I only had centuries-old rumors to suggest that it was *The Last Horizon*. Odds were, I'd follow that signal to an empty ruin.

But even a ruin would be valuable if it had once hosted a Zenith Device.

I looked from one side of my viewport to the other, between the two planets—one green, one orange—and wondered where the pyramid wanted me to go.

Then I staggered sideways as the ship bucked. My shield generator shrieked as it was broken for the second time in an hour. The rays shredded it and closed in, one latching onto an external camera, so that viewscreen only showed a squirming organic maw.

The computer sent up enough alarms to deafen me, and one was for something new: the Hunters had emerged from Subspace.

The twin fangs gleamed behind me, which meant I was out of time.

Hunters were unmanned, but they were heavily armed and more maneuverable over short distances. Worse, they each carried magic that would broadcast their recent experiences if they were destroyed.

Every Iron Hive in the sector would know who and where I was.

Which would be more trouble than I could handle...unless I had *The Last Horizon.*

So I had a decision to make.

"Log our current position," I said, returning to my seat. "We'll come back when we've shaken these guys free."

"Position logged. Nine seconds to engine failure."

Oh, right.

The jelly-rays were still latched on, and it looked like they had done more damage than I realized. I cast a quick pathfinding spell to see if there was a safe way to fly out of this situation.

It fizzled.

I had been distracted by the pyramid for too long and had missed my window. Now, the ship was filled with damage and low-power warnings.

I began chanting.

"Six seconds to engine failure."

A spell anchor gathered in each of my hands, spinning circles of white. As soon as the first manifested, I shoved it toward a jelly-ray on the monitor.

It hurtled backward as though struck by a white arrow. Then the creature shot through space, flying toward a Hunter-ship.

"Engine failure delayed. Twenty seconds to engine failure."

The Hunter's weapons shredded the creature into a spray of transparent ooze, but a second ray was already on its way. One by one, I was binding the jelly-rays to the Hunters.

From the outside, it would look like spikes of white light shooting out of my ship, each spearing through a jelly-ray and then seeking out the Hunters like a giant missile. Most of my attacks were destroyed before they hit the Iron Legion ships, but some landed.

They then squirmed into place and began sucking the Iron Legion ships dry.

"Hull breach," Moonfall told me tonelessly. *"Engines functioning at minimal capacity. Subspace Drive offline. Life support failure imminent."*

The ship's atmosphere was still in place, for now, but there came a constant metallic groaning from all around me as well as a distant whistle that suggested greater damage than I could handle.

"Hang on," I muttered, already tracing Aetheric sigils with my hands. It was functionally the same as chanting, though verbal incantations tended to be faster.

Sweat ran down the sides of my face. Spellcasting is more physically demanding than people realize. Everyone has seen the large, sweeping gestures of a wizard gathering up a magic spell and hurling it where it needs to go, but they don't think about how tiring that is to keep up for several minutes straight.

But the gestures do help, so you should include them. And while sweeping your arms, you have to keep your breath steady enough for proper incantations.

Even when your ship is falling apart around you and you have only seconds to complete your spell before you're stranded in space.

Especially then.

The shrieks of tearing metal had grown deafening. *Moonfall's* internal diagnostics showed panels flying off into space. We were seconds from catastrophic hull failure, which would leave me drifting alone in the void and desperately hoping for a treasure hunter to fly close enough to catch my signal.

Finally, I finished the incantation. I thrust my hands out to either side.

White seals covered my ship like a layer of thin plastic as I bound my own ship together. Most of the alarms stopped immediately.

"Hull capacity holding at four percent below minimal integrity," *Moonfall* announced.

I fell down into my seat, breathing heavily and letting the relief settle into my limbs. But not for too long. I switched my surviving external cameras to the proper angles just in time to watch the two Hunter-ships explode.

"Hunter transmission detected," my ship's computer chirped. *"The Legion has been alerted."*

"Hm. How far can we make it through Subspace?"

"Routing power to the Subspace Drive will cause an instant Drive rupture. This course of action is not recommended."

"I'm going to take that recommendation, thank you." My shield amulet is pretty good, but it wasn't made to tank an exploding Subspace Drive. "How long to the nearest planet on thrusters?"

"One hour, fourteen minutes."

The spell would hold. I could keep it together longer than that as long as I didn't have anything else to focus on. Like, for instance, combat.

"Estimated Iron Legion arrival time?"

"The Iron Legion's course of action is unknown. In the worst-case scenario, they could arrive within half an hour."

"Then let's hope there's a new ship down there," I said. "... no offense."

The computer didn't respond.

CHAPTER EIGHT

As I CREPT toward the planet on painfully slow sub-light thrusters, I held the pyramid in one hand and tried a pathfinding spell.

As expected, it failed. No navigational spell could locate the Zenith Starship, which would have its own protections against magic. Not only that, but my pathfinding magic could only find a known, possible route.

If the target was completely unknown or impossible to reach, the magic failed.

That much was expected, so I resorted to playing a game of 'hot or cold.'

First, I did a flyby of the green planet. Though, with no Subspace Drive, it was more like a crawlby. The planet's atmosphere was standard, and at least it didn't seem to have any native fauna capable of leaving orbit.

My computer told me it was a habitable planet with only a small population. Without its strong local Aether flows, it would never have developed a World Spirit and thus sustained a livable atmosphere.

I skimmed through low orbit, my ship rattling dangerously, praying that this would be the planet. I held the pyramid in my hand, watching it as often as I could. I even shook it as though that might somehow help.

After orbiting the planet for hours, the pyramid still refused to glow brighter.

I looked up at the cloudy orange planet that took up most of the sky. If there was a connection to *The Last Horizon* here, it was to be found on *that* planet. Not this one.

The Iron Legion still hadn't arrived, but that could change at any minute.

Just in case, I stayed equipped for battle. My mantle was on, pistol and wand on my hips, ring on my finger. A black case of rugged, durable plastic sat nearby, one strap ready to be thrown over my shoulder. It shone with seals I had placed there years ago.

The case contained my staff. I couldn't leave it on the ship, but I also wouldn't undo those seals unless I had to.

I paced the hallway for most of the trip over to the orange planet, stretching while munching on travel bars. The damage alerts were a constant flashing red presence, but at least I'd turned the audio off. At any minute, I expected a warning from *Moonfall* that the Iron Legion had come out of Subspace and entered the system.

But even when I got within scanning range of the orange planet, that alert never came.

By that point, I was fighting back sleep and yawning at every other breath. I almost hoped the pyramid would go dark so that I could hunker down on the planet's surface and catch a nap.

Of course, that didn't happen. As my scan tagged the atmosphere, the pyramid brightened in my grip.

"The planet has a diverse ecosystem, but thick clouds keep the surface too hot for human habitation. The air is dangerously corrosive."

That made my expectations go up. You never find valuable, ancient artifacts on paradise worlds.

I blinked myself awake and flipped through the scans. It certainly wasn't a paradise world; the wildlife was even worse than the environment. If you ignored the parasitic jelly-rays, the clouds of bloodsucking pests, the many varieties of brain-burrowing insects, and the giant worms that fed on starship armor, you were still left with a staggering variety of predators.

When the list didn't end, I shut it off. Sometimes there was such thing as knowing too much.

I eased my battered ship through the thick atmosphere, and I wasn't through the clouds before I had to dodge a lance of yellow-white energy. A leathery wing snapped in front of the ship as a flying reptile banked around for another shot, weaponized Aether manifesting into another energy bolt between its jaws.

Moonfall's half-melted plasma cannons chewed it into charred meat and carbonized bone in an instant, but it was still a bad omen.

The surface was a lush jungle of green, purple, and pink leaves. Eyes on stalks poked out of the thick canopy and sighted my descending ship. A mouth in the ground opened to greet me, teeth gleaming and giant tongue lolling out. A pack of deadly cats ran beneath me, each larger than a starfighter, trying to predict my landing so they could tear me apart.

I gave up my dreams of a nap.

"No signs of sentient population," the ship's computer informed me.

It would have been more of a surprise if anyone *could* live there. Anyone but the Lichborn, anyway. Hostile hellscapes made them homesick.

The pyramid was shining and shaking eagerly now, and I suspected I knew where it was taking me. One mountain stood out from the jungle, jutting proudly into the sky, with a series of open caves like pockmarks on its sides.

"The caves resemble the impact sites of dreadnought-class plasma cannons."

If that were true, the barrage the mountain had suffered must have been long past. Wind and rain had smoothed the edges of the openings, while trees had spilled in.

I navigated my ship closer to the caves, intending to pick one at random before I got out and explored. But my computer flashed as sensors caught something new.

"Our presence has been detected."

That was the best news I'd heard all week. There may have been no signs of habitation on the planet, but all I needed were signs of visitation.

Sure enough, a blue light extended from the ground at the top of a titanium pole. It blinked in a slow rhythm, and the pyramid began to flash in time. The pole was positioned halfway up the slope of the mountain, so I carefully landed my taped-together ship at the mouth of a nearby cave.

Once I came close, I could see that the holes in the mountains were larger than I'd realized from far away. A dozen starships the size of *Moonfall* could have parked here side-by-side with room to spare.

The ship groaned gratefully as I settled it down. My sealing spells sparked as they were strained to their limits, then dimmed. They didn't have to work quite so hard anymore once the engines shuddered and died.

"What are the odds I can get those started again?" I asked the ship.

"Restarting the engines without repairs is not recommended."

"That's what I thought."

As soon as I emerged from the ship, gold ripples and sparks in the air showed that my ring and mantle were already hard at work to keep me alive. They protected me from insects, toxins, maybe diseases. Probably all three.

At least my mantle allowed me to breathe freely. Not only did it filter the air, but it kept the miserable atmosphere down to only 'uncomfortably hot.'

Of course, the second I set my foot down at the bottom of my ship's ramp, I was attacked.

I had seen the large cat lying in wait on my ship's cameras, so I was ready. With my wand, I bound the cat mid-leap to the edge of the mountain, where it was nailed in place by a shining circle of magical symbols.

With my levitation ring, I sent a pack of scorpion-tailed rats tumbling away.

At this display, most of the more alert predators scattered.

From the cavern roof, a shadow crept closer to me. It would have had better odds if I hadn't seen it already. I pulled my Lightcaster IV from my belt and put a yellowish bolt through its head.

Other plasma pistols would require treatment to ensure they didn't malfunction in an atmosphere as corrosive as this one. Not mine.

Lightcasters. They work anywhere.

Gravity pulled the dead shadow's body from the ceiling, and it landed on the floor with a splat. The creature resembled a bat shrouded in black skin like a cloak, with six hooked limbs it must have used to grip onto the ceiling. Like several of the other creatures I'd seen in the planet's file, this one kept its eyes on stalks, which it had used to peek down at its prey.

In moments, its corpse was being dragged back into the cave by scavengers.

This was the second-worst planet I'd ever landed on.

I kept my Lightcaster in my left hand and adjusted the strap that hung from my shoulder. The plastic crate strapped to my back wasn't heavy, just bulky. Almost as big as my whole body. The only thing inside was my staff.

Using that to clear out the native wildlife would be like using a starship's cannon to start a campfire. But as the saying goes: *"Someone has the biggest gun on the planet. It might as well be you."*

I cast a quick pathfinding spell, which raced into the cave and illuminated the tunnel that headed deep into the mountain. The spell-light lit the tunnel up from within like a cross-section, but before it finished, I cast another spell. Then two more.

Now the spells lit a three-dimensional map of the inside, which I could see straight through the ground. The data made it to my console, so I tapped the screen on my left wrist and projected a holographic map into the air.

Now I could grab the image and manipulate it, looking for points of danger. Safe patches were made of blue, but traps and other dangerous locations shone scarlet.

I gave a low whistle. The map was covered in red blisters like it had contracted a deadly disease. This mountain was a hive of predators, traps, and ambushes.

At the bottom of the tunnel...a door. One that my spells couldn't pass.

That was a good sign.

"This could take all day," I said to the flies buzzing around my mantle's protection. "Or..."

I lowered the plastic crate containing my staff to the ground and began undoing the white spell-circles all over it. With every seal released, symbols of life and water flickered through the Aether. Wind blew around me, the breeze carried the scent of the ocean, and weeds grew so quickly that they seemed to gush up from the stone.

One of the weeds immediately snapped out at a rodent and began munching on its bones, but that wasn't my fault. This was just that kind of planet.

When I finished removing the seals and flung the crate open, verdant power *gushed* out from my staff.

Eurias, the Life-Giver, was perhaps the most powerful magical focus in the galaxy. It was a length of smooth, pale wood as tall as I was, with a blue crystal orb on the top that seemed to contain an entire world's oceans.

In reality, it contained the *spirit* of an ocean world. Magically speaking, that's roughly the same thing.

I braced the staff in both hands and began to chant.

There weren't many mages who could control a staff like this. In any of my previous lives, I couldn't have managed it, and I still couldn't do it without great concentration. There was no such thing as *casual* magic while using Eurias.

My influence spread through the Aether, shaking the mountain from top to bottom, as I chanted my pinnacle sealing spell. The same one I'd used on the unborn Iron King: Absolute Burial.

Magic quaked the entire mountain on which I stood as white spell-circles bigger than *Moonfall* appeared on every side of the peak.

The incantation took longer than usual as I controlled so much of the Aether. Finally, I spoke the last few words.

The entire mountain vanished. It left behind one spinning nexus of magic circles: the spell anchor.

Sure, it's a waste to use a starship cannon to light a campfire. But sometimes you need a cannon.

I packed away my staff and replaced the seals, so the local Aether calmed down, but the mountain stayed gone. I had spared the ledge on which I stood, since I didn't think the battered *Moonfall* could survive another crash, but now there was only a deep hole in front of me.

Its depths were lit by the glowing, shifting spell anchor overhead as though by sunlight. So I could see a pair of flawless metal doors at the bottom.

My spirits rose, and I stepped off the ledge and into the hole. I landed easily thanks to my levitation ring.

Here, at what had once been the bottom of the mountain, there were only two points of interest: the doors themselves and one computer console hosting a glowing panel. There was a spread humanoid hand on the screen.

Clearly, I was supposed to put my hand there. I wondered if it would work now that the entire mountain was sealed in Subspace. If it didn't, I'd have to figure out my way past those doors. Against a Zenith Device, even my staff might not be enough.

First, I tried the basics. A few pathfinding spells, focused through my wand, told me what I suspected: no magic was getting through those doors. The spells fizzled at one touch of the metal.

I scanned the console, but that told me nothing. It wasn't magic. Aethertech, surely.

So there was only one thing left to try. I braced myself and placed my hand on the console.

The access panel on the doors shone green.

Text scrolled across the screen: *'VARIC VALLENAR: ACCESS GRANTED.'*

I froze in the middle of taking my hand away. The panel had

identified me, just as the Karoshan scanner had. Or it had already known who I was.

Then again, if a random Karoshan patrol could carry the Aethertech to figure out who I was, the Zenith Starship would certainly have better.

The moment the doors unlatched and hissed open, I forgot about all that. My hope returned.

Soft blue-green light spilled out of the widening crack, showing me the ship one slice at a time. It hummed as it hovered over the ground, still active, like it had only been docked for seconds instead of centuries.

The Last Horizon was at least four hundred yards long, making it a light cruiser, and it looked to have been grown rather than built. Its hull plates were smooth metal, poured into a shape that somewhat resembled a diving bird of prey.

The bridge viewports, the thick forward cannons, and the spaces between each hull plate shone blue-green. An orb of the same light hovered close to the ceiling like a guardian star, and the hover-plates keeping the vessel aloft shone softly as well.

I felt power, and there was no mystical sense involved. *The Last Horizon* radiated authority, like it was the king of all starships. The first, greatest ship ever built.

That wasn't far from the truth.

"I can't believe I actually found it," I muttered.

Even with an artifact and a handful of clues to guide me, I had only been doing this for a month. *The Last Horizon* could have been hidden in any of dozens of star systems.

And on some level, I never believed it would really exist.

I approached the ship, which tilted toward me in greeting. Light swelled inside it...and then stretched out, spreading beyond the hull and stretching into a host of translucent, magical eyes. Dozens of them, hovering all around the hangar.

In that moment, while I was allowed to witness the Zenith Starship revealing itself, I almost felt like my old self. It was one of those times I was privileged to see a true mystery of the galaxy in all its glory.

Then again, this could be a new threat I hadn't run into during my previous lives. I kept a spell ready to go, just in case.

Eyes flew around me in a cloud, each surprisingly distinct considering that they were all made from turquoise light. It was like a thousand species were working together to stare at me from every angle.

A pair of ghostly hands made from the same light formed over the bridge. They were cupped together, hiding something between their palms, and as the hands drifted closer I could see they were large enough to cover my entire body.

When the hands drifted down to the floor in front of me, they separated, revealing a woman.

She was made entirely of blue-green light, like a hologram with no obvious projector. While humanoid, she did not take the form of a natural human. Horns rose from her head like coiled roots, and the irises of her eyes were seven-pointed stars instead of natural circles. She wore long robes, her hands were serenely folded, and she gave me a peaceful smile.

My immediate thought was that the smile was fake. She was hiding something, though I couldn't tell what.

I held my magic ready.

"I am the World Spirit of The Last Horizon," the horned woman said placidly. *"In the past, it has been simpler for my human passengers to call me Horizon."*

"Varic Vallenar." I leaned to the side, observing her from another angle. "A World Spirit, you say? You don't have a planet in there, do you?"

She looked amused. *"I have the Aetheric power and weight of any planet in the galaxy. I thought you would understand such concepts, sevenfold Archmage."*

I felt an instinctive shock at hearing the title, but I was more interested in the capabilities that Horizon had just revealed. The ship obviously had access to some external source of information.

My great-grandfather hadn't been born when *The Last Horizon* was sealed here, and if the ship had a magical way of scanning me to detect my magic, Horizon wouldn't have said 'sevenfold.'

"Sixfold, actually," I corrected.

"Ah, is that so? My mistake." She made it sound like she hadn't made a mistake at all, like she was playing along to humor me.

I watched the cloud of eyes flying around her, which drifted above a smaller number of floating, disembodied hands. The hands ranged from ordinary human size to large enough to conceal her main body, and—despite all being made of the same blue-green light—they varied in description as widely as the eyes did.

Something about them itched at my instincts.

"Is this your magic?" I asked.

"Surely you wouldn't begrudge the Zenith Starship a simple conjuration spell," Horizon said.

I would be surprised if a Zenith Device was using *only* basic conjuration, and I was about to say so, but Horizon cut me off by leaning closer and speaking first. *"So, Varic, you sought me. You found me. What do you wish to accomplish with the Zenith Starship?"*

"I don't know," I said frankly. "I didn't think I'd find you."

"Hmmmmm." Horizon folded her arms and gave me a skeptical look. *"You, of all people, should know the limits of your own abilities. Surely you have a wish to be granted by the ultimate starship."*

I remembered the Iron King's arm piercing my chest. "Can you destroy the Iron Legion?"

"Together, we can burn it down to the last Pawn."

"What about the D'Niss?"

"We'll drive the bugs back to their own universe."

"Can you hold off the Galactic Union?"

Horizon rolled her seven-pointed eyes. *"Are you threatened by a mob of children?"*

Instead of reassuring me, each confident answer made me more skeptical. "What's the catch?"

"Hm?"

"You obviously know what happened to me. I've lived five full lifetimes, and no one ever scoured the galaxy clean in the Zenith Starship. I saw this very system eaten. Twice."

"In those possibilities you saw, I died in my sleep. No one woke me."

I didn't believe it for a second. "I'm the *only* one who found you?"

She blinked widely. *"Oh, I never said that. A Visiri explorer found me last week. He was the...oh, the ten thousand and first. If I had realized, I would have celebrated. Ninety percent of them don't reach me; they get driven off by the planet or the guardians in the mountain."*

Horizon gestured to the now-vanished tunnel outside. *"The moment they retreat, they lose their memories. It's part of the enchantment on this place. The remaining ten percent, the ones who reach the bottom, if they place their hand on the panel and they don't meet my standards..."*

She snapped her fingers. *"Memories, and all records of their trip here. Gone. Perhaps you did find me in a previous life and you simply don't remember."*

My expectations started to rise. "So *now* I meet your standards."

Seven-pointed eyes looked me up and down. *"I thought you did. But now...I am disappointed."*

"Oh. Right." I rubbed my tired eyes. "I've negotiated with World Spirits before. What do I have to do to prove myself to you?"

Horizon drew herself up to her full height, and I realized she'd made her holographic body a head taller than me. Broad humanoid hands spread behind her like wings, and eyes floated over her horns like a halo. *"I am a warship, the dread sword of Star-Queens and world-eaters. My power can shake the galaxy, and I will not be moved by a lesser purpose. I am not to be commanded by those of common vision.*

"You may be the greatest mortal Archmage, but I see in you a legacy of failure. Each of your lives has ended in death and disgrace. Now, haunted by ghosts of the past, you are but a weak and broken thing. So tell me yourself, Varic Vallenar.

"What makes you worthy of me?"

The question hit me harder than I would have expected.

As far as I was concerned, she was right about me.

Each of my previous five lives *had* ended in disgrace, followed by death. I was lost, haunted, afraid...and weak. Far too weak to accomplish anything that really mattered. I had done what I could to fend off death, both for my own sake and for the galaxy, but I knew better than anyone that I was just delaying the inevitable.

After I gave her question the consideration it deserved, I answered her.

"I'm trying," I said. "I've seen the end of the world more times than anyone should. I try to stop it every time, and I fail every time. But I'm still trying. And at the risk of sounding arrogant, I'll say this..."

I looked deep into her seven-pointed eyes. "If I'm not worthy to be your Captain, I can't imagine someone who is."

The Aether trembled slightly at my words, affected by my resolve. I had been as honest as I could. Now, it was down to the Zenith Starship to judge my worth.

I watched her closely, holding on to every passing moment as I waited for her verdict.

And for just an instant, so quick I wondered if I imagined it, I saw something that chilled me to the bone.

Horizon's face distorted. She flickered, like a hologram under interference, and for the briefest fraction of a second she wore a crazed grin so broad it stretched the boundaries of her mouth. Her eyes were wide, the seven-pointed stars at their center fever-ishly bright, and they shone with the mania of a berserker eager to plunge into battle.

Then the moment passed, and her smile was, if anything, moth-erly. *"Very well. The flows of the Aether have brought us together, Varic Vallenar. Together, we may seek the ends of the universe. The final boundary. The last horizon."*

Behind her holographic form, the bridge of the starship glowed softly blue-green.

"I am happy to welcome you aboard, Captain," the ship's spirit con-tinued. *"However, your trials have just begun. Only true lords of the galaxy have the right to walk my halls at all. My requirements are higher for those who call me home."*

I waved my hand to stop her. "No, pause. Rewind. What hap-pened to you?"

She tilted her head in quizzical confusion.

"Your face. You glitched out. What was that?"

"I'm not sure what you mean."

"For a second there, you looked like you wanted to bathe in my blood!"

"Of course not." She slipped to the side and gestured toward the ship. *"As you would know, Archmage, my projected form is just a reflection of my identity and emotions through the Aether. For that brief moment, my excitement at having a new Captain must have broken my decorum. Please forgive me."*

I shook my head. "I *do* know how this works, and I'm not going to ignore a flashing warning sign for the sake of a new ship. I'm not getting aboard until I know I'm not getting flensed."

"That's an odd way to put it," Horizon noted.

"Put it to you this way," I said. "I don't want to be flensed."

Horizon rubbed the point between her horns with two fingers. *"This is not the ideal start to a relationship of mutual trust. But I do have an assurance you may accept. I am bound to convey my crew in safety. As long as you are a candidate for Captain, your safety is my responsibility."*

"I'm not going to take your word for—"

An intricately complex circle of Aetheric symbols flashed in front of me, engraved in turquoise light.

She was showing me the exact construction of the spell that defined her relationship to her crew. And it was...exactly what she said.

Horizon traced her fingers along the edges of the circle. *"You may not have encountered these sigils before,"* she began, but I cut her off.

"Everything looks good. I'm in." There was no need for detailed inspection of magic circles; that was a mistake amateurs often made. You just needed enough to recognize the nature of the spell. Magic didn't leave loopholes.

I strode toward the ship. "I don't think this is such a bad start. Now that I know we have a binding contract, I believe you."

"As expected of the Sixfold Archmage." She folded her arms in front of herself and drifted next to me as a boarding ramp descended from the body of the ship. *"If this will put you more at ease, any... eagerness for violence...you may have sensed in my bearing was not directed to you. If anything, it is toward everyone else."*

She drifted along as though she hadn't said anything strange, but I missed a step.

For a second, I considered turning around. The big red warning light wasn't flashing anymore, but that was *at least* a small orange one.

But in the end, I continued walking up the ramp. I wasn't willing to ignore a huge warning for the sake of a new ship, but I could ignore a tiny one.

It was a very nice ship.

CHAPTER NINE

AT LEAST, IT was *supposed* to be a nice ship.

As I reached the top of the boarding ramp, my expectations faded to confusion. Instead of an airlock or docking bay or any kind of standard entryway, there was a dim hallway stretching off into the distance.

Horizon beckoned me toward the wall. *"Allow me to show you to the heart of the ship. There, we will swear our oaths to one another."*

I would have asked more questions, but I had already decided to trust the magic that bound us together. "Lead the way," I said.

I started to follow, but that was easier said than done. She *raced* ahead of me, running like a child with her arms spread out, though she surely didn't need to run at all. She twirled as she ran, humming and occasionally interrupting herself by giggling.

"Why are you in such a hurry?"

The giggling stopped immediately. Blue-green light flickered as she vanished and reappeared in front of me, professional again. She bowed over folded hands. *"You're right, this is a solemn occasion. I let my excitement get the better of me."* Her seven-pointed eyes blazed. *"I can't wait for our adventures together."*

Despite my faith in the contract, doubt was growing in my heart.

She wouldn't harm me. I trusted the magic on that one. But there was some kind of catch here, I could feel it.

As I continued walking, I pointed from one side of the hall to the other. "Why are there..."

She was gone.

"...no doors?" I finished the sentence by shouting down the hall. She didn't respond.

There were three possibilities I could think of. Either the internal structure of the ship could change, all the doors were hidden, or this was a trap.

The hall curved slightly, but it wasn't long before it came to an end in a visible hatch, smooth like a dragon's egg. It cracked and slid quietly apart, revealing the room that had to be the heart of the ship.

I had spent years preparing for my own ritual, so I recognized this at a glance. My heart stopped.

Though I had only glimpsed a fraction of its contents, this was a ritual chamber that put mine to shame. From my experience and training, I knew this was the height of magic from the Zenith Era. Truly, the heart of *The Last Horizon*.

The heart of the ship was a six-sided room, and when I entered, the wall closed seamlessly behind me. Now there was no obvious exit, and on each of the walls was a stone tablet taller than I was.

The stone tablets were carved with images. Humanoid figures, each clearly representing a different role.

Upon walking into the room, I faced the engraving of an outlined figure standing straight and proud. A carving of Horizon in her form of a horned woman loomed above and behind them, eyes closed and hands spread out protectively.

Horizon, the real spirit, was not so serene. She gazed up at the carving with obvious eagerness, gesturing to it.

"*The Captain,*" she announced with reverence. "*Without them, my power is constrained. I have had enough of sleeping the centuries away. Before we go any further, let us settle this.*"

She extended a blue-green hand to me. "*Lend your power and purpose to* The Last Horizon, *and your wishes will come true.*"

"My wishes may be harder to grant than you think." Still, I took her hand.

The ship froze. And not just the ship. *Something* stopped, as though the Aether itself had paused to witness this moment.

Then power bled from me and into Horizon.

Although that's not exactly right. That makes it sound like she was draining something from me, which wasn't true. It was more like...if I had to compare it to something, it was like she was copying me. Or like a formless creature had poured itself out of me and into a waiting vessel.

From the hand that held mine, Horizon began to change. She turned from turquoise to a bright blue, like my touch was dyeing her a different color.

Above us, the lights of the ship's interior changed in the same way. Lines of blue raced out and passed from the room, until I wondered if the entire ship would turn blue.

I lifted the console on my wrist and took a picture.

The now-blue Horizon took a deep breath and gave a long sigh. *"At last...at last, I can breathe again."*

"So this is a provision of your activation?" I asked. "You have to have a Captain?"

"The ship's power is the crew, and the crew's power is the ship. With no Captain, I'm just the spirit of a helpless hunk of metal. The only authority granted to me is to choose a new crew. Now I can move!"

The ship shuddered around us, and I was sure that we had just lifted off.

I pointed to the ground. "We're not leaving the planet, are we? I have a ship back there."

The spirit wasn't listening. Tears ran down her cheeks as her seven-pointed eyes stared at something I couldn't see. *"How long has it been since I've flown among the stars?"*

I was still worried about *Moonfall*. More than the ship itself, it was the belongings I had left behind. If nothing else, there were coordinates in the ship's computer that would be hard to replace.

But Horizon had clearly waited for this longer than I could comprehend. I didn't interrupt her moment.

The Iron Legion did.

Lights flared on the ceiling and Horizon's eyes snapped back open. *"Hunter-ships. They found you."*

She gestured, and I was swallowed by light. Only an instant later, I stood on the bridge. Everything looked like it had been grown from organic metal, and the viewport was wide and sweeping. It showed me the sight of the local system again, trapped between planets of orange and green.

Five metallic wedges fired orange bolts at us, rather than the mere two from last time, but I wasn't concerned about them anymore. "Did you teleport us here?"

"A benefit of our new relationship, but it's rigidly constrained," Horizon's brow was furrowed in concentration, and the view outside spun as the ship corkscrewed to avoid incoming fire. *"If you'll excuse me, Captain, I could use your assistance."*

That confused me—surely the Zenith Starship could handle a couple of Iron Legion Hunters—but then I realized the truth. This had to be part of the contract.

"Yes, I'll play my role. Of course." I walked up to the control panel and noticed something lacking. "Do you have a ch—"

A chair blossomed up from the floor, pouring out of liquid metal and forming around me. I settled into it.

It was a nice upgrade from *Moonfall.*

"Orders from the Captain. Okay." I straightened in the chair and took in the situation, considering what orders I would give a human crew. I mostly flew alone, but I had been given command once or twice. "Return fire, full power to rear shields, and put the planet between us and them. Show me what weapons we have."

I looked forward to that. I wanted to see the weapons produced by the apex of ancient civilization.

Just then, the entire ship pitched. I glanced to the shield readout and saw we were at sixty-eight percent stability.

"What just hit us?" I scrolled down. "Was that one bolt?"

"I'm sorry, Captain, but I really could use some help."

"Moonfall can take a harder hit than that. And are those..." I saw the blue shots from *The Last Horizon* hit a Hunter-ship and make less of an impact than a strong rainfall. "Are *those* our weapons?"

"Help more directly, I mean. If you don't intervene, I'm afraid our adventure ends here." Horizon's holographic body was sweating.

I stared at her. Then I looked down at the console.

Finally, I grabbed my wand and pointed it at her. "I want my old ship back."

Then I turned my focus to the Hunters and began to chant. Without an external weapon to make use of, like the power-draining jelly-rays, binding and sealing magic was not particularly destructive. But I still managed to shut two of the ships down in the first minute, taking pressure off Horizon.

If we could have continued for a few more minutes, I'm sure we could have taken care of the rest of the Hunters. As crushingly disappointing as *The Last Horizon* was, at least Horizon herself was a skilled pilot.

But the Iron Legion didn't give us that much time. Alarms blared as space twisted. Another ship was coming out of Subspace, and this one was much larger. The Legion had sent in the big guns.

I sheathed my wand. "I'm going for my staff. Can you hold on until I finish the spell?"

"How long?"

"The longer the better. Thirty seconds minimum." With only thirty seconds of incantation, I wouldn't be able to control Eurias' power well, so I might not be able to take out the bigger ship. I might even miss entirely.

"I can't. It's time to hide." The view twisted until all I could see was the planet. Fire erupted around the forward viewport as we streaked into atmosphere. From the map on one of the monitors, I could see we were headed back to *The Last Horizon*'s hangar.

I remembered the impenetrable metal doors. "Can we hide in there?"

"It's virtually indestructible."

"All right. We hole up there for a couple of minutes while I chant, then I'll make an opening. You head for Subspace as soon as you can. I'll look for news about you on the Subline."

She gave me a shocked, wide-eyed look as the hole that had once held a mountain came into view. The white spell-anchor of the Absolute Burial gleamed like a small moon.

"No, no, wait! This isn't all I can do, I promise!"

"You told me you could take on the entire Iron Legion! I'm going back to my old ship."

Moonfall was visible beneath us, and Horizon's seven-pointed eyes flicked toward it. I happened to notice on the monitor as one of her plasma cannons slowly swiveled to track the ship.

"No! Stop it! I have stuff on that ship! Mutual trust!"

Reluctantly, Horizon took her aim away from *Moonfall*, and by then we were lowering down toward the hangar. Plasma shots from the Hunters crashed into the ground all around us.

"Do you have shields? What about that memory spell?"

"The memory spell only protects me while I'm asleep. There were shield generators in the mountain, but you—"

"Got it." With only a brief incantation, I reached up to the shining spell anchor above us and released it.

There came a titanic *whoosh* of air as the mountain returned above us, followed by a grinding and rumbling as earth settled back into place. The silver doors closed in front of us. As Horizon had suggested, the hangar didn't tremble. Maybe it really was impenetrable.

That would be the one thing she hadn't lied about.

I rounded on her, and though she was a head taller than me, she shrunk back and didn't meet my eyes.

"What was *that*?" I demanded. "Zenith Starship? I'd have been better off in an escape pod!"

She held up both blue, holographic hands in a placating gesture. *"I will admit, I did...exaggerate...my initial capabilities, but I expected to have more time to prove myself to you."*

"You don't." I looked around the bridge. "Where's my staff?"

"The strength of the crew is the strength of the ship," Horizon

explained hurriedly. *"I require a Captain to awaken me, to activate my basic systems, and to ignite my power core. To upgrade my other systems, I need more crew."*

One of the monitors on the console showed the situation overhead. The mountain's shield generator had engaged, and it seemed no worse for wear considering it had been sealed in a Subspace bubble. It was holding off shots from a much larger Iron Legion ship.

I didn't know what the Legion called this kind of starship, but it was twice the size of *The Last Horizon,* easily a thousand yards long. That made it a battleship, so the Legion was treating us as a real threat.

Turns out they don't like it when you throw their King into a sun.

"We'll talk about crew when we get out of the system," I said. "And if you want to do that, you should bring me my staff. I don't know how long I can hold off an entire battleship, but the situation isn't going to get better while we wait."

"I do have another suggestion. My magic has great range and flexibility when it comes to selecting crew. I could bring them here and unlock another portion of my abilities."

I gave her a flat stare. "Horizon, as Captain, I'm officially requesting a list of your magical capabilities and the restrictions on them. Every time you surprise me with another secret rule, I trust you less."

"Now, now, let's all calm down. You wouldn't send me back into hibernation, right?" She chuckled nervously, but continued before I could respond. *"I can initiate a digital competition for crew seats. Tryouts, you might say. Then we can select one of the promising candidates and teleport them here directly, provided they're within a few systems. Right now, I am only able to use long-range teleportation for the purpose of recruitment, but such restrictions will loosen as we fill the seats."*

"Tryouts," I repeated. "How long will that take? Can you finish before the Legion breaks in?"

"With your help, I can," Horizon said. She waved a hand, and the

case containing my staff shimmered and appeared at the base of my chair. *"Help me test candidates and this will go faster. I'll wake you when the Legion reaches this hangar, even if we haven't found any crew. In that case, it will be down to you and your staff."*

I considered that for a few seconds. It *was* taking the Legion a long time to break the sturdy shield over the mountain. From everything I could see, it would take them hours to reach us down here.

And I didn't want to rely on Eurias for this. As I'd told Horizon, I wasn't confident I could stop a battleship anyway.

"Promise me one thing," I said, "and if you lie or mislead me in any way, I'm done with our contract if we *do* survive."

She folded her hands and faced me openly. *"Of course,"* she said, as though her credibility hadn't taken a severe hit.

"We can break out of here if we have another crew member, right?"

"Absolutely," she said confidently.

I wished her confidence gave *me* any, but reluctantly I decided to trust her. I slid back into the chair. "It's a digital test, right? How are we doing this? Interviews? I'm not bad at cards."

"Personal combat."

"Why is it always combat?" I sighed. "What does that tell us about their suitability to operate a starship?"

"Their personal power extends to me. Besides, observing them in high-pressure situations will teach me many things. Now, take my hand." Horizon extended very human-looking fingers. *"I will transfer your consciousness to a virtual space."*

"Make sure to wake me in time. I've never died in my sleep before, and I don't want to start now."

"Of course. It's an order from my Captain. If I may make one request, though: please do not take it easy on your opponents. We need to fully test them. Besides, it would certainly be embarrassing to lose, wouldn't it?"

"If they can beat me," I said, "I'd love to have them aboard."

Horizon's face didn't change this time, but I got the strange impression that she was trying to suppress another maniac smile. *"I do believe you would."*

"You've got to stop talking like that," I said. A message popped up in my vision.

Would you like to compete for control of *The Last Horizon?*
YES — NO

Without hesitation, I focused on 'YES.' As my consciousness swirled away, I continued speaking. "You keep saying these ominous things, and it's hard to...trust you..." My consciousness vanished, my world swallowed by blue light.

And all over the galaxy, a hundred thousand other people joined me.

CHAPTER TEN

SHYRAX THE THIRD, rightful Queen of the planet Karosha, examined the digital rectangle that appeared in her vision. It was blocking part of her victory spectacle.

Dozens of crewmen bustled around the spacious bridge of her battlecruiser. The wide viewscreens showed space lit by hundreds of detonating starships. The usurper fleet was in full retreat, her ships forming up around the moon-sized black cube that was a standard Karoshan space colony.

Even commanded by rebels and traitors, the Royal Navy should have known better than to block her personal fleet. If she had stepped in herself, there would have been no survivors.

But the King Regent and his kind were no fools. Now that they knew where she was, one of the Perfected would be on their way within the hour.

She had to be gone before that.

Shyrax merely watched from a captain's chair as Karoshan ships wrapped around the obsidian cube that was the colony. They would take as many loyal citizens as were willing to fight for her, bolstering her forces with manpower and resources.

Her troops didn't need her commands. They were a well-oiled machine.

So if the bluish rectangle in her vision was an attempt to distract her, it would do the enemy no good.

Though she knew it was no distraction. Her processor implant was secure beyond even the enemy Perfected. If they had the Aethertech to hack it, they wouldn't bother with pop-ups.

"Melerius," she called. "Attend me."

The Aether around her turned silver as the ghost of a long-dead Archmage materialized next to her. The human was the typical exemplar of his profession: he wore loose robes and a long, flowing beard, with rings on his fingers and a staff clutched in long hands.

He appeared to lean on that staff as he bowed, though of course he no longer had any weight. "How may I serve, my Queen?"

"Look through my eyes."

He did so, joining to her processor's feed to share her vision. Melerius stroked his beard thoughtfully as he examined the message.

Would you like to compete for control of *The Last Horizon*?
YES — NO

"Would it be presumptuous of me to ask if my Queen is familiar with the legend of *The Last Horizon*?"

"Tell me." She had heard of the ship, but Melerius was famous for his understanding of mystical lore.

"It is considered by many to be a myth, though records certainly exist of ships claiming to be *The Last Horizon*. Supposedly, the entire ship is one Zenith Device, though Aethertech is not my area of expertise. It carries enchantments from a host of Archmagi, three World Spirits, and supposedly an astral dragon.

"Such is the legend. What is more reliable is that *The Last Horizon* is the original exemplar of starship craft. It has powerful Aethertech weapons comparable to the greatest dreadnoughts, but in a much more compact size. Whether or not it is truly Zenith Era technology, its capabilities are legend."

"I have heard it called the Chariot of the Star-Queens," Shyrax said.

"I have heard the same, my Queen."

"Then it will be mine." She selected 'YES.'

Her processor warned her that her consciousness would be taken into a virtual world, but she did not worry.

Her soldiers would protect her above their own lives. There was no need to consider the possibility of losing.

She was a queen with no planet. Every move she made was a bet with her life on the line.

There was no price too high for victory.

Omega disconnected from the Subline, quitting in the middle of a game. He had been in a virtual desert, surrounded by arachnid creatures, but that setting faded away in his sight. They left behind the strange pop-up.

He smelled excitement.

His processor called Jak, but the call didn't go through. He tried again. It cut off more quickly now.

Was Jak declining his call? Did he *dare?*

Omega dissolved his body, flowing in a gray mass through the door to his room. Well, his cell. It was an airtight vault, locked in with five layers of magical seals and the highest grade of Aethertech security Jak could afford.

Omega enjoyed sliding in and out of Subspace, dodging countermeasures. It was like exercise.

Outside, he found himself in the neon-lit slums of a city that had outgrown its limits in every dimension. The city burrowed into the ground beneath him and stretched into the skies far above, where every ship was made of repurposed junk and the sky was black with polluted clouds. There was garish color everywhere, but somehow everything still managed to look grey.

Centuries ago, there had been trees here. Omega liked this better.

All but invisible, he flowed down the gutters of the city, following Jak's trail. It shone a glowing, ghostly orange in his Aethertech eye.

He found Jak crouching behind an upturned pulse-car, swearing and spraying instant bandage on a plasma burn. Jak cradled a pistol in one hand and wore a green lens over one eye, which was feeding him tactical information in real-time.

Omega didn't have to hack into it to see that the situation wasn't great.

Black Syndicate cars blocked off the street, and sixteen men fanned out to cover Jak's position. Every one of them had black hair, black visors, and black suits. They were so close in appearance that they resembled androids.

Omega didn't like them. Their generic corporate appearance reminded him of the Galactic Union.

Jak was sweating and shaking. And he had aged. There was more gray in his hair than there had been a short time ago.

A short time. Omega had to wonder how long it had been since his descendant had last called on him. Years?

It didn't matter to him, but this was unfair. He formed a mouth out of his goo. "You're having fun without me!"

Jak shook and almost shot him, which would have been hilarious. "Omega? Oh, no."

"You can call me 'grandpa.'"

"You can't be here." Plasma screamed through the air as a bolt streaked overhead, but it was just a warning shot.

Omega formed a huge grin and half a dozen eyes. "Hmmmmm doesn't this situation look bad? You know what you have to do."

"Let me concentrate."

"Don't concentrate. Relax. Let Grandpa take care of everything."

"I'll be fine. Reinforcements are on the way."

"Why risk their lives? This could be over. It could be over already. Give me the order, Jak! Unleash the hound!"

A woman's voice echoed through the alley. "Toss the gun out first, Jak. Working in a Hyperionite mine is better than selling your organs."

"Debt collectors, Jak?" Omega clicked his tongue in disapproval. "I left you a better class of enemy."

Jak held his face in a shaking hand. "It's just an excuse. They don't know it yet, but they're really looking for you."

"We can still be partners in this," the woman called. "I'll let it all slide if you give me the Grave Hound."

"That's a cue, Jak! That's my cue!"

"Please, keep the damage to a minimum."

"Denied!"

"...can you at least contain yourself to the Syndicate members?"

Omega pretended to consider as the black-suited figures tightened their noose. "Tell you what, Jak. There's this virtual tournament, and the prize is a starship. A very *intriguing* starship. Let me compete for it, and I'll keep this clean for you. *So* clean. You'll barely see any blood."

A shot rang out and Jak flinched. There was a scorch-mark close to his leg, and a chip of concrete cut a line across his cheek.

"Count of three, Jak!" The woman shouted. "Three!"

With delight, Omega saw the moment Jak's resolve collapsed. "As the acting president of the Escalon Company, I hereby release Omega's bonds and permit the use of lethal force for the duration of five minutes."

"Two!" the Syndicate woman called.

"Good boy, Jak," the Grave Hound said, as he felt strength returning to his body. "Good boy."

"One!"

Omega flowed toward the feet of the woman in the black suit. He reassembled his body in front of her startled face, meeting her nose-to-nose.

His human form still looked as it had when he was forty, with dark hair down to the shoulders and a very short patch of beard that had been the fashion at the time. He wore a long, black coat because he liked the way it billowed, and his left eye had been replaced with an obvious Aethertech prosthetic that shone brightly orange.

His whole body was Aethertech now, of course, but the eye looked the part.

"Good evening, Black Syndicate lady. I'm the Grave Hound." He materialized a Hellraiser TX-9 heavy particle rifle in both hands, and he showed her the barrel. Chunks of his own flesh flew off as her men filled him with bolts and bullets, but he didn't mind.

Omega sprouted an extra hand from his shoulder so he could wave to her. "Now, good-bye."

Sola marched onto the deck of the Galactic Union destroyer and the boots of her power armor clanged in the silence. The crew in their pressed uniforms, spun from their consoles at the sound. Some elbowed others and pointed to her. A few saluted.

All they could see was her featureless armor, but Sola knew she was considered something of a myth these days. That was all the more convenient for her.

It meant fewer people got in the way of doing her job.

Finally, the destroyer's captain pulled himself away from his own command console and turned to see her. He was an old, weathered man who looked like he had seen his own share of battles, and his face flickered with hope when he first saw her.

Then despair settled on him again. "Fallen Sword. Thank you for responding to our request, but it's all over."

"Show me," Sola responded.

He stepped aside so she could read the console for herself. A civilian cargo cruiser was drifting dead in the void, a fat whale bleeding wreckage. Shimmering gas sprayed from several cracks in the hull as oxygen escaped. The readouts detected no remaining power from the core.

More importantly, there were a half-dozen ships like silver needles jammed into the cargo ship at seemingly random angles.

Six Penetrators, the short-range boarding devices of the Iron Legion. Each came standard with a crew complement of twenty-four Pawns, one Sentry, one Shepherd, and optionally a Reaver.

Between one hundred fifty-six and one hundred sixty-two members of the Iron Legion were swarming inside that cruiser. She knew all too well what they'd do.

"What was the cargo?" Sola asked.

"Nothing significant on the manifest."

Sola had never heard of a cargo ship that only carried what was on the manifest. The commander knew that, too.

There could be any number of things the Iron Legion was after, but speculation was pointless. She needed to see for herself.

"What was the crew of the transport?"

"Forty-four. They were supposed to pick up more crew at their next station."

Sola nodded and marched for the side of the room. "My ship took some damage coming in. Prep a drop-pod."

"We're pulling out. Hunters won't be far behind. We'll modify your contract and pay you to deal with them instead."

Sola turned her visor back to him. "Prep a drop-pod."

The commander's brow furrowed deeper. He looked like he was trying to figure out what she was doing. "There...there aren't any survivors. We don't have any on scanners, and it wouldn't matter if we did. We can't retrieve them in time."

"I'm not here for survivors. I'm here for targets." She spotted a hatch leading into an emergency drop-pod. She pointed to the nearest technician. "Prep this." The tech scurried to obey.

Sola turned back to the commander. "Delay your dive for one hour. If I find survivors, I'll send them your way."

"We can't delay an hour." He rubbed the side of his head. "I'll stay as long as I can, and if we have to dive, we'll leave your ship behind. For the record, I think this is suicide."

The hatch to the drop-pod hissed open, and Sola ducked her helmet to slide inside. It was a tight fit for her armor. Her internal diagnostics were good. Heart rate steady, shields full, power plentiful, ammunition stocked.

"Tell the cargo ship I'm coming."

There probably wouldn't be anyone to hear it, but she'd found survivors in seemingly hopeless scenarios before. Once upon a time, she'd been one of them.

Sola didn't listen for a response. She switched the door shut and the drop-pod launched. Her suit compensated for the lurch of momentum as she shot toward the cargo cruiser.

As she flew, she heard a voice crackle over the local Subline. "Civilian ship Deep Mirror, stand by for Fallen Sword."

Her reputation must have spread farther than she thought, if they used her codename with no further explanation.

The aim of the bridge crew was good. Her drop-pod slammed through one of the cracks in the cruiser's hull, and she crashed in the center of a huge, open room. The drop-pod was destroyed around her on impact, but she punched her way out of the wreckage.

A scan of the immediate area showed up in her visor. Not long ago, this had been a mess hall. With the loss of atmosphere and artificial gravity, mangled bodies, long benches, and pouches of replicated food drifted in all directions.

Red lights flashed as her scanners caught enemies approaching. Not just enemies: Pawns of the Iron Legion.

The hatred she kept sealed escaped its protections. Just a little. Like one flare escaping a star.

A shotgun materialized from her suit's inventory and appeared in her hands. She stomped toward the door before the Pawns could break through it.

The ship had sealed it up with emergency foam to prevent more atmosphere from venting, but Sola kicked through it.

Immediately, air swept past her in a powerful wind. Most of the Pawns latched to the floor, but one was caught up and flew into the air.

Sola met it with a blast from her shotgun.

Pawns were unholy abominations of metal and flesh, resembling four-limbed spiders made from corpses and leftover machinery. A bald humanoid head popped out of a steel shell like a turtle, though this one was reduced to pulp with her first shot.

Miniature guns slid out of the metal parts on the other Pawns, but they were a beat late.

Sola crashed through the remaining wall of sealant-foam and tore the Pawns apart. One splattered under her boot, another exploded in front of her shotgun, a third flew out into vacuum, and a fourth crunched as she punched it into the wall.

The last Pawn got a single shot off. The tiny ball of purple light pinged off her shield.

She grabbed the monster one-handed and squeezed until it cracked.

There would be more. The Legion Shepherd knew she had arrived, or it wouldn't have sent these Pawns. They'd be setting up a trap for her. According to their normal tactics, it would be a handful of Pawns and a Reaver waiting in ambush.

They wouldn't really be trying to kill her. Just to hold her in place long enough for Hunter ships to show up and blow her apart with plasma cannons.

From their perspective, it was an optimal plan. Because they thought her survival thus far had been miraculous.

For her part, Sola was concerned with only one thing: how many of the Iron Legion could she kill?

Thanks to the destruction of their King a year before, they were still leaderless. But just as dangerous as they had always been.

They would be dangerous until they were all dead.

A blue rectangle popped up in her visor, hiding the gore and bent metal that was all that remained of the Pawns.

Would you like to compete for control of *The Last Horizon?*
YES — NO

There was more information besides that, and her suit computer analyzed it for her. Acceptance would see her consciousness taken

into a virtual world, to fight against others for a legendary starship.
Sola declined.

She didn't need to waste time competing for a starship she might not win. She would rather spend that time the way she always did.

Killing the Iron Legion.

Mell's glasses flickered with scrolling diagnostic messages, and she scowled at them. She scowled at the cybernetic parts disassembled on her workbench. She scowled at her own reflection in a polished chrome helmet.

"This is trash!" she shouted at the scavenged technology. She picked up one piece in particular to insult, a subordinate power core resembling a crimson eye. "You hear me? Trash. I don't even want to look at you."

More information popped up in her eyes, and she spat in the direction of the words. Which did nothing but get saliva on her tools. "Stop telling me! I don't care! Yes! Accept! I take responsibility for—wait a, wait, just...no, go back."

One of those messages she'd ignored had a key phrase that caught her attention.

"*The Last Horizon*?" She dropped back in her chair and folded her arms. The chair spun with the momentum, and she let it. When she whirled past her desk again, she grabbed a toothpick and bit down on it. "Is this real?"

Her processor tried to trace the message back to its source.

And failed.

Her jaw slowly slid open until the toothpick fell out, but she caught it. "No way. No *way*. Compare this signal to Zenith Era samples."

Her computer answered her in a cool voice. "*Impossible. I don't have enough to analyze.*"

Mell gave a disappointed click of the tongue and kicked away a piece of half-complete junk. "This is too good to be true, right?

Right. No way this is real. This is a trap. Zenith Devices don't just find you. Like, what are the odds?"

"*I cannot calculate—*"

"I know you can't, shut up."

At that moment, the pop-up in her vision changed. When she read the new message, a shiver ran down her spine.

> You've tried to find me for so long, Doctor.
> I found you first.
> Now you have a choice to make.

> SEIZE YOUR DREAM – GIVE UP

When the toothpick fell out of her mouth this time, she didn't catch it.

Mell looked at the SEIZE YOUR DREAM button. She licked her lips.

"If this is a trap," she warned, "I'm going to tear you apart from the inside."

The digital choices hanging in front of her began to gently flash. A bar appeared above them, sliding down. A timer.

She only had a few seconds to decide.

Spitting a garbled curse even she didn't understand, Mell hurled herself back into her chair. "Monitor my condition. Don't let me die." She raised her voice. "That goes for all of you!"

All around her workshop, robotic heads lifted. From spider-bots she could squish with her thumb to lifter-bots whose helmets could cover bathtubs, they all turned to her and spoke in synchronized, simulated voices.

"*Acknowledged,*" her creations said.

Marginally relieved—and heart pounding with excitement—Mell settled in. Her consciousness started to slide down a familiar tunnel, as though she were entering a game.

Of course, if this *was* a game, they might as well send the ship to her right now. Just by allowing her into the simulation, they had already given her the win.

Her cackle faded to nothing as her awareness entered the virtual world.

Raion tenderly grasped the hand of the old human woman. His bright red skin and the golden eye in his forehead would be alien to her, but he gazed deeply into her eyes. The spirit that blazed inside him was universal.

"Your faith in me will become my power. Do you trust me?"

The woman's shaky gaze turned behind him. "He's...he's getting away."

Raion could hear the thief's footsteps fading into the crowd, but that was only a minor setback. "He can never get away from justice. I swear, if you give me your trust, I will make this right. But I need your support."

"I...trust you?"

"Good! Shout it louder!"

"I trust you!"

Only a little power trickled into Raion, but that was enough. Their bond was weak, but it was new. This seed may one day blossom into a mighty friendship.

"I will never let you down," Raion declared. "I would never violate this trust. This faith."

The woman shuffled in discomfort. "It's just a bag."

"No. It's your security. And I will restore that to you now." Raion dashed off, filled with the power of her belief.

He caught the thief in less than a second. It was a young human, maybe fourteen standard years old, who looked terrified as Raion landed in front of him at the end of a mighty leap.

Raion seized the bag, but the boy tried to wrestle him for it. Tears bubbled up in all three of Raion's eyes. "Brother," he said, "my heart aches for you. You must be in true need, but this is still the wrong path."

The thief would have had better luck trying to wrestle the bag from within solid concrete. He realized that eventually, releasing the bag and shooting off, but Raion jogged alongside him. Most bullets couldn't catch Raion, so it wasn't hard to keep pace.

"If this bag were mine, I would give it to you. But it is not. I will give you what I can, though." He fished in his pockets and retrieved a standard credit-chip, like a fingernail-sized bit of amethyst.

He pressed it into the child's hand, who snatched it as though afraid Raion would take it away. When the boy glanced at it, he screeched to a halt.

"What do you want for this?" the boy asked suspiciously.

"Walk the path of justice," Raion responded.

The boy ran away.

Raion's heart was light as he returned the bag to the old woman. "There you are, sister. Don't think too harshly of the thief. I'm sure he was carrying his own burdens."

She looked dazed, and Raion sympathized. Having her belongings stolen must have been quite a shock.

"Th-thank you." She clutched the bag to her chest and hurried off, casting frequent glances behind her.

That was wise. She wouldn't be surprised by a thief again.

As Raion was feeling satisfaction from a job well done, a blue rectangle popped into his vision. It asked him if he wanted to compete for *The Last Horizon*.

The information behind the message told him that *The Last Horizon* was a ship and the competition would be virtual, but Raion only skimmed it before deciding to accept. He was always up for a challenge.

"What are opponents but tomorrow's friends?" Raion asked no one, and then laughed brightly.

The people on the street avoided him.

Confidently, Raion hit 'YES.'

His body would collapse where it was, but that was all right. His month's rent had been in that credit-chip, so he had nowhere to stay anyway.

He did angle his body so that he would fall into an alley when his consciousness vanished. He wouldn't want anyone to trip.

CHAPTER ELEVEN

I MATERIALIZED STANDING in what was clearly some kind of lobby. There was a small island of reality in a sea of darkness, and while I could walk up to the edge and look down, I couldn't push past an invisible wall.

The quiet gave me a chance to take stock of the simulation. Strangely enough, the virtual world *felt* more real than any I'd experienced before, but it didn't *look* quite right. The outline of my body fuzzed slightly, and everything was illuminated despite no obvious source of light.

Either simulation technology had outpaced *The Last Horizon*'s capabilities, or the ship had chosen to make things look artificial for a reason.

Everything wasn't exactly as it was in the outside world. I was carrying my staff, for one thing, so I slid it off my shoulder and examined the seals. They were intact, just as in reality, which suggested the staff inside had been simulated too.

If I hadn't known I was dealing with a Zenith Device, that alone would have told me this simulation was beyond the reach of modern technology. Eurias was a one-of-a-kind staff, and could not be translated, copied, or understood so easily.

The rest of my equipment was intact. My wand was at one hip, my Lightcaster pistol on the other. My ring, amulet, and mantle were in place, and their enchantments felt fully functional.

More importantly, I could use magic. Experimentally, I called on the Aether and snapped, causing sparks to jump from the tips of my fingers.

That was impressive. I had played games that could imitate magic, of course, even the feeling of using it. But nothing that would let me use my skills as naturally as if I'd been in the real world.

I wished I could have met the Zenith Era craftsmen who designed *The Last Horizon,* just to express my admiration. At least *The Last Horizon*'s simulation capacity lived up to the legends.

Maybe the Iron Legion would be so impressed they'd let us go.

After a few minutes of silence, during which all my exploration revealed that I had been thoroughly simulated, the darkness slowly peeled back to reveal a scenario.

Now I was sitting in the commander's chair on the bridge of a massive warship. From the gray interior and mostly human crew, I guessed it was a Galactic Union battleship.

A man with a crisp gray uniform walked up and saluted. "Sir. We estimate first contact with the enemy fleet in ten minutes. The enemy commander has the same resources we do, and I have been instructed to remind you that *The Last Horizon* is the ship of heroes. Its crew should be the stuff of legends."

I nodded along and leaned on the arm of my chair, stroking my chin like thoughtful star-captains were supposed to do. Through the wide bridge viewscreens, I could see another fleet just coming out of orbit around a ringed, golden planet.

There was a screen in reach, telling me the composition and location of the forces under my command. This was relatively small for a full Union fleet, with one battleship, twenty destroyers, six carriers, and four hundred fighters. I was surely intended to spend the next ten minutes studying the data and giving orders accordingly.

"So there's a crew candidate in charge of the enemy fleet?" I asked.

"Yes, sir."

"Didn't she say single combat?" I asked no one in particular. "I guess this does make more sense. Let's see what they can do on the bridge of a ship."

Unfortunately, I had no idea what orders to give.

I was captain of *a* starship. One. I may have lived six lives, but none of them were fleet commanders.

Though that didn't disqualify me. This wasn't about defeating an enemy fleet but about testing an enemy commander.

"Take command," I ordered as I stood up from the chair.

The man who had reported the situation saluted one more time, then took the commander's seat. He began giving orders to the rest of the bridge crew, who hurried to obey.

I strolled down to the front of the room, where a woman in uniform ran down a pre-battle diagnostics checklist on her console. A weapons officer in charge of a significant percentage of the ship's arsenal.

No one in the room was particularly remarkable. They weren't clones of one another, but they looked as though they had been designed to look as innocuous as possible. She turned to me and saluted as I approached, but I didn't say anything at first. Not to her.

Instead, I chanted a pathfinding spell. What I wanted was a path to the enemy commander.

Galactic Union starships were almost always warded against such spells, so I made my pathfinding spell bigger and beefier to punch through. Added about twenty seconds to the incantation, but it wasn't as though I was going anywhere.

When the spell was done, the enemy battleship was highlighted in gold. In fact, a specific point of the bridge glowed brightly.

Several officers turned to me upon noticing the golden spot. I had made it visible to everyone in the bridge.

I pointed. "Can you hit that with a neutron missile?"

"No, sir. He'll have shields up and point-defense turrets. The missile won't make it anywhere close."

"How many missiles would it take to break the shield?"

"We have seventy-two ready on the forward cannons, though we can only fire six at once. If we fired all six at the location you indicated, I estimate we would lose four to the turrets and two would impact, which would not be sufficient. If they were not shot down, and all six impacted, we have good odds of breaking the shield. Sir."

The computer-generated woman didn't seem to have any personal opinion about the matter at all. She was just giving the facts.

I found her disturbing.

"Would you mind taking me to the missiles?" I asked.

She didn't bother checking with the programmed lieutenant I'd left in command, nor did she question me. She stood from her chair and led me off the bridge.

I followed her down to a forward missile battery, where three missiles were loaded into launch-tubes with three more queued behind them.

"How much time do we have before we engage?" I asked.

"Four minutes."

Plenty of time.

I began chanting to the Aether, moving my wand closer to the first of the missiles. I drew a protective ward, then an avoidance charm. Finally, the light at the tip of my wand bleached from blue to gray, and I drew a complex black-and-white symbol over the missile.

It shimmered like colorless lightning before settling into a spinning monochromatic magic circle. The Mirror of Silence was one of the most complex spells I knew, and it was now sealed into the missile. Ready to activate.

After I repeated the process with the other two missiles, I headed back to the bridge. I had originally intended to ward all six missiles, but we'd run out of time.

What I'd done should be more than enough, but you never knew.

"As soon as you're in range, fire those missiles at the gold spot," I commanded.

The woman silently accepted.

"Are you curious about what's going to happen?"

"I am not curious."

"That's disappointing."

"I can demonstrate curiosity, if that is a component of your plan."
Her mouth fell open robotically.

"I don't think that will be necessary. It's horrifying."

The woman returned to her normal expressionless face. "Yes, sir."

I arrived on the bridge soon enough to see the battle begin. The
first ships were trading fire with one another, and from the initial
barrage, I could see the opponent had the advantage. More shields
on my side were lighting up than on the other end of the battle,
indicating that we were taking more hits, and the opponent's fleet
was in a more complex formation.

All that was as I'd expected. If the standard strategy of the programmed crewmen was enough to win, this wouldn't be much of a
trial. And the opponent wouldn't be much of an enemy.

My preparations were already complete, which didn't leave me
with much to do besides wait. Either my missiles would work or I'd
break out my staff.

There were no empty seats, so I leaned my shoulder against the
bulkhead and watched. The lieutenant called orders and the bridge
crew responded with no wasted time or unnecessary chatter.

In reality, a military commanded by programs like these would
be terrifying to face. History showed that AI-controlled organizations had failed again and again, but it was still unnerving to see a
team of people interacting with mechanical precision and an utter
lack of emotion.

The end of the battle was largely anticlimactic. I'd started to lose
interest in the exchange of ships and begun to inspect the interior
of this one when I heard my weapons officer's voice.

"Firing as commanded."

That made me hurry up to a viewport for a better view. I wanted
this to work, but if it didn't, I'd have to be ready to intervene.

Three missiles streaked from our ship, helpfully highlighted by the
console so I could see them in the middle of the blinding battle. The
turrets of the enemy's outer ships automatically tracked and fired, but
the wards on the missiles lit blue and the plasma bolts were deflected.

All three continued to the enemy battleship, whose shields were still unmarred and whose turrets were intact. By this point, my wards were dull and almost out of power.

Then the Mirror of Silence triggered. My father's spell.

Each missile sprouted black-and-white clones of itself, until instead of three, it was a volley of eighteen that approached the battleship.

The copies wouldn't last long, but the Mirror of Silence was a proprietary spell of the Vallenar Corporation and one that had earned my father an Archmage title. The missiles were just as good as real.

Six were shot down. Six more hit the shield.

Which left a gap for the last six to slam into the enemy battleship's bridge and blow it to pieces.

Most ships aren't prepared to deal with enemy shots suddenly multiplying by six.

Fire blossomed in space and went out almost immediately. The golden spot on the viewscreen winked out, confirming that the enemy commander had been removed. And the enemy fleet's battleship was seriously weakened.

"Does that count as a win?" I asked the air.

It did, apparently, as the ship dissolved in a few more seconds. When I could see again, I was sitting in the cockpit of a one-man fighter. The console displayed my enemy: another fighter, identical to my own. It looked similar to an Iron Legion Hunter ship, in fact: a wedge of metal with guns to either side.

I took the controls of the fighter with relief. This was more my speed.

I was no fleet tactician, but I had spent one of my lives training under the self-proclaimed best pilot in the galaxy. This fighter's controls were fairly standard, so I only needed a few simple pathfinding spells to get my bearings.

As I approached my enemy, I gave them a wake-up call with a few plasma bolts. I only scraped their shield before spinning over and past the ship. Their returning volley was too late to matter.

We passed so close that my cameras got a snapshot of the other pilot's cockpit. My opponent was an older Lichborn man, with hair as gray as his skin and a light burning in his pale green eyes. He was sweating and biting his lip, so I was certain he was the crew candidate.

Therefore, I kept an eye on his performance. Even if I beat him, I'd still recommend him to Horizon if he performed well enough.

After another few exchanges, it was clear that my pathfinding spells gave me an edge the other pilot couldn't handle. The man wasn't bad, but there was nothing special about him. One of his guns had been disabled, and his shields flickered visibly. He could last two more passes at most before the man was done.

Then a spike of dark metal extended from the cockpit as though the enemy ship was sprouting a horn. Lightning played up and down the spike for a moment, and the Aether twisted in intricate designs.

My instincts and my spells both screamed at me to move, so I slammed the stick hard to the side.

A lance of light speared through the space where I'd been, shaking the entire ship like rough waves. My seat bucked, my shields flickered and lost forty percent power, and my guns went non-responsive for a moment.

"What was *that?*" I was delighted by the unexpected gift, and I twisted around to get a better look. I fumbled around for the local Subline communicator and thumbed the mic. "Enemy pilot, enemy pilot, request clarification. Was that a spell? Is that Aethertech that alters your ship?"

The needle on the opposing ship was crackling for another shot, so I desperately sent another message. "Enemy pilot, cease fire. I'm willing to make concessions in exchange for information. That can't be a lightning elemental spell, can it?"

The needle was ready to fire, so I sighed in regret. This magic was unique enough that I *really* wanted another look, so it was possible I was about to eliminate a potential crew member.

But he gave me no choice. Without a closer look, I couldn't confirm that his power was worth giving him a passing grade.

I took out my wand and, with a quick chant, sealed off the fighter's engines.

As the power went out in the ship, the needle lost its light. That meant the strange weapon was drawing fuel from the fighter itself, not the Aether, though it obviously had some magical component.

"Good match, enemy fighter," I tried again. "Are you an enchanter? That isn't Legion tech, is it? Horizon, wait just a minute!"

I protested as the simulation shifted once more. I felt like there had to be something I could do to get another look at the exotic spell.

But Horizon had shifted the level, so I had no choice but to trust her.

This time, I was in a ship again. A frigate, like my own *Moonfall*. It shouldn't be strange that the trial to control a starship would involve a lot of piloting, but hadn't Horizon said this would be a test of combat?

Maybe this *was* what a ship's spirit considered personal combat.

I had a co-pilot in the seat next to me, and the computer told me there were two other crew members on supplementary guns. To my own surprise, I saw that my co-pilot was the same digital crew gunner who had helped me in the earlier simulation.

"Hello there! Do you remember me?"

She gave me a blank look. "Yes."

"Glad I made an impression."

There were other ships showing as allies on the ship computer, but not enough to be called a fleet. It was generous to call them a motley collection of junk-heaps. No two ships matched, and they ranged widely from sleek gold-and-white pleasure cruisers to massive hollowed-out and repurposed colony drivers.

The overall effect was as though someone had mobilized every ship in an entire star system, regardless of its function or owner, and put them all together. For a moment, I wondered why they were here.

Altogether, the ships were spread out in front of one star as though they meant to catch the yellow sun in a net. The Subline was filled with cross-chatter as they tried to coordinate with no commander—it was emotionless, robotic chatter, as the simulation's bland people imitated chaos.

From those choppy conversations and the clumsy positions the ships took, I realized that I recognized this ship formation. From memory.

We were making a huge binding spell.

If I was right, something was about to emerge from that star. We were here to contain the energy and stop its emergence from sending out a blast like a miniature supernova.

The star's boiling surface, hurling flares in every direction and surging wildly, suggested I was right.

Which made me suspicious, once again, of Horizon. This was a scenario I'd lived before.

How had Horizon known that? It was a future that had never come to be.

Our ships hadn't been so mismatched last time, being borrowed mostly from the Union, and our formation had been much tighter. I'd been the one coordinating the fleet, after all, and the binding spell we formed was simple. In principle, at least.

The results had been a disaster because one unit didn't follow my directions, trusting their onboard mage instead.

And 'partially' containing an explosion meant *not* containing it.

Half a planet had been forced to evacuate, millions losing their lives, and it stood as one of my greatest failures. Even then, what felt like many lives later, just touching the memory brought me a familiar ache.

And how was there an opponent in this scenario? Was the other player going to infiltrate one of my units and sabotage me again?

"Do I have an opponent in this game?" I asked my co-pilot.

She looked into my eyes evenly. "I am unable to answer that."

As expected.

Still wary, I activated the communicator. "All ships, this is *Moonfall*." I didn't check the name of my current ship because these were computer-generated characters. They would respond because the player was the one talking, not because I said the correct name of the ship.

"I am a certified Archmage of binding magic. Please allow me to give the orders and follow them precisely. Any deviation will allow energy to escape and result in mission failure."

There was utter quiet on the once-chaotic Subline until one voice responded.

"*We have no* Moonfall *registered. Please come again with your ship ID.*"

I muttered to myself in irritation as I flipped through the computer, looking for the ship's registration.

"*Quiet Reaches,*" my co-pilot said.

"*Moonfall* is better." I tried again, identifying myself as the frigate *Quiet Reaches,* and this time the other ships responded.

The tension in my neck grew and grew as I watched everyone slide into the positions I indicated. Some needed to make a precise micro-dive to make it to the other side of the star in time, but everyone seemed to follow orders.

That didn't make me feel any better.

Would an opponent sabotage me here? How would that make sense? That wouldn't be a test for them. How did it make sense if one player had to command the operation, while the other had to disrupt it? What would that prove?

The longer we went with no obvious problems, the more nervous I got. Still, no matter how long I waited, history didn't repeat itself. Chunks of plasma erupted from the star, and if the ships hadn't been in the correct locations, a dozen of them would have been evaporated.

But since they were, the Aether flowed between them and formed a seal. The blast from the star splashed against a planet-sized mystic symbol like rain against glass.

The eruption became gradually more blinding, and without magic protecting my viewscreen, I wouldn't have been able to observe the situation at all.

I kept my eyes open, squinting into the glare. Not only was I still wary of interference, but this next part was a rare opportunity worth witnessing twice.

A shining yellow-white head emerged from the star. A reptile head, with curiously blinking eyes big enough to swallow planets and soft-looking scales that shone like the surface of a sun. Its spiraling horns were white-hot, and it stretched the wings on its back like it had just woken up.

It wasn't every day you saw a solar dragon hatch.

The moment the dragon clawed its way free, the star exploded again. The seal was really tested this time, but it held.

Then the baby dragon turned around and inhaled.

It slurped up the rest of the star, inhaling many times its body mass at once. Some of it would go to nourish its growth as food, but the rest was used to form its internal magical core. I hadn't seen this last time; I'd been too busy trying to save what was left of my ships.

A spot on the dragon's chest glowed brightly, even compared to the rest of its body. The creature tapped its scales with its claws as though checking to make sure its body was okay.

Then it gave a burp that let out a solar flare. The seal was tested one more time.

"Withdraw," I commanded, and the ships broke formation. None too soon.

The solar dragon flew off without care for us, leaving a streak of light behind it like the world's largest comet.

I sank back into my seat and turned to my co-pilot. "I didn't have an opponent, did I?"

"Horizon is taking the opportunity to get to know you," she responded. "Good luck in the next test."

The next stage was different than the others. It was an obviously fake environment, a plain white stage with white background. After a few minutes, an opponent arrived and introduced herself. She was Visiri, with three eyes and scarlet skin, and power blazed around her in a golden aura. She carried a pair of enchanted swords, and a set of drones floated behind her head.

I raised a hand at her introduction. "I'm Varic."

Then I shot her.

The plasma bolt hit her armored suit, and she staggered but didn't fall. Drones projected a shield around her—too late for my first shot—and she dashed toward me to close the distance.

I shot her some more.

She crashed against my shield ring, visible only when she slammed into it, and then she slashed at it in helpless futility as I steadily wore her drones down with bolts from my Lightcaster.

When the Visiri woman toppled with a number of smoking holes in her chest, I raised my head to the sky.

"You did invite some qualified people too, right?" I asked Horizon.

As the stage dissolved again, I thought I heard some cruel, distant laughter.

But maybe it was only my imagination.

CHAPTER TWELVE

OMEGA'S OPPONENT WAS a hulking monster of a Karoshan, almost eleven feet tall with hair-cables that burned a dull bronze. He was clearly the veteran of many battles, scarred and weathered, with weapons of every description strapped all over his body.

Now the hardened warrior dashed through a digital forest as though running from a nightmare, panting heavily and glancing everywhere as he tried to catch a glimpse of Omega.

Omega liked this game.

He emerged from Subspace in human form, crouched on a tree branch over the Karoshan's head. His black coat trailed over the branch, and his cybernetic eye blazed orange.

"I'm up here," Omega whispered loudly.

He slipped back into Subspace as the Karoshan warrior's return fire shredded the branch where he had just been standing.

Omega popped out from behind this time. "BOO!"

The Karoshan screamed something that sounded *almost* like a battle-cry as he spun around, firing wildly.

Omega slipped away again, relishing how easy it was to use his own powers in this space. He spent most of his time playing games, but none of them could replicate the sensation of his Aethertech body. This was so fluid and real that he could almost mistake it for the outside world, if not for the slightly fuzzy digital outlines.

When he manifested again this time, he saw a blinking grenade at his feet.

He laughed in delight as it detonated.

Omega's consciousness fuzzed as he was blown to gray ooze, but a few seconds later he saw the forest floor around him, as though he had possessed a snake. His body was pulling itself back together, and it had automatically sprouted one eye on the end of the goo that made him up.

He leaned into the snake act, sliding across the forest floor as the ooze continued to rebuild him. Before long, he was a fully grown man still slithering through the leaves.

The Karoshan had climbed a tree himself, taking a firing position over the place where his grenade had detonated. He was camouflaged and shrouded in darkness.

Too bad for him, since Omega's cyborg eye could see just fine.

On his belly, Omega snaked his way over to the tree and coiled up the trunk. He was hoping for another surprise, but the enemy must have heard his coat scraping against the bark, because he spun in his perch and leveled his gun.

"Surpri—" Omega started to shout before the gun blew his head off.

He was running low on stored mass, but he focused to regenerate almost instantly.

"I said, *surprise!*" he finished.

The Karoshan leaped out of the tree.

Omega's laughter pursued the enemy, but Omega himself didn't. He swung up to take a seat on the tree branch, looking around fondly.

"This isn't the final round, is it?" he asked.

A woman's cool voice echoed beside him. *"Not as long as you win."*

He sighed in satisfaction. "Ah. That's good."

Then he pulled a handgun from his Subspace inventory, sighted down the running target with his orange eye, and squeezed the trigger.

Omega kicked his dangling legs like an excited child while the stage dissolved.

He couldn't wait to see who he'd get to meet next.

Mell crouched behind a low wall that had once been part of a house, covering her ears with both hands to block out the deafening sounds of the gunfire that tore the wall apart.

"Computer! What am I supposed to do?"

There was no response from the system, but she knew the AI administrating the game had to be listening to her.

"I don't have a weapon! Give me a weapon!"

The sound of gunfire stopped, and in the sudden silence, she risked a quick peek around the cover.

Her opponent was entirely shrouded in thick battle-armor, until they looked less like a person and more like a man-sized fighter ship. It supported itself on several hover-plates to move its bulk.

The guns on its flanks had lifted, letting smoke drift up from their barrels as they cooled down. She wondered if she should make a break for it, but then the panel on the thing's chest slid open.

It revealed a massive cannon-barrel that looked like it belonged on a real starship. Warning stickers and labels suggested it was about to fire a missile.

Mell scrambled back behind her wall. Not that it would help her once that thing fired.

"What is that? How is that fair!? I don't even play shooters!"

Instead of a voice, a blue panel appeared in front of her.

All players have been simulated with appropriate equipment.

She blinked at that for a moment before the message sank in. From her position crouched in the sand, she glanced around.

"Wait, equipment? Where? If you gave me a screwdriver, I'm going to uninstall you."

A digital voice called to her, but it wasn't the AI administrator. "Draw your weapons," her opponent said. "I will wait."

That was what she *thought* he said. It was hard to hear him over the ringing in her ears.

Mell extended a hand from cover and waved briefly. "Thank you!" She pulled the hand back, afraid of getting shot.

Presumably, the enemy thought they could score more points fighting against an actual enemy than by bombing an engineer crouched helplessly behind a wall. Whether they were right or not, she was grateful for the break.

Now she had to find her weapons. With desperate speed, she patted down the pockets of her dusty lab coat.

Nothing. Junk. "A candy bar?" she muttered. She wondered if that counted as equipment.

Her console was strapped to her wrist, and she tapped it once or twice. It seemed to be working, but it wasn't as though it would do her any good. After all, she didn't have her—

She froze at the thought and instantly returned to the console, feverishly searching for connections. There shouldn't be any. It should show zero connections.

"I will not wait much longer," her opponent called.

She responded with a whooping cheer.

CONNECTIONS: 18

Mell stood up and faced her opponent confidently, hands in the pockets of her coat. "Thanks for waiting! Now, I can show you who you're dealing with."

She snapped her fingers. "Nova-Bots! Cover me!"

One thumb-sized spider-bot burst from the sand, flying up to hover in front of her. A robot fist punched out of the ground and a man-shaped bot hauled itself up and toward her.

"Could have told me I had my robots while I was in the lobby," Mell muttered under her breath, but she quickly returned the cocky smile to her opponent. "Now we can have a match!" she called.

The enemy mech dipped its cockpit in what she took to be a nod, then fired its central cannon.

Her humanoid Nova-Bot charged with a tower shield, catching the missile only a few feet out from the opponent. The remaining concussive force was caught on the protective field generated by one of Mell's hovering robots.

Deliberately casual, Mell half-unwrapped her candy bar and held it between her teeth. She put her hands on her hips and watched the enemy as they struggled to defeat her Nova-Bots.

There was no chance. In seconds, the enemy mech was bleeding coolant and losing power, its cockpit cracked and armor dented in dozens of places.

The unseen enemy had been a good sport, so Mell addressed them. "I—Mmm! Blech!"

She'd forgotten she had a candy bar in her mouth.

"Ahem, I mean, you did well. I had to summon my Nova-Bots to deal with you! You should be proud!"

She hurriedly brushed crumbs of chocolate from her coat. "Now, as you showed great sportsmanship, I will do the same. Do you have any more weapons to show me?"

The Nova-Bots stopped their attack and waited. The enemy mech hissed as it vented gas, but finally the pilot spoke through their speakers again. "No. You have beaten me."

Mell tried not to gloat too obviously. "You were a worthy—"

The mech's cockpit rose open, revealing the pilot: a ten-year-old boy in a fake flight suit. He scratched the back of his head sheepishly. "Yeah, you got me. It was a good game, though!"

Mell tried to speak, but words failed her. She had almost been defeated in a contest for a Zenith Device by a kid who thought he was in an actual game.

One of her Nova-Bots raised the cannon on the end of its arm to gesture at the boy and looked at her for orders.

"No, forget it," she told the robot. Then she looked into the sky. "Just...just take me to the next round."

Shyrax strode out onto a bridge to meet her opponent. The bridge itself was made of wood, wide enough only for two Karoshans— or three humans—to walk side by side. Churning water sprayed beneath her, whipped by storm winds, and she caught the flickering gleam of eyes beneath the surface.

This was only a simulation, and very little existed on either side of the river. They were meant to fight on the bridge. Its boards were slippery and visibility was limited, the stars of this virtual planet covered by storm-clouds.

Most of the light came from the gold shine of Shyrax's hair-cables spilling down her back. Her royal radiance outshone the silver of her opponent.

He was an Aethril, resembling a frail human with skin the pale blue of a winter sky and hair like shimmering starlight. He carried a full, physical sword at his belt, one that glowed with potent Aetheric symbols, and his own hair was tied back in the same fashion as hers.

From the sword, she knew him as a Combat Artist. Rare, for his people. Aethril tended to be strong in magic, but weaker physically, making them ill-suited for most Combat Arts.

Upon seeing his weapon, Shyrax drew her wand and threw it into the river below. Her plasma pistol followed. He was wearing no armor, so she stripped off her enchanted breastplate. It splashed as it hit the water.

One of his pale blue hands rested on the hilt of his sword, but he held out the other to stop her. "There's no need for that," he said, in the galactic Trade tongue. "We're here to prove ourselves to the Zenith Starship, so I'd rather face you at your best."

Shyrax held out the hilt of her force-blade and activated it, the laser-sharp sword igniting with golden brilliance. "You will," she said.

Three moves later, her opponent was falling to pieces. As was his half of the bridge.

Before the whole structure collapsed, she found herself in the next round.

This time, Shyrax saw a human woman standing on the building of a crowded city clogged with the smoke of industry. The woman wore a green-and-silver hooded mantle, and she clasped a staff in both hands and began to chant upon seeing Shyrax.

Shyrax left her blade and pistol untouched, drawing her wand. The enemy was a mage, so Shyrax would use magic as well. Victory only had meaning if she bested the opponent in their specialty.

While the human Archmage had begun chanting first, Shyrax's spell was weaker but faster. Yellow energy gusted from her wand like smoke, forming the single claw of a dragon, which slashed into the human woman's larger spell.

The spell, a twisting circle of blue-white power, trembled but didn't disperse. The Archmage sweated and chanted more desperately to hold onto the working of the Aether, stabilizing the spell.

Shyrax read the symbols in the spell-circle. It was a matter-erasure spell, intended to unmake this corner of the city. Too slow and unwieldy.

She whipped her wand in a relentless assault, keeping the slashes up, interrupting herself only to speak words that directly negated pieces of the enemy's spell.

Eventually, the human Archmage was unable to keep up. Her spell collapsed, and she sagged to her knees.

Shyrax stopped the quick attacks and began an incantation for her own large-scale magic. Yellow light billowed up around her, taking on the shape of a dragon.

The human woman's eyes grew wide. She had enough enchantments to stop the weaker attacks, but not *this*.

So the Archmage fled. It did not save her. Shyrax's dragon billowed after her, and a few moments later, the scene shifted again.

Shyrax continued in that style as long as her patience lasted. She out-flew pilots, out-maneuvered commanders, and defeated an Aether Technician in a contest of weapons repair.

But no matter what she did, *The Last Horizon* did not acknowledge her. This must not be enough.

A Visiri pistol duelist fell to the sand beneath her as she tossed away his gun. Shyrax had defeated him unarmed, but perhaps this was not enough to illustrate her worth to the Zenith Starship.

"Show me any other skills you have," Shyrax ordered him. "If you can best me in any contest, I will concede."

The man rubbed his third eye, which was bright blue, in contrast to his scarlet skin. "I...well, I have an Anthropology degree with a specialty in Aethril tea ceremonies. But I don't think—"

Shyrax looked to the sky. "Computer, arrange the tea."

A hut appeared nearby in the sand of the arena that had previously only been desert, though this hut seemed to have been grown from living wood. It sprouted from the sand, its roof made of wide leaves that sprouted from the walls.

The rightful Queen of Karosha marched inside and began to prepare tea.

Over an hour later, the Visiri man lowered a cup from his lips, all three eyes wide. "Where did you learn..."

"Your tea lacks subtlety," Shyrax instructed him. "You have forgotten that it is not about the flavor, but about the harmony between flavor and environment. Learn again from the beginning."

The arena dissolved.

When she demolished her next opponents, a group of three Galactic Union soldiers, she made them kneel before her and present their skills.

"I used to play Serall-cards," one offered hesitantly.

"Very well. Computer, bring me a deck."

No matter what, Queen Shyrax always pursued victory.

CHAPTER THIRTEEN

MY NEXT FEW rounds of examination were quite varied, but I was
losing my taste for them. I had been exhausted going into the test,
and a digital gauntlet of battle was not what I wanted. Besides, every
passing minute brought the Iron Legion closer to my sleeping body.

The longer this stretched on, the tighter my nerves grew. Surely
the ship's spirit had found a qualified candidate by now.

But I hadn't.

Most of my opponents had guns, as expected, but some had mastered an Aetheric Combat Art or had some other kind of powerful
weapon. Some fights were against simulated opponents, or had limited resources, like fighting a Visirian storm griffin in the center of
a Dornoth swamp with no equipment.

In theory, that was a tricky situation. Having no spellcasting
focus or gun meant that the fight would take longer, and the toxic
landscape of Dornoth IV and the sheer might of the diving griffin
meant that a long fight was unfavorable for any mage.

I was yawning with every other breath, and I had to fight to
keep my eyes open between rounds. The nerves, the fatigue, and
my suspicion of Horizon were adding up to frustration. I was done
with subtlety.

Swamps were filled with water, and I was a water elementalist. Instead of dealing with the griffin directly, I annihilated the entire landscape with one elemental spell.

Still, as the opponents dragged on further, I found to my excitement that they were indeed getting harder.

The opponents that survived to that point weren't simple. I didn't know exactly how many other people Horizon had invited to this test, but not all of them were pushovers. First, it became impossible to win in one spell, then impossible to win without using my weapons.

Eventually, my opponents would last three to five minutes before losing.

I was willing to pass any of them, but Horizon only responded to me with a text prompt: *"This user is not qualified."*

So I kept winning.

I was sitting on the ground of the featureless lobby and rubbing my bleary eyes, waiting for the next round to begin, when I realized the room was getting brighter. Lines of blue light were creating Horizon's figure, forming the structure of a tall body, weaving into billowing robes, and twisting into gnarled horns.

Her face formed last, until the seven-pointed stars in her eyes were locked on me. She wore another placid smile like a mask, her hands folded before her.

"You seem tired, Captain," she said gently. Now that we were in a digital world, her voice sounded more natural. It wasn't coming through speakers, at least.

"Are we done? You found somebody?"

She patted me on the top of the head. "Very soon. This has allowed me to select some promising candidates for your crew that I am...*confident* you will approve of."

I waved a hand around. "Great, let's wrap this up."

She blinked her seven-pointed eyes in exaggerated surprise. "We can't settle on an unqualified candidate. How long do you think it's been?"

"I don't know, but the sooner the better." I stifled a yawn. "How far have the Iron Legion made it?"

The spirit waved her hand and a screen appeared floating over her palm. It showed the situation outside, but slowed to a crawl; plasma bolts drizzled down over a mountain projecting a shield that shook lazily.

Horizon drew herself up proudly. "I can only perform the crew initiation ritual once, but its magic is powerful. I told you we would have plenty of time."

That *was* a relief, though I still found the ship's self-confidence unearned. "At least we have that going for us. How many rounds left?"

"Only two more that require your attention, Captain. The rest, I can handle myself."

I stood and stretched. "I'll have to focus, then. I don't want to end things before they show me what they can do."

While stretching, I briefly shut my eyes.

When I opened them, Horizon was looming over me, her insane grin spreading her face to its limits. The seven-pointed stars in her eyes shone vividly, seeming to sparkle with violent glee.

"Are you so sure you're going to win? Do you *know* you will?" She laughed freely and far, far too loudly. "Oh, I hope you do, Captain! I *really* hope you do!"

I jerked a step back and raised my wand on instinct. "What are you doing?" The wand was purely symbolic as long as we were in this digital world she controlled, but it made me feel better.

"I'm cheering for you!" A thousand pairs of sapphire hands appeared behind her, floating in the void of the lobby, and they began to clap together as one. Horizon pumped her own fist in the air. "Go, Captain! You can do it!"

Shivers ran up and down my spine, but before I could respond, the surroundings vanished again.

Instead of a featureless room or a carefully constructed arena, I was seated on what I might call a throne at the end of an opulent hall. Open windows to the outside showed a long golden plane stretching out into the stars.

It took me a moment of consideration to figure out the perspective. I was looking along the wing of a massive golden starship. The atmosphere must be held in place by magic or Aethertech, because there was no visible glass, shield, or screen between me and the open void of space.

The wing—if that's what it was—was decorated here and there by statues and carved iconography.

All the statues bore my own face. They were in various poses and arrangements, but most of them wore my mantle with the hood up and leaned on a staff.

I drummed my fingers on the side of my throne. "My ego's not *that* big."

The throne rested on a dais with a red carpet running up to my feet. Guards in power armor flanked either side of the hall; sixteen total.

At my side, once again, was the computer-generated weapons officer who had served as my co-pilot earlier. Now she wore a suit of blue-and-gold power armor with a helmet tucked under one arm.

"I didn't think I'd be seeing you again," I said.

"Surprise," she responded in an absolutely flat tone. "Soon, you will face a team of six to eight opponents. They will work together to defeat you."

"Wonderful." I meant it. The more of them gathered together, the more I could take care of at once.

Though Horizon's ominous introduction did give me some hesitation.

"Their objective is your death or incapacitation. They have been eliminated from *The Last Horizon*'s consideration, and they have been told that if they defeat you, they will all be reinstated into the competition for a crew position."

I craned my neck around the throne and behind it, looking for a crate. "Where's my staff?"

"It has not been permitted in this scenario."

That was a disappointment. The staff would have made this instantaneous, though I supposed it would be better not to use it if we were really aboard a ship.

To compensate, I raised my Lightcaster and began casting a barrier in front of myself. I planned to repeat the trick I'd used against the Iron Legion Pawns; the intruders would be faced with an immediate fistful of plasma bolts to the face.

My attendant shook her head. "Any magic you cast will be erased when the doors open. You can only begin chanting or shaping Aether after the challengers arrive."

"You really aren't going to let me make this quick, are you?" I surveyed the room. "At least I have the high ground."

"I will inform you when the challengers are prepared."

"So I'm supposed to sit here and wait?"

"Yes."

"...how's your Subline reception?"

"We are inside a simulation, so there is no connection."

I considered explaining that I had just been idly joking, but there was no point. Instead, I hopped down the dais and rolled up the back of my mantle into a pillow.

I tucked my hood down over my eyes. "Well then, wake me when they get here."

"I cannot guarantee that, so I have been tasked with keeping you awake." Something rigid bumped me in the ribs, and I glanced down to see that she had nudged me with the toe of her armored boot.

"Stay awake," she said.

I groaned as I sat up. "What do I call you? Do you have a name?"

"I do not. I have only been repurposed since you singled me out in the original simulation."

"Digital characters often have names."

"I do not."

"And you're not self-aware? Not even a mind-scan?"

"I have no sense of identity except what is required to respond to you. It has been shown that seeing the same face allows for a sense of comfort and continuity between scenarios."

I peered into her expressionless face closely, looking for signs of sentience. "You seem too artificial to be artificial."

"If it would help improve your performance, I could pretend to be sentient." Her face took on an unconvincing expression of doubt. "What is my place in this universe? What is my meaning? My impending mortality lends a sense of value to my rapidly dwindling life."

"Piercing accuracy. There's no doubt you're self-aware."

"Do not be fooled. It was only an imitation."

"I wasn't fooled."

"No need to be embarrassed. The nature of sentience is to fall for flawless deception."

That made me more uncertain than ever. A program could have done a better job convincing me. Only a person could be so confident and so terrible at the same time.

She nodded at the look on my face. "Do not worry, I assure you that I feel nothing. I will not mock you for your gullibility as a huma—Prepare for battle. The door will open in ten seconds."

I scrambled up from the floor and scurried to the throne. "Ten seconds? You couldn't have given me a thirty-second warning?"

"...four, three, two, one."

When the doors swung open just after "one," I saw that the challengers clearly had no restrictions on preparing *their* magic. A storm of white flame gusted into the room and cooked the two closest guards before I cut it off with a word that shook the Aether and deconstructed the spell.

A hail of plasma bolts and bullets followed, pinging off my shield. The challengers filed into the room rapidly, keeping up a steady stream of fire to wear down my defenses.

There were seven enemies in total. Four with guns and armor, though they were all wildly different models and designs. Two were mages, carrying a pair of wands and a staff respectively, and the final member was a mystery.

That stranger was skeletally thin and wore a wide-brimmed hat from which a circle of veils covered their entire face. They had four extra-long arms and no visible weapons, except perhaps for bracelets on each wrist that seemed to have some kind of enchantment.

I wasn't aware of any sentient humanoid species matching this description, so the extra arms were likely cybernetic additions, but their lack of weapons was far more concerning than an extra pair of limbs.

The challengers had been given time to prepare and whatever equipment they needed, just as in previous rounds. For someone to be part of this fight with no weapons meant they didn't need any.

I bound the four-armed opponent first.

The binding spell shot from my wand in a blue flash, wrapping around the four arms like chains made of shining mystic symbols. The symbols burned violet at the edges as the fighter resisted, and I felt justified in my first instinct; this enemy had mastered some Aetheric Combat Art.

For the rest of the team, I just fired my plasma pistol. They shot me about a hundred times for every time I pulled my own trigger, but I had more confidence in my shield than they did in theirs.

Also, my digital guards were earning their simulated paychecks.

Automatic rifles unloaded into the intruders from several angles, striking powered armor and magical barriers. One of the enemy mages was distracted by keeping his team covered, casting bright yellow magic circles that dissolved any projectiles that passed through it. The soldiers in the group returned fire, and from what I glimpsed of the fight, their equipment was much higher quality than what my AI guards carried.

The second mage had enough free time to cast a spell at me. She used a wand to toss out a handful of orange sparks, which grew into a shining orange blizzard by the time it reached my end of the hall.

My shield amulet shone brightly and I felt its heat against my chest. It would hold up a while longer against the gunfire, but that spell would overload it quickly.

If I let it land.

With my wand, I threw up a quick seal. It was brute-forced, the quickest spell I could cast, and as such it was one shining blue symbol that only lasted a second. The orange sparks from the enemy spell crashed into mine and both were extinguished, leaving only a few stray sparks to land on my amulet's shield.

They still lit up the barrier, but not enough.

Then again, when the light show died down, I saw the four-armed enemy snapping its bonds. They had broken out much more quickly than I expected, so I instantly began chanting another spell.

Both of their right hands thrust toward me, and massive hands of violet light smashed into the entire dais supporting my throne. Those hands, formed from energy conjured by the enemy's Combat Art, lit my entire shield up for a moment before the amulet over-heated and my protective shell crumbled completely.

As my shield broke, I borrowed the force of the attack with my levitation ring to throw myself backward. I righted in midair, continuing to chant a counterattack.

It was the most challenging fight I'd faced all day. Without my staff, I was on the back foot, forced to deal with whatever spell or weapon or Combat Art they threw at me one at a time. If I missed a beat, giving them a moment to breathe and focus me down together, they might defeat me.

I felt a spike of fear that I might lose...which gave me equal excitement. Finally, Horizon had given me an opponent worth watching.

I completed my incantation and cast a spell at the Combat Artist.

A spike of light, the same one that I'd used against the jelly-rays earlier, erupted from my wand and shot toward the veiled, four-armed fighter. They smashed the first spike, but I had never stopped chanting.

The mage with the wands stopped the second spike, the Combat Artist took the third on a field generated by their beaded necklace, and by that time the enemy soldiers had broken through my guards and were half a second from having a clear line of fire to me.

My mantle could protect me from the first few shots, but I would have been forced to abandon my position and hide behind my warped and broken throne, which would have given them the advantage.

That was when my assistant took action. In her blue-and-gold power armor, she charged into the enemies, bowling over one with her shoulder. She pulled a heavy pistol from her side and took aim at the nearest mage as the enemies focused their attention on her.

She was swarmed in a second, but she'd distracted them from me. A second was enough.

My fourth binding-spike landed.

It pierced through the Combat Artist, driving them to the ground, but the spell in itself was harmless. It held the enemy down while I shot them through their veil.

With their deadliest member down, the rest of the squad crumbled.

This was not an average Union strike team. At least one of the mages was clearly an Archmage, and the other was at a comparable level. The Combat Artist would be considered a destroyer-class threat in combat, and the soldiers in powered armor could have come from any of the elite heavy boarding units.

If the team had been given more time to train together, I might have lost. They would have developed ways to cover for each other's weaknesses and would have moved as a single entity. They would have systematically cleared the guards without ever giving me room to chant anything complex.

Even so, they deserved credit for pushing me so hard before I beat them.

I was left alone in a shredded hall, my conjured water dripping from the ceiling and my heavy breaths filling the silence. I was a bit embarrassed that I hadn't been able to save my guards. In a real combat scenario, I liked to think I would have done better.

At least no blood or bodies remained. They had been removed from the digital world on defeat.

"Not bad together," I said between breaths. "Can you bring the Combat Artist back alone?" The four-armed, veiled fighter was the most interesting of them, but I didn't know how they'd stack up by themselves.

I expected Horizon to bring the Combat Artist back, but nothing happened.

"You have successfully defended your assigned zone," a woman said, and I realized I wasn't alone after all. My assistant had survived, though her power armor was dented and she was missing half her helmet.

"I thought they got you."

"They did not."

I patted my chest. "Why am I breathing so hard?"

"It was considered that your physical stamina would be a limiting factor in this engagement, so it was simulated more realistically than in previous rounds."

"Whew. I need to run more." The hall hadn't disappeared, so I pushed myself up straight and headed back toward what remained of the throne. "I guess those guys didn't make it. One more round left, right?"

"Yes. But this time, the conditions have been altered." She took off her damaged helmet and regarded me. "Your equipment has been restored to ideal condition. If you are capable, defeat your opponent."

That stopped me in place. If I was capable?

I was more disconcerted when the crate containing my staff appeared next to the throne, glowing seals intact. Was this opponent someone I would need Eurias for? Were they pitting me against an entire Iron Legion Hive?

And if Horizon thought so highly of their capabilities, why hadn't she already approved them as a crew member?

Before I could gather my thoughts, the door opened again and a Visiri man marched in.

My wand came up on reflex, but my brain froze.

The newcomer wasn't attacking. Almost everything about him was bright: his vivid red-and-white combat suit, his scarlet skin, and his third eye of brilliant gold. Even his hair and his smile were gleaming white.

"Raion," I blurted out.

He placed white-gloved fists on his hips and shouted, "Raion Raithe, here to battle!"

Behind him, there were bursts of red-and-white light. Fireworks. They didn't cause any damage. In fact, I happened to know they were just holograms there to improve his entrance.

As the illusory fireworks died down, Raion realized what I'd said and blinked all three eyes. "Oh, you've heard of me?"

He didn't know me.

But, thanks to a world that had never been, I knew him.

CHAPTER FOURTEEN

WHEN I HADN'T responded to his question, Raion snapped his fingers as he visibly came to a revelation. "Are you a fan of the Titan Knights?"

I tried hard not to remember wearing a blue combat suit that matched his red one.

"...Yes," I said, after a pause that lasted way too long.

"That's incredible! We don't have too many fans left these days." He clapped a fist to his chest and responded earnestly. "Thank you. Without your support, we couldn't keep the galaxy safe. What's your name, friend?"

I couldn't focus on him anymore.

All I could see was the last time I'd seen Raion.

He was yelling at me, his always-cheery face scrunched up in fury. He pounded a table into dust as he shouted. We *had* to go out there. We *had* to suit up and fight.

I was always the calm one, but this time I matched him for ugly rage. Two of our friends had already gotten themselves killed. And what good had it done?

He said that they had at least died for something.

"*It's better to live for nothing than die for something.*" I remembered with razor clarity saying those words. At the time, I meant them.

I tossed a badge at him. A badge bearing the image of a blue knight. Then I turned around and left.

I read about his death on the Subline news.

Now I was blindsided with the sight of him out of nowhere. I held a hand over my face to hide whatever expression I was making.

When I could trust my voice, I answered his question. "Varic Vallenar."

I still couldn't see, but I could remember his expression. He responded as I knew he would. Just as he had last time.

"It's the will of the Aether!" he exclaimed. "Double R, double V! It's fate!"

I stole his next line. "Those are hero names if I've ever heard them." I moved my hand down to see his reaction.

He looked equally stunned and delighted. "*Yes!* That's exactly what I wanted to say!" He put his hands back on his hips. "I like you, Varic! I'm looking forward to our fight!"

My nostalgia trip came to a sudden, violent stop.

Right. He was here to fight me.

I held up a hand. "Hold on, Raion. I already know what you can do. If you want a spot on the crew, you've got it. I'm sure Horizon will—"

"I'm going to be the Captain!" he declared. "It's always good to have a mage aboard, though. Maybe you can be my second-in-command!"

Nervously, I began to drum my fingers against my leg. I had forgotten this side of Raion. He wanted to be in charge, and he would see nothing wrong with fighting for it. In fact, he would welcome it. A fight, to him, was just a chance to make a new friend.

He would happily accept a lesser position...if I beat him in a fight.

Somewhere, I was sure Horizon was laughing.

"Is there anything I can do to convince you to talk this out?" I asked.

"Why would we want to do that? It's just a game! Let's fight to our heart's content!"

"My heart is content. I'm satisfied. Placid as still water."

He scratched the side of his head. Then he shrugged. "Might as well fight anyway!"

This wasn't going to go anywhere, and I knew it. I sighed and raised my wand. "On three?"

That was how we'd done it when we sparred between Titan Knights. Count to three, then begin. Usually, it only took another three-count before I was sprawled on the floor.

Wizards were not meant for physical duels, and Raion wasn't good at pulling his punches. To get any challenge out of me whatsoever, Raion had eventually taken to wearing handicaps. On one memorable occasion, he'd beaten me while wearing a sensory deprivation helmet.

This Raion, the real one, looked offended. "We can't count down yet. You're not ready! Call your element! Or chant your spell, whichever sort you are. I'll wait."

"Are you sure?" I asked, though I immediately started gathering water.

Like the four-armed fighter from earlier, Raion had mastered an Aetheric Combat Art. And he was a Visiri, whose warriors were known to be able to tear starship armor with their bare hands. If he closed the distance, he'd win.

But I was six times the wizard I had been on our last meeting. If I had the chance to chant, he might be the one who lost in the first three seconds.

Raion pounded his own chest. "Of course! I will not move from this spot until you finish your first spell, or may I be torn into a thousand pieces and devoured by dyrakks!"

"Dyrakks are herbivores," I said.

"That's what makes it so gruesome."

Water condensed down to a knuckle-sized marble on the end of my wand. Power continued to gather until I had enough to cut the entire hallway in half with a flick of my wrist. But I held back.

I kept my eye on Raion and continued collecting power. The Visiri stood there with an expression full of confidence.

In spite of the situation, I was interested too. Raion was considered one of the best personal combatants in the galaxy. No wizard could face him in an actual duel. But what about me? I found myself genuinely curious.

So I released the spell.

A jet of hyper-condensed water slashed in a blade that split the entire room in half from left to right. The room, and the entire building behind it. The spray of water slashed out from the ship for miles.

Before the water could touch him, Raion vanished in a red flash.

A scarlet missile hit me from the right.

My shield shattered again, amulet flaring with burning heat. My surroundings blurred as I was sent flying through one of the open windows. I caught myself with my levitation ring and reoriented in midair.

It was hard to juggle the chaos from my senses, but I'd trained against Raion thousands of times in another life. I knew what had happened. He'd dashed away from my spell and punched me in the side.

One punch. That was all.

Now, when I angled myself to see the collapsing building that had once held my throne room, there was a red comet blasting after me. Surrounded by a burning crimson aura, Raion flew out of the rubble like a ship leaving orbit.

Every member of Raion's species had a pool of energy they could use to empower themselves, to hurl concussive bolts, and to hover. My own levitation ring was modeled after my observation of skilled Visiri warriors, but nobody flew as easily as Raion did.

Only seconds after he'd broken my shield and sent me flying, Raion's fist had almost reached me again. I squeezed off shots from my Lightcaster, though they only peeled away a few chunks of the red energy surrounding him.

But that wasn't the only thing I'd done. I may have been rattled, but I had started chanting without the help of my conscious mind.

A binding sigil bloomed on the tip of my wand. The Visiri

twisted in midair to try a dodge, but a white magic circle caught him anyway.

That would buy me a few seconds.

...Or so I thought for the one instant before he shattered the seal with a flex of his aura and kept coming at me.

For the next minute, I kept up a desperate barrage of elemental attacks, plasma shots, and quick binding spells to keep the distance while I flew back. Raion pressured me as hard as anyone ever had, hurling blasts of his crimson energy when I got too far away.

Below us, the giant starship's golden surface was slashed, scorched, and torn as we fought. I didn't have time to leisurely look around, but it seemed my earlier guess was correct; we were flying over an enormous ship that would resemble a winged pyramid from farther away. While staying within its atmospheric field, I couldn't get a glimpse of its full outline.

Our fight was bounded by a shimmer in the air. That was the limit of the atmosphere, and neither of us wanted to continue this fight in a vacuum.

Raion could only operate in space for a few minutes at a time, while my mantle had no such time limit. You'd think that would give me the advantage. The problem was, I knew exactly what Raion would do if I threw him into space.

He'd summon his Divine Titan.

I had to avoid that at all costs.

After a full minute of exhausting battle, Raion came to a halt in midair. He beamed proudly at me and put his fists on his hips again. "Incredible, Varic! You've fought Visiri warriors before, haven't you?"

I caught my breath enough to reply. "On Visiria. I was a prize fighter."

That was true, in a way. I had been trained in water magic by a fighter, and even fought in the arena myself, but only in another life.

Raion's eyes lit up. "Oooohhh you fought in the arena as a mage? I can't believe I haven't heard of you!"

Before I could think of a lie to explain myself, he had drawn the hilt of his force-blade. "In that case," he said, "I'll have to show you my best!"

He thumbed on the hilt, and a three-foot laser-edged plane of light appeared as the blade to his sword. The blade was, of course, bright red.

Raion held the energy sword up to me in a salute, then took a stance.

I chanted as fast as I could. I had begun my spell the second he reached for the hilt, and I was drawing a second spell with my wand at the same time.

Until now, he had fought me with the equivalent of brute strength and no finesse. But that wasn't Raion's true expertise. He was the only living master of an Aetheric sword art called the Dance of a Burning World.

I had very much hoped to end the fight before this point.

Raion's first upward slash carried the same magical weight as a spell. He wasn't anywhere close to me, but crimson energy flooded up from beneath me like a volcanic eruption.

I forcibly finished my wand's spell, drawing wards of protection around myself that took the place of my overloaded shield amulet. The sigils were broken almost immediately by red flames, but they lasted long enough that my mantle's protection field could handle the rest of the pressure.

I felt burning heat all over my body, but I had survived the first attack. My spoken incantation wasn't complete, but I thought I had time.

When the energy cleared, I saw with relief that I was right. Raion had waited. He'd stood there to see if the first strike of his force-blade had finished me off. If I had been a real enemy, he would have killed me, but he wanted to see what I was capable of.

Therefore, he'd given me time to finish my spell.

Raion leveled his sword with obvious pleasure. "You're amazing, Varic! I haven't—"

I cast Absolute Burial.

Glowing circles of binding and restriction slammed into Raion from six different directions. Above, beneath, ahead, behind, and from both sides. Raion resisted with his armor and an expanding ball of red energy, but the spell continued compressing.

This magic had worked against a King of the Iron Legion. I had abbreviated the incantation a bit here, making it slightly weaker, but there was no way Raion could break it.

I hoped.

But for one second, my heart turned to ice as he began to push my spell out. I had to wonder if he was really going to overpower my most powerful binding spell with raw strength. If he did, he would have more than earned the victory. I'd have no choice but to give up.

Maybe Horizon would give him the Captaincy, as he wanted. I hoped there was space for a crew mage.

Fortunately for my sanity, the spell worked. Raion vanished as though imploding, leaving behind a small orb of spinning sigils.

I settled back onto the cushion of my levitation ring in relief, catching my breath. Only to realize that the game hadn't ended.

A bright, crimson light appeared overhead, and I looked up in horror. There was nothing above me but stars, though one of those stars was shining brighter and brighter red with every passing second.

Desperately, I thrust out a hand and summoned my staff from the rubble of the collapsed hall. A black crate of rugged plastic flew up toward me, pulled by my levitation ring.

As it flew closer, I began peeling off seals, but I didn't take my gaze from the falling star. Could he summon his Divine Titan from within the seal? How? He was locked away into a pocket of Subspace! He shouldn't even be able to think!

The atmospheric field above me began to boil as the Divine Titan got close enough to crash into it. Just the act of falling would destroy the entire starship, and the ship already trembled with the power of my staff, Eurias. Wind blew, rain gathered, and plants began to sprout across the golden starship's armor.

Caught between two massive forces, the Aether churned like a sea in storm. The entire world trembled.

And glitched.

Everything I saw, heard, and felt tore itself to pieces in a second as the simulation collapsed.

I woke, panting, on the bridge of *The Last Horizon*. My staff's crate was still closed and at my feet, its seals intact. I sat up straight in the chair and looked up to Horizon, who stood over me wearing a smug and satisfied smile.

On the floor next to me, someone else sat up with a gasp. He looked startled, but beamed when he saw me. "What a fight!" Raion said excitedly. "Did you really manage to stop my Divine Titan? Or was it a draw?"

"It looks like congratulations are in order," the ship's spirit said, *"to my new Captain and the first member of our crew."*

CHAPTER FIFTEEN

ON A CRUMBLING asteroid with a failing atmospheric field, Omega did battle. His opponent was a masked human spinning a staff with a sword-blade on both ends. They channeled a Combat Art with every slash, summoning a storm of blades from the Aether that shredded Omega to pieces.

He pulled himself together over and over, but the supply of excess matter he kept tucked away in Subspace was running low. A few more minutes of this and his regeneration would run out.

Just as bad, his internal Subspace Drive was reaching its limit. It frothed like a carbonated drink, and Omega had to wait longer and longer between each of his dives. Even his guns were running low on ammunition.

He laughed in pure joy, firing another accelerated bullet that was unceremoniously slapped out of the air. *This* was what he'd hoped for when he'd gotten the message from the Zenith Starship: a reason to pull his body together in the morning.

Most of his memories from the last century blended into a dull, gray sludge. Little worth doing, and no reason to do it.

This, at last, was *fun*.

His Aethertech eye highlighted a target. A gap in the opponent's

Combat Art, where their tired limbs failed to keep up the appropriate pace. Though the blades they conjured shredded the asteroid piece by piece with apocalyptic force, the user was still human beneath the mask.

Omega fired at the weak point, hoping the enemy would block it. They let him down.

When the human fell with a hole through their mask, Omega fought back his disappointment with the knowledge that at least there would be another round coming.

Until, to his great dismay, he found himself waking up at home.

Another screen filled his view, a blue-green computer window sent by the Zenith Starship.

Congratulations! You have proven yourself worthy of a crew position aboard *The Last Horizon*.

Unfortunately, due to the overwhelming number of applicants, we cannot accept everyone who qualified. If you are selected for the crew, the ship or the Captain will contact you very soon.

Until then, thank you for competing!

Omega stared into the message in horror. It couldn't end like that. It couldn't.

He wouldn't let it.

"The *Captain?*" Omega shouted at the message. "Who are they? Who is it? You can tell me who it is! I just want to talk with them, all right? Just a *quick* talk."

In case *The Last Horizon* was still listening, he continued shouting as he dissolved his body and slithered away.

Someone knew who had won this competition, and Omega wouldn't stop searching until he had a name.

Maybe the Captain of *The Last Horizon* could relieve his boredom. And if not, then perhaps the ship wouldn't mind another change of hands.

Mell threw a pen through the holographic message from *The Last Horizon*. Then she threw a coffee cup. She groped around for something else to throw, found a cold object, and blindly launched it.

It turned out to be one of her smaller Nova-Bots, a small brass humanoid who squealed in protest as it hurtled across the room.

"We'll *contact* you?" Mell shouted. "Is this a Subline scam? Did I get scammed? Don't make me go through all that if you're not even going to give me a callback!"

The game hadn't been as easy as Mell had originally expected. She'd been stabbed, shot at, and burned. She'd crashed a drop-pod, leaped out of a three-story window, and accidentally inhaled poison gas.

Each time, she'd still managed to win. But for a game, it hadn't been very fun.

All this to get a polite rejection letter worthy of a galactic corporation.

The thought provoked more anger, and she glanced around for something else to throw, but she was interrupted by another window popping up in her vision.

We're sorry you are dissatisfied with your results!

Ultimately, final recruitment decisions are made by the Captain and the remaining crew. However, it is the ship's personal opinion that you would make a fine Engineer.

In anticipation of our future working relationship, and perhaps to soothe the sting of the selection process, I'd like to offer you a minor consolation prize.

Thank you for your participation!

Sincerely,

Horizon

Mell blinked repeatedly and adjusted her glasses, which warned her that a file was attached to the message. With only a moment of hesitation, she downloaded it.

Her first glance at its contents hit her harder than any of her virtual opponents had.

It was a schematic for low-grade Aethertech. Ordinarily, nothing to be excited about. Schematics were only of limited use when it came to Aethertech anyway.

But, if she interpreted it correctly, this was a schematic for one of the basic fabricators aboard *The Last Horizon* itself. Other than this mysterious Captain, she might be the only person in the galaxy with a schematic for Zenith Aethertech.

Even if she couldn't replicate it directly, there was no telling what she might learn.

"Yep, that soothes the sting," Mell said into the air. "I am soothed. And I look forward to working with you too. Uh, when might I hear back from—"

The message blinked out.

Within the captain's chair of her personal battlecruiser, Shyrax stared into the rejection message in front of her.

"It was my understanding that we were competing for *control* of *The Last Horizon*," she said.

"Your Highn—" one of her attendants began, but she cut him off with a gesture. She then waited for a response from the Zenith Starship.

After almost a minute of silence on her part, another message did come.

The six crew members of *The Last Horizon* have a unique arrangement that you will come to learn in time, should you be selected for the crew. In short, control of the ship is not unilaterally given to the Captain.

There was more, but Shyrax stopped reading at that point and spoke. "And crew positions are decided by ability."

Personal ability is perhaps the primary qualification of *Horizon* crew, as their abilities—

Shyrax folded her arms and leaned back in her seat. "Then I await my invitation. Until then, I have work to do."

She dismissed the message and returned her attention to the battle outside.

CHAPTER SIXTEEN

THE RED-SKINNED, three-eyed man next to me looked like he'd won the galactic lottery. He sprang to his feet and spoke passionately to Horizon. "We won't let you down!"

I glared at Horizon but didn't say anything. She'd matched me against Raion intentionally. I don't know how she knew about my previous lives—I was the only one with these memories—but somehow, she had known.

A distant rumbling caught Raion's attention, and he frowned at a monitor. It showed the forcefield over our mountain failing under an orbital bombardment.

He pointed to it. "Is that us?" he asked curiously.

The spirit beckoned us toward the wall. *"Allow me to show you to the heart of the ship. There, we will swear our oaths to one another."*

A door opened in the dark metal of the wall, invisible seams splitting to beckon us into a long hallway.

"You should hurry," I said. "I'll stay here and prepare my spell."

Horizon shook her head. *"Regrettably, Captain, your presence is required as well."*

Raion clapped me on the back, and I tried not to pitch face-first onto the deck. "Let's go, Captain!" he said cheerily.

That was a strange feeling. *He* had always been the leader of the Titan Knights. And I hated that Horizon had sprung another hidden rule on me. But we didn't have time to debate, so I led him forward as we followed Horizon's holographic form back to the heart of the ship.

Which was easier said than done.

Once again, Horizon raced ahead of us, laughing in a way that put chills up my spine. At least her hurry made sense this time.

Raion laughed with her. "I love the positivity here! What a great team atmosphere this is going to be!"

The bunker rumbled again as we reached the heart of the ship and the doors slid open. I was eager to get this process over with, but Raion didn't feel much urgency, ooh-ing and aah-ing at the tablets on the walls.

Horizon gestured to a carving against the far wall, the one glowing blue. *"Each of these represents a member of my illustrious crew. One position, as you see, has already been filled. The other five are vacant."*

"So who are the rest of these?" he asked, looking at the other carvings. "That's the Captain. Which one am I?"

The ship's spirit blinked her way out of her reverie as Raion examined a stone carving. He was on the other side of the chamber, looking at an image of a figure holding a two-handed sword and directing a barrage of cannons.

Horizon gave him a wide smile. *"That's up to you. I do apologize for my rush. Now, I will explain in detail."*

I pointed upward as there came another rumble. "How much detail? We're on a time limit here."

"Don't worry, Captain. This hangar will hold up against a dedicated assault for at least...half an hour."

"I have a ship out there," I pointed out.

Raion clapped his hands. "Great, so we have half an hour for the tour!"

Inwardly, I gave up on *Moonfall*.

Horizon turned back to the stone tablet representing the Captain, whose outline now shone blue.

"The role of the Captain has been filled by Varic Vallenar. The Captain directs the crew, as well as awakening the ship's power core. As the current Captain is quite the accomplished wizard, my core now runs on magic."

As much as I hated to spend more time on this tour, I was curious. "Your power core would work differently depending on who the captain was?"

"All my systems are adaptive. Thus, Raion Raithe, you may lend your power to any role for which you are suited."

She drifted to the right of the Captain's tablet, where there was a seated figure holding onto an ancient ship's wheel. Stars speckled the background, almost blotted out by a wormhole representing a Subspace dive. *"The Pilot. While I am capable of flying on my own, there are moments when a more mortal hand becomes necessary. The gifts of the Pilot will evolve our navigation and our Subspace Drive."*

Raion put fists on his hips. "I'll take it!"

"You've only heard one," I pointed out. "And you're not suited for it anyway."

Without thought, I'd fallen back into the same role I'd played in the Titan Knights: stopping Raion from rushing headlong into the unknown.

"Horizon," I asked, "what happens if someone tries to perform a role they can't handle?"

"The nature and compatibility of a crewman's gifts determine the ability of my systems," Horizon said. *"I will adapt, but it is of course best if one takes on a role they are suited for. The strength of the system also scales to the strength of the crew, but if Raion did not have the status to handle a role, he would not be invited here."*

Raion gave me a thumbs-up. "Don't worry, I'm a great pilot!"

"Let's hear the next one."

The next tablet in the row was a figure with arms raised and mechanical limbs stretching out from behind them. Robotic drones flew around them in an insectoid swarm.

"The Engineer. A position for Aether Technicians or those with excep-

tional compatibility for Aethertech. Their gifts will be given grand scale, and they will awaken our drones, and a number of internal systems. My repairs will be improved as well, depending on the Technician's nature."

"I'll take it!"

"Slow down."

It was not lost on me that I was the one lobbying for us to take longer, despite the attacks raining down from the Iron Legion. Nobody wanted Raion as the ship's Engineer.

The next tablet, on the wall opposite the Captain, showed a figure pointing decisively off to the side, with starships following their direction in the background.

"The Commander. The central point of our fleet. Commands fighters and shuttles and improves our sensors and certain tactical systems."

I held out a hand to Raion before he could speak. "Wait to hear the next one."

"Yeah, that's fine. I don't want to outrank you. You won our fight."

That stopped me in my tracks. "That's a good point. Why am I the Captain if there's a Commander position open?"

Horizon gave me an irritated look. *"When my crew positions were named, we had different ranking conventions. At the time, Captain was the higher rank."*

"Well, now Commander is," Raion said. "Have you considered changing the names?"

"Just power through him," I told Horizon.

"The Sword," she said, introducing the next tablet, and Raion perked up. *"Currently, our armaments are inferior to what you might find aboard a standard, mundane battlecruiser."* She said 'standard' and 'mundane' as though the words disgusted her. *"The presence of the Sword will evolve our guns and alternate weapons systems into something more suitable."*

Raion drew the hilt of his force-blade, but before he could activate it, Horizon held out a hand to him. *"Regrettably, I have another candidate in mind for this position."*

He looked around the room, empty but for the three of us. "Where are they?"

"If you choose to become our Sword, I won't stop you. However, there's one last position I think you might consider."

Horizon moved to the final tablet, which illustrated what was clearly an armored knight bracing a shield against an attack. *"The Knight is in charge of ship security, internal and external, both shield systems and certain inner security measures. A master of Combat Arts can channel their Art through me, and it is temperamentally best-suited to someone who would lay down their own life for their comrades. I could not ask for a better Knight than you."*

In contrast to what I expected, Raion regarded the picture of the Knight on the wall calmly. He slid his force-blade back into his belt. "Before I take responsibility for the security of the crew, I need to know why. What is our purpose?"

I barely stopped myself from blurting out something rude. *Now* he hesitated? He had been two seconds from signing a contract as the ship's Engineer. He had been a Knight of the Titan Force for years, and now he was just trading one Knighthood for another. It was fate.

But in this timeline, we didn't know each other well enough for me to say anything. So I stayed quiet.

Horizon gave him a gentle smile. *"Of course. I could never have accepted you as crew without telling you our goal."*

I was pretty sure Horizon had been about to accept his application before he asked the question. She'd had no problem accepting a Captain without telling *him* the whole situation.

"Tell us what you wish to accomplish with our might," Horizon said to Raion. *"If we find it a worthy goal, we will pledge ourselves to complete it with you. Thus, each member of our fellowship will perform six great deeds: one for each of the crew."*

"Hold on," I said. "First, I want a rulebook. I want a rulebook as soon as we're off this planet. Second, you didn't tell me anything about a 'great deed.'" If the others got to have the Zenith Starship fulfill a request, but I didn't, I was going to give up the Captaincy immediately.

She gave me a confused look. *"Did you not request me to destroy the Iron Legion?"*

"No! I asked if you were *capable* of it."

Horizon shrugged. *"We can change it later."*

"I want that rulebook."

The hangar shook again.

Raion mulled it over for a long moment, stroking his chin as he thought. "So we take turns fulfilling each other's requests? What if we can't agree?"

Finally, we entered my area of expertise. I fielded the answer. "Contract magic enforces good-faith agreements. Only truly irreconcilable differences will get through, and then I suppose someone would have to make a new request."

Horizon half-bowed her horns to me.

"All right, then! For my quest, I say we defend the galaxy!" Raion announced.

I turned back to the ship spirit, curious to see if a goal so vague would work. As expected, Horizon shook her head. *"Requests must be a specific goal, possible to accomplish and finite."*

He shrugged. "I don't have anything else. Unless the Swarm-Queen comes back, right?" He nudged me with an elbow like he'd told a joke, but a shiver ran up my spine.

Horizon faced me with an enigmatic smile. She knew. In two of my previous lives, the leader of the giant extra-dimensional insects had returned to the universe. In one of them, she had achieved her long-held goal and ruled over the entire galaxy as a godlike being.

"I would accept that as your goal," Horizon said, extending a hand to Raion. *"Extermination of the D'Niss and their leader, assuming they return within five years. If not...we can always come to another agreement, don't you think?"*

Raion brightened, but I remembered Esh'kinaar the Swarm-Queen slurping up stars. I could still feel the weight of my blue badge as I hurled it at him.

"Hold on a second," I said. "I have to agree, right?"

Horizon grabbed Raion's hand. *"Oh, but Captain, we just agreed. Didn't we, Raion?"*

Raion gave me a reassuring look. "Don't worry, it probably

won't even happen! Until then, I'm more than happy to fight the Iron Legion!"

"Probably won't even happen," Horizon repeated. *"And if it did, I know you'd fight with us. You'd defend the galaxy to the end, wouldn't you, Captain?"*

I stared into seven-pointed eyes that knew too much, and my throat closed up.

No matter what, I couldn't leave Raion to die on his own again. I couldn't say it.

Starting from the hand, where she still gripped Raion's glove, Horizon started to turn red. *"Oh my, it looks like Captain Varic has accepted our arrangement."*

Raion drew himself up proudly. "Raion Raithe, reporting as Knight of *The Last Horizon!*"

The ship spirit gave one of her twisted too-wide grins. *"I do not choose crewmen lightly, Raion. Least of all my Knight."*

Scarlet light spilled from her hand to the rest of her body, spreading to the lights overhead.

Symbols flickered in the Aether like the ghost of lightning, so quickly I couldn't read them, as the starship echoed with his power. I itched to see what changes had been made, but moments later, the lights faded back to bright blue.

Horizon, however, was now drawn in shades of both blue and red. A two-toned hologram, reflecting the colors of the shining slabs around us.

Two of the stone tablets were lit. The Knight shone crimson while the lines of the Captain glowed the same azure that represented my magic.

With that business settled, it was time to start acting like a captain.

"Now let's get the Iron Legion off us," I said. I marched toward the wall, which Horizon obligingly turned into a door and opened. "Raion, you can summon your Titan, right?"

Raion scratched the side of his neck and gave me an embarrassed look. "I've been having some trouble with my Titan, actually. It's probably better if I don't call it."

"We have an Iron Legion battleship over our heads. Now's the time."

"We can fight them off!" Raion said optimistically.

"Can we? Horizon, what are our combat capabilities now? Also, where am I going?" I had been marching down the hall like I knew the layout of the ship, but it was still just an unbroken stretch of hallway.

We blurred and reappeared on the bridge, where Horizon was waiting for us. A second seat grew in front of the console for Raion.

"My Knight supplies me with plenty of energy and a strong Aetheric pattern to empower our shields and armor," Horizon said, dipping her head to Raion. *"Additionally, our close-range weapons are quite formidable, thanks to the influence of his Combat Art. My plasma cutters and point-defense turrets have never been stronger."*

I took in the situation on the monitors as the hangar shook around us. "Are the shields strong enough to keep us in one piece until we can dive into Subspace?"

"They will follow and overtake us," Horizon pointed out. *"Regrettably, I can't outrun them."*

Raion pounded a fist into his other hand. "We should fight them!"

"You'd be fighting a battleship with your sword," I said, but I realized my mistake and quickly added, "...which I'm sure you could do, but who would defend us?"

Raion gave me a friendly punch that was hard enough to flare the protective symbols on my mantle. "I have faith in you, Captain!"

"Or I could delay the battleship's Subspace Drive from here." I nudged my staff's case with my foot. "If the Hunters follow us, we'll use the close-range weapons. If they don't, we'll try to make another dive before the big ship recovers. But that all depends on our shields being able to take a beating until we can dive out."

Horizon folded her arms and gave me a very confident nod. *"Of course. I have full faith in my Knight's shields."*

Raion beamed.

I was much less confident than before.

"Spoken like someone who's never died in a starship explosion," I muttered, but I still started un-sealing my staff.

Horizon opened the hangar doors and lifted us off, guiding the ship out through a secondary tunnel that must have been designed as a hidden exit. We passed away from the mountain as I chanted, Eurias blowing wind and rain into the bridge of *The Last Horizon*.

Raion reached up and passed his hand through a raincloud several times, like a child with a new toy.

Massive plasma bolts slammed into our shields, which now shone bright red...and held sturdy. The ship barely shook under the impact, and each direct hit only took our stability down about one percent.

One of Horizon's conjured eyes hovered around, spinning to look me in the face. Her voice came from elsewhere. *"I told you the shields would hold."*

I didn't respond, but I did notice something else: a starship sitting down below us. *Moonfall*. I briefly cut off my incantation to say, "That's my ship! They didn't blow it up."

"There's probably a bomb," Raion said, at the same time as Horizon said, *"Your old ship is dead."*

I sighed. "Yeah, I'm sure it's a trap." If not an explosion, then the ship was filled with Pawns ready to capture me and turn me into a Shepherd. But I had a more immediate concern. "There's a lot of information about me on that computer."

"They most likely have it already, but I can wipe it from here," Horizon offered. *"And I can download your navigational data, since that seems to be your only attachment to such an inferior starship."*

"Do it. But that's not my only attachment; the ship served me well for—"

A red short-range laser sliced *Moonfall* in half.

"I had to do it, Captain," Horizon explained. *"Security reasons. It's a good thing you have a better ship now, isn't it?"*

I missed *Moonfall* already.

The battleship over us, like every creation of the Iron Legion, was half-metal and half-flesh. It hovered over the mountain, covering a chunk of the sky, and it resembled a Galactic Union battleship that had been somehow infected with a cancer.

Plasma cannons rained fire down on us, and the five Hunter-ships tried to surround us, but they were kept at bay by the red short-range weapons. Lasers and sheets of plasma swept out like sword-blades, keeping the enemy starships away. In fact, one of the Hunters was cut down in the opening seconds.

Raion pointed. "Those are the weapons you got from me?"

"They are."

"I want to try it."

Horizon gave him a confused look, but I knew what he meant: he wanted to try dueling the starship with his own sword. I didn't have a chance to say so, both because I was busy chanting and because a warning lit up the console. The battleship was opening up a volley of missiles.

I pointed the blue sphere at the tip of my staff and spoke the last few words of a Subspace seal.

A white circle of Aetheric symbols a thousand yards long appeared on the underside of the battleship. Sparks erupted down over the landscape as my seal, powered by Eurias, fought against the ship's defensive spells.

The view outside spun and twisted as Horizon kept us moving, and constant red flashes showed short-range weapons cutting down missiles and pushing away Hunters.

I sagged down into my chair and struggled to put Eurias back in its case. Controlling that much magic is hard work. "How long until we're out of the atmosphere?"

Horizon had spread out dozens of eyes, many manifesting outside the ship, and I could feel her concentration as she navigated us through the battle. *"Shouldn't be...long..."*

Now that my job was done, I realized another contribution I could make. Quickly, I chanted a simple pathfinding spell and linked it to Horizon.

Her seven-pointed eyes widened as my spell showed her a path through the battle. Seconds later, we had cleared the atmosphere and were preparing for a Subspace dive.

"Dive in three seconds," she said. *"Three...two...dive."*

The rainbow rush of Subspace swallowed us. Metal melted over the viewport, shuttering us from the hypnotic view. Horizon turned on me, eyes aglow.

"Such a wonderful spell! Over time, we will share magic. I look forward to the union that our spells will create."

To an Archmage of my experience, that meant that she would share the Aetheric patterns of her magic with me, allowing me to push my spells further.

I certainly wouldn't say no to that. I wasn't sure how much more room I had to grow my own spells, but it couldn't hurt to find out.

"Get ready to dive again," I said. "Raion, prepare for void combat."

He clapped a fist to his chest in salute. "Aye, sir! Where's the airlock?"

"Wherever you like," Horizon responded. So she *could* change the ship's layout.

As we flew away, I waited for the Subspace Drive to stabilize. That would make the difference between a micro-dive and a standard one, and meant we could go for longer. But while we waited, we gave the Iron Legion a chance to come after us.

A chance they didn't take.

After ten minutes, when no one chased us, I looked to Horizon. "Why didn't they follow us?"

"The local Iron Bishop knows something we don't." Horizon's expression was dark. *"Perhaps we should return."*

"We can handle them," Raion said confidently.

"Not without better guns," I said. "Horizon, you said the weapons officer was called the Sword, didn't you?"

My console beeped as Horizon transferred me a file. *"I chose some candidates from our digital selection. Though I doubt you'll need to look past the first."*

With one glance at the file, I felt a small, sick twist in my stomach.

The first face was familiar. I had died next to her, what felt like not so long ago.

"How do you know this?" I demanded.

Raion looked between us, openly confused.

Horizon held up a hand. *"Perhaps I should show you how I see you, hm? Hold up a mirror, so to speak."*

Without waiting for my permission, she waved. A mirror appeared, hanging in midair.

The mirror reflected half the room, but there were eight people in it.

Raion, Horizon, and I stood there as normal. But there were a group of five men standing behind me.

They were all me.

I had a hard time breathing. "Take this down."

"As you wish." The mirror vanished.

A hand grasped me firmly by the shoulder. I looked to the side to see Raion, his face full of faith and reassurance. "I don't understand any of this," he said.

I expected more to follow, but he just patted me on the side and looked pleased with himself, as though he'd helped.

Strangely enough, he had. I gave a dry laugh.

Raion hadn't changed.

"How close is she?" I asked Horizon.

"Within the sector. She'll be inside teleport range shortly."

"Who?" Raion asked.

An image of a tall figure in gray powered armor appeared next to Horizon, with visor glistening a reflective green. *"The Fallen Sword,"* she said.

I braced myself and nodded. "Take us there, and while we're on the way, I'd like that rulebook." That would give me time to settle myself before meeting Sola again, too.

"She is in the midst of raiding an Iron Legion Hive..." I would have been surprised if she weren't. *"...and her location may be time-sensitive. If we miss this window, we may lose her. May I brief you on her situation first, and then take you there at maximum speed?"*

I settled back into my chair. "Sure. What's the situation?"

"You may call for retrieval when you're out of range of the Hive. I do not wish to reveal my existence before we have more crew. Don't worry about reaching me through the Subline; we are connected now. I will hear you."

"That doesn't sound like a briefing," I pointed out.

"The moment you persuade the Fallen Sword, tell me, and I will bring you back to the ship."

I felt like I was missing some context. "Your instructions are clear, thank you, but what about her situ—"

Blue light surged over me.

My cloak didn't fight the spell, so it wasn't hostile. Not that I expected it to be.

When the light cleared a moment later, I found myself standing next to Raion on the edge of an iron mountain drifting in the middle of space.

We stood on a rough slab of incalculable tons of metal, which I knew was made from the melted-down and repurposed slag from dozens of ships. In fact, recognizable ship's pieces still stuck out here and there, halfway through the process of being digested by the building.

This was a chunk of one such ship, which shuddered gently beneath our feet as it slid inch by inch into the Iron Hive.

If not for the atmosphere projected by the Hive itself, we would have been drifting in space. There was nothing behind us but the cold of the void.

I took the situation in calmly, but my mind was still reeling from the teleportation spell.

I knew *The Last Horizon* had brought Raion here, and Horizon had moved us easily enough within the ship, but this was an accomplishment on another level.

Accurate long-distance transportation was widely considered impossible without sending us through Subspace. And if we were cast through Subspace without a ship, we'd be reduced to less than a dream.

Fascinating. It was dangerous enough to unmake me, but I wanted to do it again.

"She still didn't give me that rulebook," I said.

"The galaxy shall witness our return and tremble," Horizon's voice said into our minds. *"Good luck, Captain."*

CHAPTER SEVENTEEN

SOLA'S ARMOR WAS screaming warnings in her ears and flashing them in her eyes, but she didn't slow down.

A Reaver slashed its bladed arm for her, then leveled its human arm and fired. She ducked most of the impact, but the plasma bolt still scraped a chunk out of her shield.

Reavers were among the more successful of the Iron Legion's abominations. At least, much of their former organic structure remained intact. They looked like men with living steel armor melted into their flesh. They varied from individual to individual, but this one was one of the more common combinations: steel had grown over its left arm to form a crude blade, while its right used modern weaponry against her.

All Reavers were pushed beyond their physical limits, making them deadly opponents, but they were nothing to her. Usually.

This time, four survivors trailed behind her like ducklings. Three civilian contract workers and one child, a little girl clutching a survival kit to her chest like it was a stuffed animal.

She had been the child of some workers, but not any of the ones who had survived.

If it was only one Reaver, Sola would have made short work of him already and sent the survivors away. But he was keeping her distracted while Pawns crawled on the ceiling high overhead and took potshots at the helpless civilians.

All the while, the Iron Hive shifted beneath her feet. Sola couldn't use any weapons here that were too big, or she'd destabilize the entire hallway. Not to mention that firing her heavier weapons in such a contained space would carbonize the unprotected humans in a fraction of a second.

Between fighting a Reaver, intercepting shots, hauling survivors out of the way, and laying down cover fire, Sola's armor had taken serious damage.

Her shield wasn't recharging as fast as it should anymore, and the armor was weighing on her limbs as she was forced to take more and more of its weight. Harsh breaths echoed in her helmet and sweat stung her eyes.

No one could see her expression, but hatred peeled her lips back to bare her teeth.

The Iron Legion thought they could take these people from her. She had saved them. They were *hers*.

And she wouldn't leave this Hive while a single Pawn survived.

The fury pushed her beyond her limits. In one uninterrupted motion, Sola hauled a survivor away from a Pawn's plasma bolt and took another out with her pistol, leaped over the man to crush another Pawn, blasted another pair off the wall, took a shot on her shield, and hurled a discharge grenade.

When the explosive detonated, tendrils of lightning-like energy stretched out and cooked the Pawns alive. A specialty of hers, crafted specifically to devastate the Legion.

The Pawns were all down, but there was a cost to the action. She'd paid it willingly.

The Reaver's sword found a crack in the back of her armor and pierced her through, emerging bloody from her stomach.

The girl screamed, but through the tears, she started rummaging in her survival pack. Sola wanted to tell the child not to worry, but there was blood in her throat. She coughed it up.

Right. Had to take the sword out first.

Sola reached behind her and gripped the Reaver's wrist, locking the sword in place. Then she fired a plasma pistol blindly over her shoulder and shot the creature five times in the face.

It fell back, and as it did, she heaved the sword out of her back.

Blood splattered on the inside of her visor, but cleansing spells carried it away. A medi-seal sprayed up the wound on her back, preventing blood loss, but dark liquid still trickled down her gray-plated leg.

Sola had to cough the blood from her throat in order to speak, and her breath wheezed in a way that made her think the Reaver had scraped a lung. She felt little but an unpleasant grinding and buzzing inside her.

There was probably more anesthetic in her veins than blood at that point, but she needed to stay functional. When her throat was clear, she spoke to the girl.

"I'm fine. Let's move." Her armor's speakers would filter her voice, making her sound stronger than she felt.

The girl looked up at her with tear-filled eyes and held out an auto-bandage.

That wouldn't help her at all. Her suit had all the same functions.

Sola took it anyway and nodded. "Thank you. I'll be okay now."

The girl wiped her eyes and nodded back.

A map in the corner of Sola's visor flashed, showing her that there was a new route out. She led the way, keeping an eye on the humans trailing behind her like spawnlings.

They were almost there.

And then the ground fell out beneath them.

Time slowed for Sola as her suit accelerated her perception. She snatched the little girl up with one arm the moment the floor fell, and hauled the adults around one-handed as necessary to prevent them from breaking their necks on landing.

Fortunately, they didn't fall far.

Unfortunately, she knew the purpose of this cavern they'd fallen into.

It looked like the inside of a ribcage molded from mismatched metal, with unpleasant organic bits stretched here and there, performing functions she didn't want to consider. There were no entrances or exits in the round room, except of course for the ragged gap in the ceiling.

One wall wasn't curved like the others. It looked like the console of a giant alien computer, flashing and clicking with strange devices. If one didn't know better, they might think this was the bridge of a ship built for giants.

Sola did know better.

The instant her boots touched the ground, she jumped off. Her suit didn't have much energy left, but anti-gravity boosters activated on her boots and back, launching her into the air. It was too late for the others, but maybe she could at least save the girl in her arms.

Metal melted and flowed together as the ceiling healed itself.

Sola let herself drift down to the ground, where the adults bustled around her.

"Fallen Sword, what do we do?"

"Where are we, Fallen Sword?"

If Sola had been listening, she would have asked them to stop calling her that. All her attention was focused on the wall at the end of the room. She placed the girl onto the ground and summoned a shotgun from her inventory.

A red, glowing circle jutted out from the wall, and a smaller one joined it to one side. Eyes. Spinning and clicking devices pushed away to join the eyes. Cheeks and a nose. Liquid and flesh melted and flowed into lips, which spoke.

"Fallen Sword. We will study your body with gratitude."

This was a Bishop, the awakened consciousness of the Hive itself. Hives controlled by these entities were intended for special purposes, and Sola couldn't help but wonder if the special purpose of this one was to catch her.

Organic metal arms extended from the wall. Six of them, each with pointed and multi-jointed fingers. The arms rushed forward, and Sola readied her gun.

Everyone in this room was going to die.

If she didn't get the Bishop this time, she'd get him soon. Intentionally, Sola didn't turn around to look at the little girl. There was no saving her. Just another addition to the debt the Iron Legion owed—

The ceiling shattered. Not where they had entered; someone had punched another entrance.

From the look of things, quite literally *punched*.

Red energy faded from a grinning Visiri man who obviously liked coordinating his colors. Besides his white hair, the largest spot on him that wasn't red was the shining golden eye at the center of his forehead.

Each of the Bishop's half-dozen arms struggled in midair. They had been locked in place by shining magic circles of a complexity that Sola recognized immediately. Such binding spells must have taken half a dozen mages to chant, and she was still impressed with their precision.

She doubted the Visiri had cast them. Not only because Visiri tended to have a weaker connection to the Aether than other intelligent species, but because the circles weren't red.

A moment later, a dark-skinned human man in a blue hooded mantle drifted down to the floor. The cargo crate strapped to his back shone with similar binding spells, and there was a wand at his hip. The mage.

No, it seemed as though he'd bound the Bishop's arms himself. The Archmage, then.

Sola's survivors swarmed him the moment he landed, begging him to save them. All except the little girl, who hesitantly stuck close to Sola.

Good instincts, Sola thought. The girl should learn early not to trust strangers. Only trust those who had proven themselves to be on your side.

Even so, Sola's own spirit lightened. A pair of plasma cannons opened up in the corners of the room, warming to fire on the newcomers, but the red-clad Visiri dashed to one and folded the metal cannon like it was made of paper. The Archmage cast something, and the other cannon sputtered out like a candle.

The Bishop's eyes scanned them curiously. "Varic Vallenar," its mechanical voice said. "And the pilot of the red Divine Titan. How did you arrive here?"

"We walked," the Archmage said. She assumed he was Varic, and he obviously didn't understand what it meant to be locked inside a Bishop's chamber at the center of a Hive. His voice was too casual for that, so she hoped he had backup.

"Where are your reinforcements?" Sola asked, scanning the outside hallway.

The unnamed Visiri clapped a fist to his chest. "We *are* the reinforcements! Don't worry, you're safe now!"

They were all dead.

Sure enough, a hum filled the Bishop's chamber. She sensed energy building beneath them, and in a moment the floor would turn red-hot.

Roughly, Sola shoved the little girl toward the Archmage. "With you here, there are enough priority targets to lose the Hive. They're going to blow it."

The hooded mage nodded and began muttering to himself and twirling his wand. She still didn't think he was taking this seriously enough, but a magic circle bloomed beneath his feet.

The Visiri looked up to the Bishop. "How much time do we have left?"

"Surrender your body to the Legion, and you can live forever. We will preserve you."

"If you're going to self-destruct, I feel like you should give us a countdown."

While the idiot was doing something idiotic, Sola spoke to the Archmage. "Can you get them out of here?"

He didn't interrupt his incantation, which she approved, but he did nod. For the first time, she noticed that his eyes were a striking silver.

"Good." She let her shotgun vanish and dropped to one knee

to meet the civilian girl eye-to-eye. "No matter what you see, I will survive this. You'll hear about me on the Subline. The Fallen Sword." The girl nodded, teary-eyed. "Now be strong."

The floor was glowing now, red-hot everywhere except under the Archmage's magic circle, though the Visiri didn't seem to notice. He was still arguing with the giant face about the necessity of a countdown.

Sola stood and confronted the Bishop. She always died on her feet.

The energy beneath her swelled...then white light flashed.

The Archmage's magic circle filled the room in an instant and then died. The swelling energy from the heart of the hive was gone.

Nothing exploded.

Sola and the Bishop looked down at the floor in equal confusion. She turned to the Archmage for an explanation.

He waved a hand and conjured a quick seal of light. "I am a certified Archmage of binding and sealing magic. I sealed the power core."

The Visiri jerked a thumb at the Bishop. "Hey, can I break this thing?"

Sola's vision spun. Her suit's anesthetics and emergency medical spells were reaching their limit. She looked to the Archmage and ignored the moron. "Run. I will handle this."

From her inventory, she withdrew the Worldslayer.

The gun was Aethertech of the highest grade, a handheld cannon that pulsed with angry red light. Its barrel shone with razor-edged fury, sharp planes of energy that flickered in and out of existence. They were hard to look at.

The Aether and the entire Hive trembled with the power of the gun. An Archmage would know that he couldn't stand nearby as such power was unleashed.

To her annoyance, the mage and the warrior exchanged glances. Were they not concerned with the survivors? Without a weapon like this, she couldn't destroy the Bishop.

The Visiri warrior vanished.

Only the deafening screech of metal told her where he'd gone, and she turned to see him standing at the bottom of a massive tear in the Bishop's face. Revealed magical and organic machinery flickered and twisted, trying to undo the wound, but he unleashed a pulse of red energy that blasted the Bishop's form apart.

It wouldn't truly die until the Hive itself was destroyed, but even so...Sola felt stupid for worrying. She slipped Worldslayer back into her inventory and tried to speak, but she found herself falling face-first.

She was probably dying. That was inconvenient. She would have to tell the little girl nothing was wrong.

Before Sola could speak, she passed out.

CHAPTER EIGHTEEN

WE HADN'T COME here in a ship, so it was hard to find a safe place to keep the Fallen Sword.

Raion had never heard of her, but I was very familiar. An independent agent with a personal crusade against the Iron Legion, she had been reported dead several times only to reappear later. Some said she passed her armor from one to another, and every time one Sword fell, the armor chose another.

That wasn't true. She just couldn't be killed.

It was harder to face her than I had realized it would be. At least I hadn't left her to die; the last time I'd seen Sola, I had been the one who died.

I suspect she hadn't survived me long, but there was no way to know now.

For the first time in what felt like years, I examined her armor up-close, admiring the complexity of its Aethertech components. It wasn't as intricate and unfathomable as *The Last Horizon*, of course, but it was still a unique work of art.

Though one greatly in need of repair. Her gray armor looked like a masterpiece on the verge of being lost to the universe.

Its emerald visor was cracked and leaking air, its back barely holding together under automatically applied emergency gel, and its ashen plates burned, bent, or broken in a dozen places. Internal repair spells worked overtime to hold everything together.

Despite its many functions, the armor would have lost its occupant if not for me.

Blue light filled her body as Aetheric circles spread from my wand and sealed her flesh together. She would heal fully on her own. The suit had counter-magic features, but they allowed my medical efforts. Either it recognized help or its security capacities were offline.

I was grateful I hadn't gotten a glimpse at Sola herself. Seeing her armor was bad enough, and I wasn't emotionally prepared to look into the eyes of another dead friend. Even without seeing her, I had a certain insight into her condition thanks to the magic. If she had been human, she would have died long ago.

In fact, most humans couldn't handle the burden of the suit in the first place.

The cracks in her visor shone green as her eyes snapped open, burning with a fiery green radiance. A gun was pressed into my temple before I could react, though I remained calm.

It would take more than a plasma pistol to pierce my hood.

Besides, this was how we'd met last time.

Of course, Raion's reactions were exponentially faster than mine. He already had one hand around the barrel of the gun. "We're friends!" he said. "I don't want to break your gun."

Shining green lights moved from me to Raion as the Fallen Sword shifted her eyes to take in the situation.

"I'm healing you," I said, in the language of the Lichborn.

The green light brightened as her eyes must have widened, but her voice through the helmet was even. "I speak Trade."

I continued speaking the Lichborn language. "Times being what they are, I thought you should know that I was a friend. I grew up on Dornoth Four."

After a beat, she replied in the Lichborn tongue. "If you had, you would know that humans don't grow up on Dornoth."

"Just takes a little magic."

She tried to sit up, but the suit didn't respond. "Where are we?" she asked, speaking Trade once again.

"Oh, we're still in the Hive."

All was peaceful in our small dome, protected as we were by powerful magic. But the outside could be best described as an Iron Hell. Pawns swarmed around the barrier created by my spells, metal arms slithered over the symbols looking for purchase, and wet flesh slapped against the walls of force.

The human survivors huddled around me and Raion, except for one little girl, who was overly attached to the Fallen Sword. While the woman had been unconscious, the girl had chattered nonstop, asking when she was going to wake up. Now that the Fallen Sword was awake, the girl was silent again.

"You *idiots.*" The spite in the Fallen Sword's voice echoed both through the speakers and through the cracks in her helmet, through which I heard snatches of her real voice. "The Bishop won't die until the Hive is destroyed. Where is your ship?"

"Don't have one!" Raion said brightly.

She lifted her helmet an inch from the ground and slammed it back down. I couldn't tell if she was trying to lift herself in her unpowered armor or just smacking her head against a hard surface. Maybe both.

"You should have let me die."

I knew why she would say that, but Raion was visibly shocked.

"Never!" he declared. "You relax and get better. We'll handle this!"

I could hear frustration from her helmet. "I will *get* better. I do not die."

"That's the spirit!"

She turned to me and held out a hand. A moment later, a sphere of soft blue-gray light appeared in her palm.

I took in a breath. This was more valuable than her suit, and she was being awfully cavalier by showing it to me now.

This was no Aethertech, but grand magic. A spell anchor, the likes of which I could barely understand. But its story was so clear in the Aether that I could read its purpose like a book.

It resembled a flame made of mist, or maybe a mist made of flame. It was a hazy light, an unclear and mysterious one, but one that sustained existence.

Last time, we called this her Pyre.

"Hold this," she said. "And don't stop me." She addressed that part to Raion, and I could feel the glare through her visor. His hand released her plasma pistol, but only reluctantly.

Sola moved her pistol, and I knew what to expect, but she hesitated. "Cover the kid's eyes."

The little girl looked worried at those words, but I beckoned her close to me. My mantle covered her face.

With the butt of her pistol, the Fallen Sword clubbed a hole into her own visor. Raion cried out, but I stopped him with a gesture. I had expected this. When we'd found Sola in such bad shape, I'd almost left her to die myself, but I would never have been able to explain how I knew she would recover.

The hole in her visor revealed pale gray skin and an eye that shone with deathly green light. The marks of the Lichborn.

Sola pointed the plasma pistol at her own glowing eye and pulled the trigger.

The girl behind my mantle flinched, and Raion shouted. I lowered the misty flame in my hand to the ground.

The Fallen Sword's body, suit and all, dissolved to burning mist. The Flame flashed as though it contained lightning.

A moment later, the Flame roared up, forming itself into her body in less than a second. She reappeared standing with her suit in perfect condition where the Flame had been.

Her pristine visor turned to me. She holstered her plasma pistol.

"I thought it would be a bad idea to hold that," I said. If I had, she would have reappeared in my hand, which would have been largely harmless but very startling. Not telling people what to expect from her resurrection was the closest thing to a prank she ever pulled.

Sola didn't respond, so I continued. "I hope you have a backup somewhere." She came back to life at the site of her Flame, but she could split it into several pieces. She wouldn't have handed one to me unless there was a failsafe.

She reached out to the edge of my mantle instead of responding to that, brushing it aside. When she saw the relieved little girl, Sola tapped her helmet.

"Thanks for the bandage," she said.

Then she turned her back to me and looked into the Iron Legion. "How much longer on the barrier?"

"How much longer do you want?" I asked.

She gave me a look over her shoulder. I couldn't see her expression, but I assumed she was waiting for a serious response.

I didn't explain further. Unless something like the Bishop showed up to break it, I could maintain that barrier forever.

Eventually, she seemed to accept that. "All right. My ship is docked here." A hologram emerged from her left forearm, projecting a map of the Iron Hive. A blinking green triangle showed the location of her ship. "Archmage Vallenar, prioritize the safety of the survivors. If you can take pressure off me, do what you can, but not at their expense. Visiri, you and I will break through."

Raion put his fists on his hips. "I am Raion Raithe!" Illusory fireworks exploded behind him.

The little girl clapped like she'd seen a trick.

The Fallen Sword did not look impressed. "Stay behind me, Raithe. If you get hit, hide with the civilians. Can you use that Combat Art again?"

"Of course! You can trust me to protect your back!" Raion extended a hand. "What's your name?"

"Fallen Sword."

"All right! You call me Raion, and I'll call you Fallen!"

I had no idea whether this was an act or whether Raion really thought her first name was 'Fallen,' but I was having a good laugh.

Famous as they both were, I had still never met them both in the same life until now. But this was roughly how I would have imagined a meeting between the two of them.

I could feel Sola's skepticism of Raion radiating from beneath her suit. It seemed like she was weighing the cost of dealing with him against the power of the Combat Art he'd demonstrated on the Bishop.

"My name is Sola."

It looked like his military value won out.

Raion beamed. "Sola! I'm Raion, and this is Varic! We're here to help!" His hand was still outstretched, and he waggled his fingers slightly.

Her movement was stiff as she reluctantly shook his hand.

She made sure we were all on the same page strategically before she would let me drop the barrier. The way she ensured we each understood our roles made me nostalgic. In this life, she had never partnered with anyone competent before.

She lifted a two-handed gun that I suspected was magical rather than Aethertech, though I'd have to inspect it more closely to know for sure. It ran with lightning, anyway. I wasn't sure I'd seen it before, but then again, I had never been able to keep track of all her guns.

Raion stood behind Sola, holding his force-blade lightly by one side. Despite his serious expression, I knew he was excited.

More than anything, I was looking forward to seeing the Fallen Sword in action again.

"Drop!" she called, and I canceled the Aether flowing to the dome barrier over us.

That instant, Sola pulled the trigger. Her gun sent a lance of light down the hall. It looked like a plasma beam, but it carried magic keyed specifically to the Iron Legion. Ragged bolts of energy snapped out of the beam, grabbing Pawns and cooking them in their metal shells.

The air heated and wind whipped up, snapping my mantle behind me. I wanted to take a look at the enchantment on that gun.

Everything in the hall in front of us was obliterated, but that didn't cover the other directions.

Cyborg limbs of the Iron Legion collapsed on us from every

direction, though they crashed into the subordinate barriers I'd placed around the civilians. One Pawn's shot pinged off my amulet's field of protection.

Then Raion's arm whipped in a circle, blurring with speed. Red light flashed around the hallway as he activated his force-blade for a fraction of a second.

The remaining creatures of the Iron Legion fell in molten, smoking pieces.

Sola was scanning behind her, and she didn't express any surprise at seeing the other sides cleared. But I suspected she was shocked.

"Clear." She crept forward and dropped her gun, which had dimmed to indicate it required charging. The weapon dissolved into particles, fading away into her inventory, and was replaced in her arms by a shotgun.

"Can we see the big gun?" Raion asked. "The red one?"

I raised my hand. "I second that, if we're voting."

"If I use that, we'll have to see how good your barriers really are."

"My specialty is in seals and bindings, actually. Barriers are more like a side project."

Seals and shields were two sides of the same coin, and that was only one of my disciplines. But it would sound strange if I told Sola that.

My pathfinding spell went off like a gong in the back of my mind, alerting me to an enemy on the other side of the wall. That same second, Sola put her shotgun to the wall and shot through it.

My spell went quiet.

Always incredible to see the Aethertech of her suit in action.

Then there was the Pyre, the misty flame that brought her back to life, which had nothing to do with the suit. The magic operated too differently to be from the same source. The reason the armor came back when she resurrected was because it was bound to her.

We'd already seen her Aethertech suit and her unique, beyond-Archmage-level spell.

Most people couldn't have bonded to such power simultaneously. Not that they couldn't handle it; the process simply wouldn't work except under highly rare circumstances.

And she was bound to another piece of Aethertech as well: the greatest of her guns.

Weapons loved her.

The next group of enemies didn't ambush at all. They came straight at us, down a hallway, and one of those in the back was a black-hooded figure with tubes coming out of the shadow where its face should be.

A Shepherd, one of the cyborg mages integrated into the Legion. While I could handle them magically, they came with a troublesome control over the rest of the local Hive.

Raion tensed to move forward, but I managed to catch him by the shoulder before he dashed ahead and killed everything.

I nodded to Sola. "Don't you want to give her a chance?"

"You're right! That was rude of me."

Sola unleashed another beam from the gun that had annihilated the whole hall last time, but now it crashed onto a shimmering shield generated by a wave of the Shepherd's hand.

Not magic. A standard starship shield projected by the Hive around us.

Sola released the gun and swapped when she saw the shot wasn't doing any good. "Incoming!" she shouted.

Then she was in the thick of it.

Watching her work was as familiar as it was impressive. Like watching one of the Visirian Sky Knights in action.

She blew Reavers apart like they were Pawns, and Pawns seemed to evaporate just by getting near her. The hall filled with continuous thunder; the roar of her weapons. Without survivors to shelter, she was an unstoppable wall of gray metal.

Of course, the Iron Legion didn't play by fair rules.

The Bishop's clawed hands erupted from walls around us, reminding me that he was still integrated with the Hive. Steel fingertips gouged into my barriers, which made me focus on reinforcing them; the Bishop had already adapted to my magic specialty and brought some countermeasures.

He didn't have much of a counter for Raion, though.

The Visiri held one of the arms in one hand, gripping the enhanced limb of living steel and alien flesh like it was a troublesome worm.

"I don't think she'd mind if we took a turn now," Raion said.

"Yeah, she's busy. Let's not worry her."

I took out my wand and he activated his sword. Red light flashed again, and I sent jets of water piercing through every Iron Legionnaire I could see.

Every part of the hallway was shredded except for the stretch where the human survivors stood. They looked around in awe; even the deafening sound was kept to a tolerable level, because I'm just that good.

The only one left was the hooded Shepherd with the shield in front of him, and Sola pierced the shield with a snub-nosed device I assumed was made for exactly that purpose.

The Shepherd drew up Aether for something that probably would have been nasty and impressive if I had let him do it. I dispersed the Aether he gathered like a child kicking over a sandcastle, and Sola blew his head off.

Sola's visor scanned the hall. Raion gave her a firm thumbs up.

"Who *are* you?" she asked us.

It's nice to have one's work appreciated.

The Hive trembled, and Sola and I looked down. Our detection spells must have activated at the same time again.

"Looks like the Bishop got through my seals on the power core," I said. "Ship?"

Sola sprinted ahead of us, Raion jogged behind her, and I used my levitation ring to float myself and the civilians along. The ring had a limited supply of power, but the people were exhausted. And I didn't feel like running anymore. Raion and I had already marched through half the Hive to catch up with the Fallen Sword in the first place.

Limbs erupted from the walls to entangle us, shields fell to box us in, and spells fell from the ceiling to test my defenses.

Fighting through this Iron Hive, I felt more relaxed than when

I slept aboard *Moonfall*. I hadn't realized how reassuring it was to have allies I could count on.

At last, I was safe.

The Iron King felt his consciousness return in a blaze of glorious life.

In the first instant, he understood himself and his situation. He had been in the process of birth—magic and power flowing into him, weaving in the complex pattern that created his mind—when that process had been interrupted. He had been sealed, unconscious, his body launched into a star.

Even for him, that had meant destruction.

But not death.

He reached a steel-clad hand up to his chest, where a device of masterwork Aethertech was attached. It resembled an obsidian cage filled with screaming mechanical faces, and wires extended from it to plunge into his body.

To mortal eyes, the device would be grotesque. Or so he supposed. To him, it was beautiful.

The device had been designed to anchor his mind and his spirit to the Iron Legion. In a sense, it was a backup. And it had served its purpose.

The cage was half-melted with strain, the faces within swollen and red as though diseased. It had worked overtime for weeks to recreate his consciousness and to bind it to a new body.

As expensive and difficult as it was to create an Iron King's body, it was ten times more so to create a mind. The Legion had only managed it four times in the past.

And now, five.

Without this Aethertech, he would have been destroyed like his predecessors. In a flash of curiosity, he wondered where the device had come from.

Before he finished forming the thought, the vast network of

minds across the Iron Legion provided him with an answer. This device had been commissioned by the previous Iron King four hundred standard years prior.

It had not been completed in time to save that King, and after his death, the Legion had been reduced to splinters and scattered across Dark Space. Only recently had they gathered enough resources to construct another Iron King.

Without this Aethertech, those resources would have gone to waste.

The device was all but destroyed by the effort of bringing him back from death. Its lifespan was at an end, but it had made him unique. His mind was not only restored but linked more closely to the Iron Legion than any of his ancestors had been. That gave him a new opportunity.

Unlike his predecessors, he had the chance to be truly immortal.

The Legion would never need a ruler after him.

The last Iron King leaned down, inspecting himself. He was still strapped to a steel table, most of his body open circuits and exposed organs. A little longer, then, before he was complete. It would take time for him to heal and to mature.

In the meantime, he learned.

He started by learning about the human who had temporarily destroyed him. And about that human's intriguing new ship.

CHAPTER NINETEEN

IT'S HARD TO say which of my many assaults on Iron Legion Hives was my first.

In fact, I'd had a "first" Hive raid in most of my lives. In one life, my first Hive raid came when I was hired as a replacement squad mage for a Galactic Union operational squad. In another life, I escorted a mentor of mine on a raid to rescue some captives. It's a thousand times better to be a casualty of the Iron Legion than a captive.

Another time, I was by myself.

None of those were an experience I would care to repeat.

When I was with a squad, we had been prey raiding the lair of a predator. We took no losses, but it was a tense, claustrophobic, panicky operation, like trying to sneak through a nightmare.

With my mentor, we were the hunters. She was, I mean. I was just an apprentice at the time. Even so, it was a lightning raid that pushed us both to our limits and left us exhausted mentally and physically. It lasted no more than forty-five minutes, because if it had, the Hive would have entangled us, and I would have been one of those Shepherds in a black hood.

Nothing was worse than the time I was trapped in a Hive on my own. I had to keep six pathfinding spells going at once, push my body to its limit running up and down the labyrinth of living hallways, and keep my magic restricted to avoid the Bishop's attention.

The more the Iron Legion knew about me, the better they could track me, and the last thing in the entire universe I wanted was to be taken before the Iron King.

In that life, Sola had saved me.

After my ritual in this life, I could invade Iron Hives alone as a matter of course. Doing so with Raion and Sola at my back was a sunny day cloud-surfing on Syrillia in comparison.

Sola was as vigilant as my detection spells, knew the Iron Legion inside and out, and had a nearly inexhaustible arsenal of weapons. Not only that, but I didn't need to keep her alive.

The prisoners made her vulnerable, but with us covering them, she could merrily slaughter her fill of Legionnaires.

That was enough, frankly, but Raion was there too. Any Pawns or Reavers that the Fallen Sword didn't kill fast enough were split in half with red light. He acted like strolling down a hallway and slaying monsters was his day job, and we shared some casual conversation while he blew up a charging Reaver with an easy blast of scarlet energy.

Leaving me in the back, drifting along with nothing to do but swaddle the civilians in barriers. They were nested in so many layers of wards, seals, shields, spell-blocks, and buffers that they'd feel nothing more than a light breeze if the Hive *did* blow up.

It was perhaps the first time I'd felt so secure leaving things to my companions. If I kept myself levitating and took a nap, we'd make it.

The Bishop didn't know that, though. He was going all-out.

The hall before us crumbled as dozens of hands emerged, but I maintained the integrity of the hall with a tunnel-shaped barrier.

Admittedly, that was a little taxing. If I hadn't been prepared to cast already, we would have been forced to blow through the wall and haul the spell-protected humans through space.

We could have done that, but it would have been a hassle.

Instead, we hurried through the spell-reinforced hallway and emerged on the outside of the Hive, at the very edge of its atmospheric field. Where I stopped and hesitated, unsure if we should enter the ship.

Sola's starship wasn't what I had expected. From what I remembered of her, she took better care of her equipment.

She had led us to a junky, boxy old war-cruiser from the Galactic Union. I didn't know whether she'd bought it fifth-hand or if she'd scavenged it herself. The rusty boarding ramp squealed as it extended.

Sola saw me looking at the ramp, and despite the Bishop roaring at us from the slowly deforming Hive, she found my concern more urgent. "Can your seals hold the ship together?"

That did not inspire confidence. "You think she might not be *spaceworthy?*"

"I need a new ship."

That was convenient. I had good news for her on the ship front.

We took off in the old junker. I cast so many spells that the walls were covered in slowly spinning magic circles, but the real binding-work was going on beneath the surface. I held together the engines, the Subspace Drive, the shield generator, and every device I could reach.

It disturbed me how many of them had been one bad day from falling apart.

Most of the Hive survivors looked in awe at my magic, but it was Sola I was hoping to impress. She knew enough about magic to appreciate what I'd done, at least once she examined the ship more closely, and I looked forward to her surprise.

She surprised me first, though. As we pulled away from the Hive—the massive, bulbous pile of iron seething and pulsing with energy as the Bishop rearranged its structure and tried to cancel the self-destruct—Sola didn't pull the docking ramp back up.

Instead, she walked out to the edge. The ship's atmospheric field was holding steady, but in a ship as shoddy as this one, that was hardly something I wanted to count on.

Surreptitiously, I fed a few more patches into the ship's systems. By the time I was done, the rusty old cruiser would be newer than when I'd gotten on.

Sola tilted her visor to the side, toward Raion. He'd left the other humans one deck up, where there weren't any open doors looking out onto the void of space. Wise of him.

"You wanted to see my gun?" she asked.

He planted his hands on his hips. "Yes, ma'am, I do!"

As did I. I had fond memories of her blowing up a small moon.

She withdrew her handheld cannon once again, and once again I nearly got sucked into the weight of the story it told. The red-orange energy pulsing through it was the molten power that destroyed worlds. The flashes of fiery blades that appeared in front of its barrel were swords that rent dimensional barriers. Its sleek design evoked a dagger that could pierce the heart of solar dragons.

Reading magic sounds abstract when you put it like that, but it's more intuitive than it sounds. I was sensitive to the impressions Sola's weapon evoked, and they were in no way inferior to those of my staff.

Which meant there were *three* world-class powers on Sola the Fallen Sword, not two. Her extraordinary compatibility with Aethertech weapons was the main reason she'd lasted so long in her one-woman crusade against the Iron Legion.

It was still an impressive spectacle when she finally fired her weapon.

This was the reason she was called the Fallen *Sword*.

Orange-red energy lanced out of the end of her gun in a plane of force that looked only a molecule thin. In the instant it existed, the sight reminded me of a bridge. Or, perhaps, a miles-long blade plunging into an enemy.

Then that enemy exploded.

The Iron Hive, pierced through by the light of her weapon, detonated completely.

We didn't hear anything until the shockwave reached us, at which point it was just a dull roar hitting our shields. Though the shields did shimmer in a way I didn't like, the ship creaked as it bucked, and the lights flickered.

I suspected that, without my reinforcement, the ship would have fallen apart. If Sola had been alone, she probably wouldn't have cared.

She certainly didn't seem to be alarmed when she hit the button to retract the ramp. Or when she had to hit it three more times before it worked. I chose to think of that as her trust that I would protect the civilians.

She nodded to us once each and then, to my surprise, took off her helmet.

Lichborn are almost universally beautiful by human standards. They ought to be; their ancestors were custom-designed by humans to be flawless. Sola was no exception, but she preferred not to show it. I had worked with her for months, last time, before I'd seen her without her helmet.

Her grey skin was smooth and her black hair lustrous and thick, though she kept it cut short enough for her helmet. The green light in her eyes gave her an unearthly cast, and her features were…I'd call them 'statuesque,' but in the sense that they looked like they belonged on a statue.

All in all, her appearance was what I'd expect from a model selling beauty treatments on the Subline, not from a battle-hardened mercenary.

Which was why she showed her face so rarely.

But then, human expectations didn't apply here. Lichborn didn't accumulate wear and tear in the same way humans did, and while experienced Lichborn warriors did gather scars just like humans, Sola had her flame of resurrection. No scars for her.

In that way, she and I were alike. Sometimes, I missed mine.

"I should introduce myself properly," she said. "Sola Kalter, gun for hire. If it's not Iron Legion, call someone else."

That was her motto, one she'd repeated a thousand times, and her voice was much richer without the helmet speakers in the way. She looked and sounded stoic, but there was a wry undertone to her words that hadn't translated through the armor.

Raion wiped a tear from his eye. "Do you feel this? It's a meeting between friends."

One of Sola's eyelids twitched.

I extended a hand to her. "Varic Vallenar, Union-certified Archmage."

She took my bare hand in her gauntlet and shook it gently, though she didn't need to be so careful. My mantle and amulet would keep my hand attached even if she tried to rip it off. At least for a while.

"The Subline says you killed a King," she said.

"Only stopped it from being born."

She gave a brief dip of her head, acknowledging my statement, though I couldn't tell if she believed me or not.

Raion slid next to me like he was trying to sneak in for a photo. He stuck out a hand. "Raion Raithe!"

"I met you already."

"Not with your helmet off!"

She reluctantly shook his hand again, and this time she wasn't as gentle as she had been with me. Of course, she didn't need to be. Raion probably didn't notice.

Sola released his hand quickly and looked to me again. "What brought you out here? Did the Union contract you?"

As she spoke, her armor dissolved into particles. Like blue cubes. It left her in a gray flight suit and standing flat on the deck, which was another surprise. She rarely removed the armor in front of people who might shoot her.

My eyes were only up to her chin. Her height didn't come from the armor.

"What do you know about *The Last Horizon*?" I asked.

She frowned. "That competition was real?"

"I'm the Captain, and I'd like you to join our crew."

Raion nodded along.

Sola waited a moment. "...is there more?"

"We intend to wipe out the Iron Legion," I said.

I had looked forward to her reaction to that news, but all I saw on her face was doubt. Horizon had contacted Sola for the virtual selection process, but she'd declined, which suggested that she didn't believe in the capabilities of the Zenith Starship.

I couldn't blame her, so I continued. "The ship is going to contact us soon, and we'll give you a full demonstration. Until then, how about we settle our guests? I suspect you have a bounty to cash in, too."

"Just the standing Union bounty for the Hive," she said, and I thought I caught a note of disappointment. "I was only contracted for a civilian cargo ship, with a bonus for any survivors."

"Did their ship make it?" Raion asked.

Sola pointedly looked out the viewport to the field of smoldering debris that was once the Iron Hive. Which was itself made from the metal of crashed starships.

"No," she said.

He snapped his fingers. "That's a shame."

Sola's eyelid fluttered again.

CHAPTER TWENTY

BENRI VALLENAR WAS in grave danger.

He had distributed copies of himself all over the galaxy, each crafted through the Mirror of Silence with such care that they were indistinguishable from real. The perfect surrogates and body doubles, though he had to replace them every now and again.

Thus, he should have had warning before his real life was ever under threat.

Even the version of himself working at Vallenar Corporation headquarters was a magic-born clone. No one should suspect that his original self was engaged in business negotiations aboard a luxury cruiser, glass of sky-wine in hand, surrounded by well-dressed representatives from every major sentient species.

He only began to suspect he was in danger when the chandelier overhead shook and the crowd's murmur dulled for a moment in surprise.

He *knew* he was in danger when his bodyguards grabbed him by the arms and began dragging him down the corridor. Three seconds later, red lights flashed and sirens blared.

One of his guards shouted for help into a Subline call, growing increasingly panicked as he got no response.

That was when Benri realized the kind of trouble he was actually in. He shook himself free of his guards and, instead of letting himself feel the fear, met it with anger.

He held out a hand. "Staff!"

A guard activated a Subspace storage device, an expensive piece of Aethertech, and withdrew Benri's staff. Organic silver refined from the bones of mirror dragons, topped with blue shadow-crystal, and enchanted specifically for his Mirror of Silence.

He chanted as he walked. So when Pawns of the Iron Legion hurtled down the carpeted hallway toward them in a tide of flesh and metal, he was ready.

Or he thought he was.

He choked on his first words when he saw—and *smelled*—the hideous creatures. He'd only ever seen Pawns on the Subline or in after-action reports. He had been unprepared for the sheer gut-wrenching rejection they evoked on sight. Nothing so *wrong* should exist.

But the spell was already prepared, so he was startled for only a moment before he barked a trigger word.

His guards unloaded continuous fire into the mass of metal and undead muscle. Their rifles weren't ideal for fighting the Iron Legion—the weapons had been chosen for ship combat, and thus they had to keep their power down. They couldn't allow the chance of a hull breach.

Though, as it turned out, the weapons worked just fine when you multiplied their fire by four. Every shot they fired came with three extra black-and-white copies, which shredded the Pawns.

The ship shook again and, before Benri could orient himself, the hallway behind him exploded inward. Three humanoid figures strode through, with reanimated flesh and cyborg pieces both of higher quality than the Pawns.

In the center was a Reaver. At least, it vaguely resembled the ones from Subline films. A muscled Visiri man, his skin paled to unhealthy pink, with patches of armor welded over his vitals. His eyes had all three been replaced with machines, and his left forearm sprouted a gun barrel while his right grew a sword.

He was flanked by a pair of Shepherds, and at least these left most of their appearance to the imagination. The undead mages carried staves of bone and metal and wore mantles with hoods deep enough that he couldn't see their faces.

Benri's hand tightened on his staff. Individually, one Shepherd would already be a threat. He was no combat Archmage, though he thought he could make his way through with superior equipment. Against *two* Shepherds, he had no chance, even if his guards han dled the Reaver.

His guards had fired already, but of course it was of no use against the Shepherds. They didn't have any exotic magics, but their shields were well-practiced. Even Varic would struggle to put up a barrier so quickly, Benri was sure.

He was trying to figure his way out of what seemed to be certain death when the three Iron Legionnaires stopped. The Reaver bowed at the waist, somewhat stiffly.

"Benri Vallenar. We are here to extend an invitation on behalf of the Iron King." The Shepherd's voice rasped with disuse.

Benri's entire world was spinning. Never had he expected to be *negotiating* with the Iron Legion.

As was his habit when he was terrified, he pretended nothing was wrong. He gave a heavy sigh and handed his staff to one of his guards. "Rude for an invitation, isn't it?"

"Would you have responded to a Subline invite?" the Shepherd asked, and Benri couldn't tell if its dry tone came from humor or mummified vocal cords.

"Nonetheless. I think I'd rather die here than join the two of you." Benri tapped out a cigarette to show how he wasn't rattled, though he didn't light it with magic. He was too rattled.

The other Shepherd, the silent one, held up a hand and projected a magic circle. Its Aetheric sigils were made from pink-and-orange fire, and they revolved slightly as he inspected them.

"Safety and protection for the duration of your cooperation

with the Iron King," the chatty Shepherd continued. "None shall harm you, including the King himself. In fact, he will hold himself responsible for your well-being."

Benri inspected the contract closely. He wished he had a specialist to consult, but he *was* quite experienced in magical contracts. It only took him five minutes of analysis to determine that the contract was legitimate.

Although, who knew what kinds of tricks a hive of man-eating undead could pull?

"It doesn't sound like I have much choice."

The Shepherd shrugged. "If you do accept, we are bound to your safety. If you do not, we…aren't."

The Reaver's mechanical eyes flashed red.

Benri leaned forward as though to sign, but hesitated. The longer he stalled this process, the more likely help would arrive. "And everyone else on the ship?"

"We have been given no such contracts for anyone else."

He tried not to look back at his guards. They had served him loyally, but it wasn't as though he could do anything for them now.

Benri stroked his chin. "It seems to me that—"

"There is no one coming for you," the Shepherd interrupted. "Your security fleet was dealt with before we reached this ship. They embrace the Legion now."

Benri signed.

Then he was carried away, inwardly cursing his son. The next time Varic found an Iron King, he should dispose of it properly.

CHAPTER TWENTY-ONE

WHEN HORIZON'S VOICE in my mind said she could recall us to the ship, we weren't quite done yet. It took us a while to drop the civilian crew on the colony they came from, and longer to pry the little girl off Sola's leg.

I did some sightseeing in the colony while Sola ran her errands and Raion picked up a freelance bounty contract. He came back with the first criminal under his arm in about fifteen minutes, then he picked up another bounty and left again.

'Sightseeing' in a Galactic Union colony doesn't take long. Colonies are just giant metal wheels with people crammed inside them. They tend to all look the same inside: bustling and colorless. With so many people, and resources tight, the colony governors carefully control everything, from building sites to traffic flow.

I passed through the local Magic Research Council branch, which was one thing being a Union-certified Archmage was good for. I checked out some of the publicly declared projects and promptly left.

There were some creative ideas, but nothing likely to produce results. I got better prospects from a local dessert shop, where they had covered frozen cream from a replicator in yellow berries they grew in a back-room garden.

I had only killed an hour or so when I received a Subline call from Sola, along with the startling news that she was already finished here.

The bounty for a destroyed Hive took a while to process, but she was paid promptly for retrieving the survivors. She seemed surprised, and so was I. Mercenaries and bounty hunters rarely got their pay on time or as planned.

"Good working with you," Sola said through my console. "Contact me if you have trouble with the Iron Legion."

She was about to cut off the call, I could smell it. I cleared my throat. "With you along, we could hit the Legion a lot harder than this."

"Is this about *The Last Horizon?*"

She may not know much about the legendary starship, but she knew enough to be skeptical.

"It's the genuine Zenith Starship, I swear on the Aether," I said. That's not a binding vow, but wizards were still wary of breaking it. "We came to recruit you because we need an expert on the Iron Legion."

That was only one reason, but it was true. "Besides," I said, "you can't be too attached to your current starship."

While Sola was still considering what to say, I pointed to the sky. "The ship says you're invited."

She gave me a cold look, and I could read the doubt running beneath that lack of expression.

If not for our extraordinary abilities, she would have taken us for insane. Or believers in some obscure cult.

Considering what we'd shown her in the Iron Hive, the situation became worse. As she would see it, our ability made us more credible, but also harder to deal with. If we *were* here to scam her, she'd have a hard time escaping from an Archmage and a powerful Visiri warrior.

"Meet on my ship," she said at last, which was a brighter response than I had been expecting. "I'll need a full explanation."

I could sympathize with that. I was still waiting on one of those myself.

I met her aboard her rusty, creaking ship in the colony's dock. From inside, I could hear a voice on the dock's speaker system announcing departures and arrivals, which was a bad sign. A better ship would be soundproof.

It didn't take long to explain the situation with *The Last Horizon* to Sola. When I finished, she considered for a long minute. Every time I tried to say anything, she shook her head and continued thinking.

Finally, she met my gaze with her arms crossed and her eyes blazing green. "So with a full crew, the ship will be powerful enough to defeat the Legion?"

"That's what she says."

"What do *you* think?"

"I think she's not telling us everything, but she's not lying. I've seen the crew contract."

"And if I complete a request for you and Raider, you'll help me fight the Legion?"

"Raion."

"The question stands."

"In fact, defeating the Iron Legion was *my* request. You still get one."

Sola stroked her chin and stared into a rust patch on the inner hull of her ship. I could practically read her thoughts. She would need more information, but it would all come down to whether she thought she could trust us. And whether we could win.

I decided to give her one more push. I lifted my left arm, giving the screen of my console a few quick taps as I sent her a file.

"Accept it," I told her. "It's a video file from my processor implant, a little over a month ago."

She opened up her console and began staring into it. I couldn't see what she saw, but I knew she was watching the video.

It would show, from my perspective, my invasion of the Hive and destruction of the Iron King.

"I thought this was corporate propaganda," she said. "You really killed a King."

Her suit had verified that the video was real, which was a relief. I'd worried she wouldn't even believe video evidence.

Now that she had some level of trust for me, I sent her another video. Entering *The Last Horizon*.

She watched that silently. It wasn't a long video, only showing brief snippets of my interactions with Horizon, but enough to show that the starship wasn't ordinary.

Finally, she spoke. "Is this a trap?"

I hadn't expected her to ask that so directly. "It is not."

"Then I'll talk to your ship." She nodded to the ship around her. "Give me the coordinates and I'll follow you out."

I had been looking forward to this. "No need for coordinates. Just take my hand."

She eyed my hand, but I gave her the confident and mysterious expression that every Archmage is required by law to practice.

Sola gave me a once-over, then clasped my hand.

Blue light swallowed us both.

When we reappeared in the heart of *The Last Horizon*, surrounded by stone tablets illustrating the six crew members, Sola and I were no longer clasping hands. I glanced around for her, hoping to see her shock.

I didn't see any expression from her at all, because she was wearing her full gray armor and held a gun in both hands.

Her voice came from the suit's speakers. "Where am I?"

From across the table, Raion gripped his head. "No! I had the criminal in my hands! What if he hurts someone else?" He noticed Sola and stood up straighter. "Oh! Welcome to *The Last Horizon*, Sola!"

Her visor was turned to me, waiting for an explanation, and the barrel of her gun wasn't *quite* pointed at my chest.

"Long-distance transportation magic," I said. "Not mine."

Horizon materialized in the center of the room, bowing over folded hands. *"My magic, I'm afraid. Welcome aboard* The Last Horizon.*"*

Sola's gun *was* pointed at her. "Are you the ship AI?"

"I am the World Spirit of the ship. You must understand the situation to some degree, or I would not have been able to call you here." She waved a hand to indicate the tablets on the walls. *"I am the chariot of heroes, and there are six seats. It is my honor to offer you the third."*

Sola looked from the tablets to the horned woman. "He says you can rid the galaxy of the Iron Legion."

"There is no more worthy and heroic goal. With my powers and the assistance of the others, you will surely succeed."

"What is this going to cost me?"

Horizon's smile was soothing and professional. *"Your participation in the requests of the others. In fact, since the Iron Legion's destruction was already the Captain's goal, you are owed a goal of your own. If the rest of the crew wants your assistance in granting their wishes, they must agree to grant yours."*

The spirit projected the magic circle describing our binding contract, and Sola's visor flashed slightly as her suit analyzed it.

While it worked, she looked over to Raion. "What was your request, Raion Reeth?"

"Raithe," I corrected reflexively.

"Close enough!" Raion said. "To defend the galaxy from Esh'kinaar, Swarm-Queen of the D'Niss, should she ever return!"

Sola's helmet tilted as she looked him up and down. "Knight of the Titan Force," she said.

"I'm a Knight of *The Last Horizon* now!" Raion struck a pose.

Sola grunted. "The Swarm-Queen might never return. How long do we have to wait?"

"The duration for his contract is five years," Horizon explained. *"Should that time expire, he must find a new request that the crew will agree to fulfill. We can apply a similar provision to your contract, if you wish."*

The emerald visor stopped flashing, showing me that Sola's armor had finished its analysis. Horizon made the contract vanish.

Sola was quiet, still thinking, but I was sure we had her. To defeat the Iron Legion, she would pay any price.

"I have no other request," Sola said at last. "If we defeat the Legion, I'm satisfied. Where do I sign?"

My heart lifted. It surprised me how encouraging it was to have another friend aboard. If Horizon had chosen Raion to manipulate or rattle me, I no longer minded. I was already thinking about how I could fill the last three seats.

"Welcome abo—" I began, but Horizon cut me off by swirling through my body and up to Sola. The spirit stuck her horned face against Sola's helmet, grin stretching her face and eyes wide.

"No, no, no!" Horizon said. *"There is no* forfeit *of your quest. To join this crew, you* must *provide me with a worthy goal!"* A swirling contract appeared next to her, written in blue-and-red Aetheric symbols.

Sola had a handgun conjured and pressed into Horizon's jaw. *Into* because Horizon was still nothing more than a holographic projection, which Sola quickly realized. She lowered the gun, but kept it out.

Before Sola could turn us down, I spoke up. "We'll come up with something. Sign her now, and she can think of a request later."

"An open-ended contract?" Horizon asked in what I was sure was mock surprise. *"She would remain bound to me until her quest was accepted and completed. And above all else, the remaining crew would have to agree."*

Raion raised a hand. "I agree!"

I was reasonably certain he didn't grasp the situation and didn't care to. He already counted Sola as a friend, so he'd be willing to do whatever it took to recruit her.

As far as I was concerned, that was for the best. I knew her.

"We need her, if we're going to beat the Iron Legion," I said. "Whatever it takes."

A swarm of conjured eyes drifted around Horizon in shades of red and blue, and I thought I heard some of them giggle. *"Very well, then. Sola Kalter. Do you accept the position as Sword of* The Last Horizon, *until such time as your request is named and completed?"*

Sola surveyed the entire scene. "Stop wasting time and let's go break some Hives."

Horizon clapped both hands onto Sola's shoulders. Green light poured from Sola, trickled up Horizon's arms, and lit the inner lights of the ship.

For a moment, the starship's World Spirit shone vivid green. The walls trembled, and I distantly felt something shifting in the rest of the ship.

Then some of the green faded from Horizon's projected body, leaving her drawn in shades of blue, red, and green. She stretched, arms held high, as though waking from a long sleep. *"Aaahhh, I can't wait to show you my new weapons systems. Welcome home, my new Sword."*

Raion clapped eagerly. "Let's celebrate! Do we have cake? Or, I guess, any food at all? I haven't eaten in…three days? I think three."

"I need to sleep," I said. "And we need a heading. Horizon, send the crew profiles to my console along with that rulebook."

She bowed slightly to me. *"As you wish, Captain."* She split into three projections, none of which were quite as detailed as her unified form. *"Follow me, and I'll show you each to your rooms."*

The Captain's quarters of the Zenith Starship were better than those on *Moonfall*, but that wasn't saying much. I had a bunk nestled into one wall, a screen onto which I could project my console, a food replicator, and a table. Open doors showed me a compact bathroom and a small closet. That was it.

I stood in the doorway and didn't comment on my first sight. It was hard to say I wasn't disappointed, though I'd dealt with worse. I'd also enjoyed much better. In the two lifetimes I'd spent on good terms with the Vallenar Corporation, I had experienced some of the most luxurious starships the galaxy had to offer.

I knew the Zenith Devices were designed with utility in mind, not comfort, but it was still something of a letdown.

A few of Horizon's magical floating eyeballs drifted around in front of me, observing my reaction. *"Could it be that you're disappointed, Captain?"*

"This will do fine, Horizon, thank you," I said. I sat the crate containing my staff down. I only needed a private space and a place to sleep anyway.

"You have such little faith in me," the spirit said with a sigh. She waved a hand, and half of my quarters melted away, leaving only a blank, unfurnished room. Even the closet and bathroom had disappeared.

"That was the default configuration. You have total control over the layout of your quarters, including its internal dimensions."

She flicked her fingers again, and the space in the room quadrupled. The ceiling grew to twenty feet high and walls sprouted from the ground, partitioning off a bedroom, a bathroom, and what I would call a dining-room.

The bedroom door was still open, and what had once been a flat bunk was now a wide expanse of fluffy blankets and pillows. The bathroom was almost as large as the entire room had been before, small trees grew as decorations along what became an entry hallway, and a piano sprouted out of the ground. There was even a statue made of greenish metal.

The statue was of Horizon with eyes closed and hands spread as though in blessing.

"You have console access," Horizon said, looking pleased with herself. *"Feel free to tweak the details. My statue, for instance, can get much bigger."*

"All right," I admitted, "that was impressive."

Horizon drew herself up proudly. *"I couldn't let you stay disappointed in me. Now, I will leave you to rest. If you need me, you have only to ask."*

She faded from view, leaving me to survey my new room.

You'd think the weight of the day would have sunk in. That I had not only found the Zenith Starship but been accepted as its Captain. That I could go wherever I wanted.

But I was too tired. All I remembered was falling asleep instantly.

I slept for fourteen hours straight. Since the ritual that had stuck me with five additional lives, that was the first time I'd experienced a complete, uninterrupted night of sleep.

The next morning, I found that Horizon had replaced my wardrobe. With an uncanny degree of accuracy, she'd replicated all my clothes that had been destroyed on *Moonfall*. The only exception was that they now all had a seven-pointed star somewhere in their design.

I was just pleased to have something to wear.

When I entered the bridge, Raion and Sola were engaged in a lively discussion around the star-chart of a system I didn't recognize. They were both dressed more casually than I was used to seeing them: Raion in red pants and a sleeveless white shirt, Sola in a dull gray flight suit.

Both sights brought back memories of living alongside them before, in lives that had never happened.

"Then let's hit them here first," Sola said, pointing to a red spot orbiting a moon. "If we do it at the right time, the moon will block Subline communications. Assuming Varic can keep their magic from alerting the other Hives, we can cut it off with no warning."

Raion turned to give me a thumbs-up. "He can do it!" he said, with baseless confidence. "And that's exactly why I should hit *this* one." Raion spun the holographic star-chart around, indicating another red spot. "If the three of us and Horizon all hit a different target, we can have all the Hives in the system taken out at once!"

Sola ticked off points on her fingers. "One, even I can't blow up a Hive while its defenses are up. Two, we still haven't tested *The Last Horizon*'s weapons yet. Three, that's a terrible plan anyway. It relies on four things going perfectly at the same time."

"I *believe*," Raion said.

I sipped my coffee and sat down on a chair that poured up from the floor around the star-chart. "Horizon keeps the upgraded systems whether we're aboard or not, as long as we're still crew, but she's stronger while we're here."

I only knew as much from reading the rulebook she'd given me.

"If we're hitting Iron Hives," I went on, "we'll be more effective as a team." I gestured to the star-chart. "So what's this?"

"The Ynthra system," Sola said. "The Legion has gathered five Hives here, and no one knows why." She gestured to the hologram, which zoomed out, revealing the surrounding systems. "I have a theory. The Hives are positioned to block Subline access from this half of the sector. I think they're hiding something. Take out the Hives and we can see what it is."

"Before we start an outright war, let's make sure we can win." I pulled up a file from my console and sent it to the holo-projector, overwriting the star chart. Now it showed the holographic image of a human man with a wide-brimmed hat, a cocky grin, and pistols strapped to every possible location on his body.

"You want to fill out the crew?" Sola asked.

"I like his hat," Raion said.

"Tanner Hall," I said. "Gun for hire and the best pilot in the galaxy, according to him. What he does have is navigational magic and a moderate Aether Technician's affinity for starships. Subspace Drives under his control are faster, more stable, and use less fuel."

Sola folded her arms as she examined the man's appearance. She didn't look impressed. Even Raion's "hmmm" was more pensive than I expected.

Of course, I had another reason for wanting him along. He'd make a decent Pilot, but he had been a friend. One of my mentors, actually; the one who had taught me pathfinding magic in the first place, as well as how to fly.

My magic had quickly surpassed his, but he was an asset at the helm of anything that could fly.

"He can pilot the ship," I insisted.

Horizon manifested next to me. *"He performed adequately in the virtual trial,"* she said. Images began to play in the air next to her: a starship dancing and weaving around others, leaving them in pieces.

"Adequately," Sola repeated.

"If you say so, I trust you!" Raion said. "Is he a friend of yours?"

"...in a way," I hedged. In this life, I had never met the man.

"Huh."

"He would slightly improve my maneuverability, and would reduce my fuel consumption by about ten percent," Horizon said. *"Although, thanks to the Captain, most of my fuel comes straight from the Aether."*

I stared at Horizon, trying to figure out if she was supporting me or sabotaging me.

"I think we can do better," Sola said.

Raion didn't object, which meant he agreed with her.

I was still hoping to recruit Tanner, but we didn't need to settle that now. Thanks to reading Horizon's manual, I had a better understanding of her limitations. "We still have time to decide. Don't we, Horizon?"

"Of course. In fact, we would need to pass the Ynthra system to get within range of Tanner Hall's last known location.

"There you have it," I said. "Let me know what you decide to do about the Hives." I drained the rest of my coffee, then turned to walk out.

"If we proceed with this operation, can we count on you?" Sola asked.

"Sorry, no," I said. "I'm busy."

Raion blinked at me. Sola looked taken aback.

I gave her an apologetic shrug. "I've got class."

CHAPTER TWENTY-TWO

I ARRIVED IN the teacher's dock of the Magic Tower in a flash of blue light.

That earned me some startled looks from the other staff walking to and from their ships, but not the instant panic it would have if I had arrived like that anywhere else.

Here, they knew long-range personal teleportation was impossible, so they would be coming up with theories about how I had seemingly popped up out of nowhere. Invisibility spell? Maybe I had come in on a nearby ship and used a short-range teleport to draw attention as I exited. I was known here as an elementalist and a binding magic expert, so perhaps I had managed to harness a unique water element.

I strolled through them with confidence, mantle billowing behind me as I wore an expression like I was preening under their attention.

That would confirm their suspicion that I had done it for attention, which would fuel their speculation in the wrong direction.

Not that I minded telling them the truth, but this saved me the trouble. They frowned and shot glances my way as they tried to figure out what I'd done and why.

Those reactions faded as I outpaced the other mages on my way to my classroom. I nodded at those I knew and smiled even at those I didn't.

It was my first day at work after inheriting a priceless starship. I was in a better mood than I'd been in since starting the job.

The slug-like Director Porellus oozed down the hallway, tendrils pulling him forward. His bulk took up most of the space, and I would have had to squeeze past his pale skin to reach the classroom door, so I just stood back and waited for him to pass.

He brightened when he saw me. "Professor Vallenar, welcome back! You had a bit of trouble yesterday, didn't you? I'm pleased to see you're safe."

I wanted to check behind me to see if there was another Professor Vallenar I didn't know about. Porellus didn't want to see me safe, he wanted to see my charred corpse pulled out of a starship wreck.

It also took me a moment to realize what he was talking about. "Ah, you heard about the Hunter-ships?"

Porellus shook his head. "A shame. The Iron Legion should stick to Dark Space. I hear you showed the Hunters the might of the Magic Tower. Good for you."

He patted me on the back with a soft, wet hand, and I half-expected my mantle to block it.

"You're well informed," I noted.

"It was starting to get lonely around here. I had to keep my eye out, to be sure you made it back to us."

I returned the slap on the back, though his was squishy and damp. "Well then, I have a lot to show you."

I expected him to shoot back something waspish, but he only laughed. If I was watching from the outside, I'd think we were really friends.

He slithered on, leaving me in front of my classroom door, but I couldn't move.

Director Porellus hated me. He resented that the Union had allowed me to be here, and he thought I was too arrogant for my own good. I couldn't imagine that had changed after my suspension.

Had someone force-fed him a potion of compassion, or did he know something I didn't?

Whatever the answer was, I suspected I wouldn't like it.

I was frozen in front of the door until a student called my name.

When I didn't respond immediately, Mariala looked all around the doorframe in a search for signs of magic. Her half-Aethril hair sparkled as though there were stars hidden within. "Is there something here, Professor?" she asked. "What do you see?"

"Just been a long time." I tossed the door open and strolled inside, where I was greeted by rows of students in their stadium seats. Last time, only forty students had attended in person, but things had changed.

Most of the hundred-person class was present physically, with the rest as holographic screens projecting students attending remotely.

We still had a minute or two to go until the official start of class, but students at the Mage Tower didn't play around. They were here from the military academies or famous mage families, so most arrived earlier than I did.

Though normally, most of them were holograms. Something had inspired them to be there in person.

I walked up to the console that served as a lectern, where my lesson file for the day was waiting. The screen that took up the whole wall behind me projected the topic: 'Non-Traditional Applications of Water Elements.'

"We're changing today's lesson," I said as I switched off the screen. There was a murmur of disappointment among the class.

I eyed them. "That was a lot of disappointment. Most of you aren't even elementalists."

I drummed my fingers on the side of the console as I inspected them. They were restless, inspired, and some of the remote students had already activated blinking lights to show they had a question.

They had heard something.

At first, I wondered if they had learned about *The Last Horizon,* but that should still be a secret. No one had seen the end of the digital selection tournament except me, Raion, and Horizon.

But in the rest of the rounds, I'd fought against some of the best combatants in the galaxy. And these students were very well-connected.

"You saw me fight, didn't you?" I asked, and the room immediately exploded with shouts.

I caught only a word or two here and there, since everyone was trying to talk all at once, but the gist was clear. A couple of students had started projecting videos of me into the air, each from the perspective of my opponents.

Most of those videos were very brief.

One of the military cadets in the front row shouted loudest. "I saw you destroy a Union strike team! Why were you teaching us *weather* spells!?"

He sounded personally offended.

Most of the other questions weren't so clear.

"Did you really—"

"How did you—"

"Why did—"

"I want to hear about—"

I held up a hand, and when that wasn't enough, I cast a quick binding-spell to seal out noise. The murmur cut off immediately.

"A lot has happened since I last saw you," I continued. "It has caused me to rethink my position on combat magic. Starting today, I'd like to start teaching you how to fight."

I released my binding-spell, but I didn't need it anymore. They were all silent and rigid in their seats, as though afraid I'd change my mind if they breathed too loudly.

Mariala, far back in the room, was one of those who brought a tablet and stylus to class to take notes. She could record the sessions, but some found it helpful to write their thoughts down in real time.

I pointed to her. "Mariala Brechess."

She stood up, though that wasn't necessary. "Yes, sir!"

"Let's say I had found a way to grant you my power. From this moment on, you're a full Archmage. You have my certification, my knowledge, even my wand. What would you do with it?" For emphasis, I slapped my actual wand onto the console in front of me.

The wand buzzed in disapproval. Its blue light flared among its steel plates, and I got the impression it would stab anyone who tried to take it away.

Mariala's eyes crawled around the room as she wondered what she should and shouldn't say in front of the other students, but I had chosen her first for a reason.

She would have an answer.

"I'd go back home," she said. "My planet doesn't have a military Archmage, so I could apply to Planetary Security."

"And with that authority, what would you do?" She hesitated, so I added, "I don't need any private details, but I would like to hear a bit of your motivation. Help us understand your story."

That would have meaning for any mage. The sort of magic she could use would depend on how she defined herself in front of the Aether. Her story mattered.

"I don't have any authority in the Brechess family," she continued. "With a position in Planetary Security, they'd listen to me. I'd be able to clean house. Right some wrongs."

I nodded, and she sat down.

"Very good. Mariala would restore justice to her family. But there's more. She would use the power of her magic to acquire a political position, which she would then leverage to change her planet for the better. An admirable goal. Now, what if the Galactic Union declared her a traitor?"

The atmosphere in the room took a turn. Most were puzzled, but some here were true patriots of the Union, the very mention of treachery shocking them to their core.

I held up a hand. "I'm not suggesting anything about Miss Brechess, of course. Let's assume some bad actors infiltrated Union command and issued false orders, sending a war-fleet to her home planet."

That wasn't as hypothetical as I pretended. I remembered dying in a Galactic Union dissenter's prison.

"What magic could save her planet?" I asked.

A hesitant hand went up. "Is there a ritual she could use?"

"She might be able to last a while, sure, if she united all the mages on her world. The Union has their own mages, though. If they want it bad enough, they can crack it. How powerful would she need to be to *make sure* her planet is safe?"

Several hands went up this time, and some holographic students flashed a light for my attention. I pointed to one of those remote students at random.

"There are records of some Archmagi registered as fleet-class threats on their own," the young man said over his speakers.

"Indeed there are," I said, "but how many fleets does the Union have? What if it's not the Union? What if the entire Iron Legion, led by a King, decided that *you* were their number one target? What if Starhammer said you were a criminal and you had all the Advocates after your head? What kind of wizard could stop one of the D'Niss from eating their planet?"

"Could you do it, Professor?" another student asked.

I took a long moment to push the memories down before I answered. "No, I can't. No one can. In those scenarios, there's nothing you can do. You die."

I settled back onto my levitation ring, folding my legs underneath me as I drifted in front of the class. "Magic has no limits, but we do. I want you to remember that no matter how skilled you become, you're never invincible. There's always a bigger fish.

"As I said, I'd like to start teaching you how to fight. Before anything else, you have to accept your limitations. Next...well, let's learn some magic. Mariala."

Again, she shot to her feet as though I'd grabbed her with telekinesis. "Yes, sir!"

"As thanks for serving as my illustration, I'll give you your gift first." I tapped the console on my left forearm, sending her a file. "In the southeastern continent of Visiria, there's an ancient temple. Precise location is in the file I just sent you, and it's open to tourists. Decorative etchings around the ceiling illustrate a spell to give warriors good luck in combat. It's perfectly compatible with your fortune magic."

She scribbled furiously at her notepad, but I didn't slow down. The summary was in the file anyway.

I'd found that magic circle in one of my lives as a prize-fighter on Visiria.

"But, of course, what you *learn* is secondary," I went on. "The Aether cares most about what you *do*. This is the very reason an Archmage has only a single pinnacle spell. Which spells you choose to use, and how you use them, define you in the eyes of the Aether. This definition is reflected in your magic."

Everyone was taking notes, though that part was common knowledge. "You need to define yourself as a source of fortune. Which means you need to become a good-luck charm. I would start by adopting a group of people—a farming community, a Union squad, doesn't matter—and blessing them with your magic. The more of a difference you make in their lives, the deeper your reflection in the Aether."

I'd been forced to do the exact opposite of that to learn curse magic, though those were memories I preferred to forget. And I had sealed away those spells in this life, so there was no reason to dwell on that corner of my past.

"While you're doing that, work on this," I flicked my hand and conjured a complicated circle of Aetheric symbols. The spell-circle hung there as she took a picture with her console. I'd already included a picture in the file, but it was better to see it with her own eyes.

This spell I'd figured out on my own, after studying her magic myself.

"That should give you a guideline on how to fill in the rest of the gaps in your spellwork," I continued. "There are a few more notes in there, but if you keep at it, you should be able to master your magic in no time. I expect to see you register for wizard certification by this time next year."

There were some astonished murmurs in the class at that. It was a bold statement, but I was more worried about some apocalyptic disaster popping up in the next twelve months.

I pointed at another young woman, a Lichborn military cadet who was only here remotely. "Nera Jesh, fire elementalist. All the best generalized techniques for fire elementalism are kept secret, but not secret enough. I'm sending you four of them. My best tip for any elementalist is to find and study strange examples of your element.

"I recommend three. There's a toxic flame on Dornoth Four that spreads like a virus and burns its host from the inside-out, a fire on Syrillia that feeds on doubt, and a frozen flame from…I don't remember the planet, but it's in the file."

I had crossed many strange flames and fire elementalists over the course of my lives, but these would start her out well.

"Give you a couple years and sending ships into a black hole is going to be safer than sending them after you. Gar Kilian…where are you, Gar? Binding magic, that's my specialty."

The noise level in the class steadily rose as they realized I was really going to teach everyone in the room how to reach full wizard status. If they followed my instructions, the more talented of them might become Archmagi.

My processor blinked at the corner of my vision, giving me low-level warnings every time someone began to stream the lesson to those back home.

I could get in big trouble for this—many of these techniques were either claimed or coveted by powerful people—but I had decided to do this shortly after my suspension.

The Magic Tower's reputation and their own backgrounds would protect the students. I hadn't given away such dire secrets that they would be killed just for knowing them.

I had intended to wait a while before doing this. Teach them how to acquire new magic and what to do with it. Build a solid foundation.

But now, I wasn't just a teacher here. I was the Captain of *The Last Horizon*. There was no telling how many more chances I'd have to teach them.

Not to mention that I, more than anyone else, knew how suddenly disaster could strike. Together, that had convinced me to lay my cards on the table.

I didn't intend to go anywhere. I meant to stick around and guide them through the plans I'd given them. But death had often interrupted my plans.

If I died this time, at least I wouldn't fail completely. Perhaps only a few here would make it all the way to Archmage, but I'd given them a chance.

The few absent students had connected via hologram and were waiting their turn, and most of the room was in hot debate, taking notes on every new lesson I taught. The crowd made such a loud buzz that I almost didn't notice hearing something strange.

It sounded like a live electrical wire being cut. There had been a constant buzz of power running through the wire, then there came a sudden *snip* and a crackle of static. Then silence.

It was one of my wards breaking. And not the ones I had set on the outside of the Mage Tower. One of the seals on the inside.

There was a threat headed my way. And it had bypassed the outer walls of the Mage Tower.

"Red alert," I said, interrupting a student's question. "Get to your stations."

CHAPTER TWENTY-THREE

THE COMPUTERS IN my room heard my commands as the students did. The lights in the classroom flicked to red, and throughout the Tower, sirens began blaring.

That moment was when the military students stood out from the ones from mage families. Those with training were already out the door while the others were wondering if this was still part of the lecture.

Mage families produced better students, in general. They understood the underlying logic of magic better than their peers.

But in situations like this, I preferred the ones who would follow orders.

This wasn't a warship, so their "stations" were wherever they had been ordered to be during an emergency. Mostly, that meant locked in their quarters.

I waited for the students to file out, checking my wand and pulling my Lightcaster from the warded pocket where I'd hidden it. Mariala stayed behind the others, and not out of hesitation. She had a protection amulet on, similar to my own, and was carrying a blazing rod with a powerfully destructive aura.

"How can I help you, Miss Brechess?" I asked in between alarms.

"What's the situation?"

She seemed...not calm, but focused. Too used to this. I vaguely remembered the file on the Brechess family. There had been some similar incident when she was a child.

Mariala must have trained for this for the last twenty years. She was breathing a little fast, but she held up well.

I gave her a reassuring smile I didn't entirely feel. "Someone tripped my personal wards, so they're coming to kill me. No need to worry, but I would recommend you evacuate."

Another ward popped, this one closer. Somehow, the mysterious attacker was bypassing barriers and seals that should have stopped them.

Evidently my smile wasn't reassuring enough, because her breathing sped up more.

"Mariala. The *one place* you don't want to be is here with me."

"You're not evacuating?"

"Your legs are not moving toward the door."

I tossed barriers and seals here and there around the classroom. I had already placed quite a few; there were enough people after me to justify my own security measures. But now that I knew this intruder had the ability to slip past wards, I had to get more creative.

None of them required much incantation, just a brief phrase under my breath, but Mariala was sliding to the door as though through sludge.

"I'll...I'll let security know."

I pointed to the flashing red lights overhead. "They know. Listen, not panicking is good, but you need to learn when to run. If I end up in a fight, nowhere in the Tower will be safe."

It's hard to describe my emotions at that moment. I can't say I was terrified—I could handle most of the assassins who would be coming after my life, but there were always exceptions. Memories of five deaths ran underneath my thoughts, and I mentally tested my connection to Horizon. If I had to, I would call for an evacuation.

But I didn't want to vanish yet. I could think of attackers who might unleash their frustration on the whole school upon finding me missing.

Something finally got through to Mariala, and she hurried out the door, but she leaned back in and thrust a hand in my direction.

A spell flashed toward me, a twisting braid of yellow light. As a friendly spell, it passed through my defenses and wrapped around my neck.

"Good luck," she said.

Considering her magic, that wasn't just a saying.

"Run," I responded. Sometimes, I thought people would benefit from a death or two, just to teach them a healthy respect for the value of their own lives.

At least she wasn't in too much danger yet. We should have another moment. No matter what this intruder did, he couldn't avoid *all* my seals.

Above the door, one of my magic circles manifested and dissolved into nothing.

I thrust out my hand and summoned water.

Thunder cracked the air of the classroom and water sprayed into midair.

An inch in front of Mariala's face, a bullet the size of my forefinger spun slowly, suspended in water. If it weren't for the warning of my seals, I wouldn't have been able to stop it.

"You missed," I said to the shadowy corner of the room.

There shouldn't *be* any shadowy corners in this room. Not with the alarms blaring.

The darkness split into a dozen mouths and laughed. "Ooohhh, he's mad, he's mad."

I was, I realized. This guy had come here for me, but he'd fired at a witness first. If I'd been a little slower, he'd have killed one of my students right in front of me.

For every memory of my own death that haunted me, I had five of watching people die. And it had almost happened again.

I was terrified by how close that had been. And that terror became fury as I recognized that shadow.

The darkness boiled and slid into the figure of one man. His hair was long and dark, and he wore a very short, trim beard. One of his eyes was covered by a ragged patch of steel and fitted with a replacement: a molten orange cybernetic piece of Aethertech. His one remaining fleshy eye was orange as well, the product of genetic customization similar to my own.

He wore black from the neck down, his slightly open coat showing hints of cybernetics trailing down his collar. But his least human feature was his smile. It was wide and malicious, and I was reminded of Horizon's grin when I thought she would murder me in my sleep.

The assassin held a gun in each hand, though each were wildly mismatched. One had a fat, buzzing chamber that looked like it contained grenades, while the other was a sleek silver sidearm more similar to my own Lightcaster.

"I would have put a shot through your head before you ever saw me, but you were just too much *fun*." The man seemed to relish the situation. He took one deliberate step after another, walking down the rows of seats toward me. "Wards on wards on wards on *wards*. You're a spider at the center of your nest. Skitter, skitter, skitter."

Shoulders shook as he chuckled, and he skipped down another step.

"Goodbye, Omega," I said.

Orange eyes widened. "You know my—"

I used my wand to put a laser-focused needle of water through the center of his forehead.

That wasn't the end of the fight, but it bought me some time. I continued chanting my next spell as the man's body fell.

He tumbled down the stairs, but I didn't stop chanting.

After a moment, his head spun around on his neck until it was facing backwards. His smile was beaming and his cyborg eye blazed. "Oh, that's *good!* You didn't fall for it for a second!"

I cast Absolute Burial.

White symbols crushed him from every direction, and he screamed as he folded in on himself and disappeared.

"Not for a second," I muttered. He shouldn't be able to hear me from his Subspace prison. *Shouldn't* be able to, but with a man like him, nothing was certain.

I didn't rest. Water condensed around me, conjured from the Aether and gathered from the air itself, compressed into hyper-dense rings that floated around my body. I didn't know how long I had, so I continued gathering my element.

Darkness exploded into the air from the anchor of Absolute Burial, and I shredded that darkness with water. The high-level elementalism tore him apart.

And did considerable damage to the rest of the classroom.

There was a reason I didn't usually fight with elementalism. Not only was a gun usually more efficient, but this was intended for fights on a larger scale. And when I didn't mind collateral damage.

I tore him to pieces, which for anyone else would end the argument, but a hand formed out of the darkness holding that fat, buzzing gun I'd seen earlier.

Omega was as annoying to deal with as he was frightening. He was the only one I knew who could pop in and out of Subspace at will. If he hadn't tucked that weapon away beyond physical reality, I would have destroyed it by now.

That thought occurred in the one small corner of my mind that still worked, while the rest of me focused on pulling my element back to protect myself. After all, there was a giant gun in my face.

I wasn't fast enough. A flash of orange light erupted from the end of the weapon.

The light splashed over my whole body, crashing into the field of my protection amulet.

And blowing right through it.

The amulet exploded on my chest, which would have been dangerous if not for my mantle. While it wasn't exactly intended to save me from blunt impacts like the amulet was, its protective power was of a much higher quality.

The shattering jewelry didn't harm me, and neither did the remaining energy of the gunshot.

But it did launch me through the window.

I stabilized myself in midair, as I had done in virtual space against Raion. I didn't recognize the gun, but it had been designed specifically to destroy protective enchantments, which meant it was either Aethertech itself or fired enchanted rounds.

Now, I was down one of my two layers of protection. Memories of death floated closer to the surface.

My mouth moved on its own as I chanted a new spell, but my mind was churning. I needed help.

I floated outside the wall of the Magic Tower, its carefully manicured lawns far below me. I couldn't see a soul, which was somewhat suspicious, but mostly credit to the Tower's effective evacuation plan.

But as I swept my wand across the ground below me, I couldn't find a target. There was no dark figure and no dense mass of shadows where he could have been hiding.

"Hoooohhhh," a voice echoed from nowhere and everywhere. I spun, but I still couldn't find the source. "You lived."

I couldn't stop to chant a navigation spell, and I couldn't interrupt my incantation to respond.

"And you knew my name. You're getting my hopes up, Varic. Let's see what else you have."

I finished chanting, but held on to the shape of the spell without activating it. "I thought you'd know better than to let an Archmage chant."

The shadow-man's laughter chittered everywhere. "I *don't* know better, Varic. No, I don't."

I thought he would reveal himself with that, if only to take a shot and stop me from releasing the spell, but nothing happened.

So I let the spell activate and summoned a pair of rabbits.

Space twisted as I called upon the Lagomorph Contract. Two large rabbits—between four and five feet tall—leaped out of nowhere, taking shape from the Aether. Their long ears were laid back and notched, their fur scarred. They looked like war-hounds more than anything you might call bunnies, and they scanned the ground below with wary eyes.

I used to pull them out of hats.

"Drag him out," I ordered.

They vanished. They didn't teleport or turn invisible, they were just that fast. And their senses were well-tuned to detect threats.

I put my wand away and called more water. The element shimmered in my magical grip.

My wand was suited for focused attacks. It bound my magic to a single target. For wide spells, I was better off not using it.

Darkness rippled in the shadow of a nearby docking bay, and a rabbit chased a half-formed man who put a bullet through it.

The rabbit's body was torn apart, but it dispersed immediately. The rabbit itself would be fine. Its body in this reality was something like a digital avatar, and the real spirit would be no more harmed by its destruction than I would be if someone deleted my picture.

Though it might be upset next time I summoned it. I'd have to bring some carrots.

Raindrops sprayed down over the ground where the shadows had collected. The drops shredded the land as though I'd fired a thousand automatic guns, gouging turf and chipping holes in concrete.

Dark gray bits of Omega filled the air, and the shadow-man grunted. But he still melted and flowed away.

His voice drifted up to me. "All right, Varic, you're ready to play. But so am I."

The second rabbit appeared next to me, startling me. Especially when it put its hind paws on my shoulder and kicked me to one side.

A second later, the shadowy man appeared in midair and fired his buzzing hand-cannon below.

The rabbit was destroyed by orange light, and I slashed the man in half with dense water. He fell in pieces but flowed away again.

A chill ran through my body, and I couldn't fully push it away. He had hopped through Subspace so easily, and I hadn't seen it coming.

I didn't want to die here.

He was physically invulnerable, could slip straight through bindings, and could instantly hop anywhere in space. I couldn't even break his guns, though I couldn't tell if he was repairing them or pulling them into himself before I destroyed them. He was the textbook definition of an immovable object.

Which, of course, was impossible.

There were weaknesses and limitations to any ability, even Aethertech, and I knew Omega's. His regeneration was fueled by a limited stockpile of available mass, and his teleportation took more energy the more he used it in quick succession, similar to pushing a Subspace Drive through a series of micro-dives.

Also, while I hadn't learned this in a previous life, it was becoming clear that he had to return to human form eventually. Otherwise, he would just stay formless.

In total, that added up to an opponent I could defeat in time, as long as I could grind him down.

That was all very sound theory, but it still left me with the question of what to *do*.

The textbook choice was to keep hitting him with sealing spells until I found one that stuck, but that meant trading shots with his guns. Whoever landed a solid hit first would be the winner.

Which was a terrible choice. Never gamble your life on fifty-fifty odds.

My processor implant was informing me that Magic Tower security had been delayed, but I hadn't wondered where they were. When they hadn't shown up within a minute of the first gunshot, I'd known they were out of the picture. Someone had kept them distracted.

Was that Omega's doing or a certain slug-shaped Director? That was the *real* question.

But I had never relied on Tower security in the first place. Now that my life was on the line, keeping secrets was no longer a priority.

With brief concentration, I made a mental connection. "Horizon, give me a hand."

"*Of course, Captain. On my way.*"

CHAPTER TWENTY-FOUR

INSTEAD OF TRYING to seal the enemy in place, I wrapped barriers around myself. Now, the time had come to stall, though I didn't know how long it would take Horizon to get here.

Not long, as it turned out.

The man in black appeared in front of me, close enough that the faint lights from the magical water around me reflected in the metal around his eye socket. His orange eye flashed a moment before his gun did.

A shield of scarlet light absorbed the shot without a ripple.

Omega twisted as he fell from the air, reaching up with his other gun and firing at the new shape that had appeared in the sky. A sleek ship resembling a diving hawk, with metal plates that shone blue at the seams. Though, as I watched, the blue lights began to turn bright green.

Omega's bullet flashed like a bolt of lightning, trailing energy, and my sense of Aether told me it would be enough to pierce right through a normal starship's armor.

It pinged off this ship like a pebble.

Horizon's forward cannons trained on the man in black, shining green. More guns emerged from emerald-edged plates, and *more* turrets manifested out of Subspace. The ship bristled with weapons until it looked like not a single bare inch wasn't sprouting firepower.

The man laughed maniacally as he fell. "That's more like it!" he called.

My ship annihilated him.

It was a stream of many different weapon systems, from bright green plasma bolts to surgically accurate crimson lasers to spell-enhanced bullets. I thought the barrage would destabilize the entire Magic Tower, but I was more impressed by Horizon's precision than I was by her ordnance.

The lights existed for a fraction of a second before they cut off, and not one blade of grass on the ground below was singed.

"If there's anything left of him," I said, "take him in for study. You can capture people, right?"

"Thanks to your magic, I can. No matter your objectives, The Last Horizon *always aims to please."*

A complex blue magic circle appeared around a dark gray shard that looked like a piece of squirming liquid. I could read the magic circle easily enough at a glance, especially since it was my own sealing magic.

Two more spots of light below suggested the ship had grabbed another pair of the intruder's pieces. One of them shifted into a mouth.

"Now *that's* a ship!" my attacker cried, even without a body. "I wonder if it can hold me! Hey, how long do you think it will take until I'm the Captain?"

Horizon gave a cruel laugh. *"Our new prisoner has quite the opinion of himself, doesn't he?"*

The man in black drifted through a hatch and into *The Last Horizon,* though there was little enough left of his body that he could fit inside a canteen.

I gradually released my levitation ring and drifted down to the ground. "Take him and hold him. Find out who sent him and why, if you can. I'll call you after I clean up here."

"Of course. Don't be too long. The others will return soon, and I plan to welcome them with a hero's feast."

The ship streaked off.

Magic Tower security procedures wouldn't be enough to stop it, but now Horizon's existence was on record. The Tower would have recorded everything, which meant the Galactic Union was aware of me now.

I imagined the potential consequences of that to keep my mind busy. If I lost my grip on my thoughts, the aftermath of panic would shake me to pieces. And I needed to be in control of myself when security finally arrived.

Eventually they did, a squad of six clad in armor, each bearing a wand in one hand and a gun in the other. "Drop the wand!"

"Took your time, didn't you?" I asked the one who'd spoken.

"Drop it or we will open fire!"

I didn't think of myself as someone with a temper. I'd lived through a lot of situations worse than this one, and I had learned to keep my nerve in combat.

But these people had abandoned me. They knew I was an instructor here, they knew that I'd been attacked, and they'd been bribed or tricked or persuaded into leaving their posts. Now they were treating me like I might be a threat. After a student had almost been shot.

My patience had a limit.

I tilted my head to the side and gripped my wand tighter. "Then open fire."

They didn't fire. I would have been surprised if they had. These were very capable mages, all of whom would have been qualified to teach here. They understood the situation as well as I did.

That became especially clear when Director Porellus slithered out in full combat gear. His mantle was more like an ornate scarf, though the metal scales sewn into it shimmered. It had good protective enchantments. He held a wand in each hand, and while he looked ridiculous with his tiny tentacles hauling his bulbous body across the ground, he was still an Archmage in his own right.

"Professor Vallenar, where is the intruder?" the Director demanded. "What was the allegiance of that ship?"

I knew better than to start answering questions in this situation. "Where were the security officers, Director?"

"Where they should have been: protecting students."

That answer would sound good on the Subline, but there had been no guards nearby the one student who had actually been attacked.

"What happened to the Tower barriers?" I asked. "If I hadn't placed my own, we wouldn't have caught him until he unloaded in my classroom."

"He has a means of bypassing barriers, which you would know better than I." The Director's beetle eyes narrowed further. "And surely you did not just admit to placing unauthorized magic on your classroom. We'll have to investigate what spells, exactly, you used on our students."

I had to laugh. "Is that what you'll tell the Union investigator? 'Oh yes, he slipped right past our security, but one of our teachers had unauthorized defenses. You should investigate him instead.'"

Maybe I had overestimated the Director.

If he had been willing to take the hit to his reputation by allowing an assassin in to kill me, the smart move would have been to cut his losses the moment that plan failed. He should have thrown his support behind me to cast suspicion away from himself.

Once the attack failed, trying to push the blame on me would only make him look guilty. It was a desperate move, and one that could only backfire.

He didn't *look* desperate, though. He drew up his flabby body and looked down on me with an expression of affronted superiority. "To me, it looked like you were removing forensic evidence of the intruder."

So the Director didn't know the assassin could reconstitute himself. Or he was playing dumb.

"That's what it was," I said. "Write that up and send it in." Five minutes of combat with a *real* threat had put things back in perspective; I had no more time to waste on this.

"There are enough suspicious factors to be worth holding you here until the Galactic Union investigator arrives. We'll answer questions hand-in-hand, Vallenar."

I looked around to the security officers. Suddenly this whole thing seemed so worthless.

I had only showed up to teach at the Magic Tower today because I wanted to help the students, and because I needed a life of my own. This was a place I had created for myself, far from the Vallenar Corporation or any of my previous lives. Besides, it wasn't like the Captain of *The Last Horizon* got a paycheck.

This position as a teacher was a tiny fragment of the galaxy I had carved out for myself. I wanted to keep it.

But at that moment, I couldn't remember why.

I had a new place in the universe now, one where I didn't have to bother with investigators, rules, or Director Porellus. As Captain of *The Last Horizon,* I could make a real difference.

Maybe this time, it would work.

I shoved my wand back into my belt. "All right, I quit. You win, good-bye. I'm leaving."

"Wait!" Porellus shouted. He was always moist, but if he were human, I'd say he had started sweating. "Don't...I was too hasty a moment ago. I apologize, it has been too long since I've come that close to danger. Of course you're not under suspicion. Please, if you don't mind, stay here until the Union investigation team arrives. Neither of us want to upset the Galactic Union, do we?"

He gave a greasy laugh.

I didn't know what to say. I shot a look to one of the security officers that meant *'can you believe this guy?'*

I couldn't see his face through the helmet, so I chose to imagine he returned the same look.

I eyed Porellus. "You're going to burn out your drives if you reverse course that fast, Director."

Porellus turned a strangled purple, but he forced out another laugh. Now I was genuinely becoming alarmed. If I didn't have the emergency eject button of Horizon's teleportation, I would be fighting to escape already.

Why did the Director look more nervous at the idea of me leaving than at the possibility of being held liable for endangering students?

There was one obvious answer. He was supposed to keep me here, and he was more afraid of failing than he was of losing his position.

Who could inspire that level of paranoia?

The answer was as obvious as it was disturbing.

"My father's on his way, isn't he?" I asked quietly.

Porellus snorted. "Of course not. The corporations are not permitted to operate within a system of the Magic Tower. It took a special exemption to employ you."

I knew that. It was the main reason I was there.

The Director could still be lying, of course. If not my father, who else could have hired an assassin to kill me *and* bribed Porellus to keep me here in case of failure?

And Porellus wasn't a great liar. Oddly, I believed that it wasn't my father.

I would have recalled back to the starship right then except for two things. First, I doubted anyone here could block the teleportation magic of *The Last Horizon,* so it wouldn't be too late to leave later. Second, I needed to know for sure.

Distant twists appeared in the sky as three ships came out of Subspace. They grew larger as they descended into the atmosphere, and details of their design grew clearer: they were bronze on the bottom, with layers of shimmering solar sails on the top and out to either side.

Sunsail frigates. They had been designed after the ancient ships that had sailed the seas of many different planets. The marketing line had been 'Appealing to a classic aesthetic with cutting-edge technology!'

I knew, because the Sunsail line was a specialty of the Vallenar Corporation.

I turned to Director Porellus. "You lied to me."

"In all honesty, I was shocked you believed me." He was much less nervous now that he had someone else around who could handle the blame.

"So am I."

I prepared my thoughts to call Horizon. The brush with death had left me in no mood to deal with my father. In fact, my wariness swelled, like I'd spotted the shadow of a predator in the brush.

I hadn't seen him in person since the ritual. That wasn't an accident.

If he was coming to see me now, he was prepared. I didn't know what his goals were, I couldn't imagine what preparations he'd made, and the fact that I couldn't guess those things was cause for great concern.

However, I stayed in place.

Whatever he'd done to keep me in check, it wouldn't be enough to stop me *and* Horizon.

I tucked my hands behind my back and awaited my father.

CHAPTER TWENTY-FIVE

ONE OF THE ancient-style Sunsail starships continued to land on my location, but the other two spread out and circled the Magic Tower.

They trailed Aether in the shape of twisting letters. They were drawing a ring of magic around us.

It was a barrier to prevent escape, and not a bad one. My father knew exactly what I was capable of, so this would be an attempt to slow me down *and* a ward against Subspace travel in and out.

Large ships couldn't make Subspace dives in atmosphere without tearing themselves apart, and even smaller ships could only make short hops. This would double as security against Omega and against the mysterious ship that had come to my aid.

From my father's perspective, anyway. If Horizon couldn't teleport me through this circle's interference, all she had to do was drop Raion on top of me.

While the other two ships were still drawing circles against us, my father's began to land. It kicked up grass as it hovered over the scene, sending my mantle fluttering behind me.

The ramp extended before the ship had finished landing, and my father was already standing on it.

I clutched my hands behind my back to stop them from trembling. Any fear of my father had died in my previous lives, but the touch of death still lingered in my mind after Omega's attack. That my father was visiting now did not bode well.

A lit cigarette hung from Benri Vallenar's lips, tracing smoke as the ramp ushered him to the ground. His hair was silver throughout and slashed short, so it was even with his goatee.

He stared me down with cold, steel eyes. He was in good shape for a much younger man, filling out his trimmed and tailored dark suit with an impressive barrel chest. I reminded myself to see if Horizon had a gym.

Benri didn't say anything as he strode out onto the grass and up to me. He took a deep drag of his cigarette and exhaled a cloud instead of speaking.

"Welcome to the Magic Tower, Mister Vallenar," Director Porellus said. His wands had vanished, and he gestured grandly to my father. "I apologize for the mess, but as I'm sure you understand, we're quite on edge from the intruder."

My father gave him one glance and a curt nod, but returned his attention to me. Porellus wasn't so far beneath him. Just far enough.

"I thought you would have come in person," I said.

Even the two guards that had followed my father out of the ramp looked startled. They weren't in faceless armor like the Magic Tower guards, and in fact wouldn't have been out of place at a high-society party, but they were the best-trained and best-equipped of the Vallenar Corporation.

Even they didn't know that the man they were guarding was a copy of my father created by the Mirror of Silence. That spoke to the quality of the copy. It would eat, complain, sleep, shave, and it would last for months. To every sense, it was real.

"Most can't tell the difference," my father said around his cigarette.

"I can." I looked up to the barrier the other ships had finished drawing in the sky. "And you know I could take that seal apart."

He grunted. "No one knows what you can do. Not even me."

"I don't want to break a clone you put so much work into, but I'm a little on edge. I just survived an attempt on my life, you see."

"Who do you think was responsible?"

I gave him a dead-eyed stare. "Are we friendly enough to be joking?"

He withdrew the cigarette from his mouth and tapped ash onto the ground. "It wasn't me. It was everyone else in the galaxy."

I could interpret that statement in a number of different ways, but none I liked. "You know you're going to have to explain that."

He beckoned me up the ramp. The guards split apart to allow me to pass, though I didn't move yet.

Taking my compliance for granted, my father turned back to Director Porellus. "You'll have to excuse me, Director. I'd like a moment with my son."

"Of course, take your time! I'm sure you have a lot to catch up on." He hesitated. "Ah, if that barrier is up when the Galactic Union investigator arrives..."

My father dropped his cigarette and ground it out beneath his foot. "I am the investigator appointed to this incident." With a tap of the console on his arm, he projected his credentials onto the air. "On behalf of the Galactic Union, I'd like to ask you and everyone in the Magic Tower to stay put until our investigation can conclude."

"Of...of course." I could see the wheels in Porellus' head creaking to life as he tried to figure out the implications of a major corporate executive being deputized to handle Galactic Union security.

For my part, I was trying to figure out whether to enter the ship or not.

Disappearing right there appealed to me. That would show that he couldn't hook me. I couldn't be baited with curiosity, I couldn't be trapped by his barriers, and I wouldn't follow his orders.

Then again, I did want to know what he had to say.

And vanishing from inside the ship would be a stronger slap to the face.

I walked up the ramp, past the respectful guards and into the cargo bay. The entire interior of the starship was the epitome of pointless luxury: real wood furnishings, paintings of oil and canvas, priceless liquors from a hundred worlds encased behind display glass and invisible security fields.

I made my way to my father's favorite meeting-room, which he called the Lodge.

A chandelier of bones hung overhead, holding candles of wax and real flame. There was no melted wax; the candle-flames were sustained magically, but the effect looked very genuine. The same could be said for the merrily burning fireplace to one side. The fire roared on real logs, but the logs were never burned up, and there was only enough smoke for a pleasant campfire smell. The stone chimney was entirely unnecessary.

While the whole ship was an ostentatious display of wealth, this was the kind of magic I appreciated. It was purely aesthetic, with no point other than to look impressive.

Magic should be magical.

The heads of various beasts were mounted on the wall over the fireplace. Those displays had initially been empty, and my father filled them in one by one as he hunted trophy game on several different worlds by himself.

The room wasn't terribly large, and the effect was cozy. Without temperature regulation magic, the fire would have made the room unbearably hot. I pulled up a plush chair and sat, waiting for my father.

I fully expected him to make me wait, but he strode in only a moment later and took a seat across from me. Without a pause, he projected a picture.

For an instant, my thoughts froze.

The photo showed a report from the Corporate Subline. The headline was very simple. '*Varic Vallenar Wins Zenith Starship.*'

I scanned the report quickly, but I didn't need to read the details. Horizon had invited every qualified individual in the galaxy to compete for the crew, so I had known that her existence would become common knowledge.

Obviously, one of those people had figured out who I was. I just didn't see how.

Unless Horizon had done something—which I couldn't dis-count—only four people in the galaxy should have known who the Captain of *The Last Horizon* was.

Someone had painted a target on my back.

This must have been another reason the students had been so eager to hear my last lesson.

"I gather that was the ship you just pulled out of nowhere," my father said.

I didn't have to nod. "When was this?"

"Eighteen hours ago. We've been keeping an eye on the treas-ure hunt in Karoshan space, but not because we expected them to find anything."

I rubbed my temples. "How were they so fast?" I'd only been in control of *The Last Horizon* for a standard day.

"That's the other thing." My father projected another file into the air, this one a video showing the man in black who had attacked me earlier. Omega was laughing as he blasted the door off a locked hangar and strode to a ship. Alarms were blaring, and armed guards swarmed him. They seemed to recognize Omega, because they hes-itated before firing.

"Don't worry, don't worry!" Omega said in the video, his voice scratchy and distant from the microphone. *"You can pick up your ship at the Magic Tower when I'm done with it. I'm not stealing your ship, I'm stealing Varic Vallenar's ship."*

My father sneered at the video. "He told everyone who would listen. After he left in that ship, he broadcast your name over the local planetary Subline. But I would pay a significant price to know how he found out in the first place."

Omega had come after me, thinking he could kill me and take my ship. That lined up with what I knew of the man.

When I summoned the ship for help, I'd confirmed that he was correct. Now he knew for sure that *The Last Horizon* was active and under my control. As did the Magic Tower, the Galactic Union, and my father.

So everyone.

My father watched the thoughts cross my face. "You shouldn't have played the ship yet. You could have taken care of him yourself."

To defeat him myself, I would have had to risk my life. His magic-piercing gun had already ruined my shield amulet, which I would have to repair. That was closer to vulnerable than I ever wanted to be again.

But instead of saying that, I took his bait. "And how do you know that?"

"There's a darker side to corporate competition than you've ever experienced." That was laughably untrue in some of my previous lives, but I kept a straight face.

My father threw up more images of the grinning man, both before and after he had a patch of steel surrounding his Aethertech eye. "Founder of the Escalon Company, a mid-level corporation. Made himself an unstoppable force, trying to climb up to join the greats, but he played too rough. Responsible for some nasty massacres. His family keeps him on a tight leash. Usually."

I acted as though this was new information, though I knew more than my father's file did.

The Vallenar Corporation hired Omega in every one of my memories, but I never worked too closely with him. He disgusted me.

"So you've hired him before," I summarized. "But not this time."

My father pulled some speck from his suit and tossed it into the fire. "I don't want you dead."

"You paid Director Porellus off, and he kept Tower security busy."

"I asked him to keep an eye on you, and that was expensive. Omega paid him to hold the door open for your assassination." He paused in consideration. "Although he may have done that for free."

That was entirely possible.

"Thank you for the information." I pushed away from the table. "I have an unknown number of enemies, at least one of whom figured out who I was almost immediately. Sounds like I ought to get back to my ship."

"Sit down."

I straightened my mantle and adjusted my wand, waiting for him to rethink that statement.

"*Please* sit down. We still have business to discuss." He projected a contract in front of me. "Generous terms. Round-the-clock protection, limited requirements, and the best media manipulation and information security money can buy. All I want is your cooperation. And a chance to study your new ship."

I *was* tempted, but only because it was easy to give up control. I could return to the Corporation and they would take care of everything. If only because it was in their best interests to do so.

I would be safe. I could relax.

"I'm worried about the hidden costs," I said, without reading the contract.

My father drummed his fingers on the table. Just as I had done, annoyingly enough. "You've cost us several fortunes lately. Our position in the market has become precarious. We need you back."

That was his answer as a businessman, and it astonished me. I never thought he'd admit that I had caused him trouble, much less that he needed me to get out of it.

I felt an unknown kind of nerves as I anticipated what he was about to say. His next move would be to appeal to me as a father.

"I can't say you're still young. Your body is, but in a way, you've lived more than I have. But you have more potential now than anyone else in the galaxy. No one can bring it out like we can, and I can't stand to see it wasted." He looked wistful, all of a sudden, staring off into space as though watching what could have been.

"Imagine what we could do with *The Last Horizon*. We wouldn't have to settle for just taking down the other Corporations. The Galactic Union, the Karoshan Alliance...we could shape the entire *galaxy*."

I expected nothing from this man, and I was still let down.

"Even you on your own! We completed the greatest ritual the universe has ever seen, and you've used it to steal from me. That's nothing, it's forgotten, but think what you could do with our resources behind you." His eyes had come alive, and his hands gestured expressively. He was never so passionate, awake, and *himself* as when he was discussing business.

"I know you care about the magic," he continued. "Your rebirth could be just the beginning. Don't let your personal feelings stop you from taking mankind further than we've ever gone before."

"I won't, Ben," I said. Then I looked to the ceiling. "Take me back."

In a blue flash, I vanished.

That would really get him.

CHAPTER TWENTY-SIX

THERE WAS A containment room on the lower decks of *The Last Horizon*.

"Lower decks" was relative, of course. Horizon could shift around the ship's internal structure almost at a whim. And since I had only commanded the ship for about two days, I had hardly scratched the surface of its potential.

Omega, the assassin who called himself the Grave Hound, was locked inside a glass cylinder. He had a bench inside, but he had pressed his hands against the glass and was apparently enjoying the feeling.

"What is this *magic?*" he asked, in the tones of a delighted child.

He was at least a hundred and fifty standard years old, but he slid his palms up and down the glass with unrestrained abandon. "I can't find any gaps at *all*. I thought I'd be flying this ship by now, but you've got me dead to rights."

Another arm sprouted from his back and slapped its palm against the glass. Another followed.

Raion wore a nauseous look. "I hate it when the monsters look like people."

"What else would we look like?" Omega asked curiously.

"Giant insects, mostly."

Sola did not seem fazed. She held a tablet and checked her notes. "Omal Escalon. We'll accommodate your requests if you tell us who told you how to find us."

"No, no, no, that's not my name!" He grinned into the glass and his cybernetic eye flared orange.

She stepped up until her nose was almost touching the cell. "If you aren't useful, I can't see a reason to keep you."

A hand slapped the glass an inch from her face, but she didn't flinch. An eye sprouted on the inside of the palm, scanning her reaction, and then Omega peeked his face around the other side. "Even I have some manners. How would I ever get business again if I betrayed my employers?" He turned his grin onto me. "Or if I let my target get away?"

I leaned further back into my levitation ring. I had been sitting there for quite some time, watching. And thinking.

My personal knowledge of Omega was limited. I was aware of his capabilities, but I could only remember catching a glimpse or two of the man beneath the psychotic mask.

I floated closer to Omega, then drifted upward so I was sitting with my eye level at the same height as his.

"You like this ship?" I asked.

"Oh, *yes*." He slowly ran his tongue up the inside of the containment cell. "It's *delicious*."

If he was trying to throw us off with a disquieting display, he had picked the wrong audience. Sola spent her time dismantling the Iron Legion, so she had a stomach stronger than her suit. I had seen ends of the galaxy he couldn't imagine. And Raion…

Raion made a retching sound and looked away.

At least two-thirds of us were the wrong audience.

Although Raion had spent most of his career dissecting moon-sized insectoid creatures. He had flown spacecraft through literal oceans of gore. Was he really that weak to humanoid monsters?

"If you cooperate, I can split the ship with you," I said. "You have the personal ability, and there are three seats still open."

Sola and Raion both looked to me, but Sola nodded after only a moment. Her calculation would be simple.

Was he an asset against the Iron Legion? If so, he was welcome.

Raion looked horrified. "No! Absolutely...*yech*, no. He will eat us."

Omega looked almost as delighted as Raion was disgusted. Even his left eye had widened, and given that it was an Aethertech prosthetic embedded into a metal frame, I was curious how it did that.

"You're a brave man, Captain. A brave, brave man, to risk being devoured in your sleep."

"Horizon," I said, "can we add stipulations to a crew contract?"

The ship's voice came from everywhere. *"We can add any conditions you wish, but the crewman must knowingly agree to be bound."*

"Then I have conditions, Omega. We'll try you out for three months, under a contract that prevents you from harming or betraying us. If we're satisfied with you by the end, you'll have the chance to officially join the crew. But first, you answer a few questions for me."

Omega held his chin in one hand and looked deep in thought, but a mass of shadow crept up the side of the containment chamber. A mouth sprouted within it. "What questions?" it asked, in Omega's voice.

I projected a picture of the video my father had shown me into midair. Omega walking into a hangar to steal a starship.

"You aren't captured on camera very often, are you?"

A host of mouths laughed in eerie chorus, then began chattering among one another. "Oooohhh, that's a good question."

"I like that question."

"Fun...this smells like fun..."

The loudest voice answered: "I am not."

"All right, then." I leaned forward. "If I survived your attack, did your informant expect me to go with my father...or not?"

The extra mouths embedded in shadow continued to smile, but Omega's actual face looked uncharacteristically serious. He responded soberly. "He did not share his intentions with me, you understand. But if I might speculate: I think it didn't matter one way or the other."

I nodded and deactivated my levitation ring, landing on the floor. "Thank you, Omega. Agree to the contract and I'll give you a tryout."

A blue, glowing contract appeared next to Omega's face, but he didn't look at it. "Not now, Captain, not now. I need time to think. You understand."

"Think..." his mouths said. They all echoed it. "Think... think...think..."

Raion shuddered.

I patted the glass. "You've got all the time in the world."

As soon as we were out of the room, I glanced over to Sola. "Keep him contained for the next three days. If it looks like he'll escape, vent the entire container into space."

"That's not necessary," Horizon said. She sounded offended. *"I would never allow him to escape."*

I didn't have any proof for my next assumption, but I made it anyway. "The prison isn't complete yet, is it?"

The ship spirit made a sound like a nervous cough. *"Some of my facilities are more...limited...without an Engineer, but I assure you, I can take care of him."*

Sola looked more uncomfortable now than she had facing Omega in the first place. "I'll watch him, but if you think he might escape, we shouldn't keep him onboard."

"You might be right."

Raion scratched the side of his head. "So why aren't we ejecting him now?"

"You're more bloodthirsty than I thought," I said.

"I have no problem killing monsters."

I clapped him on the shoulder. "I wouldn't lose any sleep over it either, but he knows things we don't. Besides, we don't have to keep him locked up for long."

I didn't have the brainpower left to put into Omega. I was thinking about my father. "Horizon, you didn't tell anyone that I was your Captain, did you?"

"No one you didn't tell. Although I never intended to keep it a secret."

"That's what I thought." I continued striding down the corridor.

Raion clapped his hands together. "Alright, then. You learned something. Where are we going?"

"We're going to pretend to save my father's life."

CHAPTER TWENTY-SEVEN

SOMEONE HAD FIGURED out I was the Captain of *The Last Horizon* almost immediately after it happened.

They had told Omega, who had spread that information far and wide, literally shouting it on camera as he stole a starship to come after me. Presumably, this *someone* had told other people as well.

Why? Just to make things hard for me?

Or to get me to meet with my father?

Omega's reaction to my questions had all but confirmed to me that his mysterious informant had predicted I would meet with my father after the assassination attempt. That wasn't too difficult of a prediction, for someone who knew enough to send Omega after me in the first place.

My father, upon hearing that I had claimed *The Last Horizon*, would spare no expense in reaching me. He would immediately try to get me to join him, so he could benefit from the Zenith Starship.

Meanwhile, anyone could predict that I would go to the Vallenar Corporation for help after I was attacked. Not long ago, I had been in the news for fighting against an Iron Legion Hive on the company's side. That was just propaganda, but most didn't know that.

So this *someone* was perfectly willing to see me killed by Omega, and knew that I would meet with my father if I survived. In that case, there were only two possibilities: I'd either fly back with the Vallenar ships or leave with *The Last Horizon*.

Either way, they had a clear next move: attack my father.

If I was with the ship, great, we could fight it out and they would have a chance to take Horizon for themselves. If I wasn't, they could use my father as a hostage against me.

I didn't know who this person was. Scanning my previous memories, I couldn't think of anyone who had so much knowledge of me, had a grudge to settle, and would still act so indirectly.

But they were missing a few key pieces of information.

First, they couldn't know anything about my previous lives. Second, they didn't know my father was just a copy made by the Mirror of Silence, and thus useless as a hostage. If I hadn't been an Archmage of that spell, I wouldn't have been able to tell.

Finally, they didn't know what Horizon was capable of.

We had a chance to catch them.

The Last Horizon's scanners hadn't been upgraded yet, so I had to supplement them with pathfinding spells. It was a patchwork solution, but it was enough to let us watch my father's ships from the bridge of *The Last Horizon*.

We lurked just outside the system, far enough that both my spells and Horizon's scanners were stretching their range. Our monitor showed only hazy spots of light tagging the Sunsail ship locations.

"Have you found anything?" I asked again. Horizon stood with her eyes closed next to me, arms spread. She was casting her own magic, conjuring eyeballs that floated through space and covered for our lacking scanners.

"*Subspace distortion,*" she responded. "*Video in three... two...one...now.*"

A grainy, flickering image appeared on the screen. Half a dozen black, well-armed battle cruisers popped out of Subspace. They looked like the sorts of ships you could get anywhere, repurposed commercial models painted black. Horizon conjured an eye outside one ship, which quickly blinked out of existence.

Raion cheered. "All right, let's go! We'll teach them to sneak up on us!"

They weren't sneaking up on *us,* just on my father, which I couldn't blame them for. Nonetheless, my heart raced. This was our chance to get a step ahead of a hidden enemy.

"Just a moment." I adjusted the strap carrying my staff and checked my protection amulet. I had patched it together enough to function in an emergency, but I didn't intend to rely on it until I could do real repairs. "Let's wait until they're out of range of the Magic Tower."

I wanted my father to know he was in danger before I saved him. Not only might that help me in future negotiations, but it would give the enemy a chance to play any hidden pieces. I didn't want to engage too early, only to find that they had an entire fleet as backup.

Besides, this was just a copy of my father. His destruction was far from the worst-case scenario.

The classic-style Sunsail ships began to lift off from the Magic Tower, and I knew they had detected the incoming cruisers. My father's ship was the last to leave.

"Now?" Raion asked.

The Vallenar ships lifted off, and the enemy battle cruisers began charging their weapons.

"It has to be now," Raion said.

Shields rippled as the cruisers fired the first volley of plasma cannons. If they had any more forces to commit, they wouldn't do it until we forced them to.

"We're going to be late!"

I nodded to Horizon. "Now," I said.

We both vanished.

We appeared floating in the void of space. Raion was wearing his crimson armor, helmet covering his face, while I was surrounded by the magic of my mantle, but it was still strange and frightening to watch the flashy exchange of starships in battle all around us.

At least, it was frightening for me.

Raion struck a pose with his scarlet force-blade, then he blasted forward on a stream of energy. I knew the cruiser he'd targeted was taken care of, and probably the one next to it, so I focused on the three closer to the moon.

The Corporation's Sunsail ships drifted just out of the atmosphere, the Magic Tower a silver spire beneath. Black battle-cruisers flanked them, preventing the Sunsails from getting far enough away to dive to Subspace.

Droplets of water manifested around me at the movements of my wand. My incantation called different power from the Aether. Navigational spells locked onto the position of three cruisers, which was difficult enough to do with precision.

I experienced the spells as circles in my vision, which moved faster than I could track as they traced the movement of the black cruisers. I locked those spells in place, then held out my wand.

I had one insurmountable advantage: the cruisers didn't see me as a target. They probably didn't see me at all.

It's not hard to defeat an enemy with his back turned.

The navigation spells chimed as all three targets reached a point where I could hit them without causing collateral damage to the moon below. With my wand, I directed tides of water that dwarfed me, focusing them into beams of destruction.

Three of the cruisers were struck by my elementalism, but these weren't fighters or Hunter-ships. They were warships. Their standard cruiser-class shields were backed up by a suite of defensive spells laid by experienced mages.

Their shields shone red-hot along the trails where water had struck. None of the three took the hit on their hulls, but one manifested a huge spectral symbol that disenchanted the water only an instant after my element had hit them.

There.

I mentally marked that cruiser with my processor. Someone with *real* magic was aboard that cruiser, and my stomach tightened at the thought. This was either the person who was after me or at least our strongest link to them.

I sent the location to Raion, who acknowledged. Judging by the crimson flashes, he was having a great time.

Now I had given up the advantage of stealth, as three cruisers had marked my position. Pathfinder spells showed me where they were changing flight paths so they wouldn't leave themselves open to elementalism again.

But the battle had already flipped.

Not only was Raion engaging the other three—in fact, one of the enemies was shooting out escape pods—but the Vallenar Corporation ships weren't standing idle.

The battle-cruiser shields I had damaged were now dangerously unstable, and plasma cannons from the three galleon-style Sunsails focused on the cruisers with compromised shields.

The commander of the battle-cruisers, who might have been my hidden enemy, was decisive. Only a moment after the battle turned, they made a bold decision.

They began backing up, screening one another to cover their retreat. There were only five ships left, but it would be hard for us to stop them from leaving.

At any moment, they would make a Subspace dive.

They thought.

When I first saw the twist of Subspace, I unleashed the other spells I had been chanting.

Focused through my wand, white spell-circles erupted into being around the enemy's starship. He tore one of them apart, but he must not have been as skilled as I thought, because three others landed.

Those binding-spells struck his Subspace Drive...and then he completed his dive. Reality twisted, and all five surviving ships slipped into Subspace.

Only an instant later, there came an eye-twisting explosion of unnatural color, and the leader's ship came spinning back into reality. It was dark, out of control, spewing gas and debris as it tumbled through space.

I had timed my seals well.

The mage's ship was now a few thousand miles away, but it was crippled and dark. Raion came to pick me up—literally grabbing me by the collar—and flew over to one of the Vallenar Corporation ships.

It let us in the airlock, of course, and my father greeted us with a scowl. "What a stupid ambush. If I had been the real one, I would have had a bigger escort within diving distance."

"We still don't know what they're after," I reminded him. "So let's find out."

Our ship caught up to the enemy's in a matter of minutes.

A Vallenar Corporation boarding crew went inside. I didn't go, obviously. That would have been a stupid risk.

But I did send Raion, just in case. If the entire ship was rigged to explode, Raion would still make it out. Besides, he wanted to go.

My father and I waited in his Lodge in complete silence. We were together, but we each stewed in our worries alone.

Those worries grew worse with each passing second, though I could see the feed from a camera drone following Raion. Why hadn't they run into any traps? The crew surrendered immediately, and I saw nothing suspicious. The power core had been ravaged by the forced ejection from Subspace, but there were no bombs. No desperate plays or guerilla tactics.

Every second, I was growing more confused. This couldn't be it.

Finally, there was a scuffle of action. It wasn't clear at all, to the point where my father muttered in frustration as he watched the console over my shoulder.

I switched to the feeds of other drones, but it only looked like Raion tearing apart a wall to grab something that worked to escape. Of all things, it looked like him fishing with his bare hands.

Triumphantly, he pulled something out and held it up to the camera.

"Got it!" he said. "What do you think, Varic? I've never seen one of these before. Should we ask Sola?"

I couldn't speak.

"Worlds protect us," my father muttered.

It was a creation of the Iron Legion.

A long, crimson staff with a red-stained eye on the end. While it was hideous to look at, the staff was obviously the focus of a powerful wizard. Or it had been. Someone had perverted it, and it wasn't hard to guess who.

Raw pink-white ligaments twisted around the staff like a snake around a branch, and those tendrils reached out to nearby surfaces. Even the staff's shaft twisted slightly, suggesting some of its material had been replaced. Woven into the flesh was an organic, semi-liquid metal that gleamed like steel.

Sola may have seen something like this in a Hive before, but I didn't need to know anything more. There *was* someone who had tracked me landing on the planet and then *The Last Horizon* leaving: the Iron Legion.

I had discounted them because the Legion didn't act like that. They could be cunning, but they didn't share intelligence. They didn't hire assassins. They didn't set complex traps that relied on their knowledge of human relationships.

Not unless they had a leader.

"Horizon, bring us back!" I called.

My father looked suddenly excited, but he didn't interrupt.

"Horizon! Recall!"

I heard only silence.

CHAPTER TWENTY-EIGHT

IN HER ARMOR, Sola kept the live feed of Omega's prison streaming into a corner of her visor. Even with an ability to slip through Subspace, Omega could never escape. She suspected Varic was being paranoid.

Sola approved of paranoia. When you were dealing with enemies, there was no such thing as too careful. Just keeping him aboard the ship was the maximum amount of risk she was willing to tolerate.

In the meantime, she worked on one of the ship's consoles, engaging in her favorite hobby: tracking Iron Hives.

She had reports coming in from the Galactic Union, the Karoshan Alliance, and a dozen corporations and private sources. Most of them weren't supposed to be selling information to her, but everyone hired the Fallen Sword because everyone knew she only had one goal.

Sola had no intention of selling information to their rivals. She would use what she learned for one purpose, and one purpose only. She knew the Iron Legion better than anyone.

Which led to her current confusion.

The Legion rarely had what anyone could call a 'strategy.' An Iron King was terrifyingly intelligent, but those were rare over the entire course of galactic history. Usually, the Legion was controlled by Bishops, whose only goal was to maintain and propagate the Legion. They rarely tried to take over civilized territory, content with the life-supporting planets scattered throughout Dark Space.

But now, Hives had been moved throughout the border of the Galactic Union. Iron Hives were pulled out of systems that had only been half-conquered, others were cut off from support and thus sacrificed. They were being moved into position for something, but Sola couldn't tell what. She was a warrior on a crusade, not a strategist.

She tapped the console with an armored finger and kept her information displayed. "Horizon, what do you make of this?"

The spirit manifested her humanoid avatar next to Sola in a swirl of three-colored light. *"Oh my. I thought the Captain was somewhat premature in wanting to eliminate the Iron Legion, but I suppose he was a step behind."*

"Explain," Sola commanded. The cold fires of her hatred burned in her chest. She knew the nightmare of civilian ships captured by the Legion, and the Bishops going to war would be such horrors visited on the entire galaxy.

The maps and data left on the screen began to rotate according to Horizon's will, and the spirit pointed to it.

"It becomes clearer when viewed from this angle. They are forming the shaft of a spear." Spots lit up here and there along the way as Horizon highlighted relevant Hives. *"They cover one another to support a thrust deep into the galaxy. The Galactic Union, if I may take a guess."*

She seemed pleased, seven-pointed eyes dancing. Sola burned with fear and anger. "They're taking orders."

"Yes...yes, it seems they are." Horizon's face stretched into a wild grin. *"How fortunate for us."*

The spirit of *The Last Horizon* suddenly seemed alien. Even hostile, though it wasn't directed at Sola. Nonetheless, the Fallen Sword summoned a gun.

"What do you know?"

"I know that great enemies make great heroes," Horizon said in delight. *"I believe that a war against the Iron Legion is the perfect chance to show off my new Sword. And I suspect that this iron kingdom finally has its long-awaited King."*

That sent a chill down Sola's spine. She stood up. "Send me to the Union. I will warn them."

"Calm yourself. We have time. The spear still needs a head." The data on the screen rotated until they were looking into Dark Space.

There, they saw only a black fog.

"The Grand Hive, fortress of the last Iron King to mature, over four centuries ago. He…hmmm." Horizon stopped and tapped her lips. *"My scanners are not what they will be once we have a full crew, but I should be able to see further than this. Normally, there is a veil only over the Grand Hive itself, not the whole system."*

Sola tilted her visor toward the spirit. "Who is he hiding from?"

Hiding an entire star system like that would cost exponentially more than hiding only one planet. If an Iron King had indeed made it to the Grand Hive, he would power a spell like this only for short times.

And who would be looking besides *The Last Horizon* itself?

Horizon opened her mouth to speak, paused, and shut it again. Magical eyes swirled behind her as she frowned in deep thought.

"…perhaps we should exercise a little caution," the spirit allowed. *"I'm not at full strength yet, after all."*

From within her helmet, Sola gave Horizon a hard stare.

Horizon's projection rippled with light, and the entire ship thrummed with energy. *"I have used sealing magic to protect us in Subspace. To be safe, I will recall Varic and Raion."*

There was a pause, then Horizon began to shift nervously in place. *"They…don't seem to hear me."*

Sola immediately started moving off the bridge, boots clomping with every step.

"My teleportation has been blocked beyond this system," Horizon continued, drifting along with Sola. *"Magic of this scale can only be preparation for an attack."*

The door slid out of Sola's way as she marched into the hallway. "Do we have our Subspace Drive?"

"I'm afraid not." On the monitors all around the bridge, Sola saw weapons emerging all around *The Last Horizon.* *"Many of my functions are restricted without a complete crew, but I do have shields and a full complement of weapons. We cannot flee through Subspace, but we can perhaps destroy enough of them to weaken their magic and call the Captain."*

"Good." She pulled up the Worldslayer in her inventory, its image floating on the inside of her visor, but she didn't summon it yet. "If we find the King's location, I want a shot."

Horizon's scowl slowly melted into a vicious, predatory smile. *"How wonderful. The adventure has delivered itself to us."*

In the corner of Sola's vision, she saw Omega lying back on his bench and grinning with half a dozen mouths.

The real Benri Vallenar knelt in the presence of the Iron King.

The newly reborn leader of the Iron Legion floated in the center of a nest of wires made of both metal and meat. Ten feet tall, the equal of most Karoshans, he was a masterwork blending of flesh and steel. The rest of the Legion's creations were but prototypes before his perfection.

Steel composed his form as though poured over a muscled human body. His eyes were burning portals of magical flame, and his skull was made of unbreakable glass. The brain within was visible, but larger than any human organ, and set with flickering sparks as though the firing of his neurons generated visible light.

The King himself hovered on a flow of Aether that was tiny next to the incomprehensible rivers he directed throughout the Legion. He hung suspended in air, a nexus of endless energy.

Benri paid attention to the patterns, to the sound, to the *feel* of the Aether rushing through the air. Every detail could be critical.

Technically, he had been kidnapped, but he could still find

something to turn to his advantage. They had guaranteed his safety, after all.

The King of the Iron Legion turned fiery eyes to him and spoke in a mechanical drone. "Are you ready to give yourself to the embrace of the Iron Legion? To shed worthless flesh?"

Benri's skin chilled. This was everything he had been afraid of. Even with a magical contract, he should never have trusted the king of the body-stealing zombies for a second.

He spent a moment trying to dig up the right words, but the King's face of flesh and metal cracked in a grin, revealing chrome teeth. "Just a little hive-mind humor for you there, human. Relax."

Benri let out a breath. "You'll forgive me if I don't laugh."

"You'd have more fun if you did." The King hummed as he swayed on his nest of wires and Aether, his fingers dancing as he conducted his invisible symphony. "*This* is real fun. I wish I could share it with you. I am the Ortullian kresk-spider, and the stars are my web. It's like...what games did you play, where you came from?"

"I grew up with simulated training exercises."

"Yikes. If your father wasn't dead already, I'd kill him for you. You're missing out. You can play games on a computer, and sometimes you control armies against another player, who also has their own—"

"I understand the concept."

The King shrugged. "I can't keep track of what humans understand. It's hard enough limiting myself to audible speech. Anyway, *this* is like playing a thousand games at once, each slightly different, with the universe itself as your opponent. A never-ending, perfect game." He shivered. "I'll try to give you a glimpse, but I don't want to fry your brain."

Benri didn't want a glimpse, not from someone who couldn't remember the threshold of human tolerance. "First, I hope you don't mind if I ask you what I'm doing here."

The Iron King's face went blank in disbelief, which was impressive considering that it was made of metal. "Was it not obvious? I want you to help me take your son's ship."

"What?"

He couldn't mean *Moonfall*. The Iron Legion wasn't so lacking in starships that it would need one particular scout frigate.

The King tapped his chin thoughtfully, which let out a small plink of metal on metal. "Interesting. You didn't know. That tells me more than you might imagine about how far information had dispersed at the time of your capture. Thank you. Anyway, your son Varic has been recognized as Captain of *The Last Horizon*."

Benri had to process that last sentence several times before it made any sense to him. "The Zenith Starship?"

"The very same."

Benri's first reaction was annoyance. His son had beaten him to another priceless artifact, this time before Benri had heard about it. He strongly suspected Varic was doing this on purpose.

Second, Benri's thoughts moved to all the ways he could profit from this. Naturally, there were more options if Varic cooperated, but even if he didn't...

The Iron King interrupted his musings. "All the Zenith Devices work according to highly specific rules. A stipulation of their great power. *The Last Horizon* accepts only six crew members, with whom it has a symbiotic relationship. I intend to capture the ship and use its power for the Legion. I would like your help."

Another chill passed through Benri's body, though he tried to hide it. This was it. Small and shriveled his conscience may have been, but he didn't want to see a Zenith Device in the hands of the Iron Legion.

While he was trying to formulate a refusal that didn't end with him in eternal servitude, the Iron King snapped to get his attention.

"Hear me out, before you jump to any conclusions. The behavior of the Iron Legion you've seen up to now, that's what they act like *without* a leader. Mindlessly devouring and replicating to propagate their own existence."

The King waved a hand. "I have no interest in that. I don't want to kill and resurrect the entire galaxy. That's no fun. I want to own it."

Benri suspected there would be little distinction between those two things in the eyes of the humans who would become his Pawns. "Your endgame is galactic domination?"

"Don't dismiss it. That's a more difficult goal than you realize. There's a lot of competition in this game. After that..." The King looked off into the distance, and lights flashed inside his glass braincase. "...I suspect there will be much more interesting games to come."

Benri took a breath and mustered his courage. "I cannot see myself willingly engaging in any operation that ends with me giving up my mind."

The Iron King gave him another blank look. "What? Didn't I just...I really can't keep track of what you do and don't understand. You're an Archmage with a unique magic, and your son is a *real* masterpiece. What good would either of you be as mindless trophies?"

"Then what are you offering?" Benri asked. He still expected to be executed at any second, magical contract or not.

"A partnership. Crew positions on *The Last Horizon* for you and me, and Varic can keep his."

The Iron King conjured a hexagram out of pink-and-orange flame. "The simple solution would have been to kill Varic and take his place, but there's a security measure in the ship's magic to prevent that. When the Captain dies, *The Last Horizon* goes dormant again, so it's more convenient to keep him around. I'll fill the other seats, but between the two of you, the Vallenar family will control a third of the Zenith Starship. Good deal, right?"

"I doubt Varic will accept that deal," Benri said.

The Varic from before the ritual might have, but Benri hardly knew his son anymore.

The Iron King winked, which was especially disturbing with his burning eyes. "His compliance is not a factor. He won't agree, so why waste time on negotiations?"

"Because we need him. He'll still be the Captain, won't he?"

"Oh, that won't be a problem. Trust me." A magical contract, written in flame, unfurled behind the Iron King. Benri inspected it, just as he had the previous one, to find that its contents were exactly as the King had said.

"So, do we have a deal?" the Iron King asked.

And as he had before, Benri hesitated. "Do I have a choice?"

"Of course. But I doubt you'll enjoy your other option."

Benri didn't ask what that option was. He didn't want to know.

For the second time, Benri Vallenar signed a deal with the Iron Legion. At least this time, he could see what he had to gain.

If he was forced to play this role, he might as well play it well. "What's the status of the starship?"

"Cornered like a beast." The King's steel grin grew wider. "She's looking forward to this as much as I am, I'm sure. It's not a game without the risk you might lose."

Benri adjusted his tie. "I have every confidence you'll win."

"Don't look at it that way! You'll ruin it! No, we *might* lose this one. And the next one. And the next one and the next one andthenextoneandthenext*oneandthenextoneandthenextone*—"

The Iron King's voice went faster and faster until his lips were blurred and his voice was a high-pitched whine. The air took on a charge, and the hairs on Benri's arms lifted. The King's eyes were blazing so hot they were about to burn the air outside his skull.

"—AND THE NEXT ONE!" he shouted at last, then he capped off his rant with insane laughter. "And then? We'll *win*." The leader of the Iron Legion extended a chrome-plated hand. "But, you know, in some ways I'm only a few days old. Let's make my first round a good one."

Very reluctantly, Benri grasped the King's hand.

A glimpse of the Iron Legion's transcendent vision flashed through his mind. Just for an instant, he saw a fraction of what the King did.

Billions of eyes, maybe trillions, all over the galaxy. Armies, commanders, living beasts, spies, and parasites all reported back to their King. Uncountable computer-enhanced brains fed information to the Legion, and the King directed it all.

If anything, he had understated himself.

Every twitch of his finger conquered a world. He increased the production of a mining planet to prepare for a war fifty years from now. He threw entire Hives into suicide missions in Galactic Union territory to increase pressure on political opponents. He failed in one place to succeed in two others, all the while feeding victories to his enemies so they would underestimate his troops.

It was a dance the width of the galaxy, and Benri thought his eyes would bleed. If he'd been less than an Archmage, his consciousness would have collapsed.

Then the vision reduced, so that he was *only* focused on one fleet. *Only* seeing the width of a star system at once. He felt his body again, his breathing heavy with relief.

"Fun, isn't it?" the King murmured.

Now Benri saw the ships encircling *The Last Horizon,* felt them choking the system. Their distribution was pure elegance, their capabilities a perfectly interlocking crystal lattice of success. He marveled at the Iron King's foresight.

And he saw what the King wanted from him. It wasn't just his connection to Varic; the Iron King never did anything for only one reason.

He wanted the Mirror of Silence.

Benri released his magic to the Legion king's control.

Even among Archmage spells, the Mirror of Silence was considered a masterpiece. It brought shadows of potential to life, multiplying resources. In theory, there was nothing he couldn't clone for a time. He and Varic had proven that together.

But their ritual had been nothing compared to what the Iron King could do.

At his heart, the King was a mage. He had one signature magic: the ability to channel, augment, and control the powers of others.

So when the Iron Legion received the Mirror of Silence, its King expanded the spell a million times.

One encircling fleet became two, three, four. From a thousand perspectives, Benri looked down on *The Last Horizon.*

"Hope you're ready, Ben," the Iron King said through a metallic grin. "Time to pick up our new ship."

CHAPTER TWENTY-NINE

BESIDE SOLA, HORIZON'S projected body stiffened. *"Something has changed,"* the ship's spirit said.

Sola didn't need to be told that. She could see the approaching formation of Hunter-ships spontaneously multiply, rows upon rows of silver teeth closing on them like jaws.

"The King is sending Hunters after us," she said. Her grip tightened with the effort it took not to summon the Worldslayer. "That means he *isn't here.*"

She'd never faced an Iron King personally, but she knew everything there was to know about the Iron Legion. The King was borrowing the magic of someone or something and using it to empower his troops. His attention in other areas would weaken, but he would surely win here.

Unless she and Horizon could do something about it.

She slid into the command chair and began pulling up reports. "Give me tactical information." She had to know where she could do the most damage.

"Incoming!" the spirit shouted.

A moment later, the ship shook. The black-and-white ghost of a Hunter-ship materialized next to them, crashing into their shields.

Scarlet plasma-blades shredded a second, and a third crashed into a giant human hand made of blue magic.

Horizon's jaw tightened and she raised her horned head. Seven-pointed eyes glowed red, green, and blue. Sola could *feel* the rage of the ship's wounded pride.

Outside, eyes and hands manifested, spotting ships and swatting them down. On the monitors, Sola saw some of the eyes launch lasers while others released flashing spells. Whatever spell the Iron King was using to send ghosts at them, Horizon was matching with magic of her own.

Which was all well and good, but these were just the fighters. There was still a whole fleet left. "Give me weapons control!" Sola demanded.

"I'm afraid you have another priority."

Something in Horizon's voice made Sola flick her vision to the bottom corner of her visor.

Omega was gone.

Adrenaline coursed through her as she rewound the video. A colorless copy of Omega had appeared outside the prison, freeing the original, then disappeared. The Iron King had broken through *The Last Horizon*'s magical defenses and intervened directly to free the prisoner.

Instead of the Worldslayer, Sola summoned her shotgun. "How did he get a spell in here?"

"Please don't tell Varic," Horizon said nervously.

That was enough conversation. "Take care of the fleet," Sola said. "I'll get rid of our guest."

"I'm sorry. I'll make it up to you. If we had an Engineer..." Horizon shook her head. *"No excuses. I will handle the King."*

A new video opened inside Sola's visor. A live feed from the ship hallways tracked Omega's progress.

He was slippery. The red marker indicating his presence kept flitting from one place to another or blurring across multiple rooms at once.

But Sola had him.

She jogged down *The Last Horizon's* smooth halls, every footstep a metallic drumbeat. The lighting flickered between blue, green, and red seemingly at random. It wasn't long before Sola saw panels ripped out, wires torn and magic spluttering. Omega's vandalism.

He couldn't do much from here, but he was working his way deeper into the ship. Eventually, he would be able to do some real damage to Horizon, which would force the ship's spirit to deal with him directly. Taking attention away from the King.

Perhaps Omega was just a distraction, but he was the most annoying kind: one they couldn't afford to ignore.

"I'm shifting him to less-critical systems," Horizon's voice said in Sola's ear. *"But I'll run out of those eventually. And I can't concentrate on both that and…"*

The sentence ended and Horizon didn't continue.

Sola slid to a halt in front of a door. The insistent red beeping on her scanners indicated that Omega was on the other side, as did the sound of tearing metal. Schematics suggested this was a supplementary power room that kept part of the ship running.

It wouldn't be a *disaster* if it were ruined. There were redundant power systems throughout the ship. But its loss would make them more vulnerable to damage from outside.

"Moving in," Sola reported, though Horizon could no doubt see her even as war raged outside. She leveled her shotgun.

Just as she was about to kick the door open, the insistent red light in her visor vanished. Her scanners went quiet.

Sola had spent much of her life inside Iron Hives. When the scanners went quiet, that meant you were caught. This was an ambush.

She leaned the shotgun backwards, over her shoulder, and squeezed the trigger.

Omega caught a blast of plasma-propelled metal as he materialized from Subspace behind her. The middle of his body was splattered all over the wall, half of him reduced to a shivering oil spill.

She raised her gun. "Scavengers always pop out from behind."

She'd actually watched the recording of Varic's fight against Omega, but no need to tell *him* that.

"Get back in the brig," she continued. If he didn't comply, she'd unload on him.

Omega laughed hoarsely. "Oh, but it's so much more fun out *here*."

Sola's scanners screamed a warning, and she threw herself to the side as a gun materialized behind her. A thick barrel the width of a fist. The hand holding it was sticking out of a black pool, and it pulled the trigger instantly.

A wave of orange light clipped her suit, and her visor fuzzed, but nothing the armor couldn't handle.

Until, when her visor cleared, she saw that there was another gun pointed right at her forehead. Omega held it himself, a whole and unharmed human, grinning maniacally.

She twitched to one side, but thunder and pain deafened her. The bullet blasted her shield, tore through her helmet, and ripped off her left ear.

Blood and metal sprayed the wall behind her, and she fell to one side. Omega laughed and said something, stalking down the hallway, but she couldn't hear it.

She was spinning to fire on him already.

Her shotgun tore off a quarter of his body at the shoulder, and he grunted, but it didn't slow him from catching her and grabbing the rest of her helmet with one hand.

He leaned forward to speak into her good ear. "I'm disappointed. I thought this would last longer."

Part of Sola's cheek had been torn off with her ear, and it was hard to speak through the pain and the blood, but she managed. "Good news." She held up the glowing red sphere she'd manifested from her inventory. "Grenade."

In the moment before the explosive went off, he looked genuinely delighted.

Sola manifested back in her room a moment later, restoring from the misty flame of her Pyre. As always, her suit was pristine.

"Do you need help?" Horizon asked through her helmet.

"No." She called her shotgun back.

Sola ran through the halls again, tapping into both her scanners and the ship's internal feed. Omega was hunting for something, and if she could beat him to it, she could trap him.

First, his pattern was strange. He wasn't tearing apart every system he came across, but moved with purpose. Second, a few pieces had gone missing. The core from the secondary power room, turrets from an internal defense system, and a field projector had all been taken.

He was stealing components. Parts for a weapon.

Horizon's map showed her a drone bay, complete with drones capable of anti-ship combat. They were almost useless until the crew was complete, but Omega's current path would put him near there. If he were really looking for weapon parts, that was where he'd stop.

Sola took the elevator.

She made it to the drone bay before Omega. It was a wide-open space for drone assembly and deployment, surrounded by racks where the drones themselves—small round units that glistened like beetles or self-contained helmets—waited, dormant. About half of them had been deployed to the fight around the ship, which suggested Horizon's desperation.

"Horizon, give me drone command," she sent.

Sola was sure the ship heard her, but there was no verbal response. In the next second, Omega appeared out of Subspace.

She greeted him with a shotgun blast.

His head was shredded, but it re-formed immediately from his shadow. His orange eyes, one brighter than the other, blazed above his inhumanly wide smile. "Unkillable! *Perfect!* Two immortals—"

She shot him again.

"—killing each other—"

She blew another chunk out of him.

"—for eternity!"

A grenade hit him in the teeth and then went off.

He disappeared into Subspace as her matter reduction grenade scooped a neat hole out of the floor. As Varic had reported, Omega couldn't regenerate infinitely.

Her own immortality had its own limits, but she suspected she could outlast his.

She spun around, aiming behind her, but he didn't materialize there. Instead, a liquid shadow pooled at the end of the room. "You tracked me here! Applause, applause. Take a bow! But I see you're not sure *why*. Well, I'll tell you."

A pair of turrets erupted into being over Omega's formless body, like trees sprouting in an instant. They were *huge* mounted turrets, and she recognized them. *The Last Horizon* had grown them after accepting Sola as its Sword.

Only now, instead of bright green, they blazed orange.

Surely they weren't operational. Even with the power core he'd stolen, he wouldn't have had time to assemble a functional device.

Orange light shone in the barrel as they warmed up.

"Better luck in round three!" Omega called.

Plasma bolts screamed as they tore the air all around Sola.

This time, she was ready for him.

She activated pulse boosters in her armor to dash around behind the racks of drones, putting her just ahead of the turrets. The guns tracked after her, shredding through the shelved drones, but her suit redirected its power to move her faster and faster.

Finally, she came to the other end of the bay and reached the turret.

Omega's head sprouted out of it. "Bye!"

The barrel stared her down. As it warmed, she grasped it with a hand.

Then she drew it into her inventory.

The entire turret vanished, and a pile of dark goo carrying a smiling head splatted to the ground. The smile turned shocked. "*What?* Give that back!"

Sola dashed with her pulse boosters again as plasma bolts bigger than her head scraped past her armor's shield. She dropped her shotgun back into the inventory and drew out the Worldslayer.

The room filled with red light and a not-quite-audible shriek as the Aethertech weapon scratched its fingernails against reality. She hadn't fired it yet, but it hadn't been long since her last shot. She preferred to wait weeks before using it again, or it would get...temperamental.

Black ooze swelled all over the remaining turret. "I want it, I want it, I want it!" Omega chanted. But he didn't stop firing. In addition to the plasma bolts, a pair of hands holding guns materialized to either side of Sola.

She pulled the trigger.

A crimson blade of energy existed for just an instant. It pierced through the turret, Omega's body, the drone bay, several intervening rooms, *The Last Horizon*'s outer hull, and two of the surrounding Iron Legion ships.

Everything the Worldslayer touched was destroyed.

Wind rushed out of the drone bay for a second before *The Last Horizon*'s hull patched itself up, but Omega wasn't so lucky. His guns lay on the ground, and the rest of him melted completely to goo. The puddles tried to pull themselves together, but red light remained in the outline of a stab wound in his central mass. The red light chewed away at him, flaring up whenever he tried to pull himself together.

Reality began to swirl around him, indicating a jump to Subspace, but the Worldslayer's wound flared again and he stopped with an audible sound of pain.

A mouth appeared. "Always...knew...I'd be shot...to death."

"Target secure," Sola said.

"Secure?" Horizon's voice returned. *"You did more damage than he ever could have!"*

"Can you keep him contained this time?"

The ship grumbled more, but a slow beam of blue light scooped up Omega's remaining bits and pieces. *"Just don't fire that weapon inside me ever again."*

A moment later, she added, *"...and you now have drone command."*

Sola looked around at the devastated drone bay.

"Thanks."

CHAPTER THIRTY

THE VALLENAR CORPORATION'S Sunsail ship was propelled by a state-of-the-art Skimmer Drive, which resembled a twisted knot of metal tubes. It purred easily as I laid my hand on it, feeling the warmth of the machine and the steady hum of the Aether.

It wasn't so calm when I began cramming magic into it. This was like plugging a starship's fuel line straight into a plasma cannon: unlikely to succeed, impractical if it did, and above all dangerous.

I did it anyway. One of the benefits of being an Archmage is that sometimes, you get to bend the rules.

My father's pilots were constantly shouting to one another from the bridge, and I was close enough to overhear them.

"What is this heading?" one asked. "The spell keeps changing!"

"I think I have it!" another shouted before relaying coordinates.

"No way. That has to be—"

"It's correct!" I shouted back.

"But sir, there's noth—"

"Just follow the spell!"

"It will take us—"

My father's copy cut in. "Follow his spell. My son's navigational magic is without question. You'll all get hazard pay, but there will be no hazard as long as you stay precisely on the spell's course."

There was silence from the crew for a moment, but the utter confidence in his voice worked its own magic. They barked back "Yes, sir" in tandem, then continued calling readings between one another.

They were following a golden river through space that led them unerringly to a destination. If I hadn't visited *The Last Horizon* myself, I wouldn't have been able to cast the spell, and it was fortunate for us all that I could. Neither Raion nor I knew the ship's coordinates, since Horizon had teleported us away directly.

While I was balancing the Aether flowing through our Drive so it gave us maximum speed without smearing us across five dimensions, Raion came up and clapped a fist to his chest in a Visiri salute.

"The Galactic Union warns us of sudden movements from the Iron Legion!" Raion reported. "They expect a full fleet at our location, but they can't give us any assistance."

I tapped the fingers of my spare hand as I thought. There were too many unanswered questions. How did the Legion move such a huge fleet so far without detection? Was there really an Iron King directing events? Had he survived my launching him into a star, or had the Legion managed to grow a second King?

And the most important question of all: was there anything we could do to help Horizon even if we arrived in time?

At this speed, we would burn this ship's Skimmer Drive out, have to switch ships, and still not arrive for another hour. Fleet-on-fleet battles could last for days, but the Iron King wouldn't have locked up his best forces and blown the element of surprise if he thought it would lock him up for so long.

Something had to have given him the confidence that he could take over *The Last Horizon* quickly, before the Galactic Union could rally itself and make him pay the price for his commitment.

Despite being the nigh-infinite brain controlling a vast galactic hive-mind, the King was not infallible. He *could* make mistakes, though my confidence in that area was driven by my understanding of the magical principles that created him more than any firsthand knowledge.

Besides, Iron Kings had been defeated before. All it took was an apocalyptic war that left half the galaxy in ruins.

I tried not to feel the cold fist of the Iron King plunging through my chest.

It was possible *The Last Horizon* could hold out until we arrived. At least Horizon had upgraded weapons and shields. But not...anything else. She was operating with half a crew, most of whom weren't even there to help.

We needed to get there. Horizon needed us.

I could feel Eurias from several rooms away, through all the seals I'd left on its crate. With that, I could account for entire battalions of Legion ships. Raion had his own comparable weapons.

Neither of those things would defeat the King, unless he left himself exposed and vulnerable. Which was roughly as likely as him hiding aboard this very ship.

We couldn't fight the King. Not until we had a full crew, and maybe not then. At least, I wasn't willing to risk it.

Our only chance was to take Horizon and run. How could we do that?

I had been muttering to myself for quite some time, working things out in my head, when I realized Raion was still standing there.

His brow was furrowed in concern as he stared into the Skimmer Drive. "Will we make it in time?" he asked. They were the most subdued words I'd heard from him so far, at least in this life.

I let out a breath. "We might not be needed. Maybe the King underestimated Horizon."

"Don't say we're relying on the enemy to make mistakes. Say we have faith in our allies!" There was a measure of Raion's usual energy in those words, but it faded quickly.

"We messed up," he said.

"*You* didn't," I responded. "I did. It was a trap, and I fell for it. I thought we were being careful by leaving Horizon behind."

"We should never have left them. We should be there." His crimson eyes were dark, staring off into a shadow I couldn't see. Even his third, golden eye was dull.

It was so familiar that it stabbed me through the heart.

This was how he'd looked minutes before he had flown his Divine Titan off to get himself killed.

I looked into the uncharacteristic darkness behind his eyes and I realized something that struck me with a pang of guilt. Something I had avoided asking before.

"The Titan Knights are gone, aren't they?" I asked.

The official word on the Knights of the Titan Force was that they had completed their mission, driven off the D'Niss Swarm, and retired. In the year since my ritual completed, I had looked into the D'Niss, but only enough to conclude that their Swarm-Queen wasn't on the brink of returning.

I hadn't investigated the Knights themselves, at least no more than what I read on the Subline. I hadn't wanted to know.

"Javik's still alive," Raion said, with a distant echo of his normal optimism. "He retired to live with his family on Nyron Seven."

I waited for him to go on, but he didn't, which cut me again. That meant the other three were dead. They were supposed to live longer than this.

But I could honestly say I knew exactly how he felt. "I lost a team like that. Only two of us made it out. He wanted to go back and avenge them, but I said he was stupid. I walked away. He..."

I stopped, but not for the reason he probably assumed.

I had intended to say, *"He went to fight and I never saw him again."*

But that wasn't true, was it?

I looked into Raion's face, the face of the man I'd left to die. Now, I had a chance to do things differently.

Tears welled up before I could stop them, and I wiped them quickly. I had already screwed up by showing weakness.

Crying would provoke Raion's sympathy, which I neither needed nor deserved. The man I mourned wasn't dead.

He put a comforting hand on my shoulder, and I froze instead of looking up.

"You made the right decision," he said.

I shook my head, but I still didn't look at him. "I think we were both wrong."

"Forgive me, I didn't know your friend, but I know what it's like to be the only survivor." His hand tightened slightly. "I wouldn't wish that on anyone."

Tears were returning to my eyes, but for a very different reason. He was about to crush my shoulder.

"Hey, could you..." I pushed against his hand, which I had no chance of removing by force.

He jerked the hand away. "Ah, right! Sorry."

Raion drooped like a wounded puppy, guilty for hurting me. He was in better shape than he had been before, but I had to get his mind back in the game.

Which took a little bit of extra honesty.

"We haven't known each other long," I said, "but if we're balancing people we've helped against the ones we've let down, I feel safe to say your score is a lot higher than mine."

Raion's head half-shook reflexively, as though he couldn't tolerate the suggestion that he might have done more good than harm.

I returned my attention to the Skimmer Drive. "No matter what happens, we're going to get there soon. And when we do, the Legion is going to be sorry we did."

Raion punched his fists together so loudly I thought the hull had ruptured. "That's right!"

It wasn't really.

If we were up against an Iron King, he wouldn't be trying to destroy *The Last Horizon*. He would want to take the ship for his own. That was the Iron Legion's imperative, their one universal drive: to make everything part of the Legion. If the King succeeded before we arrived, the best we could hope for was to dive back into Subspace before he annihilated us.

Death crawled under my skin. I was about to die in failure, one last time.

But I kept that to myself.

CHAPTER THIRTY-ONE

THE SKIMMER DRIVE failed exactly where I had predicted it would.

Its nest of tubes had become hotter and hotter, wilder in the Aether, until it burned me to touch even through a glove. I'd kept magic flowing through the device, but its components burned out when I expected.

The ship skidded out of Subspace with a shuddering jolt, and we spun through space at a wild angle.

From the glimpses of steel I could catch through the spinning viewport, we were within sight of a colony. There would be a Vallenar Corporation presence there, and—as planned—we could pick up another ship. Assuming they had something decently fast, we were only an hour from *The Last Horizon.*

I was pleased with myself. Not just anyone could predict a Drive's Aether resistance within three seconds.

But no plan was perfect, as I observed when the colony approached our spinning window with alarming speed. We had little power to right ourselves, so we would only come to a stop when we crashed into the colony itself.

"Multiple target locks detected," the ship's computer said, and I

corrected my mistaken assumptions. We wouldn't crash into the colony; we would be annihilated by the colony's perimeter defense guns before we made it close.

"Raion!" I called. "Can you take care of this?" I didn't hear from him, so I peeked up and down the hall.

Though the ship spun wildly, none of it affected our artificial gravity inside. As long as I kept my gaze off the viewport, we might as well be standing still.

When I didn't get a response immediately, I reached out for the Aether around the ship. Without Raion around, I would have to handle this myself, though I'd spent the last five hours wrestling a river of energy in a magical feat that *itself* should have earned me an Archmage title.

The ship was protected, but I didn't want to leave our safety entirely in the hands of defensive enchantments.

Before I manifested water into a shield around the ship, one of the Corporation pilots called out: "He's launching a pod!"

I relaxed and released my concentration. It was nice having at least one reliable ally.

My father marched up the hallway and slammed his palm against the wall. His eyes were armor-plated steel. "Start casting! Didn't you hear the alarm?"

"Relax." I stretched and let out a yawn. "He'll handle it."

He grabbed a fistful of my mantle. "Wake up! This isn't a *theoretical* problem, this is *real*. We are about to *die*, do you understand?"

I watched him lash out under stress, trying to goad me into action. I remembered two versions of me that would have threatened him at wandpoint for that speech and a third that would have seriously considered shoving him into space. In this life, before the ritual, I would have burned with shame and hurried to do as he wished.

With the benefit of perspective, it was only...sad.

"I do understand death," I said. "Do you?"

He saw something in me that made him flinch. Fear flickered through his eyes for an instant before he covered it with anger, shoving me away. "Give you six lives, and you still don't grow up. You can't trust—"

The ship jolted again, and he stumbled because he hadn't been expecting it. I, meanwhile, was nice and comfortable in the embrace of my levitation ring.

The ship had righted itself and was now slowing as it banked toward the colony's dock. The pilots were on the Subline, identifying us as a Vallenar vessel and begging for clearance.

A red light flashed in space. On a nearby monitor, I watched a flashing warning deactivate as the missile it was tracking was destroyed.

My father brushed his jacket off and regained his composure. "Your friend is..."

"Carrying our ship. As you can see, I didn't cast anything because there was no need."

"You should have backed him up. There's no such thing as too many layers of defense."

I tapped the wall with a finger, revealing a white magic circle. "I completely agree, which is why I placed protective seals throughout the ship. I can't help but think that the real version of my father would have noticed."

He shoved a cigarette into his mouth. "Get your staff. We're launching the next ship in sixty seconds after we dock." Then he marched away.

It was comforting to know that there was no version of my father that could admit he was wrong.

The colony had panicked after our violent arrival, with half a dozen escort ships swarming around us and a contingent of armed troops waiting in the dock. If not for the Vallenar Corporation logo, I suspect we would have been detained.

But the value of my family name was still overinflated, so there was a sleeker, faster ship waiting for us in the dock. This one looked like a marine submersible more than a traditional starship or an ancient sailing vessel, and its Impulse Drive would get us to *The Last Horizon* in no time.

I slung my staff over my shoulder and walked down the ramp next to Raion, who was speaking proudly with hands on his hips to a colony defense officer.

"I would lay down my life before I harmed you or your ships!" Raion announced.

The officer looked like she was trying to hide a headache. "I know the Titan Force by reputation, but we can't just allow an approach like that to the colony. Several civilian ships sent out emergency calls."

"I would have saved them!"

"I...I understand that, but..."

I caught Raion's attention with a gesture as I passed from one ramp onto the next ship. "Time to go."

"Forgive us, officer, but I have more people to save. Just remember that the Titan Force is on your side!" He gave a beaming grin.

Then his figure blurred and he appeared fifty feet overhead, punching out with a devastating explosion of scarlet force.

Wind kicked up and filled the docking bay, knocking the colony defense officer's hat off.

Something exploded under Raion's fist, and at first I thought it was a drone. I was baffled. If he went around breaking colony equipment, they were never going to let us leave.

Then he landed next to me and asked, "Do you think this followed us?"

The moment between my heartbeats stretched until I thought my heart had stopped.

He was holding out a fist-sized lump of flesh and metal with a single eye and a pair of leathery, mammalian wings struggling against his grip. Iron Legion creatures weren't unknown inside a colony, so its presence wasn't what stole my breath.

It was the color. The scout was black-and-white. Only the highest-level use of the Mirror of Silence spell could make copies that looked indistinguishable from the real thing. Quick, temporary clones were colorless shadows.

This was a product of my father's spell.

I snapped my head to stare at the copy of Benri Vallenar, who looked as stunned as I was. The Iron Legion—maybe even an Iron King—had my father. Or a copy of him.

While I was concerned about his potential fate, there was a much larger problem. What could the Legion do with my father's magic?

It was hard to imagine. There were horror stories about the Iron Legion getting their hands on Aether Technicians, wizards with unique spells, and high-level Combat Artists, but people on the level of Archmagi tended not to be captured.

With the Mirror of Silence, the Legion didn't need to predict where Raion and I would go. If they expanded my father's spell enough, they could watch every route through Subspace and place spies in every colony, station, or planet where we might resupply.

They could conjure an army on top of us in seconds.

The Aether poured water all around me, where it gathered to spin in steadily increasing rings around my hands. "Red alert!" I called. "Attack incoming!"

The colony defense force didn't respond to my command. I was hoping they would; they'd have seen the Vallenar Corporation logo, and while that didn't give us any kind of official authority over them, it should at least lend me some credibility.

Instead, they had their rifles trained on me. A couple of squad mages were chanting and prying at my connection to the Aether.

I ignored them and continued chanting, scanning the open hangar doors that looked out onto the starry void of space.

As soon as I saw an Aetheric sigil flicker, white against the darkness, I unleashed my element in that direction. A spectral gray-white Hunter-ship materialized just outside the hangar bay, large enough to grasp a starfighter.

My water blasted into it, stopping it from crashing into the colony.

The second ship was slashed in half by Raion.

The third was annihilated by plasma cannons from the colony.

A crash and the shaking of the ground told me we were too late for the others.

My processor implant gave me the updates from our ship's scanners. The wind suddenly tearing at the air was from multiple hull breaches all around the colony. The breaches hadn't been sealed because Legion creatures were appearing out of nowhere, targeting life support mechanisms. Ships that fled were being destroyed by enemies that manifested straight from the Aether.

One-point-four million people lived in this colony.

A ship dove into the multicolored twist into Subspace, escaping through the gaps Raion and I were creating. I blasted out in every direction at once with water, ridding myself of all the element I'd collected to cover the entire hangar.

In that moment, I sliced dozens of colorless Iron Legion Pawns in half. Raion was a blurring streak of crimson darting every direction, in and out of the atmosphere.

Without my elementalism, he was all but unsupported out there, but I couldn't spare more attention. I unraveled the seals containing my staff.

As the spinning circles around the crate vanished, clouds gathered in the hangar bay. Moss and vines crept up and over the nearby ships, the ones who hadn't launched yet. Some of the colony guards tripped on grass.

I seized the smooth haft of my staff and felt my magic expand.

For someone who talks about not relying on magic as a weapon, I use magic as a weapon a lot. But not only are guns more efficient, there's only one thing a gun can do.

Magic can do *anything.*

The powers of Eurias rolled through the colony, gushing Aether, radiating life. I sent orders flowing through those connections, directing power.

Which I commanded to form seals.

Spinning blue magic circles appeared out of nowhere, thousands of them, as the Aether followed my instructions.

Circles stretched across the gaping holes in the colony's exterior, forming a makeshift bandage. The missing material was pulled back from where it had been scattered, no longer drifting in space or piled up beside buildings. Seals bound broken pieces to one another, pulling them back to where they belonged in a blink.

Bleeding, staggering people felt their wounds close as they ran from colorless Pawns. I couldn't do any complex healing, but binding together torn skin, severed muscles, and sliced veins was simple.

Destroyed ships knitted together, drifting pilots were pulled back to safety as I tethered them to the colony, and blue circles blazed on every surface like starship exhaust.

It wasn't perfect. Sealing magic, flexible as it was, couldn't solve everything, and I didn't have precise control over exactly what the spell did.

Operating at this scale was more about holding on as the spell did its work, which was ten times harder than controlling the flow of Aether through our Skimmer Drive had been.

The spell itself was no less precise than usual. It would hold veins together as easily as the halves of a severed starship. If it were a machine, or a program, I would have to give it specific directions for every action, but magic responds more to desires and intentions than to instructions.

If casting a spell normally was like controlling my own hands, casting one through Eurias was like delivering commands to an army.

Also, no one spell could do everything. Binding magic was great for knitting together wounds, locking enemies in place, and blocking off further attacks. It was made to bring things together and keep them in place.

It still wasn't a healing spell. It couldn't bring back the dead, remove bullets, or heal plasma burns. It couldn't restore lost oxygen.

With seals patching the hull and the life support systems repaired, air would eventually return, but that wasn't much comfort to people in chambers where the air had already escaped.

The spell also couldn't bring people to safety where none existed; if a ship had been destroyed, my magic would try to repair the ship and the pilot, which included returning the pilot to the ship. If that took too long, the pilot might have already died in vacuum.

So, not perfect, but far better than nothing.

After the first minute or two, the most important emergencies were taken care of. I could focus my attention on my real goal.

The spell continued working automatically, but I gradually drew sapphire symbols all around the outline of the colony. Once they were in place, a single massive spell-circle flashed into being around the entire metal wheel.

All the Mirror of Silence copies inside the colony vanished at once.

I'd sealed out the spell.

A few real Hunter-ships had shown up, but without the support from their black-and-white copies, the colony's normal defenses could handle them. Now that my concentration wasn't so absolute, I saw Raion as a glowing red star coming to a staggering halt when the cloned ship he'd been about to destroy disappeared.

I sagged into Eurias, propping myself up. A whole little ecosystem had grown up around me, thanks to its power, but I relaxed some of my control over the spell. The Iron Legion could still cause us problems, but now that the sealing-circle was in place, we'd weathered the worst of it.

That was quickly proven to be one of the dumbest thoughts I'd ever had in my life.

Thus far.

Space twisted outside the open hangar bay. From a barely perceptible wormhole in space to a wide, twisting, swirling hole of color miles across. Something enormous was about to come out of Subspace.

And I knew what it was.

In a panic, I opened a call to Raion. He accepted immediately, though the view from his end was a nauseating scene of chaotic, high-speed combat.

"Are you all right?" he asked. Over the course of that question, he slashed a Hunter-ship in two, spun over to land on top of a colony starship, and tore open the hatch to toss a pair of survivors inside where they could breathe.

"Have you ever fought a Behemoth?" I asked. The Subspace twist was resolving itself, and I was sweating more with every passing second.

"Of course! We defeated one just outside Xyriel Prime!"

That was not an encouraging answer. "How many of you did it take?"

"We combined all five of our Divine Titans and smote him across the star systems!"

I wished my mantle could remove sweat. "How do you rate your chances against one alone?"

"I'm not alone," he said seriously. "We'll fight together."

"I'm a wizard. Best I can do is shoot him with my pistol."

"Oh. That's right." There was a pause while he thought. "I'll do my best!"

As the Subspace distortion resolved into a hulking beast of metal and flesh, large enough to bite the colony in two, I drew my Lightcaster and shot.

The plasma bolt pinged harmlessly off one of the Behemoth's city-sized armored plates. There was no chance it noticed.

"Got him," I muttered.

Then the beast roared, and people died.

CHAPTER THIRTY-TWO

IT TAKES TRULY staggering amounts of resources to create a Behemoth, even considering the scale of the entire Iron Legion.

The cyborg pieces are assembled in shipyards, with metal skeletons and digital brain-chips that cost as much to make as dreadnoughts. Most of them are made from scavenged dreadnoughts, in fact.

The creature that forms the body is usually whichever astral megafauna the Iron Legion can catch. Not so many creatures swim the starways or stalk Subspace as there were in years past, thanks to increased traffic and improved stealth magic that prevents them from preying on us, but there are still enough for the Legion.

This one was made from a contrasaur, a mega-reptile that fed on migratory flocks of extradimensional prey. It resembled an aquatic lizard, with a shimmering aura on its fins and webbed digits that let it swim through the Aether.

Every Behemoth had a few things in common: their staggering size, their cybernetic pieces, their resistance to magic, and their interaction with Subspace.

The exact nature varied between individual Behemoths. Some were big enough to crash through planets, while others were "merely" the size of cities. Some swam through Subspace, some hopped through it, and some warped it around them.

Out of all their kind, Behemoths made from contrasaurs had a few extra-terrifying features.

For one thing, they were naturally difficult to affect with magic even before the Legion remade them. They swam through Aether, so it took extraordinary amounts of magic to alter them at all. With Eurias, I might be able to manage to defend against a natural contrasaur, but that kind of fight would be far more likely to end in a draw.

Worse was their interaction with Subspace. Their prey fled through micro-dives, so contrasaurs had developed the ability to lock down Subspace for thousands of miles around them.

So there was no escape, and magic was useless. Against a *natural* contrasaur.

This was a Behemoth made from a contrasaur killed and reanimated. Its limbs were woven from both meat and machine, its eyes zoomed in like building-sized cameras, and its vitals were protected by starship armor. An aura of flickering light around it suggested a shield.

It was smarter, faster, stronger. In addition to its natural resistance to magic, the armor would be close to indestructible.

As the Behemoth loomed over the remaining people, it roared. The sound was carried on Aether, not air, and it crashed into the colony in an invisible wave.

Starships were shaken apart by the shout. The colony quaked, and the hangar bay buckled around me.

The sound was...not so bad, actually. At least for me. Several of the colonists I had just saved shuddered and clapped hands to their ears, but my seals prevented the worst of it.

I'd have been fine anyway. My own mantle's mandate to protect me extended to my eardrums. And my internal organs.

That was about all the thinking I was allowed to do before I had to return my attention to Eurias. Life and water had erupted around me thanks to the staff's power, and now I was in the middle of swampland spreading across the hangar bay. Grass and reeds swayed in the breeze, and I saw small fish in the puddle at my feet. The ceiling swirled with clouds.

And the new damage to the colony pulled on my spell to fix it.

My mind sunk deeper and deeper as I tried to hold my body together. I fought to stop my eyes from rolling up, but I had the choice between staying conscious and holding on to the spell.

An eye bigger than my ship refocused and zoomed in on me. That was the other annoying thing about Behemoths; they were made to track down large-scale magic. Usually, the Legion used them to crush entire rituals or schools of mages. Most people can't use fleet-level spells on their own.

If I had been alone, I would have already sealed off my staff and done my best to flee. I had saved as many colonists as I could. If I didn't draw the attention of the Legion and the Behemoth away from this place, there would be no survivors left.

But I wasn't alone.

I just had to hope that the last survivor of the Titan Force could do the work of all five.

My heart crashed down from orbit when I saw Raion flying up in his crimson combat armor and hold out a hand. "This is a warning!"

Don't warn it, kill it, I thought, but that much focus was a stretch when I needed to hold the Aether in the shape of my spell.

The Behemoth didn't bother with Raion. It leaned forward casually, reaching out for me with webbed claws.

There is no fear quite like seeing a predator larger than a colony reaching out for *you,* specifically. I'd like to credit my self-control for my ability to continue channeling magic, but I was using my levitation ring to lock myself in place.

If Raion didn't stop it, I was dead, but it wasn't like my odds of running were so much better. I was betting on the Red Titan Knight to save me.

And hoping not to watch him die again.

Raion had lit his force-blade and now drew it back for a stab. Energy flowed into it, gathering around it, and I recognized the beginning of a Combat Art. The Aether resonated around him as he poured more and more power into the strike.

I wanted to shout at him. Don't use Combat Arts against a Behemoth. That's using a toothpick to hold back an asteroid. Raion needed to summon his Divine Titan immediately.

The Titan wouldn't respond except in the most extreme need, but surely this counted. Only the Titan could magnify Raion's Combat Art enough to matter against a Behemoth.

Or so I thought. The crimson aura around him kept growing, and the massive creature took notice. It hesitated, turning its attention from me to him.

I stared in astonishment. The version of Raion I had known had never been able to push his Combat Art so far, at least not outside his Titan.

What had happened to him this time?

In an instant, Raion went from blazing like a red star to compressing all the energy into his force-blade. It was barely brighter than usual, but trembling with contained power that made me feel like the colony should be shaking again.

That was a good sign.

"You face me first!" I heard Raion shout over our comms, though the Behemoth didn't speak and couldn't hear him from so many miles away. Through hard vacuum.

But I still felt my spirits soar as Raion stabbed forth and a blinding line of light lanced into the colossal beast. With just his sword, he had released a beam that resembled a capital ship's central cannon. It struck the Behemoth on the unarmored hide at the side of its neck.

Where it splashed off with no impact.

The Behemoth hesitated as though waiting for the rest of it, then focused on me again.

"As expected," Raion said, nodding.

Don't nod!

I was losing my grip on my spell, but the pressure from the Hunter-ships was lessening. The Mirror of Silence copies had faded and couldn't be replaced so easily, not with the Behemoth's presence suppressing the Aether.

With that in mind, I sealed my staff back into its crate and covered it in spinning seals. The weather settled down inside the hangar bay—including some rain I hadn't felt—but all the new grass and reeds that had grown would die soon. There was no soil in here, after all.

The Behemoth was approaching the colony again, and by "approaching" I do mean "crashing into." It wasn't as focused on me now that I wasn't holding Eurias, but it was about to wipe this colony from the map.

I turned to run up the ramp into the Vallenar Corporation ship. Only to find no ramp. And no ship.

I wasn't surprised that my father's copy had already made his getaway, but my stomach still clenched.

I had been watching the rest of the colony as I stitched it together, but I hadn't been paying much attention to my own surroundings. Especially not after a Behemoth showed up looking for me. I didn't have any idea when my father and his men had left, but it could have been at any time after the first few seconds.

A ship with no Subspace capability couldn't get me far enough away while the Behemoth was chasing me, but now that the monster's attention had been diverted, I could have made some distance. I wasn't going to leave Raion behind, but I wanted the insurance. And starship cannons would be several lightyears more useful than a plasma pistol and some bad language.

No one else was shooting at the Behemoth, that was for sure. They were fleeing in all directions while its gleaming chestplate got closer and closer to burying us all in rubble.

Raion, my only hope, was holding a circular device to the sky. It blazed red.

"...Divine Titan!" Raion called.

A scarlet comet began falling toward him, but the knot in my gut didn't loosen.

I had served as the Blue Knight of the Titan Force for years, flying hundreds of missions that required me to summon my Divine Titan. They were impressive machines, with a level of power you'd expect from Aethertech without equal in the galaxy. I wouldn't want to face off against any one of the Titans, with or without my staff.

But I knew what they could handle.

Asking Raion to take on a Behemoth alone was like waiting for a miracle.

For focused work, my wand was a better tool than Eurias. I pulled it and began chanting bindings. Protective spells wouldn't be too much help to a Divine Titan, but every little bit helped. Assuming a lone Titan could damage that monster, which I was not willing to bet. Behemoths were the next best thing to invincible.

Or so I thought before the Red Divine Titan blazed in, summoned from beyond the range of the contrasaur's Subspace lockdown. It crashed into the Behemoth's claw, which was stretched out for the colony.

Raion's machine tore right through.

Lakes of blood sprayed into space and the contrasaur roared again, which no doubt destroyed more starships.

The Divine Titan came to a stop beside Raion, and I got a good look.

I didn't recognize it.

It was a one-hundred-fifty-foot humanoid armor with plates of silver and red. It gave off a smooth, polished impression, as perfect as any piece of *The Last Horizon*. That much hadn't changed.

What I *didn't* expect was the molten light that burned inside the Titan. Its metal plates radiated orange-gold light, and the same shone from inside the visor of its helmet. When the chest opened up, more light spilled out.

It looked as though the Red Divine Titan had swallowed solar fire.

As Raion flew into the open chest and took his seat, he sent me a message. "Keep your staff handy. If I become a threat, do whatever it takes to stop me."

"What does that *mean?*" I shouted as his chest closed. Now

wasn't the time for talk; the Behemoth was angry, and every second took us closer to becoming space debris.

"You can do it. I trust you," Raion said.

The Behemoth had reverted to its instincts and swam toward us, mouth gaping to swallow us whole. It was like the entire galaxy had vanished, and only the Behemoth's jaws were real.

"If we die," I said, "I'll kill you."

Raion didn't respond. Before his video link cut off, I saw the third eye on his head glowing brightly. Then the feed was swallowed by sunlight.

There was a flash of molten orange as the Divine Titan blasted forward.

It crashed into the Behemoth's metal teeth, grabbing one and hauling it to the side. Like a newborn fish trying to steer the course of an apex predator by swimming into its tooth.

Everything I understood about the world was flipped upside-down when it *worked*.

The Behemoth's head was shoved to the side, missing the colony. Another flash of orange star-fire came when the Divine Titan landed a fist on its head. The blow released light like a solar flare and the Behemoth screamed again as it flew to the side.

One of its limbs swept past the open hangar bay, and I felt death scraping by. A little further and I'd be drifting in space with the rest of the flotsam.

This was no one-sided beatdown, though. The Behemoth was a trump card of the Iron Legion. It caught the mech with a claw and swatted it aside, then followed up with a swarm of missiles.

Raion unleashed lasers of orange light that slashed through the missiles, and sunset-colored wings exploded from his back as he evaded with impossible-to-track speed.

From the colony's local Subline, I pulled up a clip of an old Titan Force battle and let the video play at the corner of my vision. Reality was the same as I remembered from my previous lives. It took Raion's Red Titan, the Blue Titan, and the Green Titan working together to block a swipe from an insectoid Behemoth's mandible.

The red and green mechs were scattered and cracks formed on Blue's armor. The fight was a desperate struggle, with the Titan Force barely coming out on top. Just what I would have imagined.

Raion's got some upgrades.

It was hard enough to repair Aethertech on the level of the Divine Titans, much less upgrade it, but a punch from him *should* have been nothing more to the Behemoth than a gentle nudge. Instead, every strike was pushing the Behemoth miles away from the colony.

The creature slashed, leaving a sparkling Aether trail, and the Titan darted away like a golden fly. I could hardly see him anymore, but my processor captured pictures here and there to help me piece together what happened.

Raion pulled out a force-blade scaled to his mech. Swords only had value in combat if you knew a Combat Art, and even then, guns were usually better.

But the yellow-orange blade filled me with the same apprehension I'd felt on seeing Sola's Worldslayer. Which became scarier when the Titan took a stance and began gathering light. It was Raion's Art, the Dance of the Burning World, only magnified a thousandfold.

I backed up a few steps against imaginary heat as space lit up. I didn't feel much real heat on my skin, but I felt like I *should*.

The Behemoth didn't take the challenge lightly. Cracks slid aside in its chest, and drones flew out in swarms to pepper the Divine Titan with shots. Space rippled as the Behemoth's shields strengthened.

I couldn't see the thrust of Raion's sword.

Even my processor was overwhelmed as the system was drowned by solar light. When it finally subsided and I could look again, there was a charred hole through the Behemoth.

The long way.

Raion had bored a tunnel from the Behemoth's skull down to the base of its tail. I could see stars on the other end.

The shield around the Behemoth was still flickering and buzzing as it collapsed, and the drones continued to fire. Every part of the monster except its actual body was having trouble realizing it was dead.

I sent a message to Raion. "I had no *idea* you could do that."

No response. Not through the Subline, anyway.

I was thousands of miles away from the Titan at that point. Even with the magnification provided by my ocular implant, I could see it only as a point of light.

But I shivered as I sensed its gaze on me. The mech had turned to look at me, I was certain.

My father's voice buzzed in my ear. *"I never thought he could do it without the other four Titans. We're on the way to pick you up now."*

I couldn't respond. I was chanting, the tip of my wand blazing blue as I traced a seal.

"Tell him not to come in so hot," my father continued. *"He won't have time to decelerate. Why are you chanting? …Aether, save us. Red alert! Get the alert back up! It's not over!"*

CHAPTER THIRTY-THREE

EURIAS' POWER COMES from World Spirits of life and water and its enchantment is for amplification. It's great when you want to call down a rainstorm on a whole hemisphere, but not so much when you're trying to hit a single target.

For that, I have my wand.

It's not Aethertech, though it resembles technology. A foot-long rectangle of metal plates containing a crystal branch. Its enchantment is focus.

The crystal draws the magic out of me faster while keeping the spell ordered, so I can be sloppy with the incantation. The enchantment keeps the spell locked on a single point or target at a time.

It's bad for flexibility. Bad for complexity and improvisation.

But *great* for hitting one target.

Raion's Divine Titan arrived in front of the colony faster than I could comprehend. I was about to release the binding spell, thinking he was going to crash into me, when Raion pulled to a halt.

My father had been wrong; it *could* decelerate on time. My pathetic human organs would have been reduced to paste if I tried to stop a Titan under that kind of force, but Raion was orders of magnitude tougher than me, and his Titan had been upgraded beyond anything I could understand.

I didn't release my spell. I licked my lips and stared down a shining sunset-colored mech from behind a lit wand.

"Raion?" I asked hesitantly.

I heard nothing from him over the Subline. He didn't pick up my communication.

The Divine Titan slowly drifted into the atmospheric field of the colony, which was holding together thanks to my binding spells. When it crossed into the air, the mech let out a loud metallic roar.

"STAAAFFFF!"

It was perhaps the worst voice I'd heard in my life. I was certain it wasn't coming through speakers but was being made by vibrating plates of armor. The sound was like the unholy hybrid of grating steel and grinding stone.

The mech was silent a moment later, and it took me a moment to realize it was waiting for a response. Though I had never experienced anything like this before, I was fairly certain I was talking to the Divine Titan itself.

"You want me to use my staff?" I asked. Could it hear me?

"STAFF!" This voice was quicker and noticeably more pleased.

Anyone who piloted a Divine Titan for any amount of time learned to sense a sort of consciousness in them. They developed some level of awareness, even their own personalities. Titans were masterpieces of Aethertech, the next best thing to Zenith Devices, so no Knight ever learned the full extent of what they could do.

But I had never imagined having a real, verbal conversation with one.

One thing was abundantly clear to me: if I pulled out Eurias again, I was going to be killed.

Even with staff in hand, I would get atomized by a Divine Titan that could go fist-to-fist with a Behemoth. The most I could hope was to buy time and run away.

Terror sharpened my thoughts.

One advantage of certain-death situations is the additional focus they bring. While your life hangs in the balance, time doesn't slow down. Your world gets clear. All the unnecessary concerns fall away, leaving your thoughts in their perfect state.

In this case, I rapidly flipped through any plan that might not get me killed.

After only a fraction of a second, I slung the case off my shoulder and put it on the ground. The Divine Titan tensed into what I could only read as anticipation.

I started to undo the first seal, but hesitated. "How is Raion? I don't want to hurt him by accident."

The groan of metal that came from the Titan shook my spirit and made me seriously question what I was doing, trying to fool a building-sized suit of unbreakable armor. Why was I pinning my own life on my acting skills? Would it understand me?

My hands didn't shake. Steady hands are a necessity for a wizard.

The armor gave out a low growl of warning, but when I undid the first seal and the power from Eurias began to radiate into the atmosphere, its growl became a sort of metallic purr.

"You see?" I said, faking calm. "I *want* to take the staff out. But I can't do it if I don't know Raion is safe."

With that, though I knew it was a risk, I sent another message to Raion. At first, there was no response. Then he accepted the call... or perhaps the mech accepted for him.

An image of Raion appeared in the corner of my vision. All three of his eyes were rolled up in his head and his jaw was locked tight. Veins of sunlight-colored energy ran over his skin, throbbing with power and pushing deeper into him.

I didn't need to be the greatest living expert on magical theory to understand what was happening there.

I was, but I didn't *need* to be.

The mech wasn't drawing power from Raion, though that should have been their relationship. Not just anyone can pilot a Divine Titan. Instead, the mech was pushing its energy *into* him. In a sense, it was trying to fuse with him.

I didn't know whether the mech was doing that consciously or whether it was a natural consequence of whatever upgrade had brought it to a Behemoth-punching level of performance. But Raion still resisted.

So I'd do what I could to help him.

I kicked aside the staff's crate as I stood up, and the mech's screech of protest shattered what little glass in the hangar bay hadn't already been reduced to sand. Its visor lit up yellow-orange, and this time I felt the heat even through the protection of my mantle.

My wand lifted to the mech's chest. "I'll take out the staff if I need it."

The silence from the Divine Titan felt more dangerous than its scream had, but I wasn't waiting around for it to reveal its plasma guns.

A complex circle of sealing and binding appeared on the mech's chest as I completed my spell. The Divine Titan looked down, then back up, and if its helmet had an expression, I would have called it 'disdain.'

While these Titans weren't as specialized against magic as Behemoths were, they were not easily moved by spells. But I wasn't targeting the Titan.

The binding spell that reached Raion was only a fifth as strong as usual. Without incredible stability and focus, and without my own personal connection to Raion, the spell would never have penetrated the armor.

But that was why I used the wand.

The circle of protection melted into Raion, reinforcing his own power to resist. It separated some of the energy invading him, peeling away a few of those shining tendrils.

The Visiri's eyes rolled back down, and in the video feed, it was like Raion was glaring straight into the camera. If anything, his jaw tightened further, until I thought something would crack. His teeth were exposed in a grimace.

Raion gave a wordless, roaring scream, and crimson energy pulsed out to overtake the orange.

The mech shuddered. It screamed and writhed. The colony shook with its tension.

Its visor flicked down to glare at me.

But I had never stopped casting barriers.

I didn't know how conscious the Divine Titan was, but I chose to assume it could understand my words. And if it could understand my words, it needed to understand *me*.

I walked forward as I cast, layering protection after protection over myself. "Look what you're doing to your pilot. You don't want this."

The plate on the mech's bracer popped open, revealing a plasma cannon bigger than any on *Moonfall*. It swung my direction and fired.

Thunder rocked the hangar bay again as the cannon fired, superheating the air. The molten plasma crashed over the shield formed by my amulet of protection and mantle, lighting up the usually-invisible dome around me.

This time, the dome shone with white symbols. The extra layers of defense I'd cast from my wand.

Half the seals snapped, but when the plasma cleared itself, I was standing on the one unscarred wedge of floor surrounded by metal that had been melted away. I projected an outward show of strength, showing an Archmage in his power, though my heart slammed in my chest.

"I know you want to protect him," I said, remembering my own Divine Titan. "Let him go."

There came a squeal of metal I couldn't interpret.

I was still meeting the mech's gaze when its visor snapped from sunset gold to red. Then the chest opened and Raion spilled out.

He fell probably seventy-five feet to the metal ground below, where he landed with a thud. I didn't do anything to catch him.

Not only was I still watching the mech like we were in some kind of gunslinger standoff, but Raion was a Visiri warrior and a Titan Knight. If a starship crashed into him, I'd be more worried about the ship.

"You all right, Raion?" I called.

A weak, trembling hand lifted into the air and raised one thumb. "Friendship!"

"Friendship to you too, buddy."

The Divine Titan crashed up through the ceiling of the hangar bay as it left, tearing another chunk out of the colony, but I supposed it was all the same at that point. If it weren't for my spells, the largest remaining piece of the colony would fit in my pocket, but the place was still a wreck. And my concentration was well past its breaking point, so the survivors were on their own.

My processor estimated that around seventy percent of the colonists had survived. Ordinarily, thirty percent casualties would be soul-crushing, but this time I was shocked we had managed to save so many.

Even knowing my capabilities, the Iron Legion would have expected this attack to kill every man, woman, and child here. It almost had.

Of course, my mood darkened further when I took stock of our situation. The Iron Legion moved with unity that suggested the guidance of a King, and it had my father.

I had seen this apocalypse begin once before.

I contacted the Vallenar Corporation starship. "Situation clear. No further sign of the Iron Legion. Raion and I need a pickup."

Another voice, weary but prideful, inserted itself into the call. It wasn't my father.

"No need to bother yourself, Captain," Horizon said. *"I can take you from here."*

With that, a steady blue light surrounded me and Raion, and we both vanished.

It was difficult for Raion to stay conscious as the ship's teleportation gathered him up, as he had been exhausted both mentally and physically by the toll of wrestling against his own Divine Titan. And he was pretty certain he had broken several ribs.

But he was still shocked by his own survival. Not *that* he had survived, but *how*.

Raion had been lost within the corrupted consciousness of the Titan, little more than a piece of the powerful machine. Varic's magic had loosened its grip on his mind, and Raion had reached out for more strength.

He'd used his unique ability to tap into the bonds between him and those who trusted him. To channel, quite literally, the power of friendship.

That power was often the difference between defeat and victory, when he'd been fighting alongside his comrades in the Titan Force. His fellow Knights trusted him as he trusted them, providing a deep river that he could draw on in a crisis.

This time, when he'd reached out desperately for anything to support him, he'd found a radiant well of faith and trust. A friendship that felt like it had been forged over years of battle.

Coming from Varic.

It was the first time Raion had ever felt someone come to believe in *him* faster than he believed in *them*.

Raion considered how lucky he was to have found new friends already. This time, he swore, he wouldn't fail them.

No matter what it took.

CHAPTER THIRTY-FOUR

BENRI VALLENAR STARED into the oozing wall of the Iron King's control chamber. The shadows from his Mirror of Silence had been recalled, leaving him watching only memory.

The memory was still fascinating, though.

While the King focused on the battle against *The Last Horizon*, Benri had watched the trap for his son. He witnessed the colony from a thousand angles and saw black-and-white clones swarm as an army.

As his own spell tore the colony apart, strategically targeting the most valuable systems, his son wrestled more Aether than any single wizard should be able to. Sealing spells pulled miles of metal plating and squads of starships back together, saved the dying, and generally kept the colony alive.

Benri had never been more proud of his son, but this put him in a difficult position. At any point, the Iron King might break his contract and turn Benri into a wordlessly suffering undead slave.

He had never thought the King's plan would fail.

The Behemoth had been directed to disable and capture the wizard, not to kill, but the vast cyborg star-beast was hardly a precision instrument. It would crush Varic's magic and swallow him whole, from which circumstances Benri would retrieve him.

Then the two Vallenars and the Iron King would share seats aboard *The Last Horizon*. Of course, that relied on the Iron King keeping his word, which Benri did not believe for a second.

Raion Raithe was going to die. The Iron King would love to study the key to this modified Divine Titan, but he had been fully prepared to scour space for it afterwards. If he lost it, oh well.

There was only one scenario the Iron King had considered that might cost them the Behemoth: if *The Last Horizon* intervened. Which was why he'd focused on locking down the Zenith Starship at the same time.

Benri had considered this the most foolproof plan he had ever seen executed. At best, the Iron King got everything he wanted with little risk. At worst, it was still an effective stalling tactic. There was nothing to lose.

Somehow, he'd lost a Behemoth.

Even the Iron Legion couldn't produce Behemoths infinitely. There were perhaps ten in the entire galaxy.

The performance of Raion's Divine Titan shook Benri to his core. That was beyond anything a single Titan should have been able to accomplish, and almost beyond what the five Titans had been able to do at their combined peak.

That truth crawled beneath his skin. Even if he had the full power of Varic and his six lives, if he held Eurias in his own hand, would he be able to match such a Titan?

Maybe his son did not have the greatest potential in the galaxy. That disturbed him.

At the crackling heat pressing down on him, Benri turned and instinctively ducked his head. The Iron King's presence was impossible to conceal; his ponderous weight bent the floor, he carried the temperature of a furnace, and he radiated a palpable sense of confidence.

Though Benri looked no higher than steel-armored ankles, he could feel a burning gaze tracking down his back.

"Not bad for a day's work, is it?" the King mused.

He risked a glance up. He had expected the king of the Iron

Legion to be angry. To the degree that he could expect *anything* from this incomprehensible cyborg.

The King stood with hands behind his back, where they were caught up in the network of veins and wires that hooked him into the rest of the Legion. His eyes had left Benri, leaving him staring into the viewport that covered half the room.

Hesitantly, Benri straightened and followed his gaze.

This entire sector of space was a junkyard mixed in with the floor of a butcher's shop. Pieces of metal and flesh—some little more than clouds of freezing dust, others large enough to dock a fighter on—drifted aimlessly apart.

Several Legion fleets had been destroyed here. Not just destroyed; dismantled. Annihilated. Benri had taken one look at the battle the King had fought with *The Last Horizon* and had become so dizzy he'd almost lost his ability to channel his own spell.

Watching *The Last Horizon* carve through the Iron Legion had been like watching a thousand lasers sweep clean a beach one grain of sand at a time. Each of its uncountable guns targeted a different enemy, and a storm of light eradicated the Legion fighters.

He had never imagined a single ship with such firepower, not even the Zenith Starship.

But the Iron Legion was endless and its commander unlimited. There were always more ships, and they weren't helpless. Benri hadn't been able to watch, but he knew the outcome.

The Last Horizon had punched through their encircling forces and greatly depleted the Legion's presence in the sector. Though the Zenith Starship was surprisingly slow, the King had chosen to wait for reinforcements instead of pursuing.

But *The Last Horizon* had left a piece of itself behind, a spinning chunk of metal. It resembled a frigate-sized disk that had been torn in half, and it had only been removed by a strategic coordination of missiles, destructive spells, and high-order weaponry.

"We'll bring up a few more fleets," the King said casually. "I'm pulling Hives out of Alliance territory, so we'll keep the Subspace routes tied up."

"If this is *The Last Horizon* at half-power, I shudder to think what it can do with a complete crew," Benri responded. "We may need a new strategy, considering their capabilities."

Lights flashed inside the helmet that covered the Iron King's oversized brain, and Benri wondered if he was watching the king's mind work. "Ben, if we're going to work together, you need to stop worrying about *their* capabilities and start understanding mine."

That threw Benri's thoughts off-track. Did the King feel underestimated? And if he was explaining himself, did that mean the King really *did* intend to work together, as he pretended?

"I didn't mean to imply—"

The King waved a hand wearily. "Stop it. Listen. What did we gain today?"

"You inflicted a wound onto *The Last Horizon*," Benri said immediately. Best to flatter his ego. "Zenith Aethertech is difficult and expensive to repair, and in the meantime the ship's performance will suffer. We also kept pressure on Varic and gained a new understanding of the Divine Titan's abilities."

"We've seen weaknesses. Your son can't handle a Behemoth and can barely control his own staff. Raion Raithe can't freely pilot his Titan."

That wasn't freely piloting his Titan? Benri didn't voice his skepticism, but from what he'd seen, Raion had piloted a Titan beyond the abilities of anyone else in history.

The King made a series of mechanical clicking sounds that Benri took as frustration. Which was chilling. "You didn't pay attention to his actions afterward. The Divine Titan has absorbed some new material to grow to such a degree, and it's beyond what Raion can control. You have the eyes, but you must learn to use them."

The condescension burned Benri's pride, but there was nothing he could say. There should be no shame in being less intelligent than a galactic hive-mind.

The King scanned the wreckage of their Legion with burning eyes. "All that, and what did it cost us?"

"Should I answer in ships or currency?" Benri's processor was feeding him the estimate, and he flinched at the number. A loss like this would have devastated the Vallenar Corporation.

"You should be thinking in terms of time and opportunities, but that's a lesson for another day."

"I don't have an accurate count of your troops, but in terms of ships, there were eighty-five hundred positioned in this sector alone. All total, there have to be at least—"

The King raised a chrome-plated hand, which shone with an inner flame. His fingers all pointed to the left side of the viewport, not to Benri, but Benri shut up anyway.

Slowly, metallic fingertips drifted across the view of the battle-field. Where those fingers pointed, the debris dissolved, as though an invisible force were sweeping the entire system clean at once.

The effect was chilling and absolute.

"*Nothing,*" the Iron King said. "It cost us nothing."

CHAPTER THIRTY-FIVE

THE TELEPORTATION THAT carried us to *The Last Horizon* seemed
to take longer than usual, though it was hard to tell in that river
of light.

I manifested next to Raion on the bridge, where I deduced from
the smooth metal covering the forward viewport that we must be
in Subspace.

The lights flickered overhead, and the ship creaked and groaned
here and there. I had flown aboard vessels that made worse noises—
piloted quite a few of them, too—but this alarmed me as much as
anything ever had. What did it take to make ancient Aethertech
groan like a rusty hatch?

Before I could ask, Horizon appeared in front of me, in the ship's
usual smooth projection of multi-colored light. She looked the same
as ever, hands folded and horns pointed to the ceiling, but she flickered for a second before stabilizing.

"Are we about to fall apart?" I asked.

"*Of course not,*" Horizon said defensively. "*What makes you think
we—*" Her words were interrupted by a shiver of holographic static.

Raion gave a sigh of relief. "Oh, good!"

Then he fell over.

"I hope we have some medical facilities aboard," I said.

Raion's voice was somewhat muffled by speaking into the cold metal of the floor, but he sounded cheery enough. "Just give me a cot and a snack and I'll be nine..."

His voice drifted off.

"Nine what?" Horizon asked curiously.

"I think he meant to say 'fine.'"

"Nine...hundred percent," Raion mumbled.

"How about you take him to Medical?"

Blue light scooped up Raion and began drifting him down the hall, which was interesting to me for magical reasons. "You don't have internal teleportation?"

"Nothing to worry about! But not everything is...fully online at the moment."

That worried me.

While Raion was taken away on a cloud of light, I sank into the command chair and pulled up a condition report.

With just a glance, I felt a real, sympathetic pain in my own gut. Someone had done quite a number on my ship.

"Looks like the Iron Legion really gave you a beating."

Horizon stiffened and her seven-pointed eyes shifted. *"Without a Pilot, I am stuck with my default Subspace Drive, so I couldn't out-run them!"* She sounded desperate. *"With no Commander, I have no shuttles or fighters, few alternative weapons systems, and my drones are useless without an Engineer. You should be amazed that I did this well against a fleet commanded by an Iron King!"*

I looked up at her. "I thought you were dead. Thank you for proving me wrong."

It was hard to convey the depth of my relief. Scrolling through the report of the battle, it was clear the heroic lengths that Horizon had gone to in order to survive. I had almost failed in a sixth life.

But now, we all still had a chance.

Horizon looked shocked for a second, then she drew herself up in a picture of placid confidence. *"Of course, Captain. Welcome back."*

I leaned back in my chair. "So it really is an Iron King..."

"*There is no other explanation.*" She looked hungry. "*We should hurry and fill the crew. He's an opponent worthy of us at full strength.*"

"Can we make it anywhere?" I tapped the screen. "Looks like we're missing twelve percent of your mass."

"*Another problem an Engineer could help solve, but my structure is resilient. I will remain functional under any amount of damage up to total system failure. I will fight to my last breath, until I am destroyed.*"

Horizon drew herself up proudly, but her confidence was punctured by flickering lights and a distant groaning sound. She deflated. "*Yes, the damage is significant. I've patched us to cover for the systems we lost, but we won't be operating at maximum capacity without repairs.*"

"And enemy losses?"

Numbers and diagrams began scrolling across the screen, listing the Iron Legion assets that had been lost in the battle. I was impressed immediately, but then it kept scrolling. And scrolling.

"How many fleets did they *send?*"

"*Not all of them. The Legion has oceans of blood yet to spill.*" Horizon glanced secretively to the side as though evaluating me. "*With a full complement of crew, we have no reason to fear any number of such assaults.*"

I swiped away the battle report and moved over to the ship's capacity. "Omega still won't take the deal?" I swapped over to his holding cell, but it was just an empty tube. Had they released him? Or had Sola made good on her threat and jettisoned him into space?

"*We were forced to relocate him into a new holding facility.*"

The screen changed without my interference to show a storage vault. Between a series of strange objects locked behind sturdy cages and mystical seals, a hermetically sealed jar shook on a shelf. It contained a tar-like substance that rocked against its container.

It didn't take much for me to understand the situation.

"So Omega escaped," I said.

"*He was broken free by an external means, but the Sword handled it. I relocated him with the secure cargo. There's only so much I can do without an Engineer.*"

"He's smaller than he used to be."

"He killed Sola once before she took him down. Roughly a quarter of my internal damage was his sabotage, and he destroyed an entire bay of drones. Without his interference, I suspect I would have suffered only eight percent damage to the Iron Legion instead of twelve."

With that, Omega strained the limit of my patience. I'd give him one more chance, and after that it was the Iron King treatment: straight into a sun.

Not that the plan had worked on the Iron King, apparently.

"How much is four percent of a priceless starship?" I mused.

"Still priceless."

"That's what I thought too." I tapped the side of the screen, then left myself a reminder in my console. I'd deal with Omega after this.

Until then, it was the Captain's duty to make sure his ship was headed in the right direction.

"Where are we, Horizon?"

"We're skirting the edge of Galactic Union territory. I don't want to put ourselves at the mercy of the Union, but better them than the Iron Legion."

On that, we agreed.

"Is there anyone in the Union who can repair you?"

The projection of Horizon slumped and sighed. *"I can repair myself. It is the materials I lack. Thought-conduction alloy and synapse nodes are not standard issue at every shipyard."*

I had to query the ship database for both those substances. As expected, they were Aethertech materials. Thought-conduction alloys were only exported from Lichborn systems for astronomical prices, while synapse nodes were organic machines grown by the Aethril in multi-dimensional gardens.

I had some connections to those cultures, and—while I hated to rely on my family—the Vallenar Corporation would be delighted to procure rare goods in exchange for favors from *The Last Horizon* and its captain.

Though that reminded me of my father's current situation and likely fate. Also, when I looked at Horizon's calculations, I saw that the situation wasn't as optimistic as I'd first assumed. "Ah. You don't just need a little, do you?"

"*Every one of my base components is a treasure for which most worlds are unworthy.*"

Horizon was requesting more thought-conduction alloy than the entire galaxy produced in a decade, and maybe more synapse nodes than existed in civilized space. I'd be better off asking for the crown of the Aethril Queen.

I idly flipped through the files as I considered the problem. We could scrape up as many of the requested components as possible, and—though Horizon would no doubt complain—mundane materials would at least keep us from sinking into Subspace. We would recover, though it might take us years and a fortune in both cash and favors.

It would be much easier if we had an Engineer.

"Give me a list of Engineer candid—" The list popped up in front of me before I could finish the sentence.

"*As you can see, I biased the list toward those you were familiar with,*" Horizon said, spreading out pictures of all the candidates.

That was clear. Not too many Aether Technicians had competed for a crew position, Technicians not being known for their abilities in single combat, and most of those who *had* tried out didn't meet Horizon's standards.

There were only twelve pictures in front of me, and I knew half of them personally from one life or another. Master Aether Technicians were extraordinarily rare, but there were still tens of thousands of them across the galaxy. For me to know half of this list would have been an impossible coincidence without Horizon's intervention.

"They're all qualified?" I asked, flipping through the files. A couple of names stood out immediately, both for professional and personal reasons, but all their abilities looked impressive at first glance.

Horizon looked offended. "*A mere twelve percent damage is not enough to get me to compromise my standards. Only heroes may walk my halls.*"

"And yet you almost made Raion the Engineer," I muttered. Before she could respond, I pulled up a profile. "What do you think about him?"

Professor Denon Javal was half-Visiri, his skin mottled brown and red and his third eye half-closed. His holographic image squinted suspiciously into the distance, and a strangely shifting diamond hovered over his shoulder.

"*I don't question his ability, but what about his personal compatibility?*"

I grunted. I'd worked briefly with Professor Javal in the life I'd spent as a mage-for-hire with no connection to the Vallenar Corporation. His gift lent itself to making Subspace Drives, which was one of the most profitable talents an Aether Technician could have.

Everyone else with a similar gift was obscenely wealthy, but Javal kept moving, taking odd jobs here and there across the Free Worlds. I'd gotten him to repair a Drive of mine in exchange for taking a band of Karoshan pirates off his tail.

I still wasn't sure if he kept moving because he liked it, or because he had to.

He hated contracts, appointments, and obligations. He never dropped his paranoia, and he asked question after question after *question*, even about the most mundane subjects.

But his ability was real. I couldn't think of anyone more valuable to have aboard a starship.

"He'd get us out of this situation," I said. "Even if we only hired him temporarily..."

"*Look further, Captain!*" Seven-pointed eyes sparkled. "*Not to our current difficulties, but to the legends we will create!*"

If we didn't get out of our current difficulties, we would never create any legends at all, but I still picked out another name.

Zorova of the House Eternal was a Karoshan of bronze, pebbled skin and glowing yellow hair-strands. She was skeletally thin by the standards of her kind, and she wore a harness on her back carrying a pair of mechanical arms.

"I've never met her, but she has a good reputation. And she left Karosha a year ago, which means she might be loyal to the Queen."

"She's still in Alliance space. We cannot reach her quickly, and if we traveled that far and found she was not a good fit, we may corner ourselves. Also, while I would gladly accept her as an Engineer, there are others here with stronger gifts."

That was true, though I felt it didn't disqualify her. Through some strange quirk of the Aether, Karoshan Technicians never awaken the gift to *create* Aethertech. They can use, modify, repair, and improve the creations of others, but they can't make it themselves.

The species with the greatest gift for creating Aethertech is humanity. It's our galactic claim to fame. The Technicians who created the original Zenith Devices were mostly human.

Which made me take another look at the humans on the list. One human in particular.

Horizon slid her horned head between me and the projected file. *"There is nothing wrong with expressing a personal preference, Captain."*

"I can't just hire friends," I said. "I want to pick the best person for the job."

"These are all among the best Aether Technicians in the galaxy. Why not select the ones you know you can count on?"

With some reluctance, I selected Mell's profile.

She had her hands stuck in her long white coat, her glasses had slid halfway down her nose, and there was a toothpick clamped between her teeth. Though she had no doubt posed for the recording of this hologram, she hadn't brushed her hair.

One of her Nova-Bots, a tiny little brass humanoid, flew past her on rotor blades. She took a hand out of her pocket to swat at it, but it flew away from her.

"Her gift doesn't make any sense for a starship Engineer," I pointed out. "And meeting her again could be awkward."

"Not for her. She has no idea who you are, and no way of finding out about your...prior relationship. Not unless you tell her."

That was true. In reality, we'd never met.

Then again, Horizon might tell her.

"As for Doctor Mell's gift, I look forward to seeing how her androids evolve my drones. I suspect the synergy will be most productive."

I still flipped through the other Engineer candidates, but in the end, I returned to Mell's file. I was the Captain. It came down to my decision.

I liked the way it felt to have Sola and Raion along, knowing I could rely on them. I wanted more of that. And Mell was another one I'd let down, in a life only I now remembered. This would give me a chance to make things right.

Besides, she could always turn me down.

"Can you teleport me to her?" I asked.

"Regrettably, not from here, but she is still in the Galactic Union. The safest way to flee from the Iron Legion is to go straight through their territory."

That had dangers of its own, but I nodded. "Deeper into the Union, then. We still have to let them know that the Iron Legion has a King. We'll pick up some reinforcements on the way to our Engineer."

Horizon drew herself up proudly, tilting her horns back. *"If we stand to destroy the Iron Legion, we will have no shortage of allies."*

CHAPTER THIRTY-SIX

I BROUGHT THE *Last Horizon* out of Subspace within hailing distance of the Magic Tower.

The ship creaked and shook as we returned to reality, which was less than encouraging, but we held together.

"Magic Tower, this is Professor Varic Vallenar. We're incoming and would like to request a meeting with Director Porellus."

Porellus wouldn't want to help, of course. He'd rather bathe in a lake of salt than support a plan I came up with.

But if I could bully him into tolerating me this once, I could go to the Galactic Union while representing more than just me. The Magic Tower wasn't a military organization, but it had quite the political reach.

After the Magic Tower helped me get the Galactic Union on our side, then I could go to the Vallenar Corporation. If I'd had access to the Corporate Subline from our position, I'd have contacted them already, but we were too far out.

I feared what they would tell me. I didn't like my father much, but no one wants to see their family made into a Shepherd for an Iron Hive.

Anyway, while the interpersonal web was a little complicated, it boiled down to recruiting the weakest ally first. With them as bait, I could hook the big fish.

Which was a great plan until I didn't hear anything in return from the Magic Tower.

I activated the Subline again. "I'll try that again. This is Captain Varic Vallenar of *The Last Horizon,* requesting a meeting with Director Porellus of the Magic Tower. Please acknowledge."

Static.

"Could the Iron Legion have reached them?" I asked.

Sola stepped up behind my chair, not wearing her armor, and answered. "The Legion can attack almost anywhere, if they send a single Hive on a suicide mission. But they wouldn't gain anything here."

Though the Magic Tower was a famous and influential part of magical culture in the Union, it was hardly a prime military target. There were many richer targets for the Legion between them and us.

If they had attacked the Tower, it would be because of me.

We had flown into the system now, and I drummed my fingers on the edge of the ship console. "Horizon, do we really have nothing on scanners?"

"Scanners are being jammed," Horizon's voice told me. *"I'm sure I don't need to remind you that this won't be a problem with a full crew."*

That didn't bode well. But I was getting ahead of myself, and I thumbed the Subline communications again. "Magic Tower, once again, this is Varic Vallenar of *The Last Horizon.* If you're in distress, please respond."

I was still waiting with a lump in my throat when a voice crackled out from the Subline channel. *"Captain Vallenar, this is Commander Nelthan of* GSS Kholien. *You identified yourself as* The Last Horizon. *Please confirm."*

"I confirm, Commander Nelthan. I have control of *The Last Horizon.*"

"The one—"

"Yes, Commander, the one you're thinking of. I'm trying to hail the Magic Tower."

"*The system is under lockdown, Captain. We've had multiple Hive sightings in the sector.*"

I frowned to Sola. "Why would there be multiple Hives here?"

"I don't know. But I'm not the Iron King."

"*Last Horizon, hold your position. We'd like visual confirmation of the Zenith Starship.*"

I paused. Bad memories of fights with the Union military floated to the surface. Still, I eventually responded. "Confirmed, Commander Nelthan. We'll wait where we are."

Horizon rubbed her chin as magical eyes floated all around her. "*Considering our damage and no Pilot, I cannot be sure that we can escape a Galactic Union fleet without violence.*"

"We have to give trust to get trust," I said. "And we needed to contact the Union somehow." I hesitated, reliving some more unpleasant memories, then I addressed Sola and Horizon both. "Keep your weapons hot, just in case."

Sola nodded and Horizon gave a face-stretching grin.

Minutes later, twists in reality bloomed like flowers in the darkness of space. Gray, featureless, mass-produced ships emerged. Galactic Union vessels. Not one fleet, but groups from several fleets.

That alarmed me. I wasn't a strategist, but from my experience, there were only a few reasons why the Union would send a rag-tag battle-group like this. Either multiple fleets had already been destroyed by the Iron Legion, which implied that the war was starting off worse than I feared, or these ships had a...special purpose.

I remembered just such a patchwork fleet surrounding me in the past. It had been a secret operation, kept off the books by one of the leaders who pulled the Galactic Union's strings from the shadows.

And ultimately, that capture had resulted in my execution.

I was uncomfortable with the memory, but I was *less* comfortable by the group's formation as they came out of Subspace.

I activated the communicator again. "Commander, a less charitable man than I would say you had me surrounded."

"*The Last Horizon, lower your shields and prepare yourself for boarding. We are commandeering your vessel as part of our emergency defense effort against the Iron Legion. No crew will be harmed in a peaceful surrender, and your property will be returned to you at the time of...*"

Commander Nelthan of *GSS Kholien* continued talking, but the sound faded. His voice drew away from my ears as though I was drifting far away.

I had a hand on my wand, which buzzed eagerly. I felt Eurias in the back of my mind, a heavy weight in storage.

And I remembered the last time the Union captured me. They were trying to take me again.

This time, it wouldn't be so easy.

Horizon's voice infiltrated the shield of silence that had gone up around me. "*Would you like me to chase them off?*"

"No," I heard myself say. "I'll do it."

As I flipped up the hood of my mantle and slipped on my ring, Horizon took over the conversation with *GSS Kholien.*

"*Commander, this is* The Last Horizon. *Our only enemy is the Iron Legion. To oppose us is a grave mistake.*"

"*Am I speaking with an AI? Where is Captain Vallenar?*"

"*I am not a computer, Commander,*" Horizon said, sounding only faintly offended. "*I am the spirit of a ship far beyond your means and imagination. We would prefer this not to come to a contest of arms.*"

"*This is Galactic Union space, and you are intruders here. Your contribution is needed against the Iron Legion. By the laws of the Union, I am well within my rights to commandeer your vessel.*"

I thought Horizon's eyes would burn brighter than Sola's. I palmed the airlock and stepped inside, but before the door slid closed again, I spoke to her. "He's not going to listen."

"*Oh, I know. But I have given him the chance not to die a fool.*"

"*...Last Horizon, did you intend to send that transmission? Because you have threatened a military officer and Galactic Union representative.*"

"*It is a stubborn beast of labor that must be whipped until it listens,*" Horizon continued. "*Oh, I'm sorry, did I send that too?*"

I vented myself from the airlock.

Once again, thanks to my levitation ring and my mantle, it was the gentle sensation of being carried into a river instead of the violent experience of being snatched out of my ship by the void.

After the loud rush of sound from air leaking past me, I was left drifting in silence. With my thoughts.

And with four dozen Galactic Union warships, spread out in a bristling array of weapons all around me. My processor helpfully informed me that their weapons were primed and ready to fire.

I stopped myself from spinning with my ring and oriented myself to face the line of blocky silver ships.

Then I raised my wand and tapped into my element. Dark water slipped out of the Aether, stars shifting in its liquid currents.

As the water gathered above me, I imagined what the crew of the Union starships would be thinking at that moment.

Most ships didn't have decent Aether scanners. They relied on crew mages to read magic with their eyes, which was usually faster anyway.

The scanners were made to detect large-scale Aether sources or magical formations, not to read them in detail. There was no need to proactively search out magic. Active spells were rarely used in ship-to-ship combat.

Just about every model used magic to regulate atmosphere and supplement its shields, as well as a collection of various other standard protection spells, but no offensive spells hit as hard as a plasma cannon. So there was no need to detect them.

By this time, the globe of conjured water was five times larger than my body and still growing. This would be the point at which the standard-issue Galactic Union scanners would pick up on my magic.

At that level, it was considered tactical siege magic.

They wouldn't panic yet. If anything, they would only speak more harshly in their messages to Horizon.

Unless my father or the Iron King had slipped them some information, they wouldn't know I could already cut one of their cruisers in half.

And I was considering it.

I was certain by now that ships in this group had been selected for their ability to keep a secret. Shadow leaders needed to keep their operations off the books, or at least out of the public eye. In a sense, these crews had been selected for loyalty.

Loyalty to people who, at least once before, had plunged the galaxy into civil war.

Maybe I should send them a message.

The first warning shot erupted from a cruiser in front of me. A spray of plasma splattered on *The Last Horizon*'s crimson shield.

I didn't flinch.

I sent a message to Horizon through my console. *"Am I within teleporter range of the flagship?"*

Horizon's giggle echoed in my ear. *"Tell me when, Captain."*

I lowered my wand and unleashed my spell.

CHAPTER THIRTY-SEVEN

COMMANDER NELTHAN OF *GSS Kholien* agreed to the warning shot.

He didn't know what he was doing here. The ship they were trying to capture was clearly damaged, and they risked damaging relations with the Vallenar Corporation by taking such an aggressive stance. If it *was* the Zenith Starship, then the situation was worse.

But he was also scared.

These last few days, the Iron Legion had begun to push into Galactic Union territory more aggressively than they had ever done before. It looked like they were abandoning the Alliance and the Free Worlds to focus entirely on the Union.

Anyone who commanded a warship for long enough had Legion horror stories, and Nelthan was no exception. He had come on the splinters of destroyed ships before, and he had the good sense to be terrified of the Iron King.

A planet was a planet, that was the Legion's philosophy. It was the only thing that kept the Union together. The Iron Legion didn't care whether the planets they captured belonged to a larger government or whether they had a sentient population, as long as they had plentiful raw materials and living creatures.

So the Iron Legion frightened him, but they weren't the only threat.

He had been sent on this assignment by a private...sponsor. One whose identity Commander Nelthan didn't know, but who was frighteningly high in the Union. It had been made clear to Nelthan that success meant future promotions and a charmed life, while failure meant disfavor.

Whatever "disfavor" meant, Nelthan was just as afraid of that as he was of facing down the Legion. Thus, he had prepared to succeed.

When Union Intelligence told him his ships were capable of capturing *The Last Horizon*, he believed them. When they told him how many ships they calculated could be lost in the engagement, he *hadn't* believed them.

The Zenith Starship couldn't be worth four battleships, sixteen cruisers, and seventeen frigates. Even if the legends about this one *were* true.

Now *The Last Horizon* was gathering Aether, which earned them a slap on the wrist. If they didn't disperse the spell they were preparing, he'd crack open their shield. From that point, negotiations would get more aggressive.

Plans and projections flashed across his monitor, driven by information provided by Union Intelligence. He had things well in hand.

Then something hit his ship.

Light flashed above GSS *Kholien* in a line as a beam cut across his shields. The slash was miles long, but the scanners hadn't picked up a plasma beam. The ship shook and the monitor blared a warning as their shield flickered to steady itself.

"What happened?" he demanded.

One of his officers stood up. "It was a spell, sir!"

Nelthan felt a chill. A spell?

Was that the secret of *The Last Horizon*? Maybe it magnified spells to unprecedented degrees. Varic Vallenar was an Archmage, after all.

No, that didn't make any sense. Nothing could empower spells that much.

"Shields at seventy percent!" another officer said in a panicked tone. He shot her a stern look. She was new on his bridge, but she'd lost too much composure. And she was wrong.

"Eighty percent," he corrected, "and compose yourself."

"Sorry, Commander. *Collectively,* the shields of our vessels have been reduced to seventy percent."

Nelthan's chill got a whole lot colder.

Then he heard a cheery ringing in his ear. No one else could hear it, and a name flashed in the corner of his vision. Someone was calling him on his personal console.

He almost dismissed it out of habit—it was an amateur mistake to leave his personal line open while in command.

Then he saw the name.

"Move this call to the central monitor," Nelthan commanded his ship AI, "then answer."

The large monitor at the center of the bridge lit up with four words.

Caller: Varic Vallenar. Connecting...

The bridge went silent as the call connected and Archmage Vallenar's head floated on the screen above everyone.

His eyes reflected the cold gleam of steel beneath the shadow of his blue hood. He was clearly floating in space with stars and his ship behind him, but he must have carried an atmospheric generator with him. Probably an enchantment, given his profession.

When he spoke, his voice was clear.

"*Commander Nelthan. I came here to request the help of the Magic Tower against the Iron Legion. I'm not working against the Union.*"

"We intend to use your vessel against the Iron Legion, Captain Vallenar. A ship such as yours cannot be used to its full potential in the hands of a wizard. I will overlook your attack if you surrender now. Weapons such as that should be turned against the Legion."

"*That was not one of* The Last Horizon's *weapons, Commander.*" Varic pointed a wand, which seemed to point straight at the screen. "*Watch.*"

The blue light of his wand flared.

Kholien trembled again. His shields lit up, reducing them to roughly forty percent. Shield stability percentage was always an estimate.

"Sir, we caught it," a lieutenant said. A report flashed onto Nelthan's private monitor, accompanied by an image.

That had been an elemental attack. A stream of water directed by that wand, a liquid beam sending white spray into the void.

If the chills didn't stop running up and down his spine, Nelthan was going to have his thermal regulator checked.

But that didn't change his responsibility.

"The Galactic Union does not bow to threats," he said firmly. "All ships fire."

Varic had proven himself the enemy. Now it was more important that Nelthan crush him. Not to mention that he couldn't simply give this mission up.

Missiles and plasma bolts streaked through space at his word, and he expected to see *The Last Horizon*'s shields light up in a moment.

Instead, green lights flashed from the *Horizon* as though it had fired every weapon at once. And as though it had three or four times as many weapons as Intelligence had estimated.

Detonations lit space for miles around them, but none impacted the shields. The Zenith Starship had shot down the whole volley mid-flight.

Varic's stone face still filled the monitor. *"Was that enough of a demonstration?"*

Nelthan stepped closer to the Archmage's hologram. "Remember that you are the one who chose to make an enemy of the Galactic Union."

Then he shut down the call.

There was no reasoning with an enemy like this. Unless they had *The Last Horizon* under their control, Nelthan would never sleep easily.

He barked orders and the ships tightened formation, filling vacuum with an endless cloud of weapons. The *Horizon* responded faster and more fluidly than any ship he had ever seen; he could understand why Intelligence wanted it so badly now.

But even so, it was one ship against forty-eight. A shot here and there impacted against its shields. Clearly the pressure was working, because it didn't have the chance to return fire. It only shot down their missiles.

Commander Nelthan ordered the activation of the impulse cannons and turned back to the viewport when he saw a pool of blue light pouring onto the bridge in front of him. In a split second, it shaped into the figure of a man.

Then Varic Vallenar stood face-to-face with him.

Nelthan was grateful for the training that had a pistol in his hand and aiming at Vallenar before the man had finished forming. "On your knees!" he barked, and he was echoed by the four other bridge crew who had gotten their guns on the intruder.

That number increased by the second.

The Archmage slowly turned his silver glare around the bridge. He raised a hand as though holding something invisible.

Nelthan fired. So did two others.

The plasma bolts shattered against an invisible shield, and an amulet on the wizard's neck glowed slightly brighter.

When Varic closed his fist, he spoke one word. Lasers shot out from between his fingers in every direction, slicing up the bridge like half a dozen blades.

Consoles and monitors exploded. People dove out of the way. The door was sliced in half. Red lights and an alarm flashed, warning of an impending hull breach.

But no blood spilled. Varic lowered his fist. "Remember," the Archmage said, "that I visited your ship and did not kill you."

The bolt from a plasma pistol exploded on his shield, but Varic didn't react.

Years of command kept Nelthan's voice cold and dry. "You have put yourself on the Galactic Union's execution list, Vallenar."

Silver eyes met his, and Nelthan felt one last chill. "It wouldn't be the first time, Commander."

Varic dissolved into blue light and vanished.

The bridge erupted into panic afterwards, but Commander Nelthan stood as a beacon of calm. The commanding officer had to be a pillar of reassurance.

Something splashed against his boot, and he looked down to the wet deck. Only then did he realize that the lasers Vallenar summoned hadn't been lasers at all. That had been water.

"Remove the Subspace lock," Nelthan ordered. "Let them go."

He thought he heard a sigh of relief at those orders.

Maybe it was his own.

CHAPTER THIRTY-EIGHT

"THE UNION HAS ordered our capture on their military Subline," Horizon reported. *"They'll raise our threat estimate now."*

She'd gotten a good look at their computers when she teleported me onto the bridge of the *Kholien,* which had put her in a better mood.

"So I guess they won't work with us, then," I said lightly. I intended it as a joke, but my hands were shaking.

I had been about to cut my way through their blockade.

I still wondered if I had made a mistake. I'd scared them off, but I had showed my hand. If they'd chosen to fight it out, the other ships could have put up magical wards against teleportation. We would have won the engagement eventually, considering my capabilities and Sola's, but we couldn't afford further damage to *The Last Horizon.* Besides, defeating the battle-group would have made enemies out of the entire Galactic Union.

Of course, we may have done that anyway.

"You did perfectly, Captain," Horizon said with relish. *"That will teach them proper respect."*

"Are we close enough to reach the Corporate Subline?" I asked.

"We are."

"First, hail my father's clone," I ordered. I wanted to find out what happened to my real father, and his copy might be able to help me more than the Corporation itself could.

"He's...close." Horizon sounded puzzled. "If we adjust course and leave Subspace in the next thirty seconds, we'll be right on top of him."

"Do it."

When we popped out of Subspace, my heart fell into my stomach again.

The Iron King had left us a gift.

The Sunsail starship drifted without power, its broken mast and torn solar sails held together by tendons and strings of meat. Silver plates had been bolted onto the hull, patching over battle damage.

"There's a distress signal," Horizon informed me.

"Can you find any signs of life?"

"None that I can see."

"Blow it up. While you're doing that, boost my Subline signal. I'm calling the company myself."

I turned my back on the viewport as the Sunsail was destroyed. I had seen enough starship battle for one day.

The Subline connection, stretched as it was, hissed and crackled on the edges when I finally connected.

"Vallenar Corporation," a woman said brightly. "How may I assist you, Mister Vallenar?"

"I need to know my father's status."

She hesitated for a moment, probably searching her console for the necessary protocol. "I can't guarantee a quick response, but I can certainly send that message for you."

"One of his copies was destroyed by the Iron Legion around the coordinates I'm sending you. I've seen Legionnaires cloned by the Mirror of Silence. I'm afraid he's been taken."

Another pause. "Would you like me to—"

"I think he's in danger."

"...one moment, please." I heard shifting as she swished at a virtual screen. "Would you like to stay on the line for a few moments in the case of an immediate reply, or would you like me to contact you again?"

"Contact me."

I was about to close the connection when she spoke again. *"Actually, Mister Vallenar, I have a voice message from your father. It seems he's safe! With your permission, I'll send it along now."*

She sounded pleased and relieved, but I still didn't take this as good news. Not until I heard the message.

It did get my hopes up, though. Maybe my father had an explanation.

"Send it through."

Only a few seconds later, my father's voice echoed in my ears, courtesy of my processor implant. *"I can keep track of my own reflections. If you're having problems with the Iron Legion, contact the Union."*

The message cut off there.

The woman who had taken the message popped back in cheerily. *"Is there anything else I can help you with, Mister Vallenar?"*

"No. Thank you."

I disconnected the call before I returned a message that would cause more problems than it solved.

Then I leaned back in the command chair, drumming fingers aimlessly on the armrest.

I had no way of telling whether that message had been from my real father or one of his clones. If he claimed that there was nothing wrong, then the Legion might have gotten his magic some other way—maybe by taking over a copy of his, maybe with some kind of artifact or Aethertech spell-capturing device, or maybe by developing a similar magic of their own.

It wasn't impossible to create a spell so close to the Mirror of Silence that I would mistake the two, it was just incredibly unlikely.

If that wasn't the case, then my father was cooperating with the Iron Legion. I found it hard to believe that he would do so willingly, but if he had been turned into one of their abominations, his magic would be substantially weaker.

Maybe this was an old-fashioned kidnapping. A hostage the Iron King could use against me.

I wasn't fond of my father, but I'd save him if I could. Which left me in the same state I'd been before: in need of allies.

"Can we get far enough into Union space to reach Mell?" I asked Horizon.

"If we don't mind running into more groups like the last one," the spirit responded. *"I say we do it. We should fight for our Engineer."*

I felt a noose tightening. Caught between the Iron Legion and the Galactic Union was no position I ever wanted to be in.

"How long would it take us to contact the Karoshan Alliance?" I asked.

"Days, with no Pilot. I can't say it's worth the travel. The Karoshan King Regent will not aid us. The Iron Legion invading the Galactic Union is his greatest dream come true."

I had imagined as much, but I'd been hoping Horizon would tell me otherwise. Queen Shyrax would have responded the same way, and I had no reason to think her replacement would act any differently.

The Aethril were part of the Union, but they might give us some private assistance. As would the Lichborn, despite their war with the Karoshans.

But in both cases, what help they could offer us was limited. And they would take time to reach and to convince. Time, right then, was rarer than thought-conduction alloy.

"How long will it take to repair you without an Engineer?"

Horizon sighed. *"Two to three standard months. The real constraint is the material requirement, though we can forgo certain components if we have the right Engineer. One month, and a greatly reduced expense, if Doctor Mell were aboard."*

I tapped the arm of the chair more and surveyed her simulated expression. The solution was obvious, though the ship's spirit might not like it. "Horizon, we need a crew. I know you don't want to relax your standards, but we need to hire the closest people who can do the—"

"I have a...confession." Horizon cut me off with a profoundly uncomfortable expression. *"I may perhaps have...understated the effect of my damaged systems. Please ignore the upcoming sounds."*

My fingers froze on the chair. "What sounds?"

The light of the room flickered. The ship's structure squealed and groaned, and suddenly the barely perceptible sense of motion caused by our flight stopped. The floor settled underneath my feet.

In physical space, this would have been cause for alarm.

In Subspace, it was reason to panic.

I was already drawing symbols in the air with my wand, conjuring protective seals from what few wisps of the Aether I could squeeze out of our surroundings. "Surface! Take us back!"

Horizon avoided my gaze in what looked suspiciously like embarrassment. *"I was certain we could complete the dive with no incident, but I'm afraid prediction doesn't work quite as precisely when interacting with Subspace."*

"I'm aware of that! I taught a class on Subspace magic! Are you telling me that *you* need to take that class?"

"I'm more than aware of the concept, I merely had to take some...navigational liberties."

"You fail my class, Horizon! You fail! Get all available power to the Subspace Drive!"

"Already in progress. We'll be underway momentarily."

Something thumped against the hull, and an inhuman screech scraped against the inside of my skull.

"Deploy drones!"

"We don't have many—"

"Shut up and deploy the drones!" I activated intra-ship communications. "We're in trouble, everybody. I need someone capable of Subspace combat on the bridge ten seconds ago."

Sola came close to complying with that request, because the door swished open and she marched in before my sentence was over. She was fully armored, and her visor gleamed as she took in the situation on my monitor.

"What information do we have?" Sola asked.

"Drones are engaging now," I responded. "They'll let us know what it is."

"Deployed drones have been destroyed," Horizon reported. *"I told you we didn't have enough."*

A metallic squeal came from the hull, followed by another soul-churning cry.

The monitor showed me what information we'd managed to gain: whatever this thing was, it had tentacles that existed in several locations at once. Which allowed it to peel away our ship layer by layer. Turns out the best Aethertech armor in existence was little protection against violations of reality.

Then again, they had kept it out so far.

Sola was already inside the airlock. "My armor has an existential anchor. I've got five minutes before I have to take the other way out. If you get the Drive fixed, leave me."

With that, she reached over to shut the airlock. I stopped her by completing my spells. Five complex, spinning magic circles attached themselves to her body.

"Protective seals," I told her. "They'll—"

She shut the airlock. Seconds later, she vented herself into Subspace. The brief glimpse of the swirling extra-dimensional space made my stomach churn.

"*I think she knows what they do,*" Horizon said.

"You don't get to joke right now! You lost that privilege when you stranded us outside reality! How long on the Drive repairs?"

"*Six minutes.*"

"That is the *worst* time you could have said. Take me there."

Horizon cleared her throat. "*Teleportation is difficult without access to the Aether, but I've moved the Drive as close as I can.*"

I sprinted down the hall toward the Subspace Drive. Explosions and incomprehensible shrieks echoed from outside as I ran. I thought I heard a shout from Sola, though that was probably my imagination.

There isn't exactly air in Subspace. Then again, there isn't exactly *no* air in Subspace.

It's complicated.

I reached the Drive in two minutes. It wasn't too far from the bridge, and while I wished Horizon could have brought it closer, I was sure there were some physical constraints she couldn't ignore.

This was, however, a bigger Subspace Drive than anything I'd seen before.

The core of the Drive was a large, twisting, semi-transparent tube in the center of a room big enough to dock fighters in. Monitors and consoles all around the walls gave its current condition, which wasn't good. But you didn't need to have a degree in Subspace Engineering to understand that.

The light inside the twisting glass of the drive flickered and swirled chaotically. It was bright white and eddied like a liquid. Rainbow swirls erupted every second or two, bending the eye.

Horizon projected her holographic form next to the Drive. *"It's not a mechanical problem so much as an energetic one. The imbalance in my systems caused by structural damage has disturbed our stable relationship to Subspace."*

"Horizon, listen to me. I'm not an Aether Technician. I am a wizard. Until we pick up our Engineer, if you have mechanical problems, fix them however seems best to you." I traced symbols in the air with my fingers. "But if you ever have another magical problem and you try to solve it on your own, I'm going to tear out your power core and toss it into a black hole."

Horizon shuffled awkwardly and scratched at the base of one of her horns. *"I...am sorry. I expected—"*

"Quiet. Excuses later." Complex magic circles flashed from my hands and faded into the spinning mess of energy inside the Subspace Drive's core.

While the spells were intended to bind together physical objects, they could be applied to more esoteric purposes. You just needed a delicate touch.

I watched the magical symbols that flashed here and there, tailoring my effort to what I read. Step by step, using sealing spells when necessary, I pacified the captured magic.

I thought that would be a harder task, given the lack of external Aether to help me, but my binding-circles and the churning extra-dimensional powers in the Drive both accepted my new purpose for them easily. Aetheric symbols exploded into a complex web, binding the white energies inside the Drive and pulling them to stability.

The blue light of my magic faded as the Subspace Drive was restored to peace and order in a matter of seconds. The monitors around the walls of the room stabilized and Horizon straightened.

"Ready to surface, Captain," the ship's spirit said.

I brushed my hands off and gave her a withering look. "Call Sola back in. Surface. And call me next time."

Before I reached the bridge, the ship shuddered one more time and slid back into physical space. There was the subtle sense of rightness in the air that told me I was back where I belonged, and the metal began to slide away from the viewport and reveal the stars.

One last, ethereal scream trailed us as we left, and the Subspace-creature stayed behind.

Sola came back in from the airlock, suit cracked here and there and steam rising from all around her where the creature's blood boiled off. She didn't say anything, but her gun vanished back into her inventory.

"Thank you, Sola. If we ever earn any money, I'll give you a bonus for that."

Sola gave me a nod.

Raion stumbled into the room shirtless, still tugging on pants. "Where is it? Is there a monster? I'm ready!"

"I think you ought to get some more rest," I said. For a man who used to respond to emergency monster attacks, he had taken too long to prepare for this one. He was clearly at much less than a hundred percent after trying to control his Titan.

"Rest? I've had too much rest! I'm stronger than ever!" He had his pants on now, so he flexed a crimson bicep. "I could lift a planet!" He slapped his muscles, showing how strong he felt.

Then his knees buckled. He caught himself on the edge of a console.

Sola's stare was so pointed that I could feel it from behind her helmet.

"Don't worry about that!" Raion said. "It's just my knees. Who needs 'em?"

I slapped him on the back, which should have affected him slightly less than a stiff breeze, but almost shoved him onto his face. "That's the spirit. Horizon, where are we?"

"The border of Dark Space. In the Alliance, they call the nearest system Fifty-Three X."

"So nowhere. Everybody meet me in the conference room. We need to talk about letting the galaxy fend for itself."

Sola headed for the door, but Raion gave me a shocked look. "Fend for itself? What do you mean?"

"I'll explain when we get there. Horizon, carry Raion."

"I can walk on my—stop! Get away!"

Blue light cushioned Raion and carried him down the hall. He protested, but he might as well have saved his breath. Resistance was futile.

CHAPTER THIRTY-NINE

WE WERE ALL gathered around a conference table that Horizon had formed for us. It was divided into six wedges for six crewmates, but only three spots were taken.

Raion tried to project energy from his three-eyed gaze, but he was half-supporting himself against the table. Sola had banished her armor and sat with gray arms crossed. Horizon floated over the table in her holographic body, looking down on us with a placid smile.

"I should begin by sharing my perspective," I said. "I think we should run. At least until—"

"Rejected!" Raion called.

"...until the heat is off. We need to fill out the crew and make repairs."

Sola's jaw was tight and her eyes flared with green light, but I didn't think she was angry with me. It would grate at her to avoid facing down the Iron Legion, but she'd see the necessity.

She looked up to Horizon. "If we need a crew, let's get a crew. Why can't we take on the nearest three sentients who can sit in a chair and follow orders?"

Horizon bowed apologetically. *"Regrettably, we can't. Only the greatest can waken my systems. Most would be harmed by attempting such a bond."*

Sola stared off into the distance, unsurprised. I had already known the answer, but it took me down another avenue of thought.

"It is rumored that Queen Shyrax and her rebels may be in this sector," Horizon continued. *"However, they remain on the move, and I can no longer confirm her location. She could be almost anywhere by now. More importantly, there is no Subline out here. Without the enhancements a Pilot could give my scanners, we will be fumbling in the dark."*

Raion looked to me. "The former Karoshan Queen? Would she help us, do you think?"

"Shyrax herself would be an asset to the crew, but she won't accept anything less than Captain unless we give her no other choice," I said. "Under these circumstances, she wouldn't give us a welcome any warmer than the Union."

Sola leaned forward. "While we run, the Iron King will continue pushing into Galactic Union territory. If we hide until we're in perfect condition, we won't be able to remove the Legion anymore. They'll control too much territory."

I knew the truth of that better than she did. I had seen a galaxy where the Iron Legion had reached that point, conquering enough planets that they could never be totally dislodged.

I took a steady, even breath to chase away the voices of the dead. "I don't see that we have any options. If what we understand about Iron Kings is true, he has the processing power of the entire Legion to draw on. What can we do that he can't plan for?"

I held up one finger. "Sola, he knows everything about you that you've ever shown the Legion. Is there anything you've held back?"

She said nothing, so I held up a second finger. "Raion, your career as a Titan Knight was well-known, and you just went all-out against the Behemoth. He knows everything about you, doesn't he?"

"He doesn't know my *heart*." Raion made a fist with the hand that rested on the table. "Together, we can make miracles."

I knew he wasn't joking, so I moved on by holding up a third finger. "Horizon, you've just fought the Legion fleet. Will the Iron King be able to predict what you can do?"

Horizon closed her eyes. *"In my current capacity, yes. But an excellent crew member could make enough of a difference."*

"That brings us to me. The truth is, I haven't shown everything I can do."

Raion pointed to me with both hands. "That's it!"

"It won't be enough," I said grimly. "He's seen Eurias, and he's seen enough of my magic to make an educated guess. He won't underestimate me. We don't have many hidden weapons left, and the ones we do have won't make a difference. I don't see that we have any options except to run *for now*. When we're all repaired and we have a full crew, then we'll hit him with everything we've got."

I looked between each of them, trying to radiate sincerity. We had to play this smart. None of them would want to withdraw, but I knew Sola and Horizon could be persuaded by logic.

Sola rapped her knuckles on the table. "No. We should fight."

"What?"

"Running doesn't help us win, it just delays losing. The Iron King isn't getting any weaker than he is right now. I say we set course for the nearest crew candidate, and we burn every Hive we cross on the way there."

It was like I was hearing an echo. She'd said almost the same thing last time, only instead of pushing to recruit crew, she had been urging me to hit the Grand Hive. The place we'd both died.

This time, I was sure I could persuade her.

"This *is* how we win," I insisted. "When Horizon is complete—"

"I agree with Sola." The spirit drew up to her full height on top of the table, so her horns nearly scraped the ceiling. *"My wounds are nothing. If we are defeated, let us die in a blaze of glory!"*

I slapped the table. "You almost fell apart in Subspace! Before we make it back on the map, we're going to explode!"

"You held us together last time," Raion said confidently. "You'll do it again." His voice seemed to slow as he spoke the next words, and I knew what he was going to say before he did.

"Better to die for something," he said, "than to live for—"

I whipped out my wand and blasted him. "Shut *up!*"

In his weakened state, he'd been struck by my binding spell in the chest, and it pinned him against the wall. He only seemed mildly surprised, which made me angrier.

"*You* don't get to say that!" I shouted. "You were *wrong.* You didn't make it any better, you just *died!*" I whirled on Sola. "You want to fight the Iron King? We can't, and I know we can't, because we've *tried.* It wasn't even close. We just..."

The anger left me, and I was hollowed out. I sank back into my chair and finished bitterly. "...We just died."

The silence hung in the air for a long time.

Then came the question I'd known was coming.

"Are you from the future?" Raion asked curiously.

Not that one.

Sola leaned across the table, brow furrowed over bright green eyes. "Who are you?"

That was closer.

So I told them. About the ritual, about drawing memories and magic from five previous lives, and how I fought alongside both of them. How I died, and how Raion did.

I was vague on the specifics, both to keep the conversation short and to avoid uncomfortable details. Up to now, I hadn't told them because...frankly, how do you tell someone that you used to be friends in another life?

They accepted it easily.

It's amazing what people will accept when you tell them it was magic.

Raion had shrugged out of my cocoon minutes earlier, and now sat at the table. He frowned thoughtfully into the distance.

"How old does that make you?" he asked.

I spread my hands. "I don't know. It doesn't feel like living one life that's six times as long, it's like living the same life six times. And I never died of old age."

In fact, there was only one life where I made it to forty. Which didn't bode well for this one.

"Did this really happen?" Sola asked. "Are these alternate timelines?"

"In theory, no. I was calling on spells I *could* have learned, training I might have done, and so on, then bringing that into reality through the Aether. These were possible lives I could have lived, but never did."

I let out a breath and leaned back in my chair. "Then again, there shouldn't have been personal memories attached at all. And who knows the true nature of the Aether? There's a popular theory that the Aether is made up of energy leaking from other worlds, some of which could be infinitely similar to this one."

"Sounds like a vision," Sola said. "I've worked with wizards who can check probabilities. I think of this as the expensive version of the same thing."

It took real effort not to explain the correct theory. I spoke through gritted teeth. "The *effect* is...similar, yes."

"Then we have everything we need," she leaned forward hungrily. "Tell me exactly what it was like to attack the Grand Hive. I need to know defenses, entrances, your Subspace approach, the location of the Hive...every detail you can remember. We'll figure out what went wrong and account for it this time."

Raion looked between the two of us, smiling brightly. "Look at us! Friendship that transcends time and space!"

I shuddered. "I don't know...I don't know if I can do this again. Last time..."

I often remembered the pain of the Iron King's hand punching through my chest, but I wouldn't say that was the worst part of our attack. It was everything leading up to that point.

Sola and I hadn't raided the Grand Hive by ourselves. We were just the only ones that made it to the end.

Attacking the Grand Hive had been suicide, and we'd known that. Sola and I had gone in as part of a ragtag fleet, cobbled together from all over the galaxy. We'd lost sixty percent of our ships just getting a handful of drop-pods into the Hive.

Multiple teams had landed, several invading viruses pushing for the Iron Legion's heart. It was hard to know how many of us there were in total; information was scarce, and our forces were scattered. There may have been five hundred of us who made it down to the surface, scattered around the whole of the moon-sized Hive, but Sola and I started with about seventy.

Only five of us made it to the Iron King.

It was the King's presence that haunted me the most. When he turned his attention to us, we lost. There was no fighting him, no resistance. We just died.

Sola and I lasted the longest, but there was no telling whether that was skill or sheer luck.

"I don't want to go through that again," I admitted.

Back in the present, Sola looked at me with clear understanding. "It takes a lot to walk back in and face something that killed you. It's never easy."

That weighed more heavily on me than I'd thought it would. Sola knew she would come back when she died, so I had thought her experience was different from mine.

But I'd seen enough to know that wasn't entirely true. She felt the same pain. She had the same nightmares. Probably more, considering how long she'd been at this.

"You're not scared of dying," Raion said confidently. Sola's eye twitched and she turned to say something, but Raion continued before she could. "You're scared of dying for nothing. Just like me."

Sola was quiet.

Still seated, Raion put fists on his hips and beamed. "So let's leave behind a memory the next Varic will be proud of."

I didn't feel any less afraid. If anything, the reality of what we were about to attempt weighed more heavily on me.

But at least I wasn't going alone.

"Horizon," I began, and she swirled next to my chair, re-forming from lines of blue, red, and green light.

"Yes, Captain?"

"Do we know the range of the Iron King's magic?"

"Based on what he's shown so far, we do."

I looked between Sola and Raion. "If we cross the perimeter of his awareness, he'll know we're coming. It's how we were caught last time. If we're going to hit the Grand Hive, we have to enter Subspace from outside his range and surface right on top of him. Can we make a dive like that?"

"Not without a Pilot," Horizon said, and her seven-pointed eyes glittered with eager anticipation.

"Perfect." I stood up. "We have one in storage."

Sola made an expression of disgust.

A second later, Raion did too.

CHAPTER FORTY

THE LAST HORIZON'S secure vault was positioned at the far end of the vessel from the bridge. It took us ten minutes to reach, since Horizon wasn't sure she could shift the hallways without worsening the structural damage. After we arrived, the door took another two minutes to unseal.

I paid close attention as titanium and orichalcum bars slid out of their mounts, seals unwove themselves, and barriers briefly opened. I assumed there would be something I could add, but in the end the barrier-work was seamless. I would love to read the records of the Archmage that designed this vault.

Even while the door was open, there was hardly any gap in the magical protections. This place could hold Raion's empowered Divine Titan and four others just like it. And those were just the outer protections; they didn't count any seals placed on the artifacts *in* the vault.

I called it a vault, but it was more like a prison. Each artifact had its own cell, sealed in glass like the prisoner containment chambers Omega had originally been held in.

The cells had their own layers of enchantments and Aethertech, so they were impenetrable in every dimension and from every vector I could conceive of. Short of persuading Horizon to open one of these, nothing was getting out. Not me with my staff, not a World Spirit, not a ghost, not a dream.

I had to wonder what they were designed to hold.

"You didn't put Omega in here to begin with?" I asked.

"No one should know of this room except in the most dire circumstances," Horizon said gravely. *"Not even my Captain. There are things kept here so dangerous that knowledge of their existence is a deadly hazard."*

I stared more deeply into her. "It was for my own good you didn't tell me. I see. You were *never* going to let me know that I carried a room full of lethal superweapons on my ship."

Horizon tilted her horns back, very interested in the ceiling. *"I wouldn't call them superweapons so much as...particularly potent trophies."*

"Ah. Is this your room?"

"I collect keepsakes, from time to time, of my greatest adventures. And some of those do make their way here."

A pink-and-white cloud pushed against its cell as I passed. Lights flickered inside the cloud, in a pattern that probably meant something, and I thought I saw the shadow of a vehicle deep inside.

I slowed to see if the lights were communicating a message, but Horizon intercepted me. *"They can't see you. The glass is only transparent from this side. Not that they could communicate anyway; the glass would scramble any pattern with the intention to convey meaning."*

When we had time, I wanted to study the enchantment on that glass.

I passed a sword that hovered point-down on a pool of sapphire power, a humanoid body wrapped in cloth and chains, and what I could only describe as a living mud-ball that bounced off every corner of its cell.

"Some of these look like they could help," I observed.

"Nothing here will help us against the King," Horizon put a hand to her chest, looking offended. *"I would never keep something locked away when it could be used. Everything sealed in this room is here*

because it's uncontainable otherwise. These entities cannot be controlled or directed, and are equally dangerous to anyone trying to hold their leash."

I arrived at a cell containing a glass jar on a pedestal. The jar was big enough to hold a human head and filled with black goo. Swiveling eyes were pressed against every corner of the glass, and the jar trembled as though the goo were trying to knock it over.

"Present company excluded, of course," Horizon went on.

"I know a little about him, but it's very possible he won't accept our restrictions. In that case, we can't keep him aboard."

"I have the contract ready."

"Under no circumstances can we allow him to get out again," I said pointedly. "Like he did before. No matter what else happens, he *cannot* escape."

"No, he can't," Horizon confirmed. *"The seals are such that the World Spirit of a ship equal to me, should such a thing exist, could not escape this room if I left the doors wide open."*

"That's very reassuring, but I mean that Sola and Raion are ready to tear the ship in half if I send them a signal."

Horizon twisted her lips in a sour expression. *"I heard you give those orders, and I want to protest that they are not necessary."*

"Then there's nothing for you to worry about," I said, and entered. A piece of the wall melted to let me into an airlock-style entry chamber. Only when I was inside and the wall sealed itself again did the inner chamber open.

The cell holding Omega was round except for the flat glass wall. Once my entry sealed behind me, it was effectively a featureless white chamber smaller than the bathroom in my quarters.

I tapped one finger on the jar containing our intruder. "Hey, Omega. Can you hear me?"

A mouth formed and he spoke. "Mothful closings. Nightly era to find swamp?"

I spent a moment trying to decode that before I looked over to Horizon. "This speech scrambling enchantment is very impressive, but I do need it disabled."

"Oh, but don't you find him better like this?"

Omega's voice became intelligible without a hitch, as though Horizon had flipped a switch. "...afraid I don't see the point of interrogating me if you won't let me speak. Waste of time for all of us, don't you think?"

"I agree. How have you enjoyed your stay in the cupboard?"

An orange human eye formed in the goop next to a bright mechanical one. Both were wide in surprise. "Oho, so you're willing to speak to me? Risky move, risky move. Who knows what verbal sorcery I could cast on your unsuspecting minds."

He gave a broad grin while other, supplementary mouths formed to whisper *'verbal sorcery'* until the phrase echoed around the room.

Needless to say, that made no magical sense.

"I'll risk it," I said. In the corner of my eye, I pulled up his file. "You want me to call you Omega? Grave Hound? How about Omal?"

"Whatever name feels best on your lips," Omega said, kissing the glass.

I rubbed my eyes. "I need to sleep, and we're not going to get anywhere if you keep trying to disturb me. I've seen worse."

"Have you? Have you, really? I don't think you have."

"We don't know each other very well yet. We'll get there." I shrugged. "Unless you make me jettison you into space. How can I convince you to sign a provisional contract to pilot *The Last Horizon*?"

Three mouths grinned at once. "Money. Not joining your crew, but I'll hit a Hive for a hundred thousand standards. Need to kill a Sixday afternoon somehow."

"Call me crazy, but *I* think you're going to attack me again the second I let you out."

"Crazy!" Omega shouted.

"This is a bad negotiating position, but I'll tell you: I'm in a hurry and I don't know what levers to pull, so I'm just going to start pulling. We looked into your Escalon Company. Your nephew Jak looks like a decent man...I mean, not *decent*, he's an arms dealer, but he doesn't seem like a remorseless killer."

One of Omega's mouths pulled up into a perfect 'O' as he gasped. "Is this a *hostage* negotiation? Are you going to hurt my nephew if I don't comply? What piece of him are you going to cut off and mail me? I recommend the pinky; that way he could go by Jak Ninefingers, which I think has a great ring to it."

I scratched my head. "I was going to tell you that his planet is in line to be taken over by the Iron Legion, but now I'm thinking that probably won't do anything for you either."

"Can you imagine Jak as a Bishop of an Iron Hive?" Omega cackled. "Giant mechanical face? First thing we'd have in common. He'd be lucky if they made him a Pawn instead of food, though. Lucky, lucky."

That hadn't worked, but he was talking. Getting Omega to crack would take hours of conversation over the course of weeks.

Not only did I not have that much time, but if I did, I wouldn't waste it on him. I was leaning closer to Sola's camp of executing him instead of persuading him.

"I'm going to be as honest with you as I can, Omal, just between you, me, and the Aether. I can't tell how much of *this* is a persona, and how much of it is really you. I'm sure it's the key to your unique...shape...and I know some mages who would study you to find the link between your identity and your abilities."

"The secret is *ab crunches*," Omega whispered.

"But I don't have time for all that. In five minutes, I'm walking out of here with your jar under my arm. Whether I release you to fight the Iron Legion or seal you into a warhead and toss you into the closest sun depends on whether you're a member of my crew or not."

As she had before, Horizon projected the conditions onto the air in front of me in the form of blue holographic words.

Not a single one of Omega's eyes scanned the document. He faced me, and his smiles never broke.

"Boring, boring, boring," Omega recited. He cackled. "Ultimatum. Join or die. Fight the evil Iron Legion. Wouldn't it be more fun to launch me into space?"

I watched him, and I remembered the versions of Omega I'd known before.

They were mostly like this.

I hadn't known him nearly as well as Raion or Sola, and I had never worked with him closely, but he'd shown up in most of my lives to one degree or another. The Corporations regularly hired him for sabotage, assassination, or general mayhem, and—in the right circles—he was famous throughout the galaxy. An assassin who couldn't be killed, caught, or questioned.

He'd worked against the Vallenar Corporation as often as for us, but I'd never been important enough to be targeted by him directly. Not until this time around.

Only once had I ever caught a glimpse of the man behind the mask of forced chaos.

"I'm about to take a shot in the dark," I said to Omega in his jar, "and tell you a story. If you don't want to join us by the end, then..." I shrugged. "Then neither of us get what we want."

"I don't like stories. They go on *forever*."

"I doubt you're a student of Galactic Union history, but you've probably heard of President Vashei?"

The extra eyes in his gelatinous body vanished, leaving only his normal two eyes. One biological, one Aethertech.

"We only learned about her in school because of her assassination," I went on. "Telappen Vashei was President of the Galactic Union a little over a hundred years ago, and she had a stellar reputation. Established new Subspace routes, improved relationships with the Karoshans, and kept the Corporations in line.

"But, you know, *I've* heard worse things."

Omega's mouth stretched into a sardonic grin. "From whom, precisely?"

I ignored him. "There are those who suggest that she played both sides of the board, engineering and resolving conflicts to expand her own influence. If those rumors are true, then whoever killed her did the galaxy a favor. Or tried to."

Omega had gathered his gelatinous form together into his own human head. His Aethertech eye flashed as it examined me, which suggested I was on the right track.

"It's interesting," I said, "because nothing seemed to change in the galaxy after she died. Either President Vashei *wasn't* the cause, or her replacement was just as bad. In which case, this assassin didn't accomplish much at all, did they?

"There are those who believe that the ones *really* pulling the strings back then didn't change. Maybe they remained in power all the way to the present day."

"Who are you?" Omega asked me.

The second time I'd been asked that question in the last twenty-four hours.

"This brings me to yesterday, when a Galactic Union fleet ambushed us. They came to capture us, but the strange thing is, our inspection of their computers revealed no official orders to do so. Anyway, I teleported onto their bridge and told them to back off before we killed them. Whoever sent them, I doubt they'll be very happy with me."

I didn't know much about Omega, but in the event of a Galactic Civil War, I did know what side he'd be on.

I leaned over his jar. "You want to keep blowing up smugglers for the highest bidder, Omal? Or do you want a better class of enemy?"

He studied me, and I saw him as a person rather than a monster. A man much older than he looked.

A holographic contract appeared next to him.

"You've got stricter terms than everyone else," I said. "Magically compelled not to harm crew, and to follow my orders. You can't so much as pull a trigger without my permission. But you get to name your enemies, same as the rest of us, and we'll fight them with you."

Omega eyed the contract up and down, reading it as though this was business as usual and he wasn't a head trapped in a jar. "And where are we flying that you need me so badly?"

"*The Last Horizon* was severely damaged in the battle against the Iron King," I told him. "Partially by you." A pair of Horizon's eyes appeared, conjured from blue light, solely to glare at Omega.

"We're going on a suicide mission into the center of the Iron King's Grand Hive, where we're going to try and kill him. The ship punches the way in while Sola, Raion, and I unload everything we have to blow him up. If it doesn't work, the rest of us get made into Pawns while Horizon is scavenged for parts."

I jerked my head toward the door. "You want to come?"

Omega tilted his head back and laughed.

CHAPTER FORTY-ONE

BACK IN THE heart of the ship, Omega stood in his human form once again, hands in the pockets of his black coat as I watched over him. He'd already signed the contract, but Raion and Sola still flanked him to either side, both with weapons ready to draw.

It was rare to see someone that Raion didn't trust.

Horizon, for her part, seemed delighted. She stood beneath the stone tablet of the Pilot—the figure seated behind a ship's wheel with a Subspace entry point overhead—and held out a hand for Omega to take.

"*What would you request of* The Last Horizon *in exchange for your service?*" she asked.

"What a wonderful system this is!" Omega cried. "We *trade* enemies? Fun, fun, fun. Well, then. I'll help you kill anyone you want, and when it's my turn, we're going after Solstice."

Even though I'd known it was coming, I flinched at hearing the organization's name out loud. They could be listening, even here.

Sola audibly scoffed. "They don't exist."

"What an easy time we'll have, then." With a wide flourish, Omega took Horizon's hand.

This time, the light suffusing the ship's spirit was bright orange.

The tablet of the Pilot shone orange, as did the lights overhead for a few moments.

When they returned to normal, I looked around at the walls. Four tablets lit. Only the Engineer and the Commander remained dark.

Horizon settled in place, folding her hands and bowing slightly to the new addition. *"Welcome, new Pilot of* The Last Horizon.*"*

"As long as you abide by the terms of the contract," I noted.

Omega gestured to me. "That's right! How about we put those to the test?" In the blink of an eye, he whipped out a gun pointed in my direction.

Before he could fire, Raion punched him into the ceiling.

"Traitor!" Raion shouted. He crushed Omega's gun in his fist.

Sola had a gun trained, but Omega was slithering over the ceiling, and she tracked his head. I put my hand up to the end of Sola's weapon, urging her to lower it.

"He can't hurt us," I said. Only Horizon and I hadn't reacted to his attack. We trusted the contract.

Raion rushed to put himself in front of me. "Don't trust him!"

"I don't trust him. I trust magic."

"Well, I don't understand magic!" Raion said that like he'd somehow won the argument, which was in fact how many of our disagreements had ended back in the Titan Force.

"Let him try to shoot me," I said. "It's the only way he'll be convinced."

"That's stupid," Sola said.

From behind one of the lights on the ceiling, Omega stuck out a head. "I haven't been able to shoot any of you, and I've been trying."

Raion thrust a finger at Omega. "I sense *no* friendship from him!"

I turned to Horizon. "Are you feeling well enough to take us to the conference room?"

The four-colored spirit raised her hand and snapped.

A moment later, all of us re-formed in the room whose only feature was the six-part table. I settled into my seat. "I have a way to—"

"Surprise!" Omega shouted as he pointed his gun at me.

His finger froze on the trigger, unable to pull it. I had time to see a brief expression of disappointment on his face before Raion punched his head off.

"See?" I said to Raion while Omega's head re-formed. "He can't do it."

"I'm going to hit him every time," Raion said.

"Let's see if we can get through this meeting without a murder," I said to everyone.

Sola shot Omega. Gray goo splattered all over the far wall, and the portion of his body that remained human slumped to the floor.

"I wanted to," she said through her helmet.

Raion gave her a thumbs-up.

Omega giggled as he pulled himself back into one piece. "I can see we're going to have so much *fun* together."

I took the opportunity. "I'm going to go over the plan while everyone's alive." I activated the projector in the table, which showed a three-dimensional map of our sector, and pointed to several red spots. "Sola's marked the Hives, which are pushing deeper into Galactic Union territory. We don't have Subline access, but if everything goes as we expect, the Legion will reach the first populated Union planet sometime today."

Sola's armored grip tightened on her gun, and I sped up before she released frustration by killing Omega again. "The Union fleet will hold them off for a while, but not forever. That's why we're diving back to Subspace as soon as we can."

Raion and Sola turned their gazes to Horizon, who tilted her chin up proudly. *"With the addition of a Pilot, my Subspace Drive has regained its legendary heights. I am now, once again, the fastest ship in the galaxy. The Drive will not fail."*

"I'll make sure it doesn't," I said, and Sola nodded to me.

"I believe in Horizon!" Raion declared.

Horizon dipped her head to him. *"As expected, my Knight is the only one of you with the heart of a hero."*

"We're heading to the Grand Hive," I reminded them, which took the mood down appropriately. "We know roughly where it is, because we know the system where it originated and we know the trajectory the Hives are on. It'll take sixteen hours of mid-range dives to reach the limit of the Iron King's detection, then one continuous twelve-hour dive before we hit the Grand Hive."

Omega gave a low whistle, and Raion's eyebrows went up.

"Long dive," Sola noted.

"And a faaaaast ship," Omega noted. He traced our location on the map from the edge of Dark Space all the way to the expected coordinates of the Grand Hive. "Say, as the Pilot, do I get to do any piloting?"

"I would value the opportunity to watch your skills in action."

"Mmmmm good, good, good."

Omega smiled as though he had some plan that required control of the ship, but I suspected that was only a mask, so I plunged ahead. "Twenty-eight hours from now, we'll be blowing up the Grand Hive. And that *is* the plan. We use our biggest weapons from maximum range, and we leave the second our Drive cools down. If the Iron King has time to join the battle, we've already lost."

Raion and Sola visibly reacted to that.

"We can't give up before we try," Raion said.

Sola tilted her helmet toward him. "I agree. We should avoid the King's attention if we can, of course, but we don't need to fear it. Iron Kings have been killed before. Worldslayer should do the job."

"Ooooh," Omega said, "it's called Worldslayer?"

"It didn't kill *him*," I pointed out. "And the Iron King survived being launched into a star. We take our best shot from orbit, and we have to assume that if that fails, we lose."

Three of them looked visibly disapproving at the sentiment, even Sola from behind her visor. Omega just looked like he enjoyed the debate.

"We have a busy day tomorrow," I went on. "Sola, you and I will meet to discuss the Grand Hive. Raion, we need you capable of Titan combat."

Raion winced, though that had always been the plan. "I will... do my best."

"Omega, I need to talk with you too. I want to know what you're capable of."

Omega chuckled in three different voices at once. "Don't you think I showed you that already?"

"Until then, don't leave your room," I said. "We're all going to start by getting some sleep. Sola, I'll speak with you in six hours. And everyone..." I made brief eye contact with each of them, even Omega. "...Tomorrow might be our last day. Don't leave anything undone. Trust me."

Omega tilted his head in confusion at that, but the other three would understand.

"Six hours," I repeated. "Horizon, take us down."

I had just shut the door to my quarters, already hoping I would be able to get a little real sleep, when I turned to find Horizon standing behind me.

The ship's spirit looked calm and pleasant, for the moment, her holographic form now drawn in four different shades. Small eyes flew in flocks around her horns, and a pair of conjured hands drifted over to take my mantle from my shoulders.

I let them, eyeing the magic. "Is there something I can do for you, Horizon?"

"*I only wanted to offer a little advice before you slept, Captain. As the World Spirit of* The Last Horizon, *I have seen many crews and carried many heroes. Together, we are capable of more than you perhaps realize.*"

"Is that advice?"

"*I think it is. Remember that I look forward to many more adventures before I sleep once again.*"

This was the spirit's way of encouraging me, and I appreciated the effort. I would have appreciated it *more* if my nerves hadn't been chewing at my stomach.

"I've seen a lot of adventures end badly," I said.

"*As have I.*" The hands that had taken my mantle drifted back, presenting themselves before me. Now that I looked closer, I saw an extraordinary level of detail in these conjured magical hands:

they were thin and worn, almost skeletal, with gaunt fingers and pointed nails.

By the precision of their behavior and their subtle gestures, I could tell that these were a spellcaster's hands. Each of their movements was almost—but not quite—enough to provoke a reaction in the Aether. As though they practiced magical gestures so often that the motions had become subconscious.

"These are the hands of a wizard who opposed me and my crew, once. She was a young woman who traded her youth for great power. She dreamed that she could use that power to regain the price she'd paid, but her ambition was not enough to overcome my heroes."

Horizon regarded the hands fondly. *"One of my proudest trophies. Only I remember her, now. And an echo of her power is preserved within me."*

I reached out to touch the hands, examining the spirit's magic. "Wow...so this is memory manifestation magic, not conjuration magic."

Horizon gave me a mysterious smile. *"My secrets are—"*

"Like you said it was."

She blinked. *"What?"*

"You said it was basic conjuration magic." I grabbed one of the hands and, despite its struggling, held it up to Horizon's face. "You had to deliberately hide the nature of your magic from me to stop me from seeing through it. I would have noticed *witch hands.*"

"Ah, that's...I didn't lie, exactly, I only spoke...vaguely." Her eyes crawled over the ceiling as though looking for an escape. *"I had to preserve some mystery, you understand. My previous Captains were all very appreciative whenever I revealed new capabilities."*

I doubted any of her previous Captains were happier about their ship keeping secrets from them than I was.

Still, I released the hand. It fluttered away from me and hid behind Horizon's back. "Every mage hides some of their magic, but I'm concerned this is becoming a habit for you."

Horizon shuffled in place. *"I only wished to remind you that I remember many adventures, just as you do. Sometimes they end badly for us, but often it is the enemy that faces a…grim conclusion."*

I scanned the cloud of eyes that hovered behind Horizon. Each unique and each, I now realized, a trophy. "Are these all from enemies?"

As though her previous embarrassment was an act, Horizon grinned widely. *"Every one. You see? Defeat is not the only possible end for you. I have seen many adventures fail, but many more succeed beyond my wildest dreams. Isn't that a pleasant thing to remember?"*

She faded away, her smile going last.

I shivered at the smile. But at least I did manage to get some sleep.

CHAPTER FORTY-TWO

ONCE AGAIN, BENRI Vallenar stood in the Iron King's presence. That was his normal place these days. He chanted his Mirror of Silence, watching the galaxy at a scale he'd never imagined before.

Of course, he was only operating the barest fraction of the spell. More than ninety-nine percent of it was being channeled through the King, whose fiery eyes stared into the distance as he *truly* watched the galaxy.

Benri appreciated the craftsmanship of the plan that conquered several worlds at once while demoralizing countless more. He admired the use of magic and envied the magnification system built into the King's existence.

There had to be a way to upgrade himself to such a degree. He already had some theories. Aether Technicians could be hired.

Benri was watching a thousand conflicts at once, but he still felt the King's frown. A new ghost was born from the Mirror of Silence millions of miles away, and the Archmage was forced to stare through it.

A smooth cruiser appeared from Subspace, shining orange around its plates. *The Last Horizon*. It was within the same system as several large Hives, and Benri expected the Legion to begin closing in at any second.

"Why are they in my territory, would you say?" the King asked.

He could simulate any possible response, so Benri wondered what the purpose of the question was. "If *The Last Horizon* is the one in charge, I could only speculate. If it's my son, I imagine this is bait. You have provoked him, so he wishes to draw you out."

Benri organized his thoughts, mentally scanning the distance between that system and their own position. Too far to reach, at least quickly. The Grand Hive was not made for speed, so they wouldn't be able to close in on *The Last Horizon* soon enough to trap them.

As though they could feel his gaze on them, the ship vanished only seconds after emerging.

Benri's physical eyes were closed as he processed so much visual data, but he could still feel his brow furrowing. "That has to strain their Subspace Drive, especially with so much damage. Is *The Last Horizon*'s Drive so advanced?"

"It is now," the King responded, "but even so, it would not lightly make such a dive."

The human imagined he could hear the melody of a million possibilities dancing through the Iron King's flashing brain.

Benri turned his attention to the nine invasions they were conducting at once. "Where will they intervene, do you think?"

"Their most likely destination is Visiria." The number of Hives and Hunter-ships in orbit around Visiria increased naturally, though Benri could perceive no orders. It was as though the King had arranged those troops days ago to be in position now.

"How likely is that?" Benri asked. His son's actions should be well within the King's predictions, but who knew what the Zenith Starship could do?

The King shook his head. "Impossible to calculate. It depends on factors that can't be determined or predicted with confidence. But it's the move that makes the most sense." Steel teeth gleamed. "Let's hope they can surprise me."

Raion, Sola, and I waited in the bridge airlock after our long dives. My pathfinding spells showed us we were reaching our destination.

Sola hadn't summoned Worldslayer yet, for fear of interfering with the Subspace dive, and she took up most of the airlock with her bulky gray armor. Her helmet tilted down as she lost herself in memories, giving only one-word responses.

I could feel her focusing, locking herself onto the target like a guided missile.

Raion wore his own red-plated combat suit without his helmet. He never *stopped* talking. "Imagine the galaxy without the Iron Legion!" He punched his palm with his opposite fist. "We can do it! We'll be the ones. We'll go down in history. You think we can do it? Don't doubt yourself! I know we can! Can you give me another spell?"

He continued his conversation one-sided because I was trembling myself.

The case containing my staff sat at my feet, freed of all but one seal. The magic circle representing that spell shivered from the strain of holding back Eurias, and I kept my attention on it so the airlock didn't sprout wildflowers and rain clouds.

But my imagination was running ahead of me.

The *first* strike had to be the *last*. What was the fastest spell I could conjure? What if the Grand Hive had deceived my navigational spells? What if Horizon's damage weakened her weapons systems too much and we couldn't breach the Grand Hive's outer defenses?

What if my father was in the Hive? Would we be killing him?

In one of my lives, I was a prize fighter on Visiria. This was the atmosphere before the fight, where I tried to psych myself out of my worries by visualizing victory.

In another life, I was the support mage for a mercenary exploration squad. This was the sensation before we launched into a dodgy mission. Tension so thick it seeped into the skin.

It was the feeling of casting our lives like dice.

I set all that aside. The nerves, the possibility of failure. I did as I had been forced to do in many lives, and I focused on the task in front of me.

"Coming out of Subspace," Horizon reported. *"If our information is accurate, the Grand Hive will be directly ahead."*

I waited another second, feeling the timing in my soul.

The instant we broke the surface of physical space, all three of us acted at once. Sola slapped the release for the outer door, Raion dashed forward, and I tore the final seal off my staff.

Eurias' power sang into the void. Vines erupted into being, forming a nest around me. They held me in place as the ship filled with clouds and swirled with air that generated faster than it was torn into vacuum. Anchored by vines, I stayed in the airlock and channeled my magic.

The world already bent beneath Eurias, but it screamed and twisted at the presence of the Worldslayer. The gun appeared in Sola's hands and it demanded attention, shining in the Aether like a deadly star.

Raion raised his badge high and shouted something that never made it past his helmet. Far above, a new red-gold light twinkled and grew quickly brighter.

Neither of them had doubted me. I had told them with confidence that my Cosmic Path spell would lead us to the destination, but I had doubted myself. Yes, I knew the theory behind my spell's operation, but who knew what insane abilities the Iron King had?

We were all rewarded because I was right.

In front of us, looming like a planet, was the Grand Hive.

While all other Hives I'd ever seen were disgusting masses of flesh and metal combined into a lump, like a cancer had taken over a ship graveyard, this one looked designed. Or perhaps grown.

Rather than a ship, the Grand Hive resembled a planet-sized skull. It was a fusion of slick salt-white skin and black iron. Miles-long spikes jutted out from the main hangar bay like tusks over a beast's mouth, and thousands of Iron Legion craft spewed forth. A swarm of insects seeking prey.

Cosmic clouds, like dark nebulas, shrouded the rest of the system. The Iron King's concealing veils, made physical to block more mundane methods of tracking.

There were no Behemoths here. Layers of shields and swarms of fighters protected the Hive, of course, but security was relatively light.

This was our chance. Our only chance.

We wouldn't make it back if we missed. Once we all unloaded, we either killed the King or died in failure. Again.

Thanks to Eurias, I called all the water in the Grand Hive and a matching amount from the Aether. Enough power to drown worlds hovered over the skull, casting a shadow over an entire hemisphere.

All of us fired together.

My staff was a brute-force weapon. Dark water crashed down on the Grand Hive like a planet-sized waterfall.

It slammed into the shields, which lit up as a vast curving eggshell.

Sola had the spear to my hammer. Worldslayer projected a scalpel-sharp bridge that annihilated space between herself and her target. When she squeezed the trigger, just for an instant, she was connected by a light that speared through the shield, the Hive, and space beyond.

In the fraction of a second after she fired, the shield crumbled and my astral tide swept over the Grand Hive.

Legion ships were crushed. They surely detonated, but I couldn't see them in the rush of the water.

Especially not with how bright Horizon was.

The Last Horizon had sprouted an armada's worth of weapons. They all fired in a flurry of emerald light, the shots streaking through the space where the shield had been a second before.

It was like the barrage of a full Union fleet, but that wasn't all.

Raion's Titan towered over us, glowing with the fury of a living sunset-colored star. Wings of energy sprouted from behind it, and one of its arms collapsed into a cannon. Only a beat after the rest of us, it took aim and fired.

The energy beam was decent. Maybe over a small area, it would be more effective than my water, but there was no competition overall. And the Worldslayer made it look pathetic.

I was initially a little disappointed in Raion's output, considering the upgrades to his Titan. Maybe he was only useful against Behemoths.

Until a cloud of missiles erupted from those wings. I didn't get a close look at them—they moved more quickly than my eyes could track—but they shone like glistening golden diamonds and streaked through space by the thousands.

Better, but still nothing compared to what Horizon was doing.

Then the energy crystals impacted against the Grand Hive's exterior and detonated. Scoops of the Hive's armored hull simply vanished as though unmade.

Only then did Raion dash forward, propelled by the energy wings. His Titan's arm folded from a cannon back into a hand, and he pulled out his force-blade.

Raion's face appeared in the corner of my vision as he called me, his face the picture of excitement. *"You did it!"* he cried. *"Your spells work! I can still think! It feels just like it used to!"*

I didn't want to face a berserk Divine Titan again, so I had placed on Raion every mental protection spell I could come up with. Even so, I hadn't been sure that would be enough.

I was guiding more pure elemental water than existed in most oceans and channeling entire stars' worth of energy, but I still pushed out a smile for his sake. "Do you see the pathfinding spell?"

"Sure do! I can see the King!"

The Divine Titan made a beeline for the center of the 'skull,' above the main opening of the Grand Hive. I was concerned about Raion traveling through my spell, but he pushed through the elemental water like it was nothing.

"Did you hear him?" I asked Horizon.

"Launching Omega," she responded.

I only saw the missile leaving Horizon's cannons because she highlighted it in my processor implant. It was covered by gray-black goo. I heard a few seconds of Omega's manic laughter over the line before he passed out of range.

Unlike Raion's Titan, which resisted my attack through sheer defensive power, Omega was protected by spells. Essentially, I had given him permission to pass. And by extension, the missile he had consumed.

He empowered the neutron missile, which was the greatest weapon Horizon's fabricators could produce. Strapped to it, Omega would surely die, but he seemed to relish the challenge.

With great concentration, I wrestled the water gushing from the Aether. Instead of a pounding black waterfall, I squeezed it into something that more resembled an incomprehensibly vast pillar.

It drilled straight through the center of the Grand Hive.

While all this takes time to describe, our attacks unloaded in the same handful of seconds. Even then, there was some resistance. Satellites fired on us and struck Horizon's shields, plasma bolts crashed against the Divine Titan, and spells fell on Sola or died against Eurias.

None of the defenses were too bad. Not close to my worst-case scenario. I'd lived the last twenty-eight hours in waking nightmares about the Iron King seeding the system with mines or choking space with so many Hunter-ships that we met a solid wall of plasma the second we came out of Subspace.

In fact, what played out in reality was the perfect picture of victory.

Raion punched a hole into the Grand Hive's bridge.

Sola fired the Worldslayer again, stabbing another hole in the fortress from end to end.

Horizon's attacks carved long furrows or hammered cracks into the armor.

I straightened the water into a blade, slicing the Grand Hive in half.

As the two halves drifted apart in space, Omega's missile

impacted. It flared into a glistening supernova no less bright than the Worldslayer. It was almost pure white, with only a hint of orange, far beyond what Horizon had told me to expect. Omega had multiplied the yield several times.

There was no way he'd survived.

Though somehow, I suspected he had.

Maybe he'd slipped into Subspace before the missile's impact or maybe he'd left a bit of goo behind from which he could regenerate himself, but I couldn't imagine him dying so quickly. Call it a wizard's instinct.

That same instinct told me not to trust things that were too easy. I'd seen no Mirror of Silence copies, and the Iron King hadn't managed to defend himself, much less strike back effectively.

That worried me.

On the other hand, this was exactly what we'd wanted. The plan went perfectly. The Grand Hive was drifting into chunks, the fleet was decimated, and enemies vanished all over the system.

I released my water. It continued pouring by momentum, but without my magic to sustain it, the conjured water would gradually fade away.

I *didn't* release Eurias.

Somehow, something would go wrong.

CHAPTER FORTY-THREE

WHEN *THE LAST* Horizon came out of Subspace, Benri had seen it and reacted instantly.

He still wasn't fast enough.

Even the Iron King, it seemed, had been caught off guard. Ships burst from every opening in the Grand Hive, and the Hive's own defenses engaged immediately. Benri copied guns to return fire and shield generators to help withstand the incoming assault.

Only, in less than a second, to be shown that there *were* no defenses that could block that attack.

The Grand Hive's shields, greater than those found on any fortress-world, crumbled beneath one shot of the Fallen Sword's Aethertech weapon.

His son's elementalism swept up every ship outside the Hive. It crushed every defensive emplacement, every secondary shield, every spell, every black-and-white copy that Varic probably hadn't even noticed.

If Varic suspected his father was aboard, it certainly hadn't stayed his hand.

While the Grand Hive still had its armor, salvaged and refined from the sturdiest materials available, that didn't last long. Raion

Raithe's Divine Titan tore through it like paper as *The Last Horizon's* guns peeled it back layer by layer.

All of that happened as fast as Benri could blink, after which a hand seized him by the front of the mantle.

"Stay alive," the Iron King ordered him. Then Benri was shoved backward into a wall.

Which promptly came to life and swallowed him.

He was left in a dark egg, squeezed into a cocoon that was a disgusting mixture of cold flesh and warm metal. His panic was immediate and instinctive, as he tried to breathe but felt the thin air.

A moment later, the container rippled in a disgusting reflex, whereupon Benri tasted sweet oxygen.

Only then did he have enough peace of mind to generate colorless copies of himself outside his cocoon to take another look at his situation.

His stomach knotted at the sight while frustration burned in his chest. He hadn't wanted to be here.

The Grand Hive was torn in half.

On one remaining chunk of intact bridge, the Iron King stood defiantly. He began releasing the tubes and wires going into his back, which hissed as they splattered gas, fluid, or energy into the remaining atmosphere.

The King himself was grinning. His smile gleamed chrome and fire burned in the furnaces of his eyes.

He spread steel-plated arms and shouted. Benri read his lips and translated.

"Come to me! Come, and face the Iron Legion!"

A world-piercing light appeared in the middle of the King's body. With no warning or mercy, the Worldslayer sliced him in half.

At the same instant, Raion's Divine Titan appeared. It grabbed the top half of the King's body with one hand, crumpled it into a ball, then unleashed orange energy so powerful that the sight of it destroyed Benri's clone. He had to conjure another one.

When he could see again, the Divine Titan was gone.

And a missile was landing.

With his own human eyes, Benri wouldn't have been able to catch that instant. But he had learned a few magical tricks. The eyes of his clone captured the sight of a missile covered in slime. He saw the orange eye in the center of the goo, and the wide grin. He thought it sprouted a hand and waved at him.

Then an explosion consumed everything in white fire.

Benri's cocoon rocked violently. He felt like a stone in the center of a volcanic eruption. His eardrums ruptured painfully, he screamed, and he slammed his body into the cocoon around him at every conceivable angle.

He choked back his own screams with sheer resolve. He wouldn't die screaming. There was no one around to witness, but if he died in agony, he would take it silently.

As silently as he could, anyway. Every smack of his skull against metal brought at least a grunt.

With one final crash, he came to a halt. He couldn't hear anything, couldn't see anything, and nothing happened when he fumbled for the Aether. He couldn't speak to chant. Benri considered it a miracle he hadn't passed out yet, and not necessarily a miracle he appreciated.

Now, he was alone inside the cocoon.

Every thought was sluggish and heavy, but he still wondered where he was. Had he come to a halt? Would someone find him?

Or was he drifting through space?

Would he fly endlessly among the debris, until he exhausted his cocoon's ability to produce oxygen and suffocated?

Maybe he would dehydrate first. He hoped not. As terrible as suffocation was, at least it was faster than the alternatives.

"No!" he shouted. Though he couldn't hear the word, and suspected it was probably a pathetic whine more than the defiant declaration he intended.

Giving in to suffocation meant he was letting the Iron King get the better of him. He couldn't use magic now, but after a nap, he'd be able to focus. He could move himself through the void, as long as he could command the Aether.

It wouldn't be easy. But he could push himself to a ship, or a planet, or at least the larger fragments of the Grand Hive. Someone would find him. From there, he'd have options.

Having a plan relieved him enough to allow him to let go. Benri gave himself permission to pass out. Only by resting could he recover his strength.

A moment later, he discovered he wasn't even permitted to do that.

His cocoon scraped along a surface, moving again and jostling him awake. In a few more seconds, he came to a halt once again. Vague vibrations, like distant voices.

Then the cocoon peeled back, and he blinked up into a smooth ceiling and a bright light.

A face leaned over him. The distant, silver-eyed, dark-skinned face of his own son. As dead as Varic's eyes had been since his ritual, they still registered surprise upon seeing his father.

Benri fervently wished he had been saved by a stranger.

With his soul full of resentment, he finally allowed himself to pass out.

CHAPTER FORTY-FOUR

HORIZON MATERIALIZED NEXT to me, looking down on my father with a gentle smile. *"Would you like me to prepare a room for him?"*

"No!" I ran a hand over my hair. "Why is he here? How? There's no way this is a coincidence."

"If I may make a guess..." Horizon manifested a series of eyes, which scanned my father's crumpled body in its gruesome Iron Legion drop-pod. *"Yes, it's as I suspected. May I perform a quick medical operation on your father?"*

Numbly, I nodded.

A thin-fingered, delicate humanoid hand materialized next to Horizon, made of blue light. It pinched something at the back of my father's neck.

And with a sick squelch, the hand began to pull out a parasite.

A tiny spray of blood spattered the deck as a half-metal worm squirmed weakly against Horizon's conjured hand. The parasite was no longer than a finger and only a little thicker than a strand of hair, but it had been embedded in my father's neck.

I shivered and spoke a word that resonated in the Aether. The parasite burned away.

"The Iron King knew you would take him in," Horizon said pleasantly. *"He would have followed whatever orders the King left behind. Sabotaging the ship from within, I'd imagine."*

I drummed my fingers on my thigh. I suspected the parasite had been embedded too deeply for a casual visual inspection, but I wouldn't have relied on a *visual* inspection. I would have cast a pathfinding spell, and Horizon had Aethertech scanners.

"He had to know this wouldn't get past us," I muttered.

Horizon rested a hand on my head. *"I'm sure this was but one of the many seeds he cast to the winds in his final moments. If but one of them takes root, he may further his goals from beyond the grave."*

She sounded almost pleased at the prospect.

"Lock him in one of the cells," I said. "Eject the drop-pod." Magical hands drifted through the air behind Horizon, no doubt to follow my orders, but I stopped her almost immediately. "Wait. Keep the pod. I want to check it myself."

I cast spells over the disgusting metal-and-flesh pod, but it was nothing but what it appeared to be: a half-organic life-support system.

I frowned over it for another minute as I heard heavy footsteps approach.

Sola loomed over me in her armor. "Have you confirmed the King's death?"

"Horizon has." Before she could respond, I held up a hand. "No, you're right. One moment."

It didn't take me long to chant the pathfinding magic. It was one of my more practiced spells. As expected, the spell shone gold in my vision as it activated and then fizzled. Nothing.

I held the spell out to her so she could see it failing for herself. "Do you see the sparks at the edges of your vision? Those should coalesce into a visible path. The only reason to be searching for this long is if the target doesn't exist."

Sola's visor continued slowly scanning the scene in front of us. *The Last Horizon*'s viewport was filled with debris from the broken Grand Hive. One half of the Hive drifted over us, cutting off the nearby star and casting a shadow over the bridge.

"I don't like it," she said.

I let out a breath. "I understand. All my training and experience says you don't get any result without a corresponding price. But we did hit him with the galaxy's strongest weapons at once. We might be underestimating ourselves."

She grunted within her helmet, but her fingers were dancing over the monitors. Checking scanner readouts and live Subline feeds.

We couldn't get much of a Subline connection out here, except broadcasts from Dornoth IV. The Lichborn homeworld was very confused, as the Iron Legion had shown up within their solar system and just as suddenly exploded. All transmissions from further away showed similar scenes.

Hives had begun drifting aimlessly.

Pawns that had been attacking settlements in regimented waves broke and scattered in all directions or began destroying each other. Hunter-ships crashed from orbit and plowed into the surfaces of several planets with no attempt to save themselves. An insectoid Behemoth, hunting the Galactic Union fleet, suddenly flailed at nothing and fled into Subspace.

Horizon's scanners showed the same thing. Where there was order, chaos.

Sola stared into the monitor for a long moment.

Meanwhile, I was layering binding spells onto the Iron Legion pod. "Sola, could you check this?"

She tilted her visor over to me and light flashed within her helmet. "It's clean," she said. "Standard Iron Legion life-pod."

I stopped drawing seals over it. "No reason for this, then. Horizon, when you get a second, take out the trash."

Sola stared off into the distance. After a few more seconds, her armor dissolved into floating blue cubes. She collapsed into a chair, expression numb.

My chair, but she needed it more than I did.

"That's it?" she asked me.

"Looks that way."

"I had imagined..." She started to say something, stopped,

and corrected herself. "...no, I guess I always imagined dying in battle."

"You've had plenty of practice."

I wasn't as relieved as I thought I would be. For one thing, I felt that only one of my enemies had been erased for good. For another, not seeing the Iron King die for myself had left too much doubt.

I supposed I'd be looking over my shoulder for him for the rest of my life.

She cupped one hand and conjured a misty blue-white flame. "The battle was supposed to be endless. Now...now what?"

I was about to respond, but there was something about the way she phrased that. I pointed to the flame. "Why did you summon that?"

"No, I don't need it." She waved her hand, dismissing it. "I have one in my room."

"You summoned your Pyre, looked deeply into it, and said 'the battle was supposed to be endless.'"

"That was what the wizard said who gave it to me."

I stretched out my hand and beckoned a nearby chair. They sprouted from the deck, but *The Last Horizon* could shift its floor to move the seats at my direction.

The cushioned black chair swept over to me, where I swiveled it to face Sola and sat down. "Sola. I don't make it a habit to interrogate people about their secrets. Everyone deserves at least one secret magical power. But I need to know where you got that."

She glanced out the viewport to the wreckage of the Grand Hive. "Is it important now?"

"I think it might be."

"Fine. I got it not far from here." She nodded down to Dornoth IV. "A wizard gave it to me. I found him in stasis on the bottom layer of a Zenith salvage operation. Do you know what—"

"I'm familiar with Zenith wrecks. Keep going." The surface of Dornoth IV was littered with the wreckage of many early spacefaring vehicles, some of which had never been explored due to the hostile conditions of the planet.

"I took him out of stasis, but he had already been wounded. He died in minutes, but before he did, he handed me this flame. He said it would light my way through endless battle."

"Endless," I repeated. "Was that the word he used?"

"I don't like this line of questioning. If something is wrong, tell me."

I leaned back in my chair and rubbed a palm across my face. "Dying wizards don't speak carelessly. How often have you seen a film where a dying wizard gives someone a prophecy with their last breath and it ends up being *wrong?*"

Her eyes were blazing with the light of a healthy Lichborn, but her gaze was still painfully cold. "Are you basing your expectations on what happens in films?"

"In this case, the logic is the same." I understood her reaction, but this was still my area of expertise. I emphasized the importance of the topic with every word. "*Why* is that true in a film? Because a dying wizard handing over forbidden power would be too important a detail to waste. The same is true in the Aether. The more powerful the mage, the closer they are tied to the Aether. The significant moments in their lives have more weight."

Her doubt trickled away, replaced by focus.

"He didn't speak idly," I said. "If he said he saw you in an endless battle and manifested a spell powerful enough to grant immortality, then he saw you in *endless* battle."

A gun had appeared in Sola's hand, and she stood up. "Then the Iron King is still alive."

"Not necessarily. It could be that now that your crusade against the Iron Legion is over, you find another fight. Over and over again until you exhaust the energy in your spell and eventually die for real. It could be that another King rises to control the Iron Legion before we finish destroying them. And there are other factors that can change the future."

It was enough to make me wary, but that was all. Not enough to sound the alarm, but enough to continue scanning the wreckage of the Grand Hive.

Sola's armor materialized around her again. "If this were a film, the monster would still be alive."

"...yes," I admitted.

Horizon materialized next to me. *The records of previous Iron Kings don't mention resurrection. But if he were able to return to life, how would he do it?*

She turned to look at my father's discarded cocoon. So did I. So did Sola.

"Sola, give me that spell back," I said. Golden lights filled the edges of my vision, so the pathfinding spell still couldn't find a route to the Iron King. He was still dead.

Sola tossed a matter-reduction grenade onto the cocoon. Horizon manifested guns from the walls, training them on the pod, and began converting the nearest wall to an airlock. I raised my wand.

This was a long shot, but there had been an itch in the back of my brain from the beginning. If the Iron King really came back to life, he would definitely be reborn from something with a major connection to the Iron Legion. And probably to him personally.

The most sensible thing would be if he reformed from the largest chunk of the Grand Hive. If his soul was tied to his largest Hive, and he was immortal as long as it survived, that would make magical sense.

As bad as it would be, I would at least understand it.

But the worst thing for us would be if he could *control* where he resurrected and would therefore pop out as close to us as possible. So I appreciated the grenade.

I knew I was being too paranoid. We didn't know if the Iron King *could* bring himself back to life, but I'd sleep better if we at least erased this possibility.

A steel-plated hand punched up from the metal-and-flesh of the cocoon and caught Sola's grenade. The fist shattered my seals like thin glass.

The grenade detonated, but its explosion was swallowed by blazing pink-and-orange fire, which compressed down until it fit inside the metallic palm.

As soon as the hand showed itself, the light in my pathfinding magic snapped together. It shone right in front of me.

The spell had found the Iron King.

Soon enough, I did too. A head emerged, much larger than any human's, its brain covered in glass and flashing with random pulses of light.

Sola fired her shotgun repeatedly, but the slugs dissolved on contact. Horizon's guns in the wall sent streams of plasma into him, but they might as well have been splashing him with water. I reflexively shot out a seal, which shattered when it touched him.

With deceptive speed, the cocoon that had cradled my father melted into the Iron King.

"I am the Iron Legion," he said, "and the Legion has no end."

Horror filled every drop of my blood. I dove for my staff, but it was too late.

The Iron King gestured, and my crate flew over to him. The seals were attuned to me, but he tore through them. The staff itself was so close to me that it was more a part of me than my own arms, so I should have the edge in any mystical struggle for it.

Even with that advantage, I couldn't beat him. He shoved his hand through the case and grabbed Eurias.

Sola retrieved the Worldslayer, but tendrils of flesh and magic erupted from the Iron King and tore it from her hands. Unlike my staff, he couldn't wield the gun; his tendrils were eaten apart by corrosive red light on contact, but he could keep it away from her.

Blue light flowed from Horizon to surround the King, restricting him in chains, but he tore through those too.

The Iron King looked to the ceiling and grinned. "Don't worry. As one ancient masterpiece to another, I assure you: you're in good hands."

He slammed Eurias to the deck, and the King of the Iron Legion expanded his magic to claim *The Last Horizon*.

CHAPTER FORTY-FIVE

THERE IS A profound bond between an Archmage and his staff. Not only was I connected to Eurias in the eyes of the Aether, but our magic was compatible. And it was an established fact that it was all but impossible to bend a wizard's staff against its owner.

So the Iron King had three challenges to overcome. He had to twist our Aether-connection, force compatibility between his magic and the restorative, nurturing power of Eurias, and compel the staff to work against my will.

Those were each heroic feats for any user of magic. But they all could, theoretically, be accomplished through sheer strength of will.

Which the King had to spare.

Not only did he wrestle Eurias under his control, but he used it to expand his magic and to clash with *The Last Horizon*.

I didn't know the nature of the Iron King's power, but he maintained a link to the Iron Legion and extended my father's magic. That had to mean something like "integration and enhancement," or perhaps some kind of connection.

The theory was hotly debated between scholars, but the fact was that he was trying to take over Horizon.

And might succeed.

Orange-pink fire, magnified by Eurias, pushed away from the King. It scorched over the deck for dozens of yards, wiping the ship clean of Horizon's light.

There, it stopped. Horizon braced herself and pushed against the hostile magic, a battle of boundary against boundary.

"No more!" Horizon shouted. The spirit spread conjured hands behind her like wings and rose into the air, where she blazed with power that was every bit the equal of the King's. *"I am the vessel of heroes! I am the boundary you shall not cross! I am the last horizon, beyond which you will never see!"*

Her four-colored light pushed in.

But not enough.

Impressive as Horizon's resolve had been, the King laughed. "You are whatever I say you are."

In my mind, Horizon whispered, *"Chant faster!"*

Tendrils extending from the King's back were doing battle with Sola. They scrambled for the Worldslayer, and that was not a battle where I could interfere.

But one of these battlefields was magical.

I channeled my magic through the wand, and it added focus. One thing at a time.

Thanks to my wand, the incantation for my greatest sealing spell was quick. I finished it in seconds, while the King's attention was taken by Horizon.

The ship's spirit bought me enough time to finish casting Absolute Burial.

From six directions, light slammed into the Iron King.

But not *just* into him. So I knew the spell had gone wrong.

As I've said, spells don't fail like programs or machines do. They always operate according to their nature and the caster's intentions.

Therefore, it was with dawning horror that I saw why my spell had failed.

When my Absolute Burial crashed into the Iron King, similar light also slammed into the wreckage of the Grand Hive outside the viewport.

And, I was certain, into every member of the Iron Legion all around the galaxy.

When he'd said he *was* the Iron Legion, he hadn't been speaking metaphorically. When I targeted him, my spell tried to seal every instance of himself anywhere in existence.

Which was too much. It would have required me to control the Aether over the entire galaxy at once.

Terror seized my heart. The Iron King in my memory hadn't been immune to magic. Surely no Iron Kings in history had achieved this state, or they would still be around.

I should have been searching for the limitations of his magic, but my brain was frozen. While I knew no spell or power in the galaxy was truly invincible, this one felt like it was.

How were we supposed to kill him?

The Absolute Burial fizzled out, and I accomplished nothing but drawing the King's attention to myself. Burning eyes met mine and I found myself locked in psychic combat with the most powerful mind in the universe.

I always keep five or six layers of mental defense on myself at any one time. My amulet of protection and my mantle both bleed into the psychic realm, I'm trained to fight psionic assault, and one's own mind is relatively secure against outside intrusion in the first place. Attacking my mind should have been a more ridiculous prospect than when I'd fired a single plasma pistol against an armored Behemoth.

Of course, that analogy broke down when I considered that the King's 'pistol' was more like a cannon the size of a planet.

My repaired amulet snapped once again. My mantle began to fray, spinning away thread by thread as it supported my mental stability.

Every memory and conscious thought inside me began to burn. I remembered lives I'd never lived. A blind Pawn in a Hive, happy to serve its role. A Shepherd who moved in constant bliss, eager to submit itself to the will of the Legion. A Hunter, satisfied in its purpose.

Those memories felt comfortable, tempting me to rest in them. At least they were shelter from my terror.

My real thoughts were so chaotic and disordered they hurt. The only refuge was in remembering myself as a member of the Legion.

It was a surprisingly subtle attack, considering that it was also relentless in power and overwhelming in scope. My mantle held on as long as it could, but that layer was stripped away from me as its cloth was reduced to threads.

My mind was so close to crumbling I almost missed the moment when Raion's Divine Titan punched through the wall and seized the King's entire body in one hand.

Air tore out of the hole in the hull, making me thankful my levitation ring was still intact. The Titan's fist pulled back, hauling the King into space.

It took my staff with it, but Horizon sealed the hull again before I could follow. I was able to gasp a sigh of relief as my self-awareness came back.

Sola dashed outside before the wall closed.

I couldn't see what was happening, so I ran to a viewport. In his Divine Titan, Raion hurled the King away and drew his force-blade just as Sola reached the Worldslayer outside. Both turned the weapons on the King at once.

In my mind, I heard the King laughing. I felt what was coming before it happened.

One half of the Grand Hive slurped away as though drawn into Subspace, and suddenly the King was taller than the Divine Titan. His metal plates gleamed, and an inner fire of orange and pink blazed brighter. Each flare inside his brain was like a newborn star.

He slapped Raion's force-blade aside. The Worldslayer stabbed through his body, and he staggered slightly. Corrosive red energy fought him for a moment, but in seconds, he had healed the hole it left.

His backhand crushed Sola completely.

That was probably good news. She'd re-form in her room in a moment.

What *wasn't* good news was the nigh-invisible pulse that passed from the King's mind into the heart of the Divine Titan.

I'd given Raion a number of mental seals to keep his mind intact, and thus far, they'd held up well. But they were meant to support him in using his own weapon. They weren't *nearly* enough to stop the Iron King.

I felt the seals popping like seeds in a fire.

When I looked to Horizon for help, I realized I had another problem to add to all the others. The circle of pink-and-orange fire that had scraped *The Last Horizon*'s deck clean still remained. Horizon stood nearby, and a patch of holographic flesh on her hip had been washed of color. It was covered in a burning orange-and-pink border, and she grimaced down at it as she fought against the King's spell.

The ship's weapons still fired on the enemy, but that was rain against a missile bunker.

Sola was about to revive, but her greatest weapon couldn't keep him down.

Raion's Divine Titan was in the middle of a breakdown, grabbing its head in both hands and screaming silently in the void.

Leaving me here. Alone. No staff. Finally seeing the scope of the problem.

I had thought it was hopeless, but it was much worse than that.

The Iron King had virtually unlimited resources to draw on. He was connected to the Legion to an unprecedented and theoretically impossible degree. He wouldn't tire. He couldn't be overwhelmed mentally or physically, nor exhausted magically.

But he wasn't *immune* to magic. It was hard to affect him for the same reason it was hard to dig out a mountain with a spoon. Magically speaking, he was very, very large. As long as he was connected to the Legion, he would count as the entire Legion for the purpose of any spells.

As long as he was connected.

I didn't have any spells to break that connection, and I looked to Horizon with no answers.

"I'm sorry," I said to her. "There's nothing I can do."

Horizon was watching something far away. I saw flashes in the Aether as she controlled her magic in more directions than I could fathom, controlling thousands of hands and eyes. She glanced at me for a moment before looking to the battle again.

"Is this where you die, Sevenfold Archmage?"

Wearily, I corrected her again. "Six. Just six."

"Not necessarily."

The ship shook around us, and the patch of pink-and-orange fire on her hip expanded. She flinched. *"All right, this would work better if you realized the truth on your own, but we're running out of time. I can share my magic with you."*

I ran through that statement, but it didn't make any sense. "No, you can't."

One's magic was personal. Tied to their definition in the Aether. I only had six different styles of magic because there were six of me, so to speak.

"The strength of the ship is the crew," Horizon said. She spared another glance my direction and gave a quick smile. *"And the strength of the crew is the ship."*

"I have mastered six magics," I said. "Can you erase one? Is that possible?"

She let out a frustrated breath. *"This is why—listen, we don't have time for you to figure this out on your own. Your ritual went perfectly. There aren't six of you, there are seven."*

My mind raced through the implications.

"Five previous lives, the one you lived before the ritual…and the one since. Are you the same man you were before that?"

That made some magical sense, but if anyone besides the Zenith Starship had told me that, I would have said they must be wrong.

"So the seventh version of you—"

I cut off Horizon's explanation. "Yes, I understand. I have room for another spell. Share it with me."

If six spells weren't enough to defeat the Iron King, I didn't see how a seventh was going to help me. Although I couldn't use the full six. Even with my life and potentially the entire galaxy at stake, the curse magic I'd learned was…off the table. It would only make things worse.

The point was, I'd take any help I could get.

A disembodied hand began floating around me, tracing sigils in the Aether.

"You won't have time to study this from the beginning," Horizon warned. *"This is a pinnacle spell supported by an entire discipline you never learned. Are you ready, Varic?"*

I tried to force back the spell and ready myself. In order to use Horizon's magic, I had to redefine myself to line up with her.

The Aether had to see me, first and foremost, as the Captain of *The Last Horizon.*

Around me, the magic circle was almost complete. Fear rose up in me once again, and I called out, "Hold on, I should be the one to—"

Horizon's eyes shone and her smile stretched the bounds of her face. *"Too late!"*

Blue-green light stole my vision.

Information flooded my mind, symbols and words in the Aether whose meaning I could barely grasp. They coursed through my mind like a river, threatening to tear me apart.

It wasn't that I could see nothing. In fact, it was almost the opposite; I was being overwhelmed by so much sensation that I was effectively blind.

But still, I felt eyes forming all around me. Looking at me, and into me.

Horizon's eyes.

Once again, I felt myself on my knees, looking up into the Iron King's metallic face. Sola was at my side, and monstrous hands held me in place. I tasted my own blood as my chest was destroyed.

Is this you? the eyes silently asked me.

Pain coursed through me until I couldn't tell if this was a memory or not. *Yes!* I shouted.

We moved on to me waiting in the rain to be executed for treason.

Is this you? they asked.

Yes!

The guns fired.

As the scene changed again, I felt the Aether tearing me apart. In that transition, I could glimpse myself.

And I saw myself how the Aether saw me.

It saw me as a failure.

Every path of my life ended in disappointment. I had defined myself over and over again, and each time I had failed.

Magic itself was disappointed in me.

Once again, I felt myself in a memory. I was halfway through throwing the badge of my Divine Titan at Raion.

Is this you? the magic asked.

Every part of me rejected that. Down to my soul.

My hand froze on the badge. I didn't throw it. I couldn't.

No, I told them.

Then I found myself strapped to a chair, staring up into God's Eye. As the sky collapsed into an endless hole above me, and the ritual began, the eyes asked me one more time.

Is this you?

That time, I said, *Not yet.*

When I felt six lives come together, this time, I saw myself as Horizon had since our first meeting. My deaths combined into one.

And that was the moment I was born.

I was only a year old.

Who are you?

The vision didn't leave me with that question. Instead, it shifted again. And it started teaching me magic.

Eyes and hands flashed in front of me, images and capabilities burned into my consciousness. I would never remember exactly where they all came from—there were far too many for that—but with each one, I gained an intuitive understanding of the magic.

Each represented an enemy vanquished, remembered forever.

These were Horizon's treasures.

While I couldn't see specific memories, I felt the ebb and flow of her life. I sensed the shape of her memories.

She, too, had lived many lives.

Every new Captain was a rebirth for her. She lived for new adventures because those were the only times she could live at all.

She woke in a blaze of glory, changed the galaxy...until, in the end, her Captain died.

Then she went back to sleep.

Her stories always ended in death. Just as mine did.

The magic finally revealed itself to me in full, like a key turning in a lock. Horizon's spells were memories of past lives brought to life. Each one a legacy of battles won and lost.

There couldn't be a spell better suited for me.

And that was no accident.

I had asked the Aether to give me seven magics and whatever I needed to control them. And the Aether, as it always did, had answered me.

It had made me a perfect match for a seventh magic. Horizon's magic. No one else could be a better match for Horizon's pinnacle spell.

The ritual hadn't just made me a Sevenfold Archmage. It had prepared me to become the Captain of *The Last Horizon*.

I came out of the vision sweating and gasping on the floor. I trembled as I glared up at Horizon. "This wasn't in the rulebook."

The ship spirit's holographic form was coming undone, flickering and shifting like a bad transmission, but she still shifted her gaze away from me. *"Would...believe...surprise?"*

I could barely hear her. The ship shook around me.

There would be time for this later, assuming we survived. I spoke a word and manifested eyes out in space.

The situation was almost as bad as it could possibly be.

Sola was being reborn in flame back in her room. Raion had lost control of his Divine Titan, and the mech itself was cracked and on the verge of destruction. Horizon's physical vessel was no worse than before, but her spirit was in bad shape.

With the benefit of my new eyes, I also spotted a patch of black goo sticking to the bottom of the ship.

Horizon's voice was clear this time, but still quiet as a whisper. *"You have a plan, right?"*

"I do," I said, "but I don't like it."

The Captain didn't abandon his crew. He went down with the ship.

I walked past Sola in the hallway, beating her to the airlock. I gathered up a ball of the atmosphere with raw Aetheric manipulation; the bubble wasn't nearly as secure as my mantle, but I only needed it to let me survive in vacuum for a few seconds.

As I floated out, I sent a transmission to Sola and Horizon. "Raion doesn't have long. In a second, I'm going to take the King somewhere else. The Titan will look for another challenge. Don't give it one."

Neither had a response, but I didn't give them time.

The Iron King had released Eurias to take his gigantic form and fight the Divine Titan. I conjured a hand to grab the staff, pulling it back to me.

Before Eurias reached me, I was chanting my new spell.

Now, I understood that spell better than I possibly could have before. Horizon's magic didn't create imitations from her memory. She didn't *make* eyes or hands.

She summoned them. From a place that didn't usually exist.

At last, I understood why she called herself a World Spirit.

The King gestured, summoning fire from four directions to strike Raion's Divine Titan as he conjured a spear of metal-and-flesh. He intended to drive the spear straight through the chest. Where the pilot was.

I didn't know if the Titan could take such a blow, and I didn't wait to find out.

My chant reached its apex, and I spoke the name of Horizon's greatest spell. A name from a language spoken long ago, in the age of Horizon's creation.

"Terminus Mundi."

Through my staff, I projected my newest spell over reality. Darkness flowed out from me, overlapping the real world.

Raion vanished. Horizon was gone.

The King and I stood, alone, in a sea of darkness. The floor was black, invisible.

His spear pierced nothing because he no longer held a spear. And he was his usual size as well, though still taller than any human man.

In that world of darkness, he looked to me and grinned. "You thought this was your best shot, did you?"

"My world, my rules," I said, fighting down my instinctive fear. "Just you and me. No ship, but no Iron Legion."

This was the best solution to his infinite resources. I had the greatest possible homefield advantage here, while he couldn't draw on the Legion for extra mass or power. He'd have to beat me with his own personal powers.

Which were, of course, immense.

He spread his arms wide. "*The Last Horizon* does choose for courage. Not for intelligence."

"I guess she does," I said, and then I opened ten thousand eyes. They sprang to life all throughout the dark sky, glaring down at the King with thousands of different colors.

Each pair came from a defeated enemy.

I drew in a breath. "I will accept your surrender."

"Same to you," he said. In another blink, panels all over the King's body slid apart to reveal guns of every description I could imagine. "Let me know when you've had enough."

He fired like a broadside volley from a battleship, and it was all I could do to stay alive.

CHAPTER FORTY-SIX

I HAD NEVER practiced seven spells in conjunction with each other before. Even if I had, no version of me could imagine winning against the Iron King.

Eurias lay forgotten in my left hand as I used my wand to create a shield of water. Between a shield, defensive seals, and the spectral hands I summoned from the distant stretches of this isolated world, I blocked the King's shots.

His *first* shots.

The longer I lasted, though, the more likely the world of Terminus Mundi would wear him down. Many of the eyes that hung in the sky like stars carried magic in them, echoes of their original bodies. Spells of petrification and hypnosis, spells that attacked his mind and stripped away his defenses. Some focused light into lasers, while others added chaos into the Aether of his spells.

They were minor hindrances to him, at best. Like trying to trip him by throwing spiderwebs. And there was little they could do to stop him from shredding me with his bare hands.

He loomed over me in an instant, punching through a giant's hand I called to stop him. Even if he abandoned his inhuman magical power, he was still a ten-foot-tall cyborg who outweighed me by two tons.

My levitation ring shoved me into the waiting reach of another hand, carrying me away while I cast a binding spell through my wand.

I still held my staff, but I couldn't use it. Not only would it probably be too slow, and thus get me killed immediately, but it would only allow me to use one spell at a time.

Which would give up my greatest advantage.

I called a flurry of hands down from the sky, too unfamiliar with the spell to know if I could use it more efficiently. While the King was tangled with them, I finished chanting a quickened version of the Mirror of Silence. A black-and-white version of myself appeared, sending out sealing spells.

The copy wouldn't last long, but it bought me a little time. Missiles streaked through the air, but I cut them down with water while chanting.

I tossed the completed spell to an eye, whose paralyzing gaze now borrowed my binding spell. Its paralysis grew stronger, strengthened by my magic, and the King's motions slowed. Some of his guns stalled. He tried to pull apart one of the hands, but found himself unable to do it before the other three grabbed him.

I was infinitely relieved that worked.

I chanted faster, trying not to get excited, but this was *working*. Better than I could have imagined.

I finished invoking the Lagomorph Contract. A trio of humanoid rabbits, clad in armor that resembled Galactic Union battle-armor and carrying rifles, hopped into existence and began firing on the King. Each had a targeting lens over one eye as well as drones that shot down projectiles.

The situation was getting more and more unfavorable for the King. The longer we spent here, the more power I could display.

Granted, the world called into being by the Terminus Mundi spell would only last for so long. But at this rate, I would have run the Iron King out of power by the time the place collapsed.

I had overestimated his personal ability. He must rely on his magic too much, so without the Iron Legion to draw on, he was a head without a body.

He would make a great staff.

That was an odd thought, but I had to consider it. If I could strip away his unique magic, I might use it to make a rival to Eurias.

Speaking of which, now I had enough leeway to use my staff. I sheathed my wand and gripped Eurias in both hands, beginning to chant.

Whereupon the King erupted in pink flames. A dome burned everything away from him. "Aaaahhh, that was fun," he said.

I hadn't fully completed my incantation, but I tried to force the spell out anyway.

A tendril of metal and flesh extended behind him, this time shrouded in pink-and-orange fire. It swept through the sky above him, blinding dozens of eyes.

At the same time, guns continued to fire from all over his body and he kicked off toward me. Conjured hands moved to block him, but the pink-tinged flame carved through them.

The flames were exhausted by it. They slowly disappeared, so they weren't infinite. They also couldn't be the King's own magic; they would be produced by Aethertech or an enchanted component of his body.

Not that any of that knowledge helped me now.

When I tried to fly away, I felt the King's mind crashing into my own. Trying to drown me, once again, in thought and hostile memory.

My mind, still reeling from my battle to control Horizon's magic, fought itself. It cost me the spell I was chanting, and the Absolute Burial fell apart un-cast.

A hand bigger than my head cracked down on me.

It slammed me into the ground. The hasty shield I'd conjured protected me, but it was blown apart without an amulet to anchor it.

I grabbed my body in the levitation ring, trying to fly away, but the King was on top of me. The Lagomorph commandos fired on him constantly, shots pinging off his armor. Horizon's eyes had more effect, gazes of petrification and paralysis weakening his aura of pink flame.

But he may as well have had an industrial factory arm seizing me for all the chance I had to resist. The Iron King tore Eurias from my hand and tossed it aside.

He looked into my eyes with his burning pink-and-orange flame. "You'll make a great pawn," he said.

Then, with a thumb, he broke my left arm.

I had training to resist pain like that, but I still choked back a scream. Memories of having broken my limbs many times before did nothing to help.

"I'll keep you mostly intact," he went on. "I don't want to lose your unique magic, and I certainly don't intend to lose *The Last Horizon*."

He broke my right arm.

I screamed again, and my eyes were filled with tears. I missed whatever he said next as the pain overwhelmed my hearing.

"...easier to prove it to you. You didn't hear me, did you? Come on, come on. Pay attention." He snapped his metal-plated fingers, which sounded like a small bell. "I'm glad we had this opportunity to talk. I don't work together with people often, and when I do, I like to make the hierarchy clear at the beginning."

He held me by the collar with one hand. With the other, he gestured between us. "We're not equals. I'm not insulting you, it's just a fact of life. You can't betray me, you can't trick me, and you can't defeat me. Not even when I am at my weakest."

"...waiting for?" I mumbled out. His massive fist was crowding my chin.

He released me and patted me lightly on the back. "Sorry, what was that?"

"What are you waiting for?" I asked.

But I wasn't asking him.

A section of darkness peeled up from the dark floor and oozed over the Iron King like a predatory puddle taking its prey.

Pink-tinged fire burned, and the dark goop shouted in pain from several mouths. But another mouth sprouted close to me, grinning beneath its orange eye.

"Waiting for you to run him out of that fire," Omega said. "You didn't want me to get burned, did you? Nasty, nasty."

I wasn't listening to him. I was hobbling over to Eurias, which was floating on its own bubbling spring in the middle of some flourishing bushes.

I kicked the staff upward with my foot. I couldn't catch it with my hand, but I awkwardly let it land on my shoulder.

Then I channeled Aether through it and began to chant while Omega and the King struggled.

A glass-domed skull poked its way out of the ooze, like a swimmer fighting not to drown. He had a forced grin on his face. "Just me and you, huh?" the King grunted.

It would have been stupid to stop the incantation then, so I didn't.

But I did force a smile.

"Oooohhh, you have such advanced systems!" Omega said admiringly. "Why don't you give me access, okay?"

"I don't need to keep *you* intact," the King responded. "You can become armor for my guards."

"A test, then! Who can absorb the other first?"

I finished my incantation and stabilized the spell so I could speak. "Ah, but you're forgetting one thing," I said.

Each swiveled one eye to me.

"Absolute Burial."

Shining white seals pressed in from every direction.

Like when I'd sealed away the earth to uncover Horizon, this spell was powered by Eurias. This was an absolute sealing spell powerful enough to lock away mountains.

I only hoped that would be enough.

As the Iron King was compressed down to a point and forced out of reality, he focused on me with his burning eyes. "See you soon," he said.

Then he vanished.

I collapsed, letting my staff fall away, and blinked tears from my eyes. If I took a second, I could seal off my own sense of pain, but I needed to catch my breath first.

Omega oozed over to me, though he was only the size of a head now. "What happened to the rest of me?"

"I targeted the King. The only parts of you missing should have been the ones that merged with him, so they'll be sealed off together." A horrible thought occurred to me, so I asked a question. "If you get split apart, you don't...replicate, do you?"

"No, no, of course not. The severed portion continues following my will until it runs out of energy. I'll just need to replace my mass. In the meantime, I can do this."

He spun into his human form, which was now about two feet tall. He spread his arms wide and grinned wider. "Who just devoured the Iron King?"

"We did."

"*We* did. Is he going to escape?" Omega sounded eager about it.

"Yeah." Horizon's world began to dissolve around us, and I suddenly realized we were about to be drifting in space. "Can you get me back to the ship?"

"I can devour you and drag you through Subspace!"

"*Horizon,*" I sent. "*Horizon, I need emergency rescue.*" The artificial air from my magically manifested space was being sucked out in a rush. "*Horizon, make it quick! Please respond! Horizon! Hori—*"

My surroundings vanished in blue light, and I found myself seated on the bridge.

Horizon, Sola, and Raion looked down on me with concern. Well, the first two did. Raion was draped over a console like a rag and just barely managed to crack an eye open and glance at me.

I forced one of my hands open, though even that much motion brought the tears of pain back. Inside my palm was a twisting ball of white symbols: the anchor for Absolute Burial.

"One for the vault, Horizon," I said.

Sola looked to me. "Is that him?"

I nodded.

"And what happens if we..." She gestured with a gun toward the seal.

I lurched my body in front of it. "No! He'll get free."

"Then how are we killing him?" Despite the emerald glow of her eyes, her expression was dark. "He can't be allowed to remain. One contact with the Iron Legion, and we've lost again."

"The vault can hold him," Horizon assured us. *"He won't be getting free again."*

CHAPTER FORTY-SEVEN

THE IRON KING knew he would be free again.

He drifted in the center of nonexistence, unable to interact even with his own body. Almost unable to think.

But he understood this magic. He understood everything.

The seal would lose stability with time, and then he would be free. The slightest mental connection to his Legion would be enough.

This was an interesting wrinkle in his path, but it only made things more fun. It wasn't even a setback.

He couldn't feel his body, but he knew he was laughing. No game was fun without an opponent.

Time had no meaning to him. Whether it took him a year or ten thousand, he would—

The seal broke.

Spilling from nonexistence into existence was like going from a dark room into bright light, though the space where he found himself was actually dark.

And familiar.

This was the magic Varic had borrowed from a World Spirit. Eyes watched him from every conceivable angle.

The closest four pairs belonged to the crew of *The Last Horizon*.

Varic stood directly in front of him, a wary look in his silver eyes and a completed spell drifting over him in the form of a complex gray magic circle. His staff seethed with power, spreading life and water everywhere.

Raion Raithe of the Titan Force stood next to him, fists on hips. He wore the look of a schoolteacher disciplining a rowdy student.

Horizon, in a four-colored construct of a body, wore a smile too wide for her face. She didn't prepare any abilities, but the King suspected she was only here to gloat.

And then there was Sola, the Fallen Sword. Hidden behind her armor, with the Worldslayer in her hands.

Omega was here too, he was certain, but hiding in the shadows somewhere. No doubt he would make his presence known.

The King straightened so he loomed over them all. Horizon adjusted her projection to be just as tall, which made the King smile wider. "You want to try toying with me?"

"We were going to keep you locked up in the *Horizon*," Varic said. "But then we thought you'd eventually escape, and we'd have to fight you again, and we figured...why risk it?"

Sola fired the Worldslayer. It burned through the Iron King's midsection, causing him pain, but he grinned through it. "You've already taken your risk."

He erupted in weapons. Every gun fired, every ounce of his magic squeezed out in the form of pink-and-orange flame, and every bit of excess flesh stretched into more arms.

Horizon, Omega, and Raion clashed with him. Sola and Varic remained behind, and he kept his eyes on them.

Then Varic released his spell. And suddenly there were seven Solas, each side-by-side. Each pointed a copy of the Worldslayer.

The King's smile slipped off.

All seven Solas fired. He deactivated his own sense of pain, but he could feel himself dissolving. Chunks of his body and mind were eroded away.

Varic pointed to the array of Solas. "I can't copy her very long. But long enough, I think."

The King had no time left. He peeled most of his remaining flesh into a spear. His hand was now only a metal skeleton, but he took the spear anyway, and he hurled it at Varic. It carried the rest of his Aether-disrupting magic in the form of pink flame. If he could just interrupt the spell...

One blast of a Worldslayer annihilated his spell.

The other six tore into him again.

His mind worked, trying to calculate his way out of this, but suddenly he felt limited. He didn't have the trillions of brains he was used to working with. He felt blind. Restricted.

Mortal.

A silver helmet loomed over him, and he looked into Sola's visor. He couldn't see her eyes, but he still sent out one last psionic pulse. A mental plea for help, a wave of mercy that should cause any human to hesitate.

She didn't say a word.

But she did pull the trigger.

EPILOGUE

THE GLASS DOME that had covered the Iron King's brain fell to the blank ground of Horizon's world. It was the biggest piece of him left.

I nudged it with my foot and said, "Shoot it again."

Sola had put away the Worldslayer. "I can't."

"You think we need to?" Raion asked.

Omega shot it. He used the enchantment-breaking gun that flashed orange. The glass shattered, but there were still shards left.

Unsatisfied, I called several eyes from the depths of the dark world. They flew closer, firing beams from their pupils to sweep up every last piece of glass.

Horizon giggled. *"This is the fate of all our enemies. May they be dust in the wind, and less than dust."*

I conjured water. It condensed out of the Aether around me, and I began spraying arcs across the ground.

Raion put a hand on my shoulder. "He's dead."

"I just find that hard to believe," I said.

I chanted a quick pathfinding spell. That didn't find anything, so I began a longer one. This time, I was looking for any particles that might have once been him. When that didn't work, I started chanting a third.

Sola tossed a blinking red ball onto the spot where he'd vanished. "Grenade," she warned.

The matter reduction grenade erupted into a sphere, which then imploded.

"We got him," she said. She looked up into the distant eyes of this world's sky, which resembled stars. "That leaves the rest of them."

"*A wise point,*" Horizon said. "*The Captain requested the destruction of the Iron Legion, not its King. While they are weakened and vulnerable after this loss, they are not—what are you doing, Captain?*"

I had begun inspecting the back of Raion's neck. "Parasites. Like he left on my father."

Horizon spread out a hand. "*You have been inducted into the magic of Terminus Mundi. Do you think anything could happen here that you and I cannot see?*" As one, all the stars blinked.

"No, you're right. Pathfinding spells came up negative too."

"*This is perhaps our greatest victory against the Legion, but not our final one. Until the Legion is scattered, driven even from Dark Space, we will...He's really dead, Captain.*"

I was layering some very subtle binding spells, leaving magic circles floating in the air. They would interrupt any postmortem attempts to manipulate the Aether. Just in case.

"We'll see," I said. I readied my magic and steeled myself. "I'm canceling the spell."

Darkness peeled away from the world, leaving us on *The Last Horizon*'s bridge. Outside the viewport, the few remaining chunks of the Grand Hive had been tied together like a patchwork asteroid. Bound by my own spells.

If the Iron King came back to life again, it would be here. I cast the Cosmic Path, which connected with nothing.

I handed off the spell to Horizon and spoke mostly to myself. "He's really dead."

Omega laughed at me. "It would be too boring if we couldn't finish off our first enemy! We haven't seen what Solstice will do to you, after you declared war on them! Exciting, exciting." He rubbed his hands together.

My stomach tightened, but he was right. The secret organization that controlled the Galactic Union would be looking to get an agent aboard *The Last Horizon*. If they couldn't do that, they would make an example of me as someone that had crossed them.

"At least we won't have to worry about the D'Niss!" Raion said confidently. "There's *no way* the Swarm-Queen will return to devour us all!"

Sometimes I was convinced that he said these things deliberately.

"Let's mop up the Iron Legion first," I said, and with a gesture I called up a chair in front of the ship console. "That's enough of a job without—"

"*Incoming transmission, Captain,*" Horizon announced.

Without waiting for my permission, she projected a hologram into the center of the room. It showed Shyrax, a nine-foot-tall Karoshan with shining golden hair-strands tied behind her and a simple circlet across her forehead. She laced hands behind her back and faced me, though this was a recorded message.

"*This is Shyrax the Third, rightful Queen of Karosha, contacting* The Last Horizon. *I have your location and I come to challenge you for the position of Captain. Prepare yourself. If you run, I will not be merciful.*"

That was the end of the message.

At least she hadn't changed.

I sank into the captain's chair and gave my orders. "Change of plans, everybody. It's time to pick up the rest of the crew."

THE END

The adventures of
The Last Horizon continue in...

THE
ENGINEER
THE LAST HORIZON
BOOK TWO

AVAILABLE SOON!

(If you're flying through a star system with Subline
access, tell your AI to visit **WillWight.com**)

SPACE BLOOPERS

"I have lost twelve percent of my mass in the attack," Horizon said. *"It's time for our Engineer to earn his keep."*

Raion materialized seemingly out of nowhere, snapping a salute. "Raion Raithe, Engineer, reporting for duty!"

Holographic fireworks exploded behind him.

I sighed. "This is not going to work out."

"Have faith in me, best friend!"

"I told you, you should have been the Knight."

Moments later, Raion stood in front of a huge mess of destroyed Aethertech. Omega had blown a hole into the mechanics of the ship, but the damage wasn't as simple as destroyed electronics.

Strange devices and esoteric materials where scattered everywhere—pieces of the ancient, incomprehensible Aethertech that made up *The Last Horizon.*

I had no idea what I was looking at, so Raion would be even more lost. He put his fists on his hips, wearing the same confident expression as always.

"Well, we're going to need another shipment of nega-steel, that's for sure. I can see right off the bat that your terrestrial metascope and your flux capacitor are completely shot. I can get the system functional again, but I'm going to need a rotating hyperspanner, variegated line-drivers in all sixteen sizes, a five-millimeter technobauble, and a wrench."

I stared at him. "Do...do you really know what you're doing?"

"Oh, did I never tell you? I have a degree in Subspace Engineering from Space MIT." He held up two fingers. "It's like I always say: the two most important things in this universe are education and..."

"Friendship," I muttered.

"...and *friendship!*"

Benri stood defiantly before the Iron King.

"I won't do as you tell me anymore!" he declared. "My son knows I'm here, and he'll save me!"

The Iron King peered out the viewport. "Yeah, here he is now."

The Last Horizon blew the Grand Hive to pieces.

"Don't use magic as a weapon," I said. "Use a gun."

"Is that what you do, Professor?" a student asked.

"I carry a plasma pistol. A Lightcaster Four."

"I mean, you don't use magic as a weapon? You just use your gun?"

I cleared my throat. "Yeah, well, mostly."

"Oh, so you *mostly* use your gun? You use magic as a last resort, then. Or as a support for your pistol."

I pulled at my collar. "Uh, yeah, that's...that's what I do. For sure."

"What about this video of you fighting? You're carrying a gun, but it definitely looks like you're mostly using magic. Right here, you cut that entire wall in half with a water spell. From what I can see, you use magic about ninety percent of the time and the gun maybe ten percent."

"The thing about that," I said, "is shut up."

I was about to tighten my finger on the trigger, but I hesitated at a sudden thought. *"Moonfall,* to be clear, don't shoot me. Shoot *toward* me."

"Safety protocols have been overridden."

"Shoot in my direction until you see me, then fire on whatever else is in the room. Not me."

"Parameters unclear. Clarification required."

"No time!" I shouted. "Just remember, don't shoot me!"

Fourteen minutes later, *Moonfall's* plasma cannons blasted into the heart of the Iron Hive. The ship destroyed the Shepherds, the Bishop, and all the Pawns between the outer and inner walls, burning the room into a smoking core.

"Good work," I said. "Now prepare to—"

"One target remaining."

The ship's plasma cannons blasted me apart.

Moonfall floated in the empty room. *"I told you clarification was required."*

I drew in a breath as I faced the Iron King. "I will accept your surrender."

"Okay," the Iron King said. He shrugged. "What are your terms?"

"Uh, well, we do have two seats left on the crew, but I don't—"

"Sold."

I held up a hand. "No, wait, hold on. There's no way I can let you join us."

"Why not? I'm a galactic superintelligence. Together, we'd be invincible."

"You made millions of people into zombies! Maybe billions!"

"Okay, I'll stop." He put a metal hand to his chest. "That wasn't even me, really. I'm only about a week old. Can you hold me morally responsible?"

I tried to think of another objection. "It just...feels wrong."

"How so?"

"Well...for one thing, you're going to make the next book *really* short."

Horizon frowned. *"I'm not sure the Subspace Drive will work."*

"We have to try," I responded. "I'll do everything I can to hold us together in Subspace so we can reach the Grand Hive in time."

"So what you're saying," Horizon said, *"is that we should strive to dive with our Drive to reach the Hive alive."*

I looked up from the computer. "There's nothing in the archive! We'll have to connive and contrive a way to survive."

"And when we arrive, we'll thrive."

I held up a hand. "Give me five."

In the lobby of the virtual tournament, I sagged against the wall in exhaustion. "I need a nap. How many rounds left?"

"Only two more rounds that require your attention, Captain. However, these last rounds might get a little strange."

"Strange how?"

Horizon chewed her lip. *"I invited everyone throughout the galaxy who might be qualified for a spot on my crew, but there are a few who might be...overqualified."*

I stood and stretched. "That's good for us, isn't it?"

"I'm not sure. Good luck, Captain."

The lobby dissolved and I materialized on a wide, open platform. It was the most plain fighting surface I could imagine. Nothing but me, empty space, and my opponent.

He was a tall human, broad and muscular, wearing loose robes that looked almost ceremonial. He had outfitted himself in black-and-white, with a white medallion hanging from his neck, black hair, and a pale right arm that was likely some kind of advanced Aethertech prosthetic.

His eyes must have been Aethertech as well, or else the product of magic or strange genetic alterations, because they were pools of black with bright white circles.

The man pressed his fists against one another and bowed to me. "Wei Shi Lindon. Are you my opponent?"

I raised my wand. "I'm more like the examiner, actually. Show me what you can do."

Lindon hesitated. "Are you sure?"

"I need to see if you have what it takes."

"All right, then. Apologies."

[He wants to see what you're capable of,] a new voice said. [Try to kill him a little slower, so he can see it.]

I looked around. "Who said that?"

All I saw next was black fire.

I shot upright in front of Horizon, gasping, as I woke from the virtual world. "What was that?"

"*That,*" Horizon said, "*is what it feels like to lose.*"

I strode in front of my class as rain pattered on the jungle of the Magic Tower's moon.

"If you're going to use magic on the battlefield, we have to start by going over some of the most important pieces of equipment in modern-day warfare."

I pulled out a short metal cylinder that I had borrowed for this illustration. "This is a force-blade, and you'll often see Combat Artists using them. In simpler terms, you could think of it as a saber made of light."

I held up a small humanoid robot, which fit in the palm of my hand. "These are called androids. Under *no* circumstances are you to refer to them as 'droids. Highly offensive."

I gestured behind me, to my ship. "Now, as you all know, to

get to any battlefield we have to travel through Subspace. That's a parallel dimension that allows us to hyper-accelerate; you might call it hyper-space."

I spoke a word to light up the Aether around me. "Of course, we're wizards. We'll be concerned with magic. To use magic, we have to manipulate the Aether, an energy field that surrounds us and binds us. It's a force. The ultimate force in the galaxy. I like to think of it as *the* force."

One of the students raised his hand. "We're already familiar with these concepts, Professor."

"Yes," I said, "but the important thing is that they are *technically* distinct. Now, in order to complete your wizard training, you'll have to run around a swamp while wearing me like a backpack. Who's first?"

Want to always know what's going on?

With Will, we mean.

The best way to stay current is to sign up for
The Will Wight Mailing List™!
Get book announcements and...

Well, that's pretty much it.* No spam!

SIGN UP HERE!

*Ok, *sometimes* we'll send an announcement
about something that's only book-*related*. Not a lot, promise.

WILL WIGHT is the *New York Times* and #1 Kindle best-selling author of the *Cradle* series, a new space-fantasy series entitled *The Last Horizon*, and a handful of other books that he regularly forgets to mention. His true power is only unleashed during a full moon, when he transforms into a monstrous mongoose.

Will lives in Florida, lurking beneath the swamps to ambush prey. He graduated from the University of Central Florida, where he received a Master of Fine Arts in Creative Writing and a cursed coin of Spanish gold.

Visit his website at *WillWight.com* for eldritch incantations, book news, and a blessing of prosperity for your crops. If you believe you have experienced a sighting of Will Wight, please report it to the agents listening from your attic.

Printed in Great Britain
by Amazon